Helen Glynn Jones is an author, blogger and freelance writer. Born in the UK, she has lived in both Australia and Canada. A few years ago, she returned to her native England where, when she's not writing stories, she likes to hunt for vintage treasures, explore stone circles and watch the sky change colour. She currently lives in Hertfordshire.

tiktok.com/@helenglynnjones
instagram.com/helenglynnjones
x.com/authorhelenj
facebook.com/AuthorHelenGlynnJones
threads.com/@helenglynnjones

Also by Helen Glynn Jones

The Last Raven

THE RAVEN'S COURT

HELEN GLYNN JONES

One More Chapter
a division of HarperCollins*Publishers* Ltd
1 London Bridge Street
London SE1 9GF
www.harpercollins.co.uk
HarperCollins*Publishers*
Macken House, 39/40 Mayor Street Upper,
Dublin 1, D01 C9W8, Ireland

This paperback edition 2025
25 26 27 28 29 LBC 6 5 4 3 2
First published in Great Britain in ebook format
by HarperCollins*Publishers* 2025

A catalogue record of this book is available from the British Library
ISBN: 978-0-00-869542-2

Printed and bound in the United States

For my loves

Playlist

willow - Taylor Swift
Tainted Love - Soft Cell
Ever Fallen in Love - Buzzcocks
vampire - Olivia Rodrigo
Map of the Problematique - Muse
Lonely in Your Nightmare - Duran Duran
Run the World - Beyoncé
Electricity - Suede
Don't Blame Me - Taylor Swift
Same Old Scene - Roxy Music
Bring Me To Life - Evanescence
Secret Oktober - Duran Duran
Changing - Sigma, Paloma Faith
Sign Your Name - Sananda Maitreya
Fly on the Windscreen - Depeche Mode
Far From Home - Sam Tinnesz
The Crystal Ship - The Doors
DAUGHTER - Beyoncé
Hallucinate - Dua Lipa
Love Like Blood - Killing Joke

Chapter One

DAYBREAK

Warmth. It wraps around me, better than the softest of blankets. The wonder of a human body, holding me close.

Michael stirs. 'What time is it?' His chin-length blond hair is tousled, his blue-grey eyes sleepy.

'I don't know.' My voice is a rasp. We're lying on a velvet sofa, tangled together. 'It's morning, though.' Pale light slants through timber shutters, striping the wooden floor, the colourful rug, the pale blue walls.

'Hmmm. We should probably get up.' He doesn't move, though, running lazy hands down my spine, waking flickers of pleasure.

'We probably should.' I absolutely do not want to get up.

'Morning, lovebirds.' The whispered greeting is accompanied by a giggle. Laurel, my roommate, tiptoes across the living room towards the adjoining kitchen. Faint trails of glitter are visible on her neck above her grey sweatshirt. I'm sure there's more elsewhere on her body, hidden beneath the matching sweatpants.

I sit up, running a hand through my hair, straightening my crumpled skirt. 'Shall I make coffee?'

'Already on it,' Laurel replies, accompanied by the hiss and whirr of the coffee machine, the buzz of beans grinding.

'Did we even watch the end of that film?' Michael swings his long legs around, sitting up.

'We didn't watch much of any of it.'

He grins, then leans in. 'I suppose not.'

I close my eyes, my lips meeting his. He smells like butterscotch and smoke, with a faint hint of violets. I could breathe him in for ever.

It's been two months since I moved to the Safe Zone. I've been with Michael for one of those months, slowly getting to know him. Slower, perhaps, than he would like. But there's still a part of me that's healing. He knows, and he understands. About Kyle, how I loved him, how he betrayed me. And how I had to kill him. I told him everything.

Well, almost everything.

When you're getting to know a boy it's difficult to find the right moment to tell him your family killed his father. I know there was no love lost between Michael and Mistral, that he barely knew him, and what he did know of him was cruelty and abandonment. But he was still his father.

So, I haven't told him that Mistral was behind the North Wind rebellion, and my kidnapping. Or how he'd burned in a throne of metal on a field of snow, blood spreading like a flower beneath him. I know I *should* tell him. I don't know why I can't.

It's not like he doesn't know Mistral is dead. It was big news, when it happened. The heroic lieutenant, giving his life to protect his ruling family. That was the story we spun to the press, anyway. No one needed to know that Mistral was a traitor, that there was such weakness at the heart of Raven. Everyone who witnessed the actual execution was sworn to secrecy; there were still rumours, of course, about the extent of Mistral's involvement in the rebellion, but we shut them down, the families closing rank to protect us. And Michael doesn't seem to want to talk about his family or his past. The fact it happens to be convenient for me is something I probably need to address.

It's the only thorn in what's been pretty much a sea of roses since we started dating. Even when I told him who I was, he didn't back away like I expected him to.

'I'm with you, Emelia Raven,' he said, as we stood on the beach at the turning of the day. 'Your secret is safe with me.' Then he took my face in his hands and kissed me.

We haven't really stopped kissing since.

I mean, we have. But when we're together, it more often than not involves us being wrapped around each other, as though we can't get enough of each other's warmth. I think he's been with human girls before; at least, he's hinted at it. But I've never been this close to another human.

Not that we're truly human. Vampire born, both of us, though we appear like everyone else. Yet we hold a faint scent of violets, echo of our dangerous kin. Heal faster, run faster, than regular humans. I thought myself weak for so long, it was strange to find out that I do have power. I suppose I have Kyle to thank for that.

Laurel reappears, holding a tray with three steaming mugs. She puts it on the coffee table and takes one of the mugs, cradling it to her. Her auburn hair is sleekly curled, her make-up flawless. But there are purple circles under her eyes and her cheeks are pale.

'Long night?'

'Hmm.' She takes a sip of her drink. 'Your parents had guests.'

'There should be more iron tonic in the fridge. I got some last time I was home.'

'Already had a shot.'

'You want to watch a movie with us? We won't mind if you snore.' Michael grins, picking up the remote and flicking on the TV.

His smile slides away. We all stare at the screen. Horror blooms in my stomach, a cold and vicious flower.

The vampire newsreader is shadowed, illuminated only by faint silver light. There's nothing unusual about this; vampires can only handle low-strength light, like that of the moon, or the electric candle-lamps that light my parents' home. Darkness is their natural habitat. There's enough light on-screen, however, to see the bodies bobbing, face down in dark waters. Then shadowy dark figures, like fleeing ghosts, a few seconds of grainy footage captured by one of the coastal guard towers. I clutch Michael's arm. The newsreader's voice, cool and seductive, fills the room.

'The attack on Safe Zone Seven-Alpha is one of several recent atrocities on the South coast, all of which resulted in significant stock casualties, as well as the loss of five vampire guards. Seven-Alpha is, of course, close to the Southern edge of the Great Forest, home to lawless Reaper gangs.'

The newsreader pauses, their dropped fangs the only sign of their agitation. 'The timing, for the House of Raven, is not ideal, with the recent rebellion and the coronation of the heir just months away. This newsreader would like to know when they're going to step up and put an end to this Reaper scourge once and for all. Lives are being lost, their attacks becoming bolder, and—'

Whatever else they're going to say disappears in a click, as Michael turns off the television. Laurel puts down her mug. Her hands, pale against the dark crockery, are shaking.

'I had … I think I had family there, once,' she says. 'Before.'

Before. Before the Red Rising, the great vampire conquest of the planet, a single night of carnage where every human country was subjugated beneath the might of the four families. Before vampires turned towns into farms, caging humans in one place, forced to donate blood every month for the rest of their lives in return for light and power and safety, for the chance to live as they once did. I know, now, that they do nothing of the sort. Seven-Alpha, I also know from my research into conditions at Safe Zones, was once a port where people could catch ferries to the Channel Islands and across to France, back when they were allowed to do so. The fact they no longer can is something I'm trying to change. Along with everything else.

'It's not Reapers.' Michael frowns, his jaw tight.

'Who the hell else is it, then?' Reapers, vicious vampire gangs hunting the Great Forest and its environs, who hold fealty to no one, are rapidly becoming a problem. It's something I've been following, as much as possible, along with all the other learning I'm trying to cram in before I take the crown.

There's a sound like a sob, then Laurel's footsteps padding down the hallway, followed by the click of her bedroom door. I stand, but Michael catches my hand.

'Leave her, E,' he says, his voice gentle. 'Give her a moment.'

I'm only really starting to grasp the enormity of what vampires did to humans. The shattered lives, the trauma, the loss of almost everything they held dear. It's a weight of guilt that almost drags me under, some days. It's why I've vowed to dedicate my reign to undoing as much of the damage as I can.

'Come here.' Michael gets to his feet, pulling me into his arms. I try to relax but can't get the image of those floating bodies out of my head. *Stock casualties.* They were *people,* like me and Laurel and Michael.

'It's not your fault,' he murmurs, as though he can read my troubled thoughts.

'I know,' I mumble, even though I feel like it is. I love living here as Emily Reynolds, just another human. But this latest news is a reminder that I can't do it for ever. I bury my face in his shoulder, feel the press of his lips on my hair.

'You okay?'

'I'm fine.' I'm not fine.

'Why are you so tense, then?'

Why do you think it wasn't Reapers? I don't say anything, though. Just hug him a little more tightly.

'Is it because you're going home later?'

I still don't speak. He's right. It's not just Reapers playing on my mind. But I can't tell him why this particular trip home is making me so nervous. Not yet. It's also, if I'm honest with myself, why I haven't told him about his father. It feels as though he's slipping through my fingers. As though everything is. In a few months I'll be eighteen, and crowned Raven. My life will change completely. And that's why I can't tell him all my secrets, not yet.

Because I don't know if he can be part of who I'm going to be.

Chapter Two

HOMEWARD BOUND

'If you could travel anywhere, where would you go?' Laurel bumps me with her shoulder. We're heading for the shift bus, both of us wearing pale grey sweats, the Raven emblem embroidered in black on the front. The only difference is that she has a heavy down coat over hers, protection against the winter chill, while I have just my leather jacket. Another apparent advantage of my vampire blood: a resistance to colder temperatures.

Or maybe it's because I grew up with vampires, and I'm used to it.

'You know I'm still on Paris. You choose somewhere.' We walk up the hill, our breath puffing like clouds in the cold afternoon air. It's a game we often play, poring over atlases, watching old movies, then choosing a place to visit. Conveniently ignoring the fact that I can go pretty much anywhere I want, and Laurel can't. When we first started living together it took a while before she could see me as anything other than Emelia Raven, daughter of her employers, heir to the throne. But now we have a real friendship, the first I've ever had with a human. It's wonderful.

'Uh, I think I'd like to go to Bali.'

'Bali?'

'It's an island, on the other side of the world. Scorpion territory, now. But apparently it was once a popular place to visit, all golden beaches and blue sea.'

'We have the beach here.'

'Not like this. Water like blue crystal. Soft sand and sighing breezes. And the shopping…'

I grin. Laurel loves clothes. I've given her quite a few things, as I have enough to wear for several lifetimes. I think my mother sometimes forgets that.

My grin fades as we pass the harvesting plant, a line of people waiting outside. Laurel glances at me.

'You going to be able to do anything about that?' She jerks her head.

'I'm trying. But it's more difficult than I thought. This is just one plant of hundreds across the realm.'

Kyle warned me, back when I believed he wanted a life with me. My father did, too. How difficult it would be to change things for humans. I knew it would be, but God and darkness, the red tape! The arguments! What I wanted, I thought, was simple. For donation to the plants to be optional, or the donation frequency decreased. For humans to be able to travel between Safe Zones, not tied to one place. We can't give up blood harvesting totally, because then vampires will start to hunt humans again. But apparently, there are vampires and humans who want that, arranging their own lucrative illegal hunts, another thing I've been furious to discover. There are also humans who want things to stay as they are, happy to be farmed for their blood in return for what they see as a safe existence. It's an almost impossible line to walk, keeping all the factions happy.

'Surely you can do *something*!'

I stare at her. 'I'm doing what I can,' I say, feeling stung. This is another thing that worries me. Once I'm publicly anointed as the next Raven, and it becomes more widely known that I'm human, it feels like the pressure on me to change things will increase.

Before I ran away, I thought a human life was one of sunlight and warmth, a place of safety. But now I see the darkness overlaying it all, the shadow of Raven permeating every aspect of human existence. And the fact that, despite the lights and guards and boundaries, no human is safe. Not so long as the blood in their veins is what vampires need to survive. There's no way around it. In no world can I take the throne and simply declare that humans are free and cannot be hunted. I'd be dead before I left the room. I can't reverse the Rising, either. My hope, instead, is that I can build something new; work out a way for everyone to get something they want, rather than one group getting everything and the other getting not much at all, under the guise of 'keeping them safe.'

My time in the Safe Zone is supposed to be for research; to figure out what humans really want, and how I can make that happen for them. It's such a massive task. I can't sleep, sometimes, for thinking about it. Yet I'm determined. I've already made a start, working with my parents to create a Free Zone for humans on the Channel Islands. It's almost ready to launch, a triumphant start to my reign. At least, that's my hope.

'I'm sorry.' Laurel's auburn brows draw together. 'I shouldn't have said anything. I know you're trying.'

I sigh. 'No, I'm sorry. I shouldn't have snapped at you. It's just…'

'I know. And it's okay.' Laurel links her arm with mine, her head on my shoulder as we head towards the pick-up point. There's a small group of people waiting already. They're also dressed in Raven sweats. And they're all food.

Not blood dancers like Laurel. Instead, they're food for guards on the Raven estate, confined to a cage in the basement for their shift, then returning home. It's horrible. I've suggested getting blood pouches like most vampires use, fresh from the harvesting plants. But apparently, one of the perks of being a guard on the estate is having live food. Another wall I'm trying not to bang my head on.

The bus pulls up with a hiss of brakes. We file on board, Laurel and I taking a seat together at the back. No one has ever recognised me, but I take as few chances as possible. I was barely acknowledged by vampires before the North Wind rebellion, and most humans weren't even aware vampires could have human children. I suppose that's because they're usually killed at birth. I survived, and Michael survived, because our mothers fought for us. But I've chosen to remain a secret until I leave the Safe Zone, which is why I refuse the car my parents offered, taking the bus instead.

Trees crowd both sides of the road as we head towards Dark Haven, the vampire town closest to my home. The Great Forest borders our estate, spreading across the entire country to the far north, enveloping abandoned cities and towns and villages. It's the same across the world, or so I've been told. Forests like this springing up everywhere, once humans were driven from their homes, killed or funnelled into Safe Zones. Our Great Forest is vast and impenetrable, a place of danger, home to Reaper gangs and darkness knows what else. There's the occasional glimpse of humped buildings among the trees as we speed past, ghosts of the world that was. I remember the human guard, driving me back to Dark Haven after I escaped Kyle and Jessie's clutches. *There are houses in there,* he said. *Whole villages swallowed up. And other things.* As I watch dark trees flash past, barren and tangled with winter, I wonder. What other things?

'Hey, are we okay?' Laurel nudges me.

I realise she was talking while I zoned out. 'Of course we are.'

She looks down. 'I shouldn't have had a go at you. I'm just … it's scary. And now we have Reapers to worry about as well.' Her voice gets quieter.

'No, I'm sorry. I do want to change things. And I will! I just can't do it all at once. It's not easy.' I mutter the last words, feel like an ass even saying them. No part of human existence is easy.

Laurel's expression softens. 'You're as trapped as we are, aren't you?'

The bus rattles to a stop, the doors opening with another hiss. Everyone gets up, exiting quickly. Humans don't tend to hang around too long in vampire towns, and our bus driver is no exception. Laurel and I are last off the bus, joining the others in a small huddle on the pavement. Even though it's still daylight, night isn't far off. Another bus will be along soon, to take us to the estate. There's no reason for it not to come, but I understand their apprehension. I remember being alone here, the sun setting as I made a desperate dash for home. I was lucky to make it alive.

I haven't answered Laurel. Because she isn't wrong. I am trapped. On all sides. By red tape and political factions and a society centuries in the making. Even though the Red Rising was less than a century ago, humans were farmed for food long before that. Just not on such an … industrial scale. I'm trying to change the world. And I don't know if I can do it.

The estate bus pulls up. It's sleek, painted black with the Raven insignia silvered on the side. The door opens and we climb on board, single file. The seats are plush, comfortable, velvet curtains at the windows. Yet I can't escape the feeling that this is more like a coffin than anything, taking these people to their slow death.

I sit down next to Laurel, and the bus starts to move. I'm going home.

But as shadows close around us, the bus taking me further from the Safe Zone, and Michael, it also feels as though I'm leaving home behind.

Chapter Three

FAMILY TIES

The gates at the rear of the Raven estate are already open, the house a towered square against the winter sunset. We pull to a stop at the back, where stone stairs lead down to the guard quarters in the basement.

I thank the driver as we disembark. As I do so, I notice a small flash of red on his collar, what looks like an enamelled pin catching the light. It sparks something in my memory.

'Come on!' Laurel grabs my arm, pulling me away. We head around the side of the house past the base of a tower, one of the oldest parts of the property. There's a door, hidden in the stone wall, that if I opened it would lead straight up to my bedroom. But too many memories haunt those secret passages, and the only one I use now is the one to the roof from the library. Even that holds ghosts, but I can deal with them. Just.

'Are we late?'

'No.' Laurel glances at me. 'I'd just like to rest for a while before your parents request me.'

'My parents?' I know Laurel works for my family. But

there's something awful about the thought of my parents feeding from her. She's my *friend*.

'They always request me at some point during the week. I guess they like to know that everything's going well in the Safe Zone. Your mother asks me questions while your father ... well... Then they swap. Anyway,' she shrugs, 'it's what I do.'

I stop walking. 'Why do you do it?' I've never dared ask her this, never wanted to remind her that she was an employee, not just a friend. I regret the words as soon as they leave my mouth. I know why she does it. What choice does she have?

She stops as well. 'My mother was a dancer. I've never known anything else.'

Laurel has no surviving family. None that she knows about, anyway. 'I'm sorry. I shouldn't have asked.'

Laurel envelops me in a rose-scented hug. 'Yes, you should,' she whispers, kissing my cheek. 'I know you mean well. And I love you for it.' She pulls back. 'I hope you make all the changes you want to make, Emelia Raven. And I'll help you, any way I can.'

I blink back tears. 'I love you, too,' I say. 'Anything I can do for you, I will. Just say the word. Even a trip to Bali.'

'Bali? Well, that would be something.' She smiles, then bumps me with her shoulder. 'Come on. Let's get inside.'

She continues around the house, opening a side door. It leads into a suite of three interconnected rooms filled with narrow beds and rows of dressing tables with mirrors, racks of skimpy clothing lined up along one wall. Glitter sparkles on every surface, trodden into the parquet flooring. There are a few dancers here already, some lying down reading, others fixing their hair and make-up, all in various states of undress. But when I enter the room, they all tense up, the conversation getting quieter, people tidying up or covering themselves.

'I should come in the other way,' I mutter.

'Nah. This lot just need to lighten up.' Laurel grins, scanning the room. A couple of people laugh, the tension easing. 'I'm heading off on the early bus,' she whispers, close to my ear. 'So, I'll see you later.' No one needs to know we live together, and I appreciate her discretion.

I squeeze her arm, then slip out to the hallway beyond. Two guards fall into step behind me, keeping pace as I glide along the shadowed hallways, my feet sinking into plush carpet. And just like that, I'm Emelia Raven again. Heir to the throne and all that jazz. I round a corner and cross the huge foyer, ascending the golden stairs. The Halloween tree is gone, packed away for another year. But Michael and I brought a sharp-scented pine in its own red pot into my little house by the beach. Echo of an older tradition, evergreen. A symbol of hope, of renewal.

Here, in my family's world, the symbols are all about power. Red moons for the Red Rising, Raven marks burned into human skin, silver and black livery like moonlight and shadow, the world of night my parents rule.

And I straddle both worlds, able to exist in light and darkness. Sometimes I feel like I don't belong anywhere; not quite vampire enough, not quite human enough. I'm still trying to work out what kind of symbol I'm going to be. A positive one, I hope.

I sigh as I open the door to my room. It looks the same as always, except for the pile of clothes on the bed. Velvets and silks and beaded chiffon, dresses and skirts and blouses and, hidden under it all, a jacket, the leather so deep purple it's almost black.

Okay, I don't mind the jacket.

The rest of it, though… I think of the markets in the Safe Zone, the second-hand clothing in neat piles, folded to hide the worn patches. Geneva's little shop, where she makes the most of what she can get, scraps thrown from the tables of her overlords.

I want to throw everything into the fire.

'My lady? Forgive me for not meeting you at the door.'

I turn at the familiar voice. 'Bertrand!' I squeal.

My personal guard picks me up in his massive, muscled arms, swinging me around, his blue eyes alive with pleasure. The guards either side of my door are smiling as well. Okay, maybe things aren't as formal as they used to be. I guess me getting kidnapped and nearly killed, then moving to the Safe Zone, has made me, somehow, more real to them. Especially to Bertrand. I knew how much he cared for me before I left; now he tells me, often, that he misses me when I'm gone. He's also pushed for better conditions in the feed hall, humans now on four shifts of six hours, rather than three of eight. It's a small but significant change.

He sets me down. 'Your father is in the library.'

'And my mother?'

'She—'

'Gorgeous girl!'

All the guards, including Bertrand, step back and bow.

My mother wraps me in her cool embrace, her hair like silk against my cheek. 'Oh, I have *missed* you,' she cries, kissing me. 'Come, tell me what you've been up to.'

'I need to get changed first.' I gesture at my sweats. My

parents don't like seeing me dressed like other humans. Which is partly the reason I do so, as often as possible.

'Oh, yes.' My mother's satin-smooth brow creases for a moment. 'Did you see the clothes I left for you? There's a beautiful velvet gown that used to belong to your grandmother. Will you try it on? It's the purple one.' She kisses my cheek again, as though unwilling to let me go.

I know she misses me. I miss her, too. She was my entire world for much of my life. There are people who wonder why she's even bothering to make me Raven. I used to wonder the same thing. But I get it, now. She fought for me since the moment I was born, and she continues to do so.

I go into my bathroom and change quickly, putting on the purple dress. My mother links arms with me, telling me of her day as we head towards the library. Father didn't come to meet me because he wanted her to have that moment, I guess. But there's no disguising the quiet joy in his face as he looks up and sees us coming through the double doors.

He's seated at a large wooden table, the gleaming polished top almost hidden by piles of books and curling maps. A smaller table nearby holds a tray; steam curls from the spout of a flowery porcelain teapot, the matching cup next to it. There's a pen in my father's hand, dark against his pale fingers. He could use a laptop, if he wanted. But I suppose old habits die hard. And his are very, very old.

He puts down the pen and gets to his feet. His lean face breaks into a smile, his golden eyes bright as he folds me into a hug, pressing a kiss to my hair. I cling to him, breathing in his scent of moss and violets. I never thought he loved me; always felt he was ashamed of me. Then he offered his life in exchange for mine, and I realised how wrong I was. How my own self-loathing had coloured the world around me. And how much I love him.

'You look well,' he says, his hands on my shoulders. 'Are you here long?'

'I'll go back tomorrow afternoon, on the shift bus.'

'You don't want to take the car?'

'You know why I don't.'

'I do. Have I told you I'm proud of you?'

I grin. 'You might have mentioned it.'

He regards me for a moment longer, then pulls me to the table. 'Before we start our lesson, I have something interesting to show you. Notes of an experimental community, a few centuries ago. Human and vampire, living together.'

My father is teaching me statecraft, among other things. But he's also researching how humans and vampires co-existed through the centuries, each scrap of information another piece of the puzzle, key to the new world I want to create.

I scan the curling parchment, squinting to make out the words in the low light. My father's finger moves across the page. 'It speaks of a place, a town where humans and vampires share the community. Vampires guard it, humans offering blood in return, but only if and when they choose. They work together, each for the good of the other. And there's something here about "dark knights" who protect the place during the day. Human champions, I suppose.'

'Really? That sounds pretty cool.'

'Yes, very cool.' My father's lips twitch as he reads from the page. '"Designed by ye ladye Morvenna, this ys a place where human and vampyres may live as free men, where reciprocity and manners keep one as civilised as the other, where balance in all things is respected and required."'

'Lady Morvenna?'

'Her name isn't familiar.' My father's brows draw together. 'What about you, my love?'

My mother places a cup of tea on the table for me, running a gentle hand across my hair, then sits next to my father. 'I've not heard of her.' She purses her red lips. 'I had a cousin called Morwen – it's one of our family names – but she wasn't born until the eighteen-hundreds.'

'I know nothing of her either, or this experiment.'

'Ah, you were probably too busy fighting wars across Europe then.' My mother gazes at him fondly. He drops a kiss on her lips, both of them smiling.

I sip my tea, breathing in the sharpness of mint, the warmth of this moment. Faint golden light gilds us, fire crackling in the fireplace. Yet it feels, somehow, like the calm before the storm.

My mother turns her attention to me. 'Are you ready for tonight?'

So, here it is. The thing that's been making me nervous since I woke up this morning. Since I first heard about it, to be honest. Tonight, I finally get to do something I've wanted to do for months. Something I couldn't tell Michael about, or Laurel.

I'm going to speak with the North Wind.

Chapter Four

THE CHALLENGE

'Name the twelve families.' My father's voice is gentle, yet has an undertone.

'Mistral, Ravenna, De Corbeau, De Raaf.' I recite the names, the rhyme familiar from childhood lessons. 'Vindhof, Ravenko, Corvosa, Andras.' There are twelve noble Raven families apart from ours, all descended from former Ravens who stepped aside for their heirs, each managing their own territory in Europe or North America, a dark network of black and silver watching over our lands. 'Darkwing, Karanlik, and there are two more, Voronov and Eligor. I already know this,' I add, unsure why he's making me run through it again.

'Knowing something and understanding it are two different things.' His golden eyes briefly dim. 'Tell me, who has the largest army?'

Every Raven territory has their own army, each with their own livery, all loyal to the Raven banner. The heads of each family also act as a council for my parents, convening when important decisions need to be made, such as Mistral's sentencing and execution for inciting the North Wind rebellion, and subsequent cover-up.

'Uh, Vindhof.' I frown as I try to remember. I'm doing my best, but between my father and my mother there's just so much information to take in. It's partly my fault. I pretty much did everything I could to avoid being Raven, despite my parents' efforts. But with my coronation just months away there's a new urgency to all they want to teach me. I know they want me back at the house full-time. And I'm increasingly aware that I need to step up. 'Ravenko. Then De Corbeau.'

'Ravenna?' Again, the undertone to my father's voice. My frown deepens.

'Ravenna don't have a large army.'

'But they ally most closely with—?'

'The house of Mistral, who do have a decent-sized force.' Makes sense, really, that they would be tight. Stella Ravenna, my cousin, has never liked me. Artos Ravenna basically insulted me to my face last time I saw him. And Mistral's two eldest sons, Jacques and Oliver, are gigantic assholes. The only reason they're still allowed to hold their titles, despite their father's treachery, was that it was a condition of them keeping quiet about what really happened to him. Birds of a feather flock together, and they are all Ravens, after all. Plus, I think my mother feels somehow guilty, even though nothing about what happened was her fault. But she was with Mistral for a long time before she was with Father, so perhaps that's why she wasn't as ruthless as she could have been with his children.

I fold my arms. 'Why are we going over this? Shouldn't we be talking about what's going to happen tonight?'

The message came through a few days ago. Via Ira, of all people. The North Wind want to meet and talk terms for a ceasefire. The huge, tattooed owner of the Dome nightclub seems an unlikely candidate to deliver rebel leaders, yet I remember how he knew Kyle from before he worked for Raven, and the human commander who helped me get home after being kidnapped telling me he was sympathetic to humans. And the boy, caged in Ira's bar, who died a violent death in a blood-soaked meadow. A death both Ira and I witnessed, though not together. There's definitely more to him than being a local club owner. I'm just not sure, exactly, what that is.

'Remind me again why Ira's involved?'

My father's lips twitch. 'Everything we teach you is important, Emelia,' he says. 'All part of a greater whole.' His voice is grave, but there's a twinkle in his eye.

'Like Ira?'

My father laughs. 'Yes, like Ira. We all have our roles to play. And tonight's meeting is an excellent chance for you to see negotiation in action.'

'Negotiation? What could there possibly be to negotiate?' When Mistral died, the North Wind began to unravel. Documents found in his home detailed plans and rebel safe-houses across the UK and Europe, including the one where Kyle and Jessie kept me captive. And where I left Jessie, frozen after Kyle tried to change her to vampire.

'That's what we're unsure about.' My mother rests her chin in her hands, her elbows on the table, her rippling black hair contrasting sharply with the red velvet of her gown. There's a strange tension to her, a flicker deep in her onyx gaze. I glance from her to my father.

'Understand, Emelia,' he says, 'that Raven broke apart everything they could in the first month after Mistral died. We are swift, and efficient, when it comes to getting things done. The North Wind has already been mostly shut down.'

I nod. I know this.

'Ira is bringing them because they surrendered to him at the Dome. Knocked on his back door two nights ago with a message, asking us to pull back our "dark forces". That they wanted the attacks to stop. Yet we *had* stopped, a month before.'

'That makes no sense.'

'It does not. And, with what's been happening recently in the Safe Zones, I'm unsure what their game is.'

'You mean the Reaper attacks?' I consider for a moment. 'Do you think it could be the North Wind, still? Some sort of double-bluff tactic to keep us on our toes?'

My father shakes his head. 'No. Like I say, Raven has essentially broken them apart. And what happened in the Safe Zones bears clear marks of vampire attacks.'

'Could they be working with vampires?'

'What makes you think that?'

'Uh.' I cast around for something plausible. They know I snuck off the estate, but not that it was thanks to Kyle swapping secrets with another guard. 'Mistral was a vampire, and he started the rebellion. Maybe there are others who still think it's a good idea?'

'For humans to overthrow us?' My father raises an eyebrow. 'I think it more likely to have been Reapers attacking the Safe Zones. The signs are all there.'

'The signs?'

'The humans were brutalised, as were the vampires.' My mother's voice is sombre. 'Their deaths were savage.'

More savage than being torn apart in a meadow? I swallow,

trying not to think of the Moon Harvest. 'There's no nice way to kill someone, I guess.' Whether a slow death trapped in a town you can't leave, or a quick death at the hands of a Reaper. 'Why do they think it's us, then?'

'We don't know,' my mother replies.

'Which is why we're wary about tonight,' my father adds. 'Even though I do believe they'd like a truce. I think they just want to live.' A shadow crosses his face. 'I understand that.'

I blow out a breath. 'So do I. But what do Raven want?'

'We'll see what they have to say and—'

'I don't know what I want.' My mother's cool voice cuts across my father's and I'm reminded, once again, that she's the head of Raven, not him. 'They almost killed you, Aleks! Took Emelia from us and would have killed her if she hadn't escaped.' Her voice shakes. She's angry. It's not surprising, when you think about it. My father was badly injured in a bomb attack; only the efforts of our blood dancers stopped him from being incinerated in the light. Several other vampires died, including the Lion prince, Daniel. And I was kidnapped. Such things wouldn't be brushed off so easily, not with her.

'Nonetheless, they have surrendered. We need to hear them out, at least.' My father puts his arm around my mother, kissing her satin hair. 'Peace, my love. We hold the power here.'

She relaxes into his embrace, her hand on his cheek. 'If I had lost either of you…' she murmurs, a catch in her voice.

'Yet you did not.' My father's golden gaze is as soft as I've ever seen it. 'We're here, all of us together as it should be. And we'll put an end to this, finally, tonight.'

I clear my throat. 'So that's what we want. An ending.' I

hadn't imagined anything else, but I need to be sure what they mean by that. 'A peaceful one, right?'

My father nods. 'Yes. And, while your mother and I will be doing the negotiating, you have a voice as well. If there's something you feel needs saying, say it. You are the next Raven, and this is as much to do with you as it is with anyone else.'

Good. Not that they could have stopped me speaking up. 'When will they get here?'

'Midnight.'

'Do we need to go over anything else beforehand?' I know there's something else. I can feel it.

My parents exchange a look, my mother shaking her head slightly. My father stares her down, then puts his hand on my shoulder. 'There is something that we—'

'My lord?'

The moment scatters, all of us turning. A tall vampire, broad-shouldered, stands at the doorway to the library. His lustrous shoulder-length dark hair is partly tied back from his handsome face, and he's wearing black chain mail moulded to his muscular form, the silver Raven crest blazoned on the chest. A long curving sword is sheathed at his side, a slender slice of darkness.

'Varin!' My father gets to his feet, glancing at the gilded clock on the mantel above the fire. 'Is it that time already?'

The vampire bows. 'It is, my lord.'

I glance at my mother. Her mouth tightens, a line between her brows as my father embraces her then comes to me, dropping a soft kiss on my hair. 'Don't worry about tonight. We have it all in hand.'

'But—'

With a whoosh, my father and the chain-mail clad vampire are gone, cool air curling in their wake. I turn to my mother. 'Who was that?'

'Oh, no one.' At my frown she relents. 'Varin is a sword-master, from India. He and your father have been friends for years, fought together in many wars.'

'And he's visiting us because…?'

My mother pauses. I can almost see her thinking. 'Your father felt he was out of practice, as he doesn't fight with his sword anymore. So, he asked Varin to come and spar with him.'

Yeah. Sure. I'm sure my father just decided one day, out of the blue, that he needed to start using his sword again. I hold my mother's gaze, until she looks away.

And there it is.

'What aren't you telling me?'

'It's nothing.'

Oh, so it's something, then. I wait.

'It's just, with what happened to Mistral. His sons are talking of reviving the Challenge.'

Chapter Five

DARK FORCES

'The Challenge?'

'It's a vampire ritual. You most likely won't have heard about it.'

'And why wouldn't I have heard about it?' I don't bother hiding my annoyance.

'Your father and I both admit we've made mistakes, Emelia.' My mother's tone sharpens. 'We should have taught you more, when you were younger, about the ways of the vampire world.'

'Why didn't you?'

It's old ground. We've been over it before. I know I shouldn't do this, know they both want me to be Raven and believe in my right to be so. But old habits, as I say, die hard.

'You know why!' My mother blinks, looking away. 'When you were born… God and darkness, we were *terrified*. I didn't leave your side for the first few years of your life. Keeping you safe was our first and only priority. And then … we wanted you to forge your own path. Be free to choose. You are unique,

Emelia, and I knew you were special the moment I laid eyes on you. Blood-borne, yet human. And with the potential for infinite change. Even though I know you didn't feel that way.'

I get it, I guess. If they hadn't been so strict, I probably wouldn't have made it past my first birthday. And it didn't stop me running away, anyway. I reach for my mother's hand, playing with her long cool fingers. 'Tell me about the Challenge.'

'It's an old custom, and—'

'They do tend to be.'

My mother shoots me a look. 'As I say, an old custom. Your great-grandfather was the last to be challenged so, and that was centuries ago. He won, of course.'

'But what is it?'

'A fight. To the death. The winner becomes, or remains, Raven.'

Darkness. 'Are you kidding me?' Every vampire ritual I've ever come across is like this. Whether it's Jaguar mocking human religion, drugging them to drink their blood in his stone temples, or Scorpion with their literal blood baths, it's all the same. A game of pain and darkness leading to one thing. Death.

It's what I ran away from, the brutality and power of my parents' world. And it's what I'm trying to change. I don't want to be a ruler who kills for sport or punishment, upholding arcane traditions from another time. Humans also used to fight to the death, centuries ago, to settle scores. But years of war were replaced by diplomacy, a desire to build a better world for their children. Vampires, though, seem to still live in that brutal past. Why change something that works for them, I guess. But it's not going to work for me.

'You have to understand, among vampires, such things are considered—'

'Normal?' I shake my head. 'There's nothing normal about this.'

My mother's dark brows draw together. 'Nonetheless, it is serious. A threat to our family name. And with everything else going on, your father wants to be ready.'

'But you're Raven, not Father. Shouldn't they be fighting you?'

'Your father is not just my husband. He's also my champion. It's how we met, you know.'

'It is?'

'Well, yes. You know I was with Mistral, of course.'

I wrinkle my nose. Mistral was very handsome, but also a terrible person. I still have no idea what my mother saw in him.

'He was my lieutenant and champion, as well as my lover.' She shakes her head as though she can't believe it either. 'Then your father arrived one night, offering his fealty. Armour-clad, sword in hand, that look in his eyes.' She rests her chin on her hand, a smile curving her lips. 'He laid his sword at my feet and looked up at me, and that was it. There was no one else for either of us. He said it was love at first sight.'

I try not to roll my eyes. 'So, Oliver and Jacques are challenging for the title of Raven? Like father like son, I guess.' Mistral's two other sons are both vampires, blond and handsome and full of themselves. And not above nipping at the human daughter of their Raven rulers, either. I've never told my mother what happened at the one Gathering I attended as a teenager.

I was told to stay on my throne beneath the canopy, anti-feed so thick around me I could barely breathe. I stared out at the bustling throng, everything painted grey and silver by the full moon, and wondered what the hell I was doing there. My parents were somewhere in the crowd, a line of Raven guards standing between me and the rest of the Gathering.

Then I heard a hiss. I ignored it. But then it came again. I turned my head. The billowing silk surrounding me moved strangely, and a handsome smiling face appeared between the folds of fabric, a boy about my age with long blond hair.

'Hey, Raven. You want to have some fun?' The words were whispered.

Did I? Anything was better than sitting there, bored out of my mind. I glanced at the guards, all with their backs to me. Fuck it. I spritzed myself with anti-feed, then slid quietly from the throne, taking the beckoning hand that reached through the gap in the silks.

Once through, I was surprised to see another blond vampire, almost as handsome as the first. They introduced themselves as the sons of Mistral. Even better. He was my mother's lieutenant; even though I didn't like him much, I figured I could trust his sons. So I went with them. And it was fun, at first. They took turns whirling me around the dancefloor, so fast at times I could barely see. Then they each took my hand and pulled me through the crowd, blocking me from sight with their tall, powerful bodies. I laughed and went along with it, enjoying myself for the first time that evening.

Then somehow it was just the three of us, among the tumbled boulders that bounded the meadow. I tried to go back, but they held on to me. Not too hard, but hard enough. Moving too fast as I tried to get away, blocking my path.

'Your mother used to be with our father,' Oliver said,

smiling. His fangs were dropped, though, and he was too close to me.

'Imagine that,' Jacques said, again too close, his cool breath sliding across the back of my neck. 'We could be siblings.'

'Though that might make this awkward.' Oliver moved closer, his teeth grazing my neck while Jacques pushed at me from behind.

'Let me go!' I struggled, but Oliver held me in place, effortless, all the while both of them touching me, their hands roaming across my body.

'I suggest you do as my lady asks.' The voice came from behind us, calm and quiet. 'I would hate to have to get her parents involved.'

Oliver snarled, but pulled away, his hands finally leaving me. Jacques did the same. And then I was in strong arms, being borne back through the crowd.

'Bertrand.' I clung to him, shaking, horror threading through me at my narrow escape. 'Oh, thank darkness you—'

'You should not have left your seat, my lady. Those boys are much older than you, despite how they look.' Vampire adolescence lasts far longer than it does for humans. I should have known, but how could I? I never got to meet anyone my age. I huddled against Bertrand, my cheeks burning at my stupidity.

He returned me to the silver-grey canopy, entering the way I left. The guards still stood there, their backs to us. And I was never so glad to be behind that wall of silver and black once more.

Bertrand sat me gently on the throne, then knelt in front of me. His hand came to mine. 'Do you need a drink, or to feed?'

'No.' What I wanted, more than anything, was to go home.

'Thank you,' I breathed, tears filling my eyes despite my efforts.

Bertrand frowned, then bit his finger, releasing a drop of blood. 'If I may, my lady.' He bent forward and pressed it to my throat, and I felt the faint tingle of healing. Then he wiped the remnants of blood from me. 'Now you are perfect once more.'

I found it so hard not to cry at the gentle concern on his face. 'Please don't tell them.'

He studied me for a moment, then his mouth curved. 'I think that wise, my lady.'

As far as I know, he never did. Dear Bertrand.

'So, Father is practising because he thinks Oliver and Jacques are better fighters than he is?' I scoff, lightly. My father is a legendary swordsman. I hope he kills them both.

'Oliver is the one making the Challenge. He holds the Mistral title now. After what happened to their father, they feel justified, I suppose.'

'You mean how he started a rebellion, tried to kill Father, kidnapped me and would have had me killed if I hadn't escaped? I think he got off lightly.'

My mother grins, a brief flash of light. 'I thought you weren't bloodthirsty.'

'Motherrrr. Tell me what this means.'

'Mistral was also a fine swordsman and trained his sons well. Your father is making sure there's no margin for error, if the challenge proceeds.'

'If?'

'There is … you have to understand, when we sent Mistral into the light, even though the family heads outwardly supported our right to do so, not everyone agreed with that decision. There are also those who are not sure a human should rule Raven. His sons are trying to build on that dissent.'

I feel sick. My humanity, once again, is a fucking liability. 'Shouldn't I have been told about this sooner?'

'It's not really been a problem until this week, when the Challenge was made. They need the approval of six noble families for it to go ahead.'

'How many do they have?'

'Four.'

Four? God and darkness. 'No wonder Father was having me go over the twelve families and their armies. Let me guess. Ravenna is one of them?'

My mother nods.

'And the others?' Anger flares in me, white-hot.

'Vindhof and Ravenko.'

Shit. The two largest armies under our banner. Vindhof and Ravenko are close, their territories bordering each other. I suppose it makes sense, if any of this can be said to do so. 'Who else?'

'Darkwing.'

'*Darkwing*? But they're in North America. They don't even know me!' There are two Raven families in North America, each holding their own territories; Karanlik in the north, and Darkwing in the south. I've never met any of them. But with Mistral, that's five noble families. Perilously close to the majority of seven they need for the Challenge to proceed.

My mother shrugs, elegant as always. 'They don't need to know you, Emelia. They just know what they're told.'

'That I'm human. And we killed Mistral.'

She nods, her perfect red lips pursed.

'So, even though Mistral started a literal rebellion against vampires, the families feel like having a human ruler is somehow *worse*?'

My mother looks pained. 'Not all the families. Only those involved in the Challenge.'

Like that makes it any better. 'Do you think they'll get the majority they need?'

'We don't know.'

I stare into space, thinking. 'And if it goes ahead and father loses, does that mean…?'

'At best, it means Oliver becomes Raven. You and I will be relegated to one of the lesser estates. And your father, of course, will be dead.' She blinks, looking away.

'That's the *best* outcome? What's the worst?'

My mother's gaze comes back to me, red lining her onyx eyes. 'It means civil war. And, with things as they are outside our borders, the fall of the House of Raven.'

Well, that sounds like a fun time.

Chapter Six

THE NORTH WIND

I head to the War Room just before midnight, massaging my temples against a threatening headache. The absolute fucking *nerve* of Oliver and Jacques! I know not everyone is happy with me being crowned. Darkness knows, I have mixed feelings about it myself. Human children born of vampire parents are rare, not because they aren't born very often, but because they're usually not allowed to live. The fact that my mother fought to keep me is unusual, especially in a ruling family. I wonder what she saw in me, what she hoped to accomplish by putting a human on the throne. My father said to me, as we sat on the steps watching a rebellion catch fire, that he and my mother had tried to protect me from cruelty, that they didn't want anyone to think differently of me. I wish, now, that they'd let me bear it, rather than keeping me hidden away. I already grew up feeling like I wasn't good enough; what difference would a few more insults have made? At least I might have had the chance to stand up for myself, and show everyone who I am. It feels like I'm coming into this on the back foot, having to prove myself even before my mother anoints me. I can understand why Oliver and Jacques want to challenge me. A human girl, responsible for exposing their father's treachery, ruling over them? I'm surprised they haven't tried to kill me already. And now I have to sit in a room with the North Wind, another of Mistral's stupid dangerous schemes, and pretend like I don't know my father's life is under threat. Because of me.

Heavy the head that wears the crown. I read that somewhere, once, and it always stayed with me. Now it makes more sense than ever. I'm not even Raven yet but I feel overwhelmed.

Moonlight paints silver shadows on the darkened carpet, the long hallway walls. Bertrand pads along behind me. The War Room is close to the Costume Room, filled with dusty maps and ancient books of strategy, weapons on the wall. A huge central table features a relief map of the world, the four realms mapped in copper and silver, jade and gold, like the one on the wall in the library.

My father waits for us, his hand on the door, a gentle gleam in his eye. There's an answering glow in my chest, comforting as a warm fire. It seems wildly unfair that we might have just mended the distance between us, only for this to happen. I cannot lose him, not now. I know how strong he is, how talented a warrior. But he's not infallible.

He opens the door, ushering me inside with a quick glance, brows raised. I hastily school my features into a calm mask. The War Room looks different, tonight. More … alive. Candle lamps glimmer in golden sconces, sparking light from the map on the table. Chairs surround it, carved ebony inlaid with silver, the Raven emblem on the tall backs. Guards are stationed against the walls, including my parents' personal contingent, flecks of red among the silver on their livery. Bertrand takes his position among them, his massive arms crossed.

Varin is already here, as is Ira. The club-owner bows to me, his hand to his chest, his ice-blue gaze warming. His tattoos are mostly hidden tonight under a tailored black shirt, though there are some visible at the edge of his cuffs and collar, including a flash of red on the inside of his wrist. With him are two humans, a man and a woman, both dressed in tidy yet worn clothing. At my entrance their eyes widen, glancing at each other. The woman's hands are twisted together, the knuckles white. It's understandable. Being in a room full of vampires, in the home of Raven itself, must be daunting. I stay close to my father, my shoulders back, my head high, conscious of the part I need to play. I might feel out of my depth, but I can't let anyone else know. *Negotiation is about appearance as much as anything.* My father's lessons float through my mind. *It is the same in battle. Arrive as though you're already the winner. Leave nothing exposed that you do not wish to have exploited.*

Mistral started the North Wind rebellion as a distraction to undermine our house, to get rid of my father and me, just so he could be with Mother again. Why he thought a plan like that would work I don't know. Mother would never have forgiven him. I suppose he was so arrogant he thought he could just breeze back in and save the day, and she would fall into his arms. I wonder whether he really knew her at all.

Yet it did almost work. If Kyle hadn't been distracted,

changing Jessie into a vampire, I would never have been able to expose him to the light and kill him, then escape. The rebellion itself was more successful than Mistral ever thought it would be; I remember him talking to Kyle about it, when they both thought I was unconscious, and his surprise that humans would fight back, and so strongly. Yet another way he underestimated them, and me.

My mother enters the room. Clad in black velvet, severely cut. Her flawless beauty shines in the dimly lit space, like a sharpened blade in the moonlight. Everyone bows, including me. She is Raven incarnate tonight.

'My lady.' Ira straightens up from his bow. 'May I present Jane, and Andrew, of the North Wind.'

My mother inclines her head, her expression cool. She pulls her chair out from the table and sits. We all do the same, the humans slightly clumsy in their haste. I hate that for them. I meet their puzzled gazes; perhaps they think me some sort of human pet. They will soon learn I am no such thing.

'I am Penelope Raven,' my mother says. 'Head of the house of Raven. My husband, Aleksandr.' She gestures to my father. 'And my daughter, Emelia, who will be the next Raven.' She places her hand on my shoulder.

'I'm sorry, Lady Raven. Did you say this was your daughter?' This is the woman, Jane. Her hands are still clenched together, but her voice is clear and strong.

My mother squeezes my shoulder, lightly.

'She did,' I say. 'The next ruler of Raven will be human.' I smile, just a touch. Jane's lips part, and she glances at Andrew again.

'Tell me.' My mother's voice slides into the room, like a

silvery poisoned blade. I think again of her rage in the library. Of blood on her face, in a darkened meadow. I know her. And she's still angry. 'What is it you would like to achieve tonight?'

'Your forces have destroyed all but a few of our settlements.' Jane's hair is greyish-blonde and curling, tied back from her fine-boned face. She looks tired, yet there's still fire in her grey eyes. 'The ones that remain … there are children there. We wish, therefore, to ask for peace between us.'

'We didn't know that Mistral's promises were hollow. Nor of his plan to harm your family. But you have to understand—' Andrew is tall, broad-shouldered, his angular face tanned, his dark hair greying at the temples, a scar across the back of one of his hands like a badly-stitched seam '—we just wanted things to be better for us.'

I wince internally. I get it. Vampires stole so much from humans when they took over the world. Their blood, of course. But also their freedom of movement. Their choices.

'I can appreciate that.' My mother's tones are measured. 'But there was always the opportunity to speak with us, rather than embark on this cycle of destruction. It was you who chose that path, and your movement is now paying the consequences.'

It's funny she thinks humans would have dreamed of approaching her to ask for changes. Would the cow in the meadow ask the farmer for mercy? My mother is ruthless when crossed. I saw her order the death of twenty humans as punishment for the attack on my father, then stood on a darkened cliff top and watched her carry out the sentence. She sent her former lover to a spiked and burning death for what he tried to do to me.

I wonder what she wants to do to these humans.

They're wondering, too. I can almost smell their fear. What will Raven demand as payment for what they've done? All at once it feels impossible, that there could be any sort of peace between vampires and humans.

But my mother just smiles, though her eyes remain dark. 'I ask again. What do you want to achieve here?'

'We want the attacks to stop. Want your dark forces withdrawn. We want…' Jane falters momentarily. 'We wish to rejoin the human community. Then, perhaps, we can talk about the possibility of change.'

Rejoin the human community?

'Our dark forces, as you call them, are no longer attacking your movement.' My father's voice is deep. 'So, I don't understand what it is you want to stop.'

Jane and Andrew glance at each other. 'But … there was a raid, just the other night. On a camp near the Darkmeadow, where you hold your Gatherings.'

A camp near the Darkmeadow? I don't understand. Humans live in Safe Zones, work in vampire towns and on the estates. At least, that's what I've always been told. I glance at my father, but his face gives nothing away.

Jane speaks. 'No one was left alive. If it wasn't Raven, then who was it?'

Shit. Surely that's not how we do things. My mind is racing. Was it Reapers again, like the attacks on the Safe Zones? I try not to think of the floating bodies, the shadowy dark figures.

'As Lord Raven said, this is not our doing.' My mother's dark brows draw together. 'We are no longer actively engaged in breaking your organisation apart. As far as we're concerned, it's already broken. Your presence here tonight is proof of that.'

Ouch. My mother isn't wrong, though. A few months ago, a meeting like this would have been out of the question. I wonder again at Ira's presence. Why has he been allowed to stay for such high-level negotiations? Again, there's the feeling of something more here, something I don't quite understand.

Jane looks close to tears. I can't hold back any longer. 'When you say, "rejoin the human community," what do you mean? Aren't you already in the Safe Zones?'

Andrew turns his attention to me. 'No. But we're willing to return and start monthly blood donations, if it means our families are safe.'

I think fast. Aside from the mind-blowing fact that these humans have been surviving outside Safe Zones, I don't feel that decanting a bunch of rebels back into them is going to be great for human morale, nor will it ensure a lasting peace. A kernel of an idea takes shape.

'What if there was somewhere else to go? Somewhere you could actually be free?' I know they've done terrible things. But so have my family, much worse and for far longer. Kyle said something about it, once. *Any animal will fight, if cornered. And humans have been cornered for a long time.*

Everyone in the room is looking at me. This might be madness. But, faced with such quiet desperation, I feel the need to do something. 'How many of you are left?'

'Around two hundred, including children.'

Two hundred? That seems like a lot of rebels. I know my father is surprised as well, by the way his hand twitches. Still, it's just about the perfect number of people for what I have in mind.

'When the North Wind almost killed my father,' I say, 'I wanted to speak with you. To find out what it was you wanted, why you were trying to hurt my family. Then I spent time in the Safe Zones, and realised how it really was for humans. Why you wouldn't want that. And why you would choose to fight back.'

Surprise ripples through the room. Ira seems to be fighting the urge to smile. Jane and Andrew stare at me, their mouths half open.

'I saw what was taken from you. How your lives were subject to Raven's power. I witnessed the Moon Harvest and I also saw humans attacking vampires. This is a cycle of violence without end, unless something changes. And that's what I'm offering. Change.'

This might not be what my parents had in mind. But it feels like the right thing to do, more than just about anything I've ever done. All the injustice, the pain and death and sorrow of the past few months well up in me. I blink away tears. My father said I had a voice here, and I'm going to use it.

'After my experience, one of the first things I wanted to do was create a true Safe Zone. A place where humans can live without blood harvesting, free to follow the lives they choose.' I pause, searching for the right words. 'I want to change things, but I know it won't happen overnight. I would like to offer you, and your community, the chance to live on the Channel Islands, in a vampire-free zone. In return, you end this rebellion. Completely. Change is coming, but it cannot come with blood. Not this time.'

The room is silent. This is most definitely not what my parents had in mind. But if they want me to lead, they have to let me make decisions, too. Not everything has to be about death. Jane has tears in her eyes.

'Is this a true offering? We lay down our arms, and you'll let us do this?'

'Yes,' I say. 'Though it must be all of you who remain, and a true surrender, rather than a ceasefire. Those who wish to return to Safe Zones may do so. Those who wish to be part of the new community will be taken there. And the North Wind ends here, today.'

Chapter Seven

RULING HOUSE

When we leave the War Room, I brace myself. I know my father told me to speak up, but my parents may have had other plans. Undoubtedly did, if I'm honest, and that didn't involve giving Raven lands to the people who tried to kill them. But I can't escape the feeling that it was the right thing to do.

My mother is quiet, walking ahead of me as we head down the long hallway. My father pats my shoulder, then goes to join her. I frown, quickening my pace. Varin is escorting the humans and Ira from the house, so I don't need to worry about them overhearing anything. Bertrand is following me, of course, and my parents' personal guards, but I know they can be trusted.

'Mother!' I hiss.

She glances back at me, slowing her pace. Red lines her eyes. Oh darkness. What now? I bite down my frustration, but honestly. First, she drops the Challenge on me, now this. Does she really think I'm just going to go to bed and not talk about it?

My father, his hand at her waist, steers her into the Costume Room, beckoning me to follow. The door closes behind us, the guards waiting beyond. My mother glides between the mannequins, clothed in family garments from across the centuries, and sinks gracefully onto the padded seat beneath the huge arched windows. Outside, feathery clouds scud across a navy sky speckled with stars, a pale crescent of moon visible above the swaying trees.

My father inspects a suit of shimmering armour, pulling the sleeve of his shirt over his hand to polish some non-existent smudge. I wonder what in darkness he's doing. Then I realise.

I sigh, then make my way between the faceless dark figures, taking a seat next to my mother, my hands braced against the cushions. I don't care what she has to say, no matter the ache in my chest. I stand behind my decision.

'How do you feel that went?' Her voice is a cool chime, moonlight silvering the curve of her head.

'As far as I can see, it solved two problems at once.'

'How so?' She glances at me.

'Well, it's the end of the North Wind, if they accept our offer. And it also solves the problem of who to send to the Channel Islands.' This has been one of the sticking points in the project. I would love nothing more than for every human in my realm to be free. But the massive fucking flaw in this plan is that vampires need blood, and if I shut down the Safe Zones and cut off their supply, chaos will ensue. The Channel Islands are supposed to be a symbol of my new reign, a place to show the world what's possible. But how to choose which humans to send there has been bothering me for a while. The whole project has, to be honest, but I can't quite put my finger on why. Nor can I think of a better alternative at the moment.

'And if they don't accept the offer?'

'Why wouldn't they accept? Surely it's better than staying wherever they are, waiting for Raven or Reapers to get them. And that's another thing. What in darkness did they mean when they said they weren't in Safe Zones?'

'Not every human in the world lives in a Safe Zone.' My father strolls towards us, casual as though what he's saying doesn't go against everything I've been taught.

'What?'

'There have long been human settlements outside Safe Zones,' my mother says. 'Mainly on the edge of the Great Forest. They usually don't last too long; either hunted dry or cleared by Reapers. Raven move them on whenever they find them.'

'Move them on?'

'Into Safe Zones, where they'll be safe. What?' She frowns at me.

My mouth hangs open. I have about twenty things I want to say, none of them particularly wise. 'Why has no one ever told me this?'

'They're small settlements, not easy to find,' my mother continues. 'Ten, twenty humans at most, some of them nomadic. We've always felt it best to focus our resources elsewhere. But now, it seems, we have to look more closely at them.'

'You know of the documentation we found following Mistral's death,' my father says, 'detailing the rebel network within Safe Zones. What's been more difficult to track are any external cells, where the remaining rebels would be. As your mother says, they're not easy to find.'

'Gods.' My throat is tight. 'So if they don't accept our offer—'

'—they'll go back to their cells. And now they know about your project.'

Expose nothing that you do not wish to have exploited. Shit. I drop my head into my hands, despair rolling over me. How am I ever going to do this? Vampires have centuries of living to hone their intellect, to learn about the world. I only have my few human decades, and I need to sleep as well. I sit up, blowing out a deep breath.

'They'll accept,' I say.

'How do you know?'

'Because I'm offering them what they're fighting for! The chance to live a normal life. To be free. They're being attacked, by Reapers. There are *children* with them.'

'That's what they told us,' my father says. 'But what else have I taught you about negotiation?'

My stomach lurches. Maybe I've really screwed this up. 'To not take every statement at face value,' I mutter. The faceless mannequins, dressed in the chain mail and silk of my ancestors, seem to be judging me, an audience for my failures. My mouth twists. Screw that. 'I believed them,' I say. 'And it just *felt* like the right thing to do. To give something back.'

My mother nods. 'Do not forget, Emelia, that you'll be ruling vampires as well as humans. We are not the monsters you think us to be. Both need to be considered in your plans.'

'I know.' I do know this. But I also feel like vampires have everything, and humans don't have much of anything at all.

My mother gets to her feet, one hand stroking my hair. 'I am proud of you, you know,' she says. 'But this will not be easy.'

'I'm getting tired of hearing that,' I snap. 'I don't expect it to be. What would be helpful is being given all the information I need.'

'I cannot cram a lifetime of knowledge into a few short months!' My mother's voice sharpens, her hand leaving my hair. 'We're telling you all we can in the time we have. I had much to learn when I gained my crown, and you are no different. So do not point the finger when you don't know something!'

'I'm not pointing the finger! But I think it would have been useful to know that not all humans live in Safe Zones, seeing as I'm trying to change things for them.'

'Changing things for humans cannot come at the expense of your vampire subjects!'

'Oh, yes, darkness forbid vampires are inconvenienced! Maybe I should start donating my blood as well.'

'Now, Emelia—'

'Do not be ridiculous.' My mother's voice cuts across my father's. 'You might be human, but you are vampire-born.'

'So *what*?' I snarl. 'What does that give me, apart from a family name? I have to rule over vampires, who could kill me any time they feel like it, and to do so I have to let humans, like me, be brutalised just to appease them. I won't do it! That is not the ruler I want to be! It's why I ran away in the first place!'

The red is back in my mother's gaze. I know my running away scared her, and she doesn't like to be reminded of it. I drop my head in my hands, angry tears hot against my palms.

'What is it, dear one?' The cushion moves as my father sits next to me, his hand gentle on my back.

'I just … I don't know how to do this. Vampires … any one of you can kill me—No, you know it's true,' I say, over my mother's rising protests. 'How the hell am I supposed to rule people who can kill me without even thinking about it?'

'Is this why you're focusing on humans?' My mother's voice softens. 'Oh, Emelia. Because they're—'

'Because they're like me. It's just … this is such a huge job. I want to do it, but I have no idea how.'

'Which is why your father and I will support you, as much as we can.' Her hand returns to my hair. I take comfort in her gentle touch, as I have all my life.

'I need to be able to rule on my own, too. To make the decisions I want to make.' There it is. Another thing that's been lurking under the surface.

'And you will. I was eighteen, like you, when I took my crown. My father was very much part of things for the first years of my reign.'

'How many years?'

My mother looks away. 'Twenty.'

'*Twenty?* Absolutely not happening.'

'Maybe you should get some rest, and we can talk about this later.' My father stands. 'It's been a long night for us all.'

'I'm staying here.' I don't want to go back to my room yet, to stare at the ceiling while frustration eats at my bones. Twenty fucking *years*? Why even bother to crown me at all?

'Come and find me, when you wake.' My mother's cool lips brush my brow. Then she and my father are gone, leaving me alone with my turbulent thoughts.

I wonder whether my parents forget sometimes that I won't live as long a life as they will. Or perhaps they choose not to remember. Of course I need guidance, still have a lot to learn. But I refuse to be a figurehead, unable to make my own decisions. I'm the only person who truly understands how it is to live both as a vampire and as a human. It's an almost unbearable pressure, moving between the two. But I need to be able to stand on my own two feet, or I risk losing everything I came back home for.

I can see why vampires felt the easiest thing to do was to farm humans; perhaps, in their own way, they thought what they offered was fair. They need human blood to survive, after all. But I cannot comprehend the kind of blindness it took to turn away from the suffering they caused in the process. Even my parents were part of it; they participated in the Rising, along with the other Great Families. It wasn't until I was born that they even considered thinking differently. However, is their way of thinking different enough to help me do what I want to achieve?

At the moment I'm still hopelessly, painfully naïve about the realities of my world, the ancient political structures I need to navigate, despite my experiences with Kyle and the North Wind. All I have to go on is my gut; I have to figure out what's right, make my decision, and face whatever consequences might come with it. It felt like the right thing for me to come home, instead of running away with Kyle. It felt right for me to give the Channel Islands to the North Wind, too. And it feels right, to my very bones, to try and make things better for humans.

I rub my eyes, trying not to think of Kyle, of dancing with

him in the moonlight. But he seems to haunt me here, a silver and black ghost in the shadows, whispering around the edges of my vision. He fucking knew, all along. Knew how hard it would be for me to do this. Even if he didn't love me, he tried to tell me the truth.

I get to my feet, trailing my hand across my great-grandfather's chain-mail tunic, the links making a soft whispering sound as though he's trying to talk to me, a voice from the past. I wonder what he'd tell me, and whether this was what he wore when he fought for his crown. Now I have to fight for mine. Rage flares again at the thought of Oliver and Jacques. The old Emelia, the one they tricked into going along with them, is long gone. They won't catch me so easily this time.

I stop at another mannequin. My mother's wedding dress. A drop-waisted concoction of ivory tulle and pearlescent beading, the lace-capped veil still with small silk blossoms attached. She would have looked beautiful in it. She married for love, of course. I want that, too. But, as I touch the delicate lace, the trembling flowers, I wonder whether it's the wisest decision. Yes, I have Michael, but for how long? Once I'm crowned, everything will change, and there's no guarantee he'll want to stay. I've been burned by love before. Perhaps I'm better to choose a consort with my head, rather than my heart.

My gaze goes to another white dress nearby. This one is corseted, silk and satin cut precisely to my measurements, the long full skirt beaded with jet black and silver feathers, the matching cloak with the Raven crest beaded and embroidered on the back, more glittering feathers decorating the long train and high collar. My coronation robes.

They used to scare me. In some ways, they still do. But it's time for me to face who I am. To step into my power.

And show this world exactly who the new Raven will be.

After a restless sleep I find my mother in the practice arena. A large, circular space deep beneath the house, the earthen floor packed hard as iron, tiered seats all around. It's pitch-dark down there. Unless I arrive.

I'm carrying a small portable candle lamp, set to low, and vaguely make out my mother's slender shape seated in the front row. When she sees me, she raises one pale hand and lights start to glow around the room, enough for me to see by.

Wow.

My father, clad in light chain mail, is at the centre of the ring. His sword moves so quickly it's like a ribbon of silver, tracing a star-shaped pattern in the air as he pivots and twists. I take in a breath, mesmerised by the beauty of his movements. There are a few guards seated around the ring, all watching intently.

'You're slow on the left side.' Varin moves forward in a blur, his sword intercepting my father's with a sound like the chiming of bells. 'Out of practice.' He laughs, the noise echoing.

Slow? If that's slow then I'm literally a snail. I sit next to my mother. We have things to discuss, but I can't take my eyes from the dance of steel.

My father moves again and Varin's sword flies from his hand, the tip of my father's blade coming to his throat. 'Slow, am I?' He laughs.

My mother gasps, her hands clasped together, the most adoring look on her face. It's almost embarrassing. Father starts the same sequence of movements again, carving shapes in the air.

'What's that called, the exercise he's doing?' I whisper to my mother.

'It is the Morningstar.' Varin, lean and light-footed, comes towards us. 'Humans have their eight-pointed star – eight precise movements designed to incapacitate an opponent. Vampires are the same, though there are sixteen movements for us.' He smiles, his hazel eyes crinkling at the corners. 'Penelope, this must be your daughter?'

'Oh, yes!' My mother, still watching Father, blinks. 'I'm sorry, Varin. This is Emelia. Emelia, this is Varin Darksolder, an old friend.'

'Emelia Raven, Lady of the Night.' Varin takes my hand and bends over it, brushing his lips against my knuckles. 'It's a pleasure to meet you. Tell me, have you done any training with a sword?'

I shake my head. 'No…' Something stirs in my chest as I watch my father. It's as though the sword is singing to me, as though it's a tune I should know but don't yet. 'I think I would like to, though.'

'Oh, Emelia, are you sure? It's so—'

'A moment, Penelope, if you please.' Varin's gaze narrows. 'What do you see, when you watch your father? And hear?'

'I see…' I watch my father again. 'I see light. I see patterns in the air. And it feels, sounds … I don't know.' I feel stupid.

'Tell me.' Varin is insistent.

'Like music.'

'Aha!' He claps. 'She is truly your daughter, Aleks,' he calls across the ring. 'She hears the steel sing.'

'Emelia.' My mother touches my hand. 'I don't know if this is wise.'

But my heart is still singing. I've never experienced anything like this … *longing* to do something. It feels as though I could step into the ring and join the deadly dance. As though I'm meant to do it.

Varin draws his sword. The blade is long and slender with a slight curve to it, the razor-sharp edge catching the light. It's utterly gorgeous.

'Please.' He holds it out to me, hilt first.

I stand and take it from him, wrapping my fingers around the worn leather. I hold the sword out in front of me. It feels like magic, like an extension of myself. 'It's so light.'

'All vampire swords are. Lightweight and razor sharp. We have no need of heavy metals, or brutal weapons. We *are* the weapons. The sword is simply an extension of that.'

I sweep the blade one way, then the other. I consider what it might be like to be a weapon, to be able to defend myself. I *want* this, I realise. So much.

'That's it. Keep your wrists straight. The power must come through you in an unbroken line.' Varin puts his cool hand over mine, correcting me as I try again. My father stops what he's doing and comes over.

'She's a natural, Aleks.' Varin glances at my father. I adjust my stance, taking the blade in wider sweeps, feeling as though I'm dancing.

'Would you like to learn, Emelia?' My father smiles. 'I confess I never dreamed you would.'

I scowl. 'Because I'm human?' Possibly a bit of a low blow.

'Human, yes,' Varin says, his hand still on mine. 'But with vampire blood, a vampire heart. Your father, like most fathers, simply wants to keep you safe, my lady.'

'I'm sorry,' I mutter.

'So am I.' My father's voice is soft.

I return Varin's sword. My father reaches over the barrier, folding me into a hug. He smells like metal and violets. Then he holds me back from him, a smile on his face.

'If you want to train, let's begin.'

Chapter Eight

A BLAST FROM THE PAST

Later that afternoon, my shoulders and back aching, I catch the bus back to the Safe Zone. My father made me change clothes, then brought me into the practice arena where he and Varin had me do push-ups, stretches and arm movements. I'd done all right, I thought.

But they'd both looked at each other. 'Sword-fighting uses these muscles,' Varin said, touching my shoulder blades and arms lightly, then my abdomen. 'You need to strengthen them before you pick up a blade. Your father and I can help with this.'

'So, I don't get to work with swords yet?'

'Not yet. But you will.'

Another thing I wish I'd started when I was younger. But I suppose letting me wield razor-sharp blades wasn't high on my parents' list of How To Keep Emelia Safe. So, just like learning the intricacies of ruling, it's something I'm coming to late, meaning I have to work all the harder. If I'd actually accepted that I was going to be Raven, instead of trying to run away, maybe I wouldn't be so overwhelmed now. But that is a shutter opened which cannot be closed. All I can do is go forward.

I spoke to my mother before I left. About how much I love her and want her in my life. But that I only have a short time to rule, compared to her. She understood, but it hadn't stopped red lining her eyes. I get that, too. There are still plenty of years left for us.

I also made a decision. One that made her smile through her tears.

It's time to leave the Safe Zone.

Time to stop being Emily Reynolds and become Emelia Raven.

I came to the Safe Zone because it felt like a starting point, a place to make a difference. But this is only one small fraction of my realm. If I want to change it, I first need to understand it. And I can't do that while I stay here. Reapers are preying on my people, Mistral's sons challenging my crown. It's time to go home, change the narrative, and become the ruler I mean to be. Time to meet a challenge with a challenge.

Speaking of Mistral's sons… I dig my phone out of my pocket and check it again. I messaged Michael before leaving; he was going to meet me at the house when I got back. But there's no reply. Huh.

I'm going to tell him everything. About his father. About the Challenge. About my plans. Then, together, we can figure out a way for him to be part of my world, if he wants that. As the human son of Mistral, I know it won't be easy. But I hope he wants to try.

Someone nearby is sobbing. I turn around. A few seats back

from me a woman is curled over, her companion, another woman, with her arms around her.

'Are you all right? Can I help?'

The woman holding her friend looks up. Her eyes are also red-rimmed, but there's a wild light in them. Not sorrow, but something else. 'She'll be all right. She's just had someone pass through.'

'Pass through?' Does she mean they died? I'm not entirely sure how humans talk about such things.

A few other people are looking at us now. One reaches to pat the crying woman on her shoulder. 'It's the best thing for them,' another murmurs. 'You know it is.'

'I know,' the woman sobs. 'I know it's the best, and I'm happy for him. I just miss him so much, you know?'

She's happy that he's *dead*? God and darkness. 'I'm sorry,' I say. 'Is there anything I can do?

'Thank you.' The crying woman sniffs, wiping her eyes. 'Honestly. I'm fine. It's fine.'

I lean my head on the cold glass, trying not to listen to the whispering behind me, the woman no longer sobbing. *Passed through*. I need to know what that means. I turn around, but before I can ask, the bus comes to a stop, the door opening with a hiss. The sobbing woman and her companion are already on their feet, and I lose them among the crowd as we head down the hill towards the seafront. I'll have to ask Michael. I hug the thought to me, the anticipation that soon his lips will be on mine.

The late afternoon sky is grey, the wind icy. I clutch my jacket closed as I continue along familiar streets, the finality of my decision hitting home. Saying goodbye to my house, to living with Laurel, to seeing Michael every day, is going to be difficult. But ruling demands sacrifice. I don't get to live a life different to every other human on the planet without there being a price. And I'm willing to pay it, if it means I can change things.

I pick up the pace, cold biting at my hands, the ground slippery. I pass the shops, Geneva's window packed with cosy jumpers, then take the small side road to my house. I'm not looking forward to telling Michael what really happened to his father, but I hope he understands why I had to keep it secret. As to what happens next, I'm unsure. My heart, battered and broken by Kyle, feels too tender to give again. But at the same time, I can't imagine saying goodbye to Michael when I leave here.

When I get home, there are no lights on, despite the grey day. Perhaps Laurel is sleeping. There's no sign of Michael, either. That's odd. He's usually pretty punctual. I fumble for my key with icy fingers, almost dropping it before I manage to get it into the lock. The door swings open, letting out a blast of welcome warmth. I step inside, stamping snow from my shoes, hanging up my jacket. Maybe I have time for a shower. I pull out my phone, about to text him, when I hear a noise like a gasp.

I put my phone in my pocket, heading down the hallway. The door to Laurel's room is ajar, her bed rumpled, but she's not there. I continue to the living area. Perhaps she's popped out for something or gone back to work.

But I just came from where she works.

Worry starts to pull at me, a claw in my chest. The house is quiet. Too quiet, like an in-drawn breath.

Then I smell it.

Blood. And violets.

The coppery smell swirls in my nostrils, my enhanced senses picking up what human noses usually can't. Like the scent of violets. Of vampires. But light still slants through the windows, striping the sofa with pale lines.

Something chuckles, a dark noise like the tumbling of grave-dirt. And I see Laurel. Or what's left of her, sprawled on the kitchen floor, blood pooling from a jagged gash in her throat, sightless eyes staring at the ceiling. Horror rises, cold as the winter outside. I only have a moment to process before something hits me, hard.

Arms wrap around me, bony and strong, and I'm lifted and spun as though in a whirlwind, unable to catch my breath. Sharpness grazes my throat, and I smell old soil and leaf loam, mixed with an eye-wateringly strong stench of violets.

Then, just as suddenly, I'm released. I drop to the carpet, landing heavily. When I put my hand to my neck, it comes away red.

Oh *shit*. I scramble backwards, one hand to my throat, the other reaching for the emergency button set into the wall near the sofas. It will drop the shutters, alerting my guard at the same time so he can come up from the basement, whether it's day or night.

'I wouldn't.' The voice is clotted, hoarse. Yet also familiar. Something skitters in the shadowed alcove next to the fireplace, nails scratching the timber floorboards.

A face emerges from the gloom. Ravaged by scars, but still recognisable. No. Nononono. Fear slides down my spine, ice cold.

'Remember me, Raven girl?'

It's Jessie.

Chapter Nine

DEAD GIRL

Fuckfuckfuck.

Jessie is supposed to be dead.

My mind scrambles to understand. Last time I saw her, she was frozen on a bed after Kyle started changing her to vampire, before I killed him. I thought she would burn when the light hit her. Kind of hoped for it, to be honest. Or that Raven guards, when they broke up the North Wind cells, would have killed her. It's not like I didn't tell them where she was.

So why in darkness is she here? *How* is she here? I reach for the emergency button once more.

'Like I said, I wouldn't.'

I remember her in a dingy bathroom, pinning me with her gaze, like a mouse mesmerised by a snake. And I fucking let her do it. Just like I'm doing now. She's quick, spider-like, as she advances on me, her body strangely twisted, the bones loose beneath her skin.

I hit the button, several times. Nothing happens. What the fuck?

Jessie laughs again, that strange rasping sound, like bone against bone. 'You think I didn't disable that, Raven girl?' Her mouth opens in a twisted grin, her fangs dropped and stained with blood. *My* blood. She leans closer. 'You think this is my first fucking rodeo?'

Disable it? My security system is state-of-the-art. It shouldn't be able to be shut down by some bitch with a vendetta. Blood seeps down the sleeve of my sweatshirt, despite the pressure I'm keeping on my neck. I refuse to give into fear, reaching for rage instead. This is *not* how it ends, not for Emelia fucking Raven. Not after all I've been through.

'Get the hell out of my house.'

Jessie's tongue, dark and rotted-looking, flicks across her lips. She smells of cold graves, her clothing tattered.

'I'm not going anywhere,' she snarls. 'Not until I get what I want.'

'I'm not giving you *anything*.' I bare my teeth. I don't understand how she isn't burning in the light. Come on, Emelia. *Think.* I look around for a weapon, something, anything. Laurel is a humped, dark shape in the gloom.

'Oh, you will.' The last word is a hiss as she leans in, licking at my fingers.

I kick her, the movement a reflex. 'Get away from me!' The scar she carried as a human still twists from her neck to her chin, more scars on the side of her face. I wonder what in darkness happened to her. Kyle was strong, beautiful. His progeny should be as well. I ignore the lance of pain at the memory of how beautiful he was.

'Bitch! Do you see this?' She hisses, holding up her arm. The forearm has an angle to it, like it's been broken then healed. 'Do you fucking see what they did to me?'

'What who did to you? I imagine you deserved it, whoever they were.'

'Those assholes from the North Wind. They broke me. Then left me.'

'The North Wind?' I'm too surprised to give her a smart answer. 'But you and Kyle were both—'

'You know *nothing* of what he was!' She lunges at me, wild-eyed. 'You killed him, you fucking bitch. And you left me there, frozen. Which is where they found me.' Her voice is a wail. 'When he died, the blood magic died with him. And now I'm some sort of half-vampire bullshit. Which is why I'm going to take your blood. Your *vampire* blood.' She licks her lips. 'I'm going to drain you dry. And finish the fucking job.'

She pulls my hand away from my neck, her fingers rough. I whimper, despite my resolve.

She strokes my hair, her head tilting like a bird. 'Cry all you want. No one is coming. I hope you feel the same fear I felt, when you left me to die. When you killed everything I loved.' A tear, watery blood, trickles down her face.

Fuck her. Any pity I might have had died long ago in a dusty bedroom, with Kyle. I should have finished her off then, as well. I'm dizzy, half my top dark with blood. But I will *not* end here. There's another security button in the kitchen. I gather what's left of my strength, pressing back into the wall.

A floorboard creaks. Jessie turns, but she's not quick enough. A blurred male figure, clad in black, swipes at her once, twice, three times. I catch a glimpse of silver. Jessie screams, the sound like the closing of a rusty metal door.

But it is not yet dark.

A hand grabs Jessie, who's still screaming, by the hair. Pulling her head back, exposing her throat. A silver blade comes to rest on her greyish skin.

And I look into Michael's storm-dark gaze.

Chapter Ten

VIOLETS AND SORROW

'You need to drink from her.'

'What?' I don't understand.

'Drink from her!' He shakes Jessie, who moans. Blood pools at her feet, pouring from deep wounds across her ankles and shoulders, her arms hanging loose. In the corner of the room a tall shadow seems to lurk, a glint of silver.

'She bit you. Her blood will heal the wound. But you must drink, Emelia. I can't hold her much longer.' Michael sounds desperate. Everything seems foggy. It's almost dark, lamps starting to glow.

Jessie growls, bucking against Michael. He snarls and tightens his grip, muscles standing out in his arms. The tall shadow detaches itself from the corner. I know that gait, those long legs, the silver gleam of his gaze. But Kyle can't be here, because I killed him. From somewhere I find a lick of strength, a last push. I lean forward and pick up Jessie's arm. It's boneless, bird-light, as I bring it to my lips. She screams, raging. Michael's blade digs into her throat, a line of blood appearing.

'Do it,' he growls.

I bite down, her flesh giving between my teeth, trying not to remember doing the same to my mother, long ago when I thought there might be a chance for me to be what I longed for. Now I just want to live. Blood gushes into my mouth, thick and cool. I try not to retch, swallowing several mouthfuls, violet perfume stuck in my nostrils, coating my tongue like the world's worst medicine.

There's a crash and a shudder and Jessie is gone, torn from my lips.

'Don't kill her!' Michael's voice is sharp.

Finally. Night has fallen. My guard is holding Jessie face down on the rug, one of her arms twisted back at an acute angle. Like he's about to tear it off.

'My lady?' The guard turns to me.

'If you kill her before Emelia heals, the blood magic won't work,' Michael says, that sharp thread of desperation still in his voice. 'The wound in her neck will reopen, and she'll die.'

I'm so dazed it's like I'm somewhere else, watching from a distance. I remember a cold night just before dawn, Kyle holding me after a guard almost drained me. Strange. I swear he's here, talking to me, but I can't quite make out what he's saying.

'Emelia!' Michael shakes me. 'Are you healed?'

'I don't know,' I mumble, fighting for clarity. Kyle pads around us, his silver gaze flickering from me to Jessie, still held on the floor. Why can no one else see him? Am I so close to dying? Part of me wants to let go, to sink into the darkness of his waiting arms.

Michael blows out an exasperated breath. His fingers brush over my skin. I curl into them, into the warmth and comfort of his touch. Gradually, reality returns. Kyle is gone, and Michael is here. Jessie is sobbing, low guttural noises. I think I hear relief in them, though.

He turns to my guard. 'She's fine. Do it.'

I turn away, wincing at the crack of bone, the wet tearing.

Michael crouches next to me. He seems … different. Darker, somehow. I reach out, putting my hand on his.

He starts, turning to me with a slight frown as though he's forgotten I'm there. 'Your rug is ruined.'

I stare at him. What in darkness? I'm covered in blood, Laurel is dead, and that's what he's worried about?

'I can get a new one,' I whisper.

He nods, no warmth in his blue-grey gaze, then returns his attention to whatever my guard is doing. My hand lies slack on his. Panic curls in my chest. Everything about this is wrong, but I don't understand why.

The rug disappears from under my feet. I flinch, letting out a yelp.

'I'm sorry, my lady.' It's my guard. He's young, his hair cropped close to his head. Blood is spattered across his face, almost black against his dark skin. 'I smelled the blood, but the light … I couldn't come upstairs.'

'I understand.' We need a way for him to control the shutters, I realise, then remember it doesn't matter anymore, because I'm leaving. My breath hitches as the guard rolls up my rug and, with it, what remains of Jessie.

'I'll dispose of this, and then…' He nods towards the kitchen.

I can't speak.

'Laurel needs to be buried.' Michael's voice is stern. 'As is custom.'

I take a shuddering breath. I'm so cold, my sweatshirt sticky against my skin. 'Y-yes,' I manage to say. 'I'm sure… Is there someone we can call?'

'I'll sort it out.' A muscle flexes in Michael's jaw.

I want him to pull me into his arms, to kiss me and tell me it's all right. But this muscled stranger, his grey eyes dark, seems miles from the gentle boy I thought I knew. I don't understand what's changed.

A short while later I'm in the shower, water swirling reddish-brown around my feet. The taste of violets still clings to my tongue, and I open my mouth under the flow, swishing and spitting several times. I'm not dizzy anymore but can't stop shaking, despite the warm water.

Fuck. That was far too close. Another reason I'll be better off at home. I don't like thinking that way, but can't deny I'm shaken. I turn off the shower, wrap myself in a fluffy towel and brush my teeth, twice. But it'll be a while before I lose the memory of how Jessie's skin gave way under my teeth. I spit and rinse, spit and rinse, trying not to think about the sound of her being torn apart.

Apart from everything else, I'm worried about Michael. Why was he late getting here? And how did he know to disable Jessie like that, or that I had to drink her blood? I rub mist from the mirror, pulling a comb through my damp hair. I'm paler than usual, dark circles under my eyes. Just like Laurel, when she comes back from work. The comb drops and I sob, bracing myself on the sink, sorrow rolling over me like a wave. I cough and hiccup, trying to hold in my grief, but can't.

There's a knock at the bathroom door.

'It's open,' I gurgle.

The door opens. It's Michael. His eyes widen when he sees me. I suppose I'm as naked as I've ever been around him. I can't find it in myself to care. I reach out and he comes to me, folding me into a hug. I curl into his warmth. I know there are things we have to sort out, but I just need this moment. 'Thank you,' I mumble into his chest. His lips touch my hair, and I lift my head. He kisses me, finally.

But something still isn't right. Aside from the whole dead-friend-in-the-kitchen and strange-vampire-creature-attacking-me situation, I mean. When I open my mouth to his, wanting to deepen things, more aware than ever that I'm only wearing a towel, he pulls back. His hand comes to my cheek, then drops to his side. Pain wars with something in his dark gaze. It looks like … regret.

My stomach lurches. 'Michael?' I watch his face, the beautiful lines of him, the long-lashed eyes, the sensual mouth I love to kiss. There's no warmth when he looks at me. None at all.

'When were you going to tell me what really happened to my father?'

Chapter Eleven

PART OF MY WORLD

'Wh-what?' I lean on the sink, feeling sick.

'My father? When were you going to tell me that your family executed him? That he was a *traitor*!'

My mouth opens and closes, but I can't find the words. Images roll over me, of Mistral bound in spikes and metal, left alone on a frosted dawn. The way his eyes met mine, as I watched him burn.

Anger rises, cutting through the shock. 'What was I supposed to say? It's not the kind of thing you just bring up in conversation.'

Michael's mouth tightens. 'You should have told me.' He growls the words. 'He was my *father*.'

'I know. I'm sorry.' He's right. I should have told him, and I'm sorry I didn't. But I cannot be sorry for his father's death.

'Sorry? I *trusted* you. Cared for you. I meant it, what I said on the beach. I'm with you, Emelia Raven. Or I was, anyway.' He shakes his head.

'I care for you, too!' Fear shudders through me at his use of the past tense. 'And I had my reasons!' We stare at each other, both breathing hard, the bathroom feeling too small to contain the energy simmering between us.

'Fuck!' He turns away, bracing an arm against the wall. 'When my brothers told me I—'

'Your brothers?' I frown.

'Yeah. They contacted me, yesterday. Told me what your family did to ours.'

Ours? Michael has never felt part of his family. But if that's how he wants to play it… 'What about what *your* family did to mine?' I hiss. 'The North Wind almost *killed* my father. Kidnapped me and would have killed me, if I hadn't escaped. *That's* who your father was. A liar and a monster, who couldn't accept that my mother didn't love him anymore. Jessie, that creature who just died in there—' I point towards the living room '—she was like that because of *him*. Laurel is dead, because of him. I had to *kill* the first boy I ever loved, because of him, and it almost destroyed me. So excuse me if I don't feel bad about the fact he got to face the consequences of that!'

Michael doesn't say anything for a moment, his throat moving. His dark gaze is unreadable. 'Did you see it happen?'

I nod. 'It was quick.'

He huffs out a small breath. 'Raven mercy, I guess.'

'There was nothing merciful about it.' Mistral died a terrible death. I don't have it in me to sugar-coat that.

'I know what he did. Who he was. But I deserved to know, Emelia.'

He's right. Of course he is. But the way he found out… 'Don't go back to them, please.'

'Go back to who?'

'Your brothers. They … they're just like him.'

'Where else am I supposed to go?' Pain flashes in his eyes.

'I just…' Fuck. This isn't how this was supposed to happen. 'I'm going home. You could come with me.'

Michael looks at me like I've grown another head. 'Come with you? And what, live in your house like some sort of pet?'

'Why do you think it would be like that? I want you to be part of my world!'

'I *was* part of your world! My mother was a Vindhof. My father was second only to your mother in rank.' His lips draw back from his teeth, his eyes wild. 'I *had* to leave! I didn't grow up with parents who coddled me, like yours. Were you even going to tell me you were leaving, or would I have just come back here and found you gone?'

I flinch. Screw him. 'Were you going to tell me about your brothers?' We're so close to each other, heat swirling between us, both of us almost snarling. But another part of me, the part that was already betrayed, is curling up, withdrawing. 'Why go back to them, if you *hate* my world so much?'

'Yes, I was going to tell you. I was going to ask what you thought I should do.' His voice catches. 'I want a home. Family. And they're all I have, now.'

It's like I'm reaching out for him and pulling back at the same time. It hurts to breathe. 'You have me! You don't have to go back to them. We can have a home together and—'

"Don't you understand? There is no more *together*.' Michael's face twists, his fists clenched. 'There cannot be. Not if I can't trust you.'

I blink, rocking back on my heels. My towel slips and I grab it. Michael's eyes widen again, just for a moment. 'I should have told you,' I say, my throat raw. 'The only reason I didn't was because I was scared of losing you. Scared you might hate me when you found out.'

'Funny how that's worked out, isn't it?'

The words hit me like a slap. My breath shudders, tears dripping from my chin.

Michael's gaze softens, just for a moment, sorrow deep in his eyes. Then it hardens, becoming the stranger once more. 'Go home, Emelia. Claim your crown. I hope it serves you well.' He turns away. A few moments later, I hear the front door slam.

I stare at the empty doorway, as though I can rewind time and bring him back to me. Bring Laurel back to life and make everything right again. I clutch my damp towel around me, sobbing.

There are footsteps. My heart lifts.

But it's my guard who appears. He blinks, looking away, when he takes in my state of undress, the tears running down my face. 'My lady, I apologise. It's just … the arrangements have been made for the human in the kitchen. They'll be here shortly. However, I need to file a report about what happened. Will you be speaking with your parents?'

I take a shuddering breath. Michael is gone. Laurel is gone. Grief waits for me, beyond my anger. I need to pull myself together, before the might of Raven descends. Because it will, of course. An attempt on the life of the heir? This place will be crawling with guards. I can't do that to the people here; can't bring any more fear and darkness into their lives.

'I'll call them, now.' I pull my towel tighter, wiping my face. 'Then you can make your report.'

'Of course.' He bows, then disappears, a faint whoosh of displaced air.

I lean on the wall, because my legs are shaking so much that I'll fall if I don't. I resist the urge to crouch down, to give into my sorrow and loss. I reach for that core of ebony and steel, the strength that helped me to kill Kyle, that got me home.

Then I go and find my phone.

Raven, as a unit, are very efficient. But even I'm surprised by the speed at which everything happens. It's as though my parents were already planning for this, I think, as I watch guards packing up my personal belongings, carrying them to a large van parked outside.

Four guards is a reasonably restrained response, I suppose. Even if they were here in less than an hour, and one of them is Bertrand. I tried to be as calm as possible when I called my mother, explaining there'd been a problem with my security system and I'd been attacked but the threat was contained. But my voice caught as I told her about Laurel, despite how I tried to hold back.

'My lady, the car is here.'

The house is almost cleared now, apart from the furniture. I stand in the living room, my stockinged feet curling on the bare floor, Bertrand waiting by the door. The space looks forlorn, without the comforts that made it home. Laurel's body is gone, sand scattered on the kitchen floor. I don't want to remember her like that.

I nod. 'Thank you.'

I put on my boots and head into frosty darkness, pausing to take a last look at the little white house. The sleek black

Mercedes is parked next to the kerb. Of course, Emelia Raven can't travel in a van with a bunch of guards. It's obvious my parents were just humouring me when I insisted on taking the feed buses back and forth to the estate. Now that everything has fallen apart, the illusion as to who I really am breaks down.

Bertrand holds the car door open. His craggy face is soft, his blue eyes gentle. I can't look at him for too long, because I'll start crying. I wish he could carry me, as he has so many times, wrapping me in safety. But one thing I've learned is that I need to carry myself.

'Did you get the tree in the pot, from the living room?'

'We did. Would you like it planted on the estate?'

'Yes.'

A memory. Of Laurel, of the brief happiness I had with Michael. Something that will live after I'm gone. As I get into the car, the door closing, it's as though the mantle of Raven wraps around me, dark as wings; protection and suffocation at the same time.

No longer a cage, though. I'm ready to lean into this power I hold. I might be going home, but it's my choice to do so, despite everything that's just happened. As we head out of the Safe Zone, leaving the glittering safety lights behind, I feel as though I am ash and bone, a creature made of the same darkness as the endless night outside the window.

I'm furious. With Jessie, with Michael, with Mistral, with everyone. With the fact that, in one night, Jessie has exposed the main problem facing me as I try to change things for humans. We're weak, almost defenceless, against vampires. And they are everywhere. For fuck's sake, the Safe Zone I'm in is supposed to be vampire-free. But it isn't, as I well know. Vampires live here freely, mingle with humans, stand around drinking their blood from plastic packets while making polite conversation, as though it isn't the most monstrous thing, like talking to a cow while eating a hamburger.

I pull out my phone but there are no messages, even though I've left three for Michael. He's read all my texts, though. I try calling again, but there's no answer. *Fine.* I block his number. If he doesn't want to talk, then neither do I. I get that I should have told him. But I also thought he understood me better than that. Understood that I'd been through something traumatic and needed time. That I might not want to share something that could be used against me or my family. That I didn't want to be betrayed again. That I'm carrying a huge weight of responsibility, and need to be careful. It was my choice not to tell him, and maybe it was wrong, but I can't change that now. My only regret is hurting him.

It's a mistake I'll have to live with.

Eventually we pull up outside the house, gravel crunching beneath the wheels. My mother hurries down the front steps, her arms wide. She pulls me close, then my father is there, his arms around us both.

I sob, just a little. My mother's hands flutter around me, my father's expression grave, his golden eyes glittering.

'I'm all right.' It's not really true but I want to go inside.

My mother frowns. 'We've called the doctor.'

'I just need to rest.'

'Then you shall rest.' My father puts his arm around my shoulders, my mother on my other side as we step into the velvet confines of the house. I kiss my parents, then head up the curving golden stairs, alone with my thoughts. Alone with my sorrow, my rage.

Alone.

Chapter Twelve

FORGE AND FIRE

Sweat beads my brow, dampens my spine, my muscles screaming. I'm breathing hard, my heart pounding. All the things I shouldn't be when I'm with a vampire.

'Again,' Varin says.

I drop into a plank for what feels like the fiftieth time, my arms trembling. I bend my elbows, grunting through another punishing round of push-ups. Varin circles me, idly twirling his sword, the slender blade catching faint shimmers of light. The earthen floor is cold, smells like iron and blood. I finish and drop onto my front, panting. I've been in the training ring for the past two hours, Varin putting me through my paces.

'Enough,' he says. 'Take a break.'

'I can keep going,' I gasp. 'We haven't hit the pads yet.'

'Are you sure?' Varin extends his hand, helping me to my feet. 'You feel very warm. Take water, at least, if you want to keep going.'

I do want to keep going. I want to keep going until I can't, until I fall to the ground and it swallows me, taking away the pain.

I haven't been able to sleep much since coming home, my dreams turning to nightmares of Laurel's staring eyes, of guilt and blood and Jessie, and Michael saying he hates me. When I do sleep, I wake each time with a pit in my stomach, grief heavy in my chest. I keep my pain caged, not letting it out. But it steals through the bars, haunting me with visions of warmth and strong arms, memories on the edge of sleep and waking.

The only thing that helps is throwing myself into work or helping my father with his research into the mysterious community he discovered. And pounding my body into oblivion in the practice ring with Varin.

He and Father have kept their promise to train me, despite my mother's concerns. I don't know what she's so worried about; I've not been allowed near a blade, apart from a wooden practice one. Father says it's heavier than the real thing, so I'm using it to strengthen my shoulders and arms, Varin taking me slowly through the Morningstar pattern of strikes. I want to do it faster, though. Can almost feel it, when my father flashes through the sequence, like a melody etched on my soul. So, for several hours a day, I push myself through exercises until I can't take any more, then fall into bed for a few hours' sleep, and start the cycle again. If I'm to be alone, I should at least be able to defend myself.

It's not just the disastrous end to my time in the Safe Zone. My trauma goes deeper, back to Kyle and his betrayal. And even before that, the years of feeling trapped, of screaming silently in the hope someone would let me out. Kyle showed me, though, that the only person who could set me free was me.

And that's tough to take. I should hate him after what he did. I gulp down some water, rub my forearm across my sweaty brow, then head back to the centre of the ring. Varin has stripped down to loose black trousers, his chiselled chest gleaming in the light from the candle lamps, his long dark hair tied back. He holds a pad on each hand, ready for me. I pull on my gloves, curling my fingers around the elastic guards, dropping into a fighting stance.

I *should* hate Kyle, I think, as I throw the first punch, my fist shuddering against the pad. But I don't. Despite how he betrayed me, he also saved me. I can't even be angry with him for lying to me anymore. Maybe about the part that he loved me. But I would swear I saw it in his eyes, felt it in his touch. That's one of the hardest things, that I can never have that closure. I wish I could ask him. But I can't, because he's dead and I killed him.

I throw a cross punch, Varin nodding his encouragement as we move around the ring. It feels good to hit the pads, like I'm scratching an itch, deep inside. I hit faster, one-two combinations, my breath sobbing in and out.

I realise I'm actually sobbing, my face wet, warmth on my cheeks. I keep going, gritting my teeth, but can't contain the noises I'm making. Varin pulls back, catching my hands between the pads, his face a mask of concern. Then my father is there, swift as a shadow, his arms coming around me.

'It's all right,' he murmurs, smoothing my hair.

I sob into his shoulder, breathing his comforting scent of moss and violets. Then I pull back, embarrassed by my outburst. 'I can keep going.' I wipe my forearm across my face. 'Let me keep going.'

'No.' My father is gentle yet firm, his hands on my upper

arms. 'I think you've done enough today. You need to feed, and rest.'

Varin is already shrugging his shirt back on, putting the pads away at the side of the ring. I guess that's it, then. My mouth twists. 'Fine. I'll eat something.'

My father tilts his head. 'Do you want to talk about it, dear one?' The love in his voice almost breaks me. But I'm conscious of the guards at the edge of the ring, Varin nearby. Everything is still so tangled. If I start talking, I don't know what will come out.

'Not yet,' I mumble. Father presses a kiss to my brow, then releases me. I leave the ring feeling drained, as though part of me is missing. Maybe it is.

Later, once I've forced down some food, I head to my room. I get into bed and flick on the TV, scrolling through the channels, hoping to find something to lose myself in. Instead, I see bodies, piled and twisted, their features mercifully blurred, shattered buildings behind them.

'…initially thought to be another attack on Raven holdings. This, however, seems to be the result of an illegal hunt, the remains found outside a Safe Zone. In other news—'

I turn the TV off. I'm so sick of this shit. But I have to tread carefully. Choose the battles I want to fight. Cracking down on illegal hunts isn't going to help my larger issue of human rights and will divert forces at a time when I need to be as strong as possible, with Mistral's Challenge. As much as it pisses me off, I need to consolidate my reign first.

There's a piece missing to all of this, something I can't figure out. Humans aren't just food to vampires, they're more than that; I saw it when I was in the Safe Zone, vampires and humans mingling socially. Kyle told me, when I thought he loved me, that vampires were banned from changing any more humans. But the only reason to ban something is because it's happening, vampires caring about humans enough to want to change them. While there are vampires who think of humans as just cattle, and humans who think of vampires as monsters, it seems to me there must be just as many, if not more, who see similarities rather than differences. We have a common origin; my existence is proof of that. If there can be love or friendship between humans and vampires, then surely there's a common ground where each side brings something to the other, rather than one side taking everything. Not every interaction needs to end with blood and death. What I need to figure out is how to get vampires to see that humans deserve dignity and freedom, just as they do. That they are more than just the blood in their veins.

I sigh, then get out of bed, grabbing the long cardigan draped across the end. If I can't sleep, I might as well keep working. There are still details to be ironed out for the Channel Islands project; plus, my father mentioned he'd found more references to the experimental community of vampires and humans. *They* seemed to know the secret of coexistence; it's a shame it seems to have been forgotten. Or perhaps it all descended into chaos and fell apart. Still, the more I can find out about how it worked, the more chance I have of implementing something similar.

Two guards fall into step behind me as I leave my room. I ask them to wait outside the library; I'm not going up to the roof, but want to be alone. The promised papers are on the huge table, a pile of curling yellow parchments. I grab the magnifying glass my father has helpfully left there, scanning the faded lettering. It's interesting stuff, though nothing terribly new. Just more references to 'a new socyetie' and the prowess of the dark knights. Considering they're human they must be pretty good, if vampires are writing about them like that. But what it doesn't tell me, frustratingly, is how they got it to *work*. I yawn, rubbing my eyes. I'll just put my head down for a minute while I try to figure this out.

Someone shakes me, gently. I struggle towards waking, wondering why I'm so uncomfortable. Michael and I must have fallen asleep on the sofa again.

'Emelia?'

The sorrow that rolls over me when I hear my mother's voice, instead of his, is breathtaking. I open bleary eyes to see her bending over me, her brow creased. I groan, lifting my head and peeling ancient manuscripts from my cheek.

'You need to go to bed.'

I rub a hand over my face. I feel stretched, broken. 'I need to keep working.'

My mother's frown deepens. 'What's going on?'

'Nothing.' The inside of my mouth feels as though something crawled in there and died.

She folds her arms. 'You've been working day and night. When you're not here, you're in the training ring with Varin and your father. You barely sleep, and you're not eating enough. You need to rest.'

I blink back tears. 'I have a lot to cover before the coronation. I need to be prepared.'

'Prepared for what?'

'For … everything.' I wave a hand. 'All of it. I'm trying to change the world. We have the Challenge to deal with. And I want the Channel Islands running smoothly by the time I'm crowned.'

'You're not going to be able to change anything if you're unwell.'

'Well, maybe if I'd started things earlier, I could have—'

'No.' My mother's tone isn't stern, but it is unyielding. 'Do not make this about the past. You have every support you need around you to achieve what you want to do.'

'Do I, though?'

'What?'

'You and Father both say you want me to be Raven. You've let me live in the Safe Zone, you've helped me set up the Channel Islands, but do you really want me to change things?'

My mother stares at me.

'Humans are your food, after all. Is change something you really want? Or do you just want it because of me, and how I am?'

'What? Emelia, I…'

'You were at the Rising, weren't you? Both of you.'

She nods.

'That was almost a century ago. The few humans who do remember it, fear it. And everyone else knows nothing different. So why are you all right with me changing that? Is it because you don't think I can do it?' Tears burn my throat as the realisation crashes over me. I'm such a fool.

My mother crouches next to my chair, her face close to mine. Up close, her beauty is breathtaking, sculpted perfection. And most definitely not human. 'I confess, it's not easy,' she says, her voice gentle. 'Your father and I … we've both lived a long time. Yes, we've seen change, yet much in our lives stayed the same. Until you came along.'

I can't speak.

'You changed me. And you changed your father. I don't

even know how, exactly, yet; all I know is that when I saw you, I knew you had to live. I cannot explain it any other way. Perhaps it was for this,' she says, stroking my hair. 'Our world isn't perfect; I'm not blind to it. The Rising was ... it was more than it was ever meant to be. I have known humans, and loved them, over my long life. And if you, my most precious daughter, can work out how to make things better for them, then I'll support you in that.'

'For twenty years?' My mouth twists.

My mother laughs, a soft sound. 'Maybe ten.'

'Mother!'

'You will need me, Emelia, in your first years as the Raven. Human or not, you cannot wield power like that alone, not straightaway. It has always been thus.' She tucks a lock of my hair behind my ear, her touch gentle. 'But this isn't the only thing troubling you. I know something else is going on.'

I fight back tears, so close to telling her about Michael, about Laurel and my aching sense of guilt and loss. But telling her about Michael will lead to more questions, and I don't want to talk about him, not until I work out my tangled feelings. 'I'm worried about the Challenge. About Father. We need our plan to work. I can't change anything if I don't have the support of the families.'

'Is that all?' A faint smile, though worry still lurks in her dark eyes. She hands me a folded piece of paper, creamy parchment with a rough edge. 'You'll be pleased to know I heard from Jennie, then.'

I look at the letter. The gold wax seal, already broken, is embossed with the entwined letters J and C, topped with a tiny raven. 'She's happy to do it?'

My mother nods. 'She is.'

This is the other thing I've been working on, with my parents. A challenge to Mistral's Challenge, because screw them.

I'm aware that my position, despite being the undisputed only child of Raven, is precarious because of *what* I am. It's increasingly clear that, despite it being an unbroken Raven tradition to anoint every heir at eighteen, I'm seen as a novelty. My reign is to be measured in decades, rather than centuries, my comparative weakness meaning I need to be guarded almost constantly. There's a real danger I could become isolated, a puppet ruler in the shadows, while others jostle for power around me. Indeed, if my mother wasn't still around, I'm sure that's exactly what would be happening. This Challenge, before I'm even crowned, is proof that I'm not considered worthy. After what happened to their father, I suppose I can understand why Mistral feel that way. But four other families agree with them. And that's what I'm going to try and change.

I asked my mother to contact Jennie de Corbeau because she's her favourite cousin. She's also incredibly well connected and, crucially, on our side. We don't have a lot of time; while Raven territory spans half the planet, we need to move quickly, before my anointing at the next Gathering in a few weeks' time. The De Corbeaux hold lands across the eastern half of France, from the south up into Belgium, while Mistral's realms lie to the west so, apart from being easy to get to, it also sends a strategic message for us to meet there. Jennie and her family live in the Palace of Versailles, and the fact it was once home to humans isn't lost on me either. Symbols hold power in my parents' world, so everything I choose to do needs to be symbolic of what I want to achieve.

We've asked Jennie to gather the other families for a ball in my honour. I know they'll come, even if they're siding with Mistral. They won't miss the chance to see me in the flesh, to gauge my weakness for themselves. And then it will be up to me to convince them I'm capable of doing the job.

The only snag is that my mother is also insisting we tour the UK, including a stop at the Channel Islands project, before heading to France. 'Can we not go straight there? I've been thinking about it, and—'

My mother shakes her head. 'You need to be seen as the heir *before* we get to Jennie's home. You've barely been in public.'

'Whose fault is that?' I mutter.

My mother's lips press together. 'We all agree that choices were made in the past that no longer work for us. But I will not drop you into a political snake pit unprepared. We need to move strategically. Plus, it gives Darkwing and Karanlik time to get here, if they accept Jennie's invitation.'

My frustration boils over. 'I want to get this done!'

'Do you think I do not?' My mother's onyx gaze flares for a moment. 'I have not held this throne for two centuries by rushing into things unprepared! I won't let you do that, either. We leave tomorrow night. I hope that's soon enough for you.'

I stare at her, anger burning in my chest. She's right, of course, but that doesn't make it any less infuriating. I'm desperate to get to France, to tell Mistral and the rest of those treacherous families to shove it. But I know she won't be moved. I sigh, too tired to fight any longer.

'Fine. What about the other great families? Have we heard from them?'

The other part of my plan is a bit of a gamble. While Raven

are close with Lion, Scorpion and Jaguar are more of an unknown quantity. My mother was unsure, at first, when I asked her to invite them to the celebrations leading up to my coronation, even though it's not unusual for representatives of each family to attend big events, such as anointings and coronations; all four families attended my mother's. But it was a different time, pre-Rising.

Keep your friends close, and your enemies closer.

I didn't need my father to teach me that. But it's not until now, as I take the first steps into power, that I understand what it means. My humanity will become common knowledge once I'm crowned, all around the world. And there will be those who see it as an opportunity. Raven took North America from Jaguar, following the Red Rising. I don't want my perceived weakness to make them think it's a good time to try and take it back.

They just know what they're told.

My mother was right. And the story around what it means to be human has been the same for far too long. It's time to change the narrative. Inviting the great families is a chance to dispel any myths about who I am. And, if I manage to get even one of them on-side, it strengthens my position further.

'Nothing yet.'

"Do you think they'll come?'

'To any of it? I'm not sure. Lion, yes. We have ties with their house. Scorpion came to my coronation, but things were … difficult. As for Jaguar…' She shakes her head. 'There's a lot of tangled history here. We can only ask the question. It's up to them if they decide to accept.'

I pick up one of the manuscripts, smoothing out the

crinkles. My mother takes it from me then shuffles the papers into a neat pile, her hand resting on top.

'Let me help you to bed.'

'I'm fine,' I protest, but she shuts me down.

'I'm still the Raven, aren't I?' Humour gleams in her dark gaze, despite her admonishment, as she helps me from the chair. We leave the library, guards following in our wake. When we reach my room she helps me into bed, tucking the covers around me like she did when I was a child. Then she kisses my forehead. 'Sleep, my gorgeous girl,' she murmurs, her hand light on my hair.

Finally, I rest.

Chapter Thirteen

A FEW MISSING SHEEP

I blink at the bright sky, pulling my jacket more tightly around me. Frost crackles beneath my boots, my breath puffing clouds in the icy morning air. Mist fills the hollows, wreathes the dark trees, stretches ghostly fingers across the shimmering landscape. It's beautiful.

I'm supposed to be getting ready to leave. I woke early, heading straight down to the practice ring for another session with Varin. He's teaching me basic self-defence as well as sword fighting, and I spent an hour trying to take a wooden dagger from him, my fingers throbbing, my arms and shoulders aching. Afterwards, though, instead of going to my room to pack, I headed outside through the dancers' quarters, careful not to let any stray fingers of light into the shuttered house. I glance back at it now, the honey-coloured stone glowing against the silver-blue morning, towers stark against the opalescent sky.

I spent so many years in darkness, only venturing out to watch the occasional sunrise. My time in the Safe Zone helped me overcome that conditioning, the feeling that, somehow, it's dangerous for me to be outside during the day, even though I know I'm safer now than I ever was at night.

I remember Ruth telling me, after the long night when Kyle carried me through darkness to safety, that we needed light. I saw her a couple of times, when I lived in the Safe Zone. The first time was at the market. She almost dropped the apples she was holding, one of them bouncing from her hands. I caught it, bringing it back to her. Then I thanked her for all she'd done. For refusing Kyle, when he wanted her help to deliver me to Mistral. And for showing me around the Safe Zone, despite already knowing who I was.

The second time was for coffee, sitting at the café where Michael worked. She skirted around things, asking me how I was, how I found life in the Safe Zone. But I was direct. Told her why I was there, and what I wanted to do. That she was part of what inspired me to choose the Channel Islands for my project, her comment made on a cold beach leading me there. Her eyes filled with tears, and she pressed her warm hand on mine. 'I'll help you,' she said. 'If you want it. Just ask.'

So I took a deep breath and asked the one thing I'd been wondering, since the moment I realised she knew who I was. 'Why didn't you deliver me to the North Wind? I know you're one of them.'

But she shook her head, frowning. 'What makes you think I'm part of the North Wind?'

'You … you knew Kyle. And you knew who I was. I thought…'

Her face creased with concern. 'I might have known Kyle, but he had his own secrets. Had I known what he planned, I would have intervened further. He seemed to truly care for you.'

Yeah, he did. Shame it wasn't true. It was Jessie he really loved. Or loved more than me, I guess.

I'm so glad we're leaving tonight.

I've come to another realisation, as well. If I survive the Challenge, my next step is to choose a consort. The family line continues with me, if my parents don't have another child, and I don't have the luxury of waiting half a century for love like my mother did. Besides, I tried love, and look where that got me. I'll choose with my head this time, not my heart. Kyle is gone, and so is Michael. He made his choice. It feels cold, but I can't take any more heartbreak.

I think of my white coronation robes, waiting in the shuttered dark of the costume room, like a butterfly in a cocoon. And, next to it, my mother's lacy wedding gown, my great-grandfather's chain mail. War, power and love, all in one place. I hope to avoid one and gain the other. The third I need to let go.

Hands in pockets, I scuff through frozen leaves, past trees with tangled branches like dark lace, following the curve of the long driveway to the rear gates. There are several entrances to the estate, including the main one, with its huge wrought-iron gates and raven-topped pillars. There's a second raven-topped gate to the side, the honey-coloured gatehouse a smaller replica of the main house, kept furnished for guests should the need arise. Then there's the rear gate, with the guardhouse where deliveries come in. Where Kyle set up a ruse to get me off the estate, trading one secret for another.

I should go back. But I'm restless, as though trying to outrun my feelings. My breakdown in the practice ring plays on my mind, even though I did nothing wrong. It's not surprising, I suppose. Only three months have passed since Kyle's betrayal, I've lost Michael, Laurel is dead, and I now have to fight for my crown. Perhaps I should have taken more time to process things. But time isn't a luxury I have.

There's a shift coach parked next to the guardhouse. Huh. They usually collect people from the main house to take them back to the Safe Zone, not from here. Perhaps they've changed the pick-up point. I'm tempted to climb on board. But Michael is with his brothers now, not waiting for me at my little white house. And Laurel's blood stains the wooden floors. There's no going back for me. Only forward.

There's movement at the door of the guardhouse. A human comes out, dressed in rough, dark clothing, followed by someone in the light camouflage of our human guards. I'm almost certain it's the driver who brought Laurel and me here, the last time we travelled to the house together. He looks both ways, pushing the human so they stumble towards the coach. What the hell? I stay still, cold seeping into my boots. The coach door opens, and both humans climb on board. A few moments later, the engine rumbles, the coach slowly rolling out through the gates.

I wait until they're out of sight, then head to the guardhouse. The door is ajar. I push it open, curiosity curling in my gut. Inside, is the small room I remember, a door leading to a second room, where once a human girl and I exchanged clothes so I could have a night of freedom. The space is deserted but there's a scent in the air, a human scent. Water is running somewhere, and everything feels as though it's just been disturbed, dust motes still settling. Frowning, I open the door to the second room.

A pile of grey clothing lies on the floor, everything crumpled as though hastily discarded. I pick up the topmost one. It's a sweatshirt, the Raven logo in black thread on the breast. It's also still warm.

Gravel crunches, voices coming from outside. Then I hear the creak of the outer door. Shit. Something tells me I need to hide. I quickly open another door, hoping it's a cupboard. But instead, it's a tiny bathroom, the toilet still running as though recently flushed. I press myself against the wall, leaving the door ajar.

'How many today?' A human voice, female.

'Half a dozen.' A male voice, somehow familiar.

'We need to be careful. Too many, and they might start to notice.'

The male snorts. 'Notice? I doubt it. A few missing sheep from a flock of millions. They barely acknowledge our existence.'

'Some do. Thank God for those guards who see us as more than food.'

Guards? I remember Kyle telling the Raven guard, vampire like him, that he would keep his secret in return for keeping ours. But what the hell was the secret?

'What about the daughter?'

'What about her?'

I go cold. What about me? This better not be another rebellion. I hold my breath.

'She'll be Raven soon. If they let her. Maybe things will be different.'

My feelings swing between annoyance and sorrow at the hope in her tone.

'She's different, I suppose.'

'You've met her, haven't you.'

He has? I wonder why the voice sounds so familiar, but I daren't move.

'I have. She was nice. Polite kid.'

'That's it?' The voices move further away, and there's the creak of the door again. 'She'll need more than politeness if she expects to rule vampires. I'm surprised she's still alive, to be honest.'

My fists clench.

'She could change things for all of us.'

'Or she could make them worse. If she survives.'

The door closes with a bang. I wait until all I can hear is the faint whistle of wind outside, then sag against the wall. *She'll need more than politeness if she expects to rule vampires.*

Damn straight, I will. And I have no problem being impolite.

Chapter Fourteen

ON THE ROAD

I head back to the house, my mind whirring. It's obvious, from the running toilet to the disturbed air, that the guardhouse was recently occupied. The clothing, when I emerged from the bathroom, had been cleared away. But who was the human I saw being pushed onto the coach? And where are they going? Is this an illegal hunt? There's obviously guard involvement; the human one I saw getting on the coach, and possibly the vampire whose secrets Kyle seemed to know. But if humans are disappearing from the estate, which I have to assume from the discarded Raven clothing, why has nobody noticed?

A few missing sheep from a flock of millions.

Yeah. That's why. Because of the shitty, shitty world humans have to live in now. My mother is still angry that people tried to kill her family. Yet there are humans out there who have lost *everyone*. What's *their* anger like?

Shit. We're leaving in a matter of hours, but this seems important. The North Wind might be over, might have said they're taking everyone to the Channel Islands, but what if they're not? What if they've left cells behind, ready to continue what Mistral started?

Choose your fight. You cannot win one, if you focus on them all.

Another lesson from my father. He's right, of course. My priority is to stop this Challenge before Mistral get the majority they need for it to go ahead. Civil war is unacceptable. The threat to my reign is unacceptable. The death of my father is *unacceptable*. This is where my focus needs to be.

But the strangeness of the guardhouse tugs at me as I sort through my dresses, piles of chiffon and velvet, like flowers strewn across my bed, ready to go in the huge travelling trunks. In the end, I decide to check the rosters. Humans are counted in, then counted out. Any discrepancy should be reported and flagged. At least, that's my hope.

But when I ask Bertrand, and he leads me to a basement office, I find this isn't the case at all. I didn't tell him what I overheard, of course. Just that I wondered how we kept track of humans working here.

'So, there are five fewer people arriving than left the estate, and that's just on yesterday's afternoon shift alone?' I frown, flipping through sheets of paper. The vampire behind the desk, a young man with unusually flushed cheeks, nods, darting a glance at Bertrand. 'It doesn't look like there are ever the same amount of people leaving as arrive. I don't even understand the point of making a list, if no one bothers to match up the numbers.'

'If you'll forgive me, my lady, the numbers change because the blood dancers work different shifts to the food hall. So, if there are dancers on the coach coming in, they won't be counted coming out with the same shift because they're still here. And if the dancers have a day off and want to go to the Safe Zone, they join the departing shift. And sometimes—' the young guard pauses, looking down for a moment '—sometimes, humans don't get to leave, if they are overcome in some way. So, the numbers are never going to match up.'

That list is never fucking up-to-date, anyway.

The words come into my head, suddenly. And the voice. It all clicks together. I take in a short breath.

'My lady?' Bertrand comes closer. 'If you wish, we can change how we track the humans. And the ones who pass away, I swear they're treated with dignity.'

'No. I mean, yes. Sorry, what?' I stare at Bertrand, my brows drawing together as I take in what he just said. 'Humans are *dying* here? While they're *working*? That's unacceptable.'

Both Bertrand and the other vampire look pained. 'My lady, it's not something that happens often. And it's most often from natural causes, rather than … any misuse.'

'I just…' I swallow, feeling a bit sick. I turn my attention to the vampire behind the desk. 'Perhaps we might take greater care with the health of those down here. If someone appears unwell, they shouldn't be made to work.'

The laxness horrifies me, as does the idea of people dying down here, alone. No wonder that blood dancer was able to come in and attack my father, if no one is properly managing who comes in or out.

Then there's the other thing. The human commander who saved me, when I was trying to get home after killing Kyle; I swear it was his voice I heard today in the guard hut, the same inflection and timbre.

And he wore a red-enamelled flower pin, just like the

driver who dropped me and Laurel off at the estate. Who was the same person pushing the human onto the coach today. It has to mean something, surely. But who can I ask? Human guards and vampires don't interact. That was clear when I was trying to get home, when the human guards didn't even know I was missing, or who I was.

'Emelia! There you are!'

Bertrand and the other guard bow as my mother sweeps into the room. Her cheeks are flushed, her onyx gaze gleaming. She's obviously just fed. 'I've been looking all over the house for you,' she continues, frowning. 'What on earth are you doing? Your father and I need to go through a few things with you before we leave.'

'Did you know humans are dying while they're working here?'

My mother's eyes widen.

I wave the sheets of paper at her. 'And the numbers aren't correct. More people coming in than leaving, dancers on different shifts to the feed hall. This must be how that dancer was able to get in here and attack—'

'That's quite enough.' My mother doesn't like to be reminded of that night. Her attention moves to the young guard at the desk. 'Is this so? How are these humans being tracked?'

'By numbers,' I say, before he can answer. 'Not names.' Another thing that sickens me. 'Even though each one of them is a person.'

My mother sighs. 'Right. Enough of this. Emelia, we have things to do. Bertrand, can you make sure that humans are now tracked by name, as well as numbers? For security purposes. I trust I can leave this with you.' She takes my arm, pulling me from the room.

I glance back over my shoulder. 'Sorry,' I mouth at Bertrand. He shakes his head, amused resignation gleaming in his blue eyes.

'Honestly, Emelia.' My mother takes me along the panelled hallway, then up the stairs into the main part of the house. I brace myself for the inevitable lecture.

'I appreciate that you wish to change things, and both I and your father are keen to see you stepping up to rule,' she says, as we cross the foyer. 'But you need to learn that not every detail needs to be managed by you. This is why we delegate. It's too much for one person to do.'

'But I just—'

'And I will remind you, again, that you are not just going to be ruling humans. Like it or not, at least half of your subjects will be vampires. They deserve the same consideration.'

'Do they?' I mutter.

'What was that?'

I know she heard me. She just wants me to repeat it. 'Do they? Deserve the same consideration? Because if that's the case, I guess I'd better herd them into towns where they aren't allowed to leave. Where they have to give up their lives, their choices, their very blood, just to be safe. Then it will be equal for everyone, right?'

'That's not—'

'I know it's not what you meant. But when there's such glaring inequality, surely the focus needs to be on raising people up, rather than knocking them down? Me checking how humans enter and leave this house is just a small thing, but it could make a difference. Not just to them. To our own safety.'

She presses her lips together, but her expression softens.

'I don't want to argue,' I continue. 'I feel like we do enough of that. I know you and Father are helping me, and I also know I wasted a lot of time when I should have been learning. But that can't be changed. If you want me to rule, you need to let me try things.'

My mother nods. 'You're right, of course. To a point.' There's a flash of warning in her eyes. 'Come. Let's sort out those gowns of yours. Image is as much a part of ruling as anything else.'

Just before sunset I hurry down the flight of steps at the front of the house. Our huge travelling coach is parked on the curve of gravel drive, silhouetted against the fading sky. A second coach waits behind, to carry guards and blood dancers for our journey. There are human drivers on both coaches, as we'll be on the road during the day. I cannot wait to get out of here.

The coach door opens with a hiss, the steps unfolding. I haven't been inside it for a few years. It still smells the same, like perfume and violets. Still looks the same, all gleaming chrome and soft velvet, plush cushions and carved timber, gilded with the faint gleam of candle lamps. It's massive, with a second storey and sides that extend outwards, all sealed against daylight.

The flight of narrow stairs at one end leads up to two doors, one of which opens into my room. It's small but comfortable, with a bed against one wall, a built-in wardrobe and dressing table with a gilt-framed mirror, a TV on a stand and an en-suite bathroom. All done in velvet and tapestry and carved timber, the peak of luxury.

I drop my bag on my bed. There's not much in it, just my notebook and a few old documents to read through, my jewellery box and toiletry bag. I unpack, putting everything away. My trunks have already been loaded, my gowns hung up, shoes lined along the shelves, glittering and shimmering.

You have more privilege than you know. Kyle's words, spoken in a darkened room in the Safe Zone, twist through my mind. He wasn't wrong. I didn't know. But now I do. And I plan to weaponise it, to use it to speak for others like me.

Outside the sky is dark navy, a few stars starting to appear. My parents are on board now; I can hear them below, talking to Varin. I open my jewellery box, lamplight sparking from the small pile of jewels. There's a small wooden acorn, nestled amongst the gleaming gems, the leaf and dimpled cup perfectly rendered. My heart clenches. Michael bought it for me at one of the night markets in the Safe Zone, after we'd been dancing. Something about it feels real, warm compared to the icy glimmer. I hesitate, then pull out my phone, my finger hovering over his number. Maybe I should just message him, make sure he's all right. Or maybe I should let him go.

I put my phone down and head out to the small landing, telling myself it's for the best. I need to move on. There's movement behind the other door, which leads to the driver's cockpit. On impulse, I knock on the door then push it open. 'Hello?'

Inside are two padded leather seats, plus a dashboard covered with dials and switches. The windscreen curves above me like a bubble, open to the road and wide sky. A young woman clad in a black and silver Raven uniform is kneeling by the dashboard, fiddling with something. A long red braid snakes across one shoulder.

At my entrance she turns, her blue eyes wide. 'Oh!' She stands, wiping her hands down her uniform. 'My lady? Can I do something for you?'

'Sorry, I don't think we've met before. You are…?'

'The driver. Uh, Sophie.' The young woman blinks, as though surprised at my question.

'Nice to meet you. Uh, so—' I gesture towards the two seats, feeling awkward '—I was wondering if I could sit with you, while we're travelling during the day?'

'Of course. Whatever you like.' There's a line between her brows, though, despite the brightness of her tone.

Right. I'm still her boss. The thought briefly deflates me. I don't want to push myself on anyone. 'Well, it's also what you like. I don't want to make you uncomfortable.'

She grins, her face lighting up. 'The only thing making me uncomfortable is that it's dark.' She glances out the window. 'We need to get on the road, if we're to make our schedule.'

'Emelia?'

I stick my head out the door. My mother stands in the curve of stairs, the pale oval of her face turned up to me. 'Are you coming down?'

'I might stay up here a while.'

'Of course.' She smiles. 'Come when you're ready.'

There's a rumble and sway as the coach starts to move. I return to the cockpit, sliding into the seat next to Sophie. Stars stream above us, the moon a lantern to light our route. I think of Laurel, with sorrow that she never got to travel like she wanted.

I'm doing this for you. I send the thought into the ether, as though she might hear it. We head down the long driveway, past the huge wrought-iron gates, my eyeline level with the stone ravens on top of the huge pillars. Excitement curls in my stomach, mixed with nerves.

My reign might be under threat before it's even started. But this Raven is taking flight.

Chapter Fifteen

AMONG THE ANCIENTS

'Was it tough, learning how to drive? I wish I knew how to do it.'

'No, it wasn't too bad, my lady.' Sophie keeps her focus on the road, turning the wheel as the huge coach curves through the woods.

'Oh, okay. And it's Emelia.' I knew it would take time for things to feel comfortable between me and Sophie, but hadn't expected it to be so awkward.

It's the second day of our journey. We drove for a few hours through the night, stopping at Seven Alpha, where my parents and I viewed the damage from the attack. There wasn't much to see; a few broken walls, already being rebuilt. I stared out at the moonlit sea, trying not to think about floating bodies. It was odd, on reflection. Why would Reapers attack houses near the shore, rather than closer to the Great Forest? And why was Michael so insistent that it wasn't Reapers? I hate that I can't stop thinking about him.

We returned to the coach in silence, and I slept for a few

hours before waking to daylight, and the coach already moving. I fed, then slipped into the cockpit, greeting Sophie as I took the other seat, excited by what I might see. But after several attempts to start a conversation, all of which left me feeling as though I was somehow saying the wrong thing, I ended up just staring out the windscreen at the grey ribbon of road, the forest a dark wall either side of us.

I get it, though. This must be a strange situation for her. If I were a vampire, I wouldn't be sitting with her during the day. And if I were any other human on this trip, I'd be working, just like she is. I feel ashamed of my perceived idleness. But telling her about the Challenge, or my worries about taking the crown, or basically anything to do with my life feels impossible. Being human in my world is burden enough; me complaining about my privilege is not what she needs.

I remember asking my mother if I was the only one. Now I know I'm not. But I'm still alone. Laurel was a friend, but part of me wonders how much of it was because she felt she had to be. Kyle was … he was someone I loved, and trusted. But he betrayed me in the worst possible way.

Then there's Michael. The only person like me I've ever met. Yet I've lost him, too.

There is no more together.

I glance at Sophie. I wasn't kidding about wanting to learn to drive. It's like sword fighting; something physical I can do to take care of myself. But this is ridiculous. There's no point prolonging her torture. 'Hey,' I say. 'I might watch the road from my room. There's a window there and—'

Her eyes widen. 'What? No, you don't have to do that.'

'I think, maybe, that I do. Thanks, though, for having me sit with you.' I smile, because I'm genuinely grateful.

A line appears between her brows. 'I'd like you to stay, if that's all right, my l—Emelia.'

'Really? Because I know it's weird, and I don't want to make you uncomfortable.'

One corner of her mouth curves, and her blue gaze flicks my way. 'It is weird, if you don't mind my saying. But good weird. Please, stay.'

I grin. 'Okay. Are you hungry?'

'Hungry?' Another azure glance. 'Sure. I mean, yes, I am. But I need to keep driving.'

'I'm going to make myself a sandwich. Do you want one?'

'Really?' She's frowning again. Shit. Maybe I've screwed up. Maybe I'm overthinking this.

'Really. I'll be back in a few minutes.' I leave the cockpit, heading downstairs. My parents are sitting together talking, while Varin reclines on one of the velvet sofas, polishing a dagger. They all look up as I appear, my mother smiling.

'Everything all right?'

'Yep. Just hungry.' I head over to the kitchen, quickly making sandwiches and putting them in the press. A delicious scent of melted cheese fills the coach.

'Those smell almost good enough to eat.' Varin comes up beside me, reaching for a blood pouch from the storage box.

'You want one?' I open the toaster, pulling the sandwiches out and cutting them.

He laughs. 'No, thank you.' He strolls away, all fluid grace. I try not to watch.

'They'll get cold if you don't eat them soon.' My father, a twinkle in his eye, winks at me.

Blushing, I grab the sandwiches and head upstairs again.

'Oh.' It's an intake of breath rather than a word, full of yearning. We're trundling along a broad, deserted highway, the road curving downwards, the land rising to one side. But Sophie's focus isn't on the road; rather, it's higher. Almost at the crest of the hill is a jumble of huge stones. It's somehow familiar. I rack my brains.

'Oh my God!' I squeak. 'That's Stonehenge. It's really, really old! We should stop!'

'Yeah.' Another word carried on a breath. Sophie changes gears, slowing the coach down.

'I'll be back.' I leave the cabin, taking the stairs to the living room two at a time.

'Is everything all right?' My father surges up from the sofa, hand to his hip as though he's wearing his sword.

'It's fine.' I pause, catching my breath. 'I just … Stonehenge is out there, and I want to see it up close.'

My father grins. 'We can stop wherever you like.'

I race back upstairs. Sophie has already pulled off the highway, taking a narrow road that curves back around in the direction of the monument. I can't see it anymore. Then it appears again, larger this time, the huge stones greyish-brown against the grass.

'This road should probably be more choked off than this,' Sophie says. 'And the forest … it should have taken over.' Tension threads her voice.

'Humans still come here, don't they.' It's not a question.

'They have been, for millennia,' Sophie says. 'And now we get to do it, too.'

A few minutes later she pulls to a stop. The wide plain is

green and brown, hills rising in the distance, the dark mass of the forest all around. The sky is gold and grey, wind ruffling the grass. Which is trimmed and tidy around the stones, as though there's still a guardian of this place.

We head downstairs. My parents and Varin are already in the next room, the door closed against any stray fingers of light. I knock as I go past. 'We'll be back soon.'

Sophie opens the coach door, and we step out. For a moment we just stand there. It's so still, so quiet. So wide open. Then she takes my hand and we run towards the towering stones. We slow as we get close, walking between the grey uprights into the circle itself.

The air in here is still, despite the breeze cutting across the plain. It feels … ancient. And very, very human. My chest aches, a pressure building I can't ease.

'Wow.' Sophie turns, her phone out, panning around the ruins.

'There's still power here,' I say.

'Yeah. And to think humans built this, all those years ago.'

We perch on one of the central stones, taking it all in. I try to imagine what it must have been like when people came here to celebrate. Something to do with the sun, I think I read once. No wonder vampires don't bother coming here.

Sophie puts her phone away and sits back, her hands braced against the grey stone. Her blue gaze is distant, and I wonder what she's thinking. It feels comfortable, though, sitting here together. Just two girls, perched on a rock.

'Can I ask you something?' Sophie's voice breaks the silence.

'Sure. Ask me whatever you want.'

'What's it like, being the Raven?'

'Huh.' I'm not sure how to answer. I decide to be honest. 'I didn't want it, at first. I even ran away.'

'You didn't?'

'I shouldn't be telling you this. Sorry.' I'm an idiot. At least I had a choice to leave. No other humans have that.

'That's not what I was thinking.'

'It's not?'

'No. I was thinking I get it. It would be terrifying, to have that power handed to you.' She glances my way. 'I couldn't do it.'

'I'm sure you could.'

Sophie shakes her head, looking down, her mouth curving. After a pause she speaks. 'I know what you're trying to do. I heard about it, on the news. How you want to help humans.'

'You do?' I don't know why I'm surprised. It's a regular story on vampire news rounds, always with a faint undertone of derision. My mother made a statement, saying that she and my father fully supported my desire to improve human conditions, but it hasn't changed much.

'Why do you want to do that?'

'What?'

'You heard me.' She grins, then her expression becomes serious. 'It's a huge job, Emelia.'

I stare across the wide plain, the grass rippling like a green sea. 'I lived in the Safe Zone for a while. And I saw how things were.'

'Really?'

'Yeah. I was … things were happy there, for me. But it was an illusion. My world is one of darkness, true. But it's one where I get to travel, learn about whatever I like, have every material thing I could wish for. I get to live a life. Make a difference. And it seems remarkably unfair that other humans don't. That they're just—'

'—cattle.' At my glance, Sophie shrugs. 'We all know that's what we are. Useful in some ways, but in the end we're all just food.'

Like it or not, we are the meat. Words spoken in a human dining room come back to me, as I gaze into the undulating green.

'I can't change that,' I say. 'I wish I could. But there has to be a better way of doing things. Of living together.'

We sink into silence, listening to the rush of wind between the stones.

'Speaking of food…'

I brace myself, wondering what Sophie's going to say.

'I still can't believe you offered Varin a toasted sandwich the other day.' She giggles.

My mouth drops open. 'What?'

'I don't blame you. His hotness is very distracting.'

I start giggling as well. I'm still blushing about it, to be honest. Sophie hadn't been able to stop laughing when I returned to the cabin, red-faced.

'I mean, it's not like he could eat it or anything,' Sophie splutters. 'Though I'd like to watch him try. Licking that melted cheese off his lips, brushing crumbs off his muscular chest. Might have to offer to help him with that.'

'Stop, stop.' I can barely breathe from laughing.

'As if he doesn't know how hot he is, walking around in those silks with his arms out.'

We both fall about laughing again, the sound echoing off the huge uprights. Something about laughing here feels right, as though it's a place of joy. I'll remember this for ever, I think, as I watch the sky change colour, light chasing shadows across the grass. As I laugh and breathe in the wild beauty of the stones, of this once sacred place. Things feel possible here, like the light of a new day. Maybe it's a good sign that my Raven rollout tour begins here, even if there's no one to see me.

'We should go back,' Sophie says, once we've both calmed down. 'The next stop tonight isn't far, but I need to check the route and radio ahead, so they're ready for us.'

'Okay.' Neither of us moves, though. We sit in silence for a while longer, the stones like grey guardians around us.

We're still quiet when we get back on the coach, as though the place cast a spell on us.

'I've never seen anything like that,' Sophie says eventually, as she guides the coach along a curving road. 'It reminded me…

'Of what we once were?'

'Yeah.'

I swallow. Shadows lengthen, the day turning towards night. As we enter the outskirts of a city built from honey-coloured stone, I wonder what it was like when humans walked these streets. And how they could walk them again.

The feeling grows as we continue north, through a countryside just turning towards spring, our route taking us through England, dipping into Wales, then further north again, the land becoming wilder, granite mountains like humped beasts surrounding rippling lakes. As we lounge in heated pools flanked by crumbling statues, as we wander around the soaring moonlit ruins of an ancient abbey, or dance in the vaulted halls of a walled castle by a river, a place where once kings were made. As we stop on a lonely road, Sophie and I transfixed by the majesty of two giant rusting horseheads rising above the trees, and weep at the futility of it all. As I'm bowed to by vampires, courted and hand-fed as though I'm a creature to be tamed, all the while aware they use my kind as food, living among the beauty humans have created as though we never existed for anything else. Receptions where I'm received with everything from reverence to ignorance, where I insist my humanity be acknowledged, rather than brushed aside. As I'm shown paintings and beautiful buildings and porcelain so fine I can see my fingers through it, each item adding to the ache in my chest, the feeling of something wonderful, irrevocably lost.

As I shake hands with vampires who could kill me in seconds and wonder whether they're humouring me simply because of who my parents are, or whether they truly believe I'm capable of ruling Raven. As I walk along crowded streets lined with Raven guards, waving, as my image fills the news feeds. As I realise why my mother had me do this, analysing each meeting with me afterwards to make sure I understood what I'd done right, and what I'd done wrong. As I see more of what it means to be Raven and understand what it is I'm fighting to defend.

As I sit with Sophie during the days and watch the landscape slide past. As we pass several Safe Zones. Dark brown towns like scars on the green and rolling landscape, all guarded, all kept apart from the wonder and beauty of the world around them.

And as I spot the red flower symbol here and there. On a crumbling stone wall next to a small bakery in a Safe Zone. Etched into a stone at yet another stone circle. On a rusting shipping container at a dark dock.

It represents *something*. Whether it's a human or vampire

symbol, I don't know. But the fact I'm seeing it in human places, rather than vampire ones, suggests it's somehow connected to them. But what does it *mean*?

Illegal hunts are one option; they're a way to make money, organisers selling spots to both hunters and humans. Perhaps they're a symbol of a hunt organisation, or a meeting point. Or maybe it's another rebellion, though things seem quiet on that front. The rebellion I'm currently dealing with comes from vampires, not humans.

Which is why I can't really focus my energy on this right now. It just feels like too many scattered pieces, that together might mean nothing at all. But there's a sense of something eluding me, of a whole world out there I don't yet fully see. I'm trying to understand my realm, but it seems that the more I learn, the less I actually know.

So, I tuck each sighting away, like a piece of jigsaw where I don't have the picture on the box to guide me. I'll claim my crown, then come back to it.

Because I want to figure it out.

Chapter Sixteen

DARK KNIGHTS

Late one evening, as we head south towards Old London, I'm in my bedroom, trying to make sense of one of the documents from the library. Sophie is sleeping on my bed, rather than in the small cubicle attached to the cockpit. I offered it to her while one of the guards was driving the coach, hastily summoned when we left the latest reception early, after the host mistook me for a blood dancer and tried to offer me to his guests. I frown, shuffling the pages, annoyance a sharp tang alongside the ache in my chest.

One thing this trip has made very clear is what a mistake it was to keep me hidden away. I'm supposed to rule over half the planet. This tour has worked, in that my face is all over the news and social media so at least people are starting to recognise me. But any respect I'm given is because of my last name. It's just as I realised on my first visit to the Safe Zone. If not for an accident of birth, I'd simply be another human. It's not surprising at all that Mistral want to challenge my right to rule.

Like it or not, at least half of your subjects will be vampires.

I sigh, trying to work out whether a word on the page says 'wings' or 'winds'. I chose to return to my parents' world because I realised that the best way for me to change things was from within. The more I learn, though, the more I realise that getting a crown on my head doesn't make me a ruler. Power handed to me is different to power that I earn. The first will slip through my fingers, if I'm not clever or strong enough to hold it. The second, though, I can wear like a mantle, like armour. Because it will be *mine*.

What I need to figure out is how to earn it. I don't want to be a ruler who stays behind walls and guards, using the iron fist of Raven to crush any opposition. I want to make an actual fucking effort to learn about the people in my realm, in the hopes we can come to a solution on how to change things.

Stonehenge, the palaces I've danced in, those rusted horses, still magnificent, still rising, yet so very alone, feel like a metaphor for all that I've seen so far. Humanity's greatness, now lost to them. Vampires seem to love all that humans have wrought; why then, do they not value humans the same way?

Because they're food.

The version of history we learn as children is what we accept, until we grow old enough to question it. I was taught that the Red Rising was a great victory for vampires, something to be celebrated each year. I grew up believing it, content with my mound of velvet-wrapped gifts, the chance to dance at my parents' ball. But now that I've actually seen how things are for humans, I don't see anything triumphant about it at all. Another thing that's clear to me is that humans can never be truly controlled. Perhaps the biggest mistake vampires have made is thinking they can be.

This is why I want to see my realm, understand what was lost, and what might be possible, once I gain my crown. Why I'm out here, letting people see who the Raven will be. I might be human, might be protected by my parents and Bertrand and the bevy of Raven guards following in the coach behind. But that's no different to how my parents live. The only difference is that they have teeth. I need to grow my own fangs, ones of steel and skill and determination. I'm getting better at the Morningstar, at least. Still slow, but it's coming along. Varin says he's pleased with me, anyway.

I frown, trying not to be distracted by thoughts of the handsome arms master, even if I have just read the same sentence four times. I continue scanning the pages. These people, whoever they were, seemed to have figured out the secret of coexistence.

> *Ladye Morvenna, and her dark knights who do reap all that threatens them. There are none can withstande her dark forces, subject to only the ladye. Anyone who tries ys cut down like so many stalkes of wheat.*

Wait. Her 'dark knights who do *reap*'? That's quite a specific word to use. Why not just say kill, or destroy?

Her dark forces. My mind goes back to a round table with a relief carving of the realms, of white-knuckled humans in chairs. What had Jane said? *We want your dark forces withdrawn*. Yet my father was adamant that Raven had stopped attacking the North Wind cells.

Fuck.

Could the dark knights be *Reapers*? No one knows where Reapers came from, or what they stand for. Apart from the fact they hold fealty to no house. What if Lady Morvenna's community still exists, and they're defending it? What if Reapers were attacking the North Wind because they got too close? But then why the hell are they targeting Safe Zones, too?

The other flaw in my argument is that Reapers are not a localised phenomenon. They're *everywhere*. Called Dragons in Scorpion lore, Vipers by Lion. And Jaguar calls them El Muerte, which apparently means death.

But if Lady Morvenna's dark knights really are Reapers, then I want to know more. The description of their community, where vampires and humans live together, is the closest thing I've found to what I want to achieve. Kyle told me Reapers were taken to the pits when they were caught – it was where he was when Mistral found him – so perhaps that's somewhere to start. But, even if I do find a Reaper, how can I get them to tell me what they know? The documents are pretty clear that they protect their community with their lives. It's a long shot.

I'm still turning it over in my mind when there's a sharp jerk of brakes. I put the paper down, wondering what's happening. Then I hear voices, and the hiss of the door from below. I get up, shoving my bare feet into boots and barrelling downstairs. The living area is deserted, the coach door open. I step outside to a scene of devastation.

We're stopped near a small cluster of buildings, on a finger of land by the sea. Homes, by the look of them, and possibly a shop. All ruined now. Glass shattered, gaping holes in the walls as though they've been ripped apart, scars in the brickwork still fresh. My parents and Varin, along with several Raven guards, are picking their way through the wreckage. I go to join them, and tread on something soft. Oh, darkness.

It's a little doll, a child's toy. Now stained with dirt and something darker, more ominous, spattered across its smiling face.

'Emelia.' My father comes to me. 'I don't think you should see this.'

'I should see it.' Even though my stomach is roiling, I need to. My father knows it, too. He takes my arm, leading me through the debris and over a shattered wall.

'Oh God.' I swallow, hard.

We're in the remains of a room, at the back of what looks like a shop. Splintered tables and chairs are tumbled together, along with piles of ash. Dark stains are splattered across everything; a faint, rotting scent. And, on the most intact of the walls, a familiar symbol. The Raven mark, scored by tattered lines. The North Wind.

'Human remains.' Varin pauses on the other side of the pile of broken timbers, looking down, his brow furrowed.

I don't need to see that. 'Was … was this one of those nomadic settlements? Did we do this?' I try not to look at the exposed upper storey of the house next door. A child's bed, the coverlets ragged and stained, hangs from the remains of a pink bedroom. As though it was ripped from it. 'Please tell me we didn't do this.'

'We did not.'

My mother comes over to us, her eyes darker than usual. 'Aleks.'

'We do *not* murder children.' My father's voice becomes a growl.

My mother casts sorrowful eyes across the wreckage. 'There's nothing we can do here.'

There never is, once death has visited. It's not something that can be turned back. Yet it seems like I always end up here, among blood and darkness and dead humans.

If you keep taking the same path, you'll end up at the same destination.

There's silence, a faint glimmer in the distance heralding the dawn. Yet it's dark, among the scattered debris. I don't bother asking the question, because I know the answer.

If Raven didn't do this, there's only one possible option.

An option that, potentially, holds the key to what I want to achieve. But, as I look around at the devastation, I don't know how I can even consider approaching them.

Reapers.

Chapter Seventeen

LIVING THE DREAM

'Humans used to fly to these places, didn't they?'

'They did.' Varin brings me a mug of tea and sits next to me on the velvet sofa. Night is almost over, but I can't sleep. We're back on the south coast, after travelling through the night from Old London, parked on the edge of a huge port, waiting for the ferry to the Channel Islands. A vampire port, so everything is gleaming and works well. No rusted hulks, no rotting buildings here. I should be excited, to finally see my project come to fruition, but can't seem to muster any joy. Only rage.

I can't get the destroyed settlement out of my mind. Or anything else I've seen. The ache in my chest never seems to fade, the feeling of a lost world, just beyond my reach. I know we can't go back there. But I don't want things to stay as they are, either.

'Vampires don't fly?'

'No. We have a horror of it. The way light comes upon us so quickly above the clouds, it's not safe. Plus, there's no point.' He shrugs. 'Time has less meaning for us than it has for humans. We're not as invested in getting to places so quickly, despite our speed. We're creatures of the earth, of blood and soil, our affinity with the ground, not the sky. It was humans who dreamed of getting closer to the stars, not us.'

'And now they waste away on glorified farms. All that talent, all that creativity. Reduced to one thing. Blood.'

'Emelia, that's—'

'How it is, right? Sorry.' I slump back on the sofa, my arms folded. He's trying, I suppose. Everyone is trying. My mother doesn't know what to do for me, buying me clothes from glittering shops, hugging me whenever she can. My father tried talking to me, but I don't know what to tell him. I can't seem to get out of this trough.

The Challenge hangs over me like an axe waiting to fall, compounding my sorrow and anger. I'm nervous about what's going to happen when we get to Versailles, whether any part of our strategy to change the families' minds will work. Lion still haven't responded to our invitation, and neither have Scorpion. Jaguar sent a single jade amulet of a snarling beast, fangs out. It's a beautiful thing, and very valuable. I'm unsure whether it's a gift or a threat.

'This has not been easy for you, has it?' Varin's dark glance is kind.

'Which part do you think hasn't been easy?' God. I should not be sassing Varin.

'Tell me,' he replies, still so kind. It's as though the words puncture something in me, my pain pouring out.

'Do any of you really know, or care, what it's like to be human? You all say you support me, but none of you ever acknowledge your own roles in the Rising, and everything that's happened since!'

Varin says nothing.

'I'm taking a crown I didn't want, because it's the only way to change things. But humans don't see me as one of them, because I'm a Raven, and vampires don't see me as part of their world, either. Meanwhile, so much that was good and beautiful has been left to rot, to be swallowed by the forest. Do none of you see that? It just feels as though you're humouring me.'

'No one is humouring you.'

'*Everyone* is humouring me!' I say. 'Each time you say you support me, but nothing changes.'

Varin's head tilts. 'You are making change happen, believe me.'

'How? By marching around in frocks in front of a crowd? Pretending I'm something I'm not?'

'What are you pretending to be that you're not?'

'A ruler. A vampire. Someone with power.'

'What makes you think you are none of those things?'

'*Stop humouring me!*' I snarl the words, baring my teeth. A strange wildness courses through me, like darkness in my veins. I pause, unsure where the surge of power came from. I feel like I could tear the coach apart.

Varin places one hand gently on my arm. I shake it off, staring at him, my chest heaving.

'You have power, Emelia,' he says, quiet. 'You are showing us all that humans born of vampires are not to be underestimated.'

'Is that all? Am I not showing you how you've fucked up everything, too? Can nobody else see what I see? Fuck!' I turn away, my hands to my head, feeling like I might burst into flames. 'We drive around and visit places and people bow to me and pretend like they don't think I'm supposed to be dead or food and it's just bullshit!'

'It is.' Varin's mild agreement stops me in my tracks.

'What?' I turn back to him.

'Ruling. Setting someone above another simply because of their bloodline, regardless of the type of person they are. It is bullshit.'

I laugh, despite my anger. 'So you don't think I deserve to be crowned?'

'It doesn't matter what I think. Do *you* think you deserve to be crowned?'

I stare at him, my mouth opening and closing, the wildness in my veins receding.

'Perhaps a walk on deck later might do you good. The ocean is wonderfully healing, or so I've found. It may give you the space you need to work out what happens next.'

'I know what happens next.'

'And what is that?'

'I face the families, face their Challenge, and succeed. There are no other options.'

Varin smiles. 'Good.'

The sea is wide and blue and the air smells of salt. Pale sunlight dances on the waves, spray like white foam hissing as the prow of the ship dips. The breeze blows through me, tangling in my hair as though it's alive, blowing some of my shadows away. A tendril of the strange darkness remains, though. I wonder again at the rush of power, and where it came from. I'm also slightly ashamed of unloading on Varin. He was right. It doesn't matter what the other families think. If *I* don't think I deserve the crown then I may as well give up now. It's a sobering realisation.

'What's on your mind?' Sophie bumps my shoulder as we lean on the railing.

'Varin.'

'And the fact that he's the hottest thing on this boat?'

'No.' I laugh. There were a few curious glances from the human crew as we came on deck, but I guess the fact we didn't burst into flames was enough to make them lose interest. 'Although, yes, you're probably right about that. No, he just said it might be good for me to come up here today.'

'You've been struggling, huh? I've seen it, but didn't want to—'

'It's just…' I wave my hand, unable to express what I want to say. 'All of this. It's such bullshit. I just want to get on with the work, you know?'

'This is part of it, though. Being human, around all of them. Having them bow to you. It'll change how they see us.'

'Yeah. That's part of it. But this is… it's my job. And I need to figure out how to do it. To be good at it. Like you are.'

Earlier, I'd watched in awe as Sophie manoeuvred the huge coach into the gaping maw of the waiting vessel, moonlit waves visible through a small porthole as the gangway clanged shut behind us.

'You will be. I had a lot to learn, when I started. Although nothing like what you have to do.'

'I yelled at him.' My voice is small.

'At Varin?'

'Yeah. He was kind about it. But he also reminded me that I need to believe in myself.' I breathe in the sea air, trying not to think about being on the beach with Michael in the early morning, when anything felt possible. A shadowy coastline rises in the distance, like the humps of a sea-monster. We're getting close to the islands. Then I notice a group of small dark shapes on the horizon. 'Are those boats?' I point.

Sophie shades her eyes. 'Maybe? I imagine there's a few loose boats floating around out here.'

'I don't think they're floating. They look like they're going somewhere.' A plume of smoke comes up from the boat at the front of the small convoy. 'And they're really small.'

'Maybe they're vampire boats?'

'During the day?'

Sophie shrugs. 'Humans aren't allowed to sail around, though, are they? So it must be vamps, somehow.' She sounds uncertain, though.

And, as I watch the small convoy disappear into the distance, so am I.

We dock a short while later, Sophie and I in the cockpit, my parents and Varin sealed in darkness below. I decided to have a daytime arrival, to make a statement. Let the news footage show humans living in the light, not the darkness. We roll onto a paved quayside, a long low building ahead of us with a sign reading 'Ferry Terminal'. I should be excited; I've worked hard to ensure the island is ready. But I'm not. Instead, I'm uneasy.

A small group of people emerge from the terminal: Jane and Andrew, accompanied by a human film crew. Sea birds call, wheeling in the bright air as I exit the coach with Sophie. I asked her to come, because I wanted her to see what was possible. And also, because I needed a friend.

'Lady Raven!' Jane hurries over, dropping into a curtsey. 'We're so glad you're here.'

'Thank you for having us,' I reply. 'This is Sophie. She'll be joining us on the tour today. Tonight, my parents will tour the community as well.'

'Of course.' Jane smiles. 'I hope you'll be happy with what we've done.'

'I'm sure I will be. How's it all going?'

The island didn't have a lot of residents when I cleared it, and those vampires who did live here were handsomely compensated, offered alternative homes on the mainland, all expenses paid. We had to start basically from scratch, making sure there was a school and a library, that shops were stocked with goods, that regular deliveries would be made for food and essentials, as well as seedlings and everything the community might need to become as self-sufficient as possible. I discovered that the attics at the Raven estate were filled with furniture, so had it cleaned up and sent over, as well as making sure every home had linens and appliances, power and water connected.

'Food deliveries are going well.' Jane ushers us towards a small vehicle with open sides, Andrew in the driver's seat. Sophie and I sit in the back, Jane in the passenger seat. 'We've also been planting our own, ready for growing season. Give us a year or so and I think you'll really see results here.' We leave the port, another vehicle with the film crew following as we head into town. 'This is our new playground,' Jane continues, as we pass an open space where parents chase shrieking toddlers across grass, push them on swings, the trees bright with spring green. A man sells drinks from a van, people sitting on benches, admiring the view of the ocean. It's beautiful.

We continue along residential streets, past homes with freshly painted trim and new front doors, some still with piles of building waste in the small front gardens. 'We're still working on these houses,' Jane says. 'They were in a bad way when we got here. But the community is really pulling together.'

More streets, more houses, some with window boxes and colourful gardens. Yet there are no people around. I get it, I guess. I remind myself that despite Jane's friendliness, these people were trying to kill my family mere months ago. Andrew is quiet, the scar on his hand pulling white as he grips the steering wheel. He smiles, though, when I catch his eye.

Sophie nudges me. 'This is wonderful,' she whispers, her blue eyes wide.

'It is,' Jane says, not missing a beat. 'You've changed all our lives.'

'It felt like the least I could do,' I say. 'I hope it's the start of positive change for everyone.'

'I'm sure it is,' Jane says, as we turn down yet another pretty street, passing a school where children play. It looks like something from the past, a scene from the old films I used to watch. But it's real. And it's the future. My mood lifts as sun breaks through the clouds, gilding everything to brightness. It feels like a good omen.

I hope that's the case.

I'm not as hopeful during the night tour, though, my sense of unease returning. The islands feel vulnerable, surrounded by dark sea, no guards or lights to keep predators at bay. And the streets, despite being lined by steel barricades and Raven guards, are once again empty of people, the houses unlit. It feels … deliberate. The human film crew are still following us but, as we pass deserted street after street, I wish they weren't.

Then I glimpse a flicker of black-and-white fabric hanging from one of the windows. Andrew, with a muffled curse, steers us away before the film crew catch up. Not quickly enough for my parents, though. They saw it, I can tell by the set of my mother's mouth, my father's frown.

A banner with our crest, the raven in a circle, slashed by three lines. The emblem of the North Wind.

Chapter Eighteen

A QUESTION OF BALANCE

'Why are we even bothering to do this!'

'Your project still has promise, Emelia. Do not let one thing—'

'*One thing?* It was the North Wind banner! You warned me, even when I trusted them, and now I've been betrayed again.'

My father's brows lower over his golden gaze as he paces the length of the coach, his arms folded.

'What do you want to do?' My mother's voice is quiet, threaded with concern. For me. Because this is my mess, and now I have to clean it up.

I feel like an idiot. Andrew cut the tour short as soon as we saw the banner, taking us back to the quayside. The film crew were taken inside, after my parents and I gave them a few quotes about how pleased we were to see the project going well. We all lie so expertly for the cameras. Afterwards, Andrew came to us.

'This will be dealt with,' he said, his voice hard.

'How? This was the deal I made with you, that the North

Wind ends.' My voice shook a little, which made me even angrier. 'I trusted you!'

'And we will not betray that trust, or our deal. The rebellion … it took everything from me. And it is *over*.' He gritted the words out. 'We have our own methods of dealing with this. Please. Don't take this place from us.' His voice caught, desperation in his eyes.

We left him on the quay, returning to the coach to discuss things. And now I'm sitting on the sofa while my father paces like an angry lion, my mother frets, Varin a watchful presence in the shadows. 'What do I want to do?' I shake my head. 'Go home. What's the point? Why the hell did either of you think I could do this?' My words curl through the room like a lash. I regret them almost immediately. My mother flinches. My father stops dead, then flashes over to me.

'You do *not* give up,' he growls. 'And we are not going home! You have a job to do, and you need to do it. Make your decision. You can end this settlement now, move everyone into their own Safe Zone where they can cause no more trouble. Or you clear the place out. Execute everyone.' His lip curls. 'Or let them stay, and work through their mistakes. What kind of ruler do you want to be?'

Not the kind of ruler who executes an entire community. I know that. But I also know something else.

It's not going to work.

I had an idea, of a world where humans could be free to choose their path. But the banner incident aside, this whole thing feels like a joke. No different to a Safe Zone, apart from the lack of vampires. What in darkness was I thinking, putting a group of humans on undefended islands? Yes, there are Raven boats patrolling the seas, but they cannot be everywhere. I was a fool to trust the North Wind. So long as the inequality between humans and vampires exists, there can never be true peace. I need to think of something else.

'It's a disaster,' I mutter, dropping onto the sofa.

'It's not a disaster.' My mother sits with me, her hand covering mine. 'It was … it's a beautiful idea.'

'But we all know why it won't work. And now this. I should just shut it down.'

'Are you sure that's what you want to do?' My father's voice softens, and he sits on the other side of me.

I think of children playing in the sunshine. Of freshly painted houses, seedlings growing, people walking on the beach. All the hard work I've done. And for what? To be betrayed? I'm sick of betrayal. But I'm also sick of things being the way they are. Shutting the project down feels like admitting I can't change anything.

'No. Not yet. I'll give them one more chance. But the place needs to be monitored. Any other signs of rebellion and it's over.' I'm exhausted, heartsore.

'We need to talk about what happens next.' My mother, still quiet.

'What's there to talk about? I know what I'm supposed to do when we get to Jennie's. Win everyone over with how amazing I am, so they don't want to challenge my right to rule and fight father. Except, I'm not amazing, and I doubt anyone will think that!' Tears come to my eyes. 'Just because you say I deserve the crown, it doesn't mean I actually do.'

'Correct.' My father's voice is grave. 'And it's important you understand that. Vampires honour the ancient bloodlines, but they still hold their rulers accountable. It's why things like the Challenge exist, why we anoint our heirs at eighteen, passing the crown on even though we are still able to rule. It is to guard against tyranny, against weakness, against a ruler who stays too long.'

'And each heir has to learn how to rule,' my mother says.

'I do not want to spend the next twenty years making mistakes while you watch over my shoulder!' I hiss. 'There are five families who think I'm not fit to rule. Maybe they're right!'

I get up, unable to take any more, heading to my room and closing the door. I sit on the bed, pulling my knees to my chest. I want to go home. More than that, I want to go back to the Safe Zone, to my little white house with Michael and Laurel. But Laurel is dead and the house is empty. And Michael, no matter how I want it to be different, is gone. Giving up is not an option.

There's a knock on my door. I ignore it. It's probably my mother. But the door opens to reveal Varin, holding a steaming mug of tea. He crosses my room, light on his feet, placing the tea next to me.

'May I?' He gestures to the end of my bed.

'Yes.' Sophie will die when I tell her about this. The thought cheers me a little. The bed shifts as Varin sits down, his raven-dark hair in waves around his handsome face.

'Did my parents send you up here to talk to me?'

'Your parents are worried about you,' he says, his voice gentle. 'We all are.'

'I shouldn't have shouted at you earlier. I'm sorry.'

'No, you should have. There's nothing wrong in standing up for what you believe.'

'It doesn't matter, anyway. Nothing's going to change. My project is a disaster. The families don't think I'm fit to rule.'

I rub the ache in my chest, my throat raw. 'I can't even do the Morningstar properly!'

'Firstly, being able to do the Morningstar at the speed of myself, or your father, requires years of practice. We're both impressed by how well you've picked things up. You're coming along quickly but can't expect to master it in a matter of weeks. I knew humans who could do it, though, and none of them had vampire blood like you. As for the rest of it … yes, what you saw tonight is a setback for your project. It doesn't mean it's a disaster, though. You will respond, and they will regret what they did. But what you've done out there, what you've created, is very much as things were. It's a shame, I think, how much has been lost in the intervening years.'

'What was it like, before the Red Rising?'

'In the old world?' Varin smiles a little, his gaze distant. 'It worked, for a long time, until it didn't. Vampires were legend to most people, and we were happy to remain separate, hunting near battlefields, in the darkness of forests and tangled city streets, generations of human families content to work for us and with us, while keeping our secrets.'

'If you were so happy, why did the Rising happen? Vampires already ruled the night.'

Varin's dark brows come together. 'It was…' His frown deepens and, in one fluid motion, he stands and draws his sword.

I tense. But Varin simply balances the blade across one finger, light catching the ribbon of steel. 'You see this, how the sword is balanced. Everything equal, held at a point of equilibrium.'

I nod.

'That's how it was, for centuries upon centuries. Vampires

ruled the night, as you say; their world mostly separate from that of humans, who ruled the day.'

'Why take over, then?'

'Night was being taken from us. We can take a little light, as you know, like the gleam of that candle lamp.' He nods to the one on the nearby table. 'But as the human population grew in both volume and technology, all of a sudden, lights were everywhere, polluting the night sky so we could no longer see the stars, their beams becoming more and more powerful, spreading across the globe. We were pushed into the shadows, relegated to pop-culture villains. It became almost impossible for vampires to hunt, our people starving. So, we took action. We took back the night.'

'But you took the days as well,' I say. 'You took everything.'

'I agree.' Varin moves his hand, and his sword drops to one side. He catches it by the hilt, sheathing it, utterly lethal, utterly beautiful. 'The balance was too far gone one way. Now it is too far gone the other.'

'All because there was too much light?' This seems hard to believe.

'Light is lethal to us. Blood is what we need to survive. It seemed logical, at the time.'

'Do you still think it's logical?'

Varin shakes his head. 'No.'

'My parents seem to think I just want to help humans. But I want something that works for both sides.' I get up and walk over to the window. The night sky is soft with clouds, a glimmer of pale moon visible. 'A world where humans are free isn't going to work. But things can't stay as they are. Not while I'm the Raven. There has to be a reason I was born this way, that my mother fought to keep me alive. I represent both sides, vampire and human. I can move freely in both worlds. If I can't fix this, then who can?'

'There are many who think there is nothing to be fixed.'

'I know.' Below us, Raven guards run through drills, flashing across the paved expanse of the quay, wielding weapons with perfect precision. I remember another dark practice ground, guards with pikes and swords. Punishment from my father, for the lie I told. I've come a long way since then. 'But it's not going to stop me trying.'

Varin is silent for a moment. Then he speaks. 'I have trained with many warriors,' he says. 'Men, women, human, vampire. Each of them with their own story to tell, their own goals. Some achieved what they wanted to do. Others did not. But what was important was that they tried. They gave themselves to the dance with their whole hearts, and they believed in themselves. It wasn't anything I could teach them; they already had to hold it, here.' He puts his palm flat on his chest. 'You said, when you saw your father do the Morningstar, that you heard the steel sing. Which is true, in a way. But what you also felt, what also resounded within you, was intention. A call to the song you carry that is unique to you. Hold on to that, Emelia. The dance may become difficult at times, the steps harder to learn. But as long as it calls to you, don't stop.'

I blink back tears, obscurely comforted. From the moment we met, Varin has always treated me as a whole person. Never pandered to my humanity, never made me feel as though we were different in any way. 'Thank you.' My voice is husky.

He nods once, smiling. 'I am always here for you, Emelia.' Then he's gone, soft and silent as a shadow, the door clicking shut behind him.

I go back to bed and sip my tea, thinking about my

intentions and what I want to achieve, as night turns to day and the coach starts moving once more. I came back for a reason, and now I'm following through, growing my fangs, claiming my power. I dream of a world where humans and vampires live side by side as equals, like the society in the old documents my father found. I imagine being a warrior, strong and capable, mastering the Morningstar. And later, as I drift off to sleep, the warrior becomes Michael, beautiful as the sun, his muscles shifting as he moves through the dance.

When I wake the sun is setting, and the coach is no longer moving. Through my window I see the bulk of a huge building, the ornate twists of an iron fence against a sky that shimmers gold and ice-blue; the clouds rumpled as though someone dragged a stick through them. Versailles. Ancient home of French nobility. Built by humans, now home to the De Corbeau family.

And the place where I will fight for my crown.

Chapter Nineteen

EYES ON YOU

I haven't seen Jennie in a long while, but she looks the same as I remember. A small, slender woman, her hair worn long and parted in the middle, her skin the same warm brown as the carved wooden doors, her face sculpted and beautiful. She has the same onyx eyes as my mother and is clad in a long velvet gown of pale blue.

She comes towards us, arms out. 'Penelope! Oh, I've missed you.'

'And I you,' my mother says, as they hug. 'It's been far too long. Come, you must meet Emelia – you haven't seen her since she was small!'

Jennie's eyes widen as she glances between me and my mother. 'Why, she's the very image of you!' Jennie's speech is charmingly accented, and she smells of violets and lilacs as she gathers me into an embrace, kissing my cheek. 'You are so welcome here, Emelia. We are cousins, after all.'

'Thank you,' I say, conscious of all the eyes on me. 'It's

lovely to see you again.' Vampires line the walls, shadowy shimmers of silk and velvet; beautiful, hard faces.

They only know what they are told.

And what they're shown. Nobody knows how close the Channel Islands visit came to disaster. And no one has to. What they're being shown, the part I'm playing, is the soon to be anointed heir to Raven, arriving at a family home after a successful tour, with the full backing of her powerful parents.

Jennie squeezes my arms, still smiling, then moves on to my father. 'Aleks! Still as tall and handsome as ever, I see.'

My mother takes my hand. 'I've been so looking forward to coming here,' she says, her dark eyes dancing. 'I can't wait for you to see the rest of it.'

Jennie escorts us through the palace, and I'm astounded. The Raven castle is luxurious, of course. But it's a luxury of dark carved wood and plush carpets; of gold and silks and stained-glass windows. This place, despite the fact we're in near-darkness, glimmers with light as though aflame. My father and Varin soon disappear, heading into the gardens with a tall, handsome vampire who I gather is Jennie's husband. My mother keeps her hand in mine as Jennie leads us through a series of rooms dripping with gilt and embroidered silks, each one more ridiculous than the last. Bertrand and several other guards follow us along with a growing crowd of whispering vampires, more vampires bowing as we go past. I keep my head high, my shoulders back, aware that every move I make, every gesture, will be scrutinised. *I* will be the next Raven, not Oliver or Jacques, or anyone else who thinks that just because I'm human, I'm weak. I'll show them that strength comes in different forms, and I'm more than capable of ruling. But as the parade continues through more glimmering rooms filled with mirrors and paintings that seem to watch me as I pass, it's harder to keep up the facade.

What if I fail here, and my father has to fight for my right to hold the crown? How will I bear the guilt of him being injured, or even dying? I wonder who, in the kaleidoscope of faces around me, thinks I'm not fit to rule. My mother was right to make me face the public before we came here, to find my feet as heir. But my feet are starting to ache. Only my desire to prove everyone wrong keeps me going. I was always taught to hide my emotions, to not make myself too appealing as prey. But my human emotions are what will sustain me here. I lean into my anger, allowing it to strengthen my resolve. Imagine I'm carrying my sword, my fangs lengthening. Feel that dark power inside me flicker. They don't want me to rule? Fine. Let them see why I deserve to.

Jennie comes to a stop in a room that shimmers as though we're inside a jewel box. She claps her hands, and the clustered vampires pause.

'The tour is complete. We will have privacy now, if you please.' There's a moment where everyone stills. Then they flash from the room in a rustle like wings, until only Jennie, Bertrand, my mother and I remain. I hold back my sigh of relief.

Jennie tilts her head like a bird. 'I thought you might like to stay here, Emelia.'

A bed against one wall is made up with white linens and a heavily embroidered silk coverlet, pink roses and green leaves everywhere. Matching drapes fall from an overhanging canopy, which has overlapping layers of fabric like the petals of a flower. Gold, woven into the draperies, also gilds the carved canopy and outlines the silk panels on the walls. There's even a gilt railing between me and the bed, a row of silk-cushioned stools against it. Vampires like sparkly things, but this seems excessive even for them.

'This was once the bedroom of a human queen,' Jennie says with a smile. 'So, I think it shall be perfect for you.' There's a knowing gleam in her eye, and I understand. I know which queen she means; a divisive figure, who died in a revolution. And I'm here in response to a revolution against my own crown. Everything, as I say, is symbolic.

Jennie opens a gate in the gilt balustrade, letting me through to the bed. It's even prettier close up, each trembling flower petal woven in detail, the colours as fresh as though made yesterday.

'We installed bathing facilities through here,' Jennie continues, opening a door concealed in the silk-panelled walls, 'and your clothes have already been hung up.'

I glance at my mother. She nods, a faint smile on her red lips, but worry shadows her eyes. Bertrand is frowning, his keen blue gaze taking in our surroundings. These rooms are all connected, one door leading to another. There's nothing to stop anyone coming in here if they wanted. Again, though, this is symbolic. A ruler should be accessible. And I have guards.

'Thank you.' I return Jennie's smile. 'It's lovely.'

'Good, good,' she says. 'There's food, if you're hungry.' She gestures to a small table, where a pile of glistening pastries sits next to a bowl of apples and oranges, and a large glass bottle of water. 'Please, rest now. And let me know if there's anything else you need.'

'I might stay with Emelia,' my mother says. 'Get her settled in.'

Jennie regards us both, then nods again. '*Bon*. Penelope, we'll be in the main salon when you're ready.' She leaves, swiftly, the door closing behind her with a click.

I sit on the ridiculous bed, testing the mattress. I feel as though I'm sitting on a cake. 'I guess sleeping on the coach is out of the question?'

My mother shakes her head, frowning. She wanders around the room, her skirts whispering on the timber floors. Night pales beyond the long windows. Dawn isn't far off.

'What happens now?'

My mother turns, her finger to her lips, her gaze darting to the closed doors, which are a far cry from the reinforced steel door of my room at home. 'A rest, I think,' she says, keeping her tone light. 'So that you're ready for the ball later. I might stay here a while and read.' She holds my gaze. Bertrand takes a position next to one of the sets of doors, facing the others with his arms folded. It will have to do.

I wake with a start to the sound of soft clapping, the rustle of silk. What in darkness? The windows are shuttered, and I can't see much. There's movement and, a moment later, the faint bloom of a candle lamp, awakening glimmers of light in the gold and silk. My mother is sitting next to the bed, a book in one slender hand. But why is she clapping?

'Mother, what—'

She widens her eyes then inclines her head, slightly, towards the foot of my bed.

I follow the direction of her gaze. And nearly fall out of bed. Vampires, probably a dozen or so, are clustered beyond the golden balustrade. All of them watching me. I clutch my covers, my mouth opening and closing. But seriously. What the fuck is going on?

'Oh, Lady Raven, she is divine. Sleeping like a human yet looking so much like a vampire.' This is a tall slender vampire clad in a tunic over fitted trousers, his face a pale gleam in the faint light. 'Fascinating.'

'What will she do next?' A plump female vampire, her generous bosom spilling from the confines of her taffeta gown, comes forward. 'Will we be able to watch her toilette?'

'Speak again, dear Raven.' This is a young male vampire. His blond hair is tied back, and he reaches a muscular arm towards me. 'I would like to hear your voice once more. I wager it's as beautiful as the rest of you.'

'Enough!' My mother gets to her feet. The crowd draws back. My mother's tone is cool, pleasant, but her hand is clenched around the book. 'I've indulged your curiosity these past hours, but my daughter is not here for your amusement. She is the heir to Raven, your next ruler. And should be treated as such.'

Several vampires bow their heads.

'I appreciate,' my mother continues, her tone softening, 'that it's long been the custom for these chambers to be open for all to enter. That the human court who once dwelled here would watch their rulers sleep, and that's why I've allowed this. But I ask now for privacy, that we might prepare for the ball alone.'

With a rustle and hiss, the vampires leave, bowing before they flash through the doors. My mother puts her book down.

I'm stunned. And more than a little annoyed. 'What the hell was that?' I murmur.

'Hmm.' My mother darts her gaze towards the still open doors. Right. Got it. 'Shall we get you ready, my darling?' Her voice returns to normal. 'I'll sort myself out while you shower. Bertrand will be here while I'm gone.' She leans in closer, her lips brushing my cheek. 'All part of the show,' she whispers. 'I'll be back soon.'

A short while later she returns, immaculate in her usual red, her gown with a layered skirt like flower petals, the fitted bodice baring her smooth creamy shoulders. She does my hair as I sit at the dressing table, her alabaster fingers braiding then coiling it into an intricate bun at the nape of my neck.

'Why were those vampires watching me sleep?' I keep my voice low. 'And why didn't you warn me?'

'That,' my mother whispers, 'was us reminding them who Raven is. Jennie suggested it, while you were sleeping; apparently it was considered quite an honour by the human courts who once ruled here.'

'It was so *weird*.'

'I hated it. Hated sitting there, watching them look at you like they couldn't decide whether to eat you or worship you. Wanted to kill them all – and would have been within my rights to do so. But I endured it. Because they will take the tale back to their friends of how they watched the Raven sleep, and what she means.'

'I'm going to get those families on our side,' I whisper. 'If I don't, and it comes to war, I want to fight. I'll do whatever it takes.'

'Good.' She reaches for a diamond flower, tucking it into my hair so it sits flat against the side of my head, close to the braided bun. I watch her reflection, the ridiculous jewelled chamber gleaming behind her.

It's such a fucking joke. Humans built this palace, lived and loved and laughed here, even if some of them did go on to violent ends. Created the artworks I've seen, laid out the ancient cities, the stone monuments. Oh, I know vampires had a hand in some of them, legends of buildings appearing overnight simply distorted truth. But this world is overwhelmingly human.

My mother smiles, her red lips almost purple in the soft light. Her eyes have a faint blood tinge as she surveys me in the mirror.

'What?'

'You look so fierce. Like a queen. What are you thinking about?'

'I was thinking that this is all bullshit.'

Mother laughs, a surprised sound. She wipes her eyes. 'Well, of course you are. What else could it be?' She giggles again, a silvery chime.

'Don't laugh at me.'

'I'm not.' She becomes serious. 'I know how you feel about this.'

'Do you? Because it seems very easy for everyone to forget that this was once a human palace. Just like everywhere else we've been.'

'What do you want me to do?' My mother's frown deepens. 'Throw Jennie and her family out on the street?'

'I want it to be acknowledged! That humans hold more value than just their blood!'

'Keep your voice down!' My mother glances towards the doors. 'We will have this conversation, Emelia, but we cannot have it here.'

I want to scream.

'Let's get you into your dress.'

A few minutes later I'm standing in the middle of the room, my feet sinking into the plush carpet. My mother laces up the silk ribbons at the back of my dress, the bodice fitted and strapless. I'm still angry. But I'll use it to get through this, no matter how it might stick in my throat to dance in a ballroom while people are dying. I have to go through with it because if I don't, Mistral will take my throne, and it will all be for nothing.

My mother fluffs out my skirt, diaphanous layers of grey tulle strewn with grey sequins that glimmer like stars, winking in and out.

'Perfect,' she says. 'This is so pretty on you. It just needs one more thing.' She pulls a black velvet ribbon from her pocket, which she fastens around my neck.

I turn to the full-length mirror, her hands on my shoulders. The Raven crest glitters at my throat, diamonds against black velvet.

'That's your choker!' It doesn't seem right to see it on me.

'It's Raven's choker. It belonged to my mother, and to all female Ravens before that. And now it's yours. Just like everything else your family name holds.' Her expression sharpens. 'For vampires, things take time; we get stuck in our ways. You cannot expect change to happen overnight. I have spoken for you, and I always will. And I promise you, we will talk further about this. Come, put your shoes on,' she continues, as I protest. 'We have an entrance to make.'

I can't deny I'm nervous as we head towards the ballroom. This is where the next phase of our plan comes into play. I'll be taken around the room to greet the families. Then it will be up to me to forge alliances, turn the heads of those who stand against me. On the surface, it seems frivolous, a party with small talk. But ballrooms and political manoeuvring have gone hand in hand for centuries. Whatever happens tonight will set the stage for the rest of our time here. If I'm shunned, if I piss off the wrong person, or show any weakness, then Mistral will likely get the six families they require for the Challenge to go ahead. I don't expect to earn the power I need tonight. But what I cannot do is let the power given to me slip through my fingers. This is a game where I have to outplay everyone. Enduring this is nothing compared to what humans endure daily.

We enter the ballroom, and my breath catches. Painted goddesses and warriors cavort on the curved and gilded ceiling, so realistic they seem to move in the faint flickering light. Mirrors, tall and arched, run along one wall, long windows opposite open onto the gardens. There are only two candle lamps, but their light is reflected over and over from crystal chandeliers running the length of the room. It's utterly magnificent. And full of vampires.

As I enter, everyone turns. I keep my chin high as the crowd peels back, people bowing as my mother and I pass. Just like the courts of old, whoever I stop to speak with confers privilege, even if it does stick in my throat to acknowledge someone who wishes to see my father in a fight to the death.

I pause at a woman. She's tall and curvaceous, swathed in jade-green silk, her long blonde hair braided. Something about her is familiar, but I can't place it. However, I know from the slight pressure of my mother's hand that I need to acknowledge her.

'So nice to see you here,' I say with a smile. 'Your dress is lovely. I hope we get the chance to speak again, later.'

The woman's eyes widen and she curtseys. 'Of course. The Vindhof family are always at your service.'

Vindhof. Okay. Well, that's a load of crap because they're one of the families currently backing Mistral. I also realise, with a pang, who she reminds me of. *My mother was a Vindhof.* Michael and I, snarling at each other in a bathroom, what seems a lifetime ago. I push the memory away. 'I'm so glad to hear it.'

We move on, to a tall man wearing black, edged with silver. I'm not sure whether it's to honour my house or declare his aspiration to the title. He takes my hand, sniffing it before pressing his lips to the ring on my finger, bowing deeply.

'Are you having a pleasant evening so far?' I say.

He nods, once. 'I am, now that I've seen you. Perhaps later I might introduce you to my son, Stefan?'

'I would like that,' I murmur, retrieving my hand as we move further down the room.

'Ravenko,' my mother says under her breath.

Traitor number two. How nice that they're all here together, apart from Darkwing. Apparently, they couldn't be bothered to make the ocean crossing. I spot a familiar face ahead and try not to sigh. Artos Ravenna.

'Emelia.' He bends low over my hand. 'You look different from the last time I saw you.'

'Do I? Perhaps it's because I'm older.' I keep my voice cool. Nope. Not here for your bullshit today. *Filthy humans.* I remember his scorn, when he thought I couldn't hear what he was saying.

'Stella was asking after you,' he says, his smile ingratiating. 'I know she misses you.'

I'm surprised my cousin isn't here, to be honest. She loves a party, and this is a big one. I'm not sorry she's absent, though. 'That's strange,' I reply. 'I don't miss her at all.'

The crowd murmurs, my mother smiling as she pulls me away from a scowling Artos. We stop to greet more people, all of whom seem pleased to speak to me. It's a beginning.

Jennie, resplendent in sapphire-blue silk, emerges from the crowd, dropping into a deep curtsey. My instinct is to raise her to her feet, to tell her she doesn't need to do that. But I know I can't. Even though this magnificent palace is her home, she's still a subject of Raven.

All part of a show.

It's like the symbols, red moons and dark ravens, evergreen pines. Everything I do here has meaning. It feels like I'm walking a knife edge, that any slip will mean sudden death, my grasp on power a tenuous, fragile thing. No wonder people want to challenge the throne. My father's hand comes to the back of my waist, light as a feather.

'Jennie.' I offer my hand. She rises, graceful as a dancer. 'Thank you. The evening is lovely, as is your home.'

A sigh ripples through the crowd. Music starts, vampires swaying to the sinuous beat. Doors open on one side of the ballroom and a group of blood dancers, wearing little more than gold paint and glitter, enter the room, mingling with the crowd.

'A good start,' my father murmurs as he guides me towards a grouping of velvet chairs, my mother at my other side.

'I agree,' she says, whisper-quiet. 'Vindhof seemed especially amenable.'

'I'm going to see if Ravenko can—'

There are gasps, exclamations from the other end of the room. I stop talking. Everything, even the musicians, seems to pause. My father moves in front of me. Then steps to the side, glancing at my mother. 'Well, this is unexpected.'

What? What's unexpected? I try to remain cool, to not crane my head. The commotion is growing.

Then I see him.

Chapter Twenty

PRINCE OF DARKNESS

A tall vampire approaches, his movements sinuous, like a panther stalking through the crowd. He's dressed in black, a suit fitted tightly to his lean, muscular form, a V of bare chest visible under the well-cut jacket. His hair is dark, cropped short.

Holy shit.

He's beautiful. Dark eyes under straight brows, a long straight nose and full lips, strong cheekbones and jaw.

Several vampires follow him, in an arrow formation. They're also wearing dark suits, the women with trailing gossamer skirts under their sharp jackets. All as beautiful as he is.

Jennie hurries over to greet him but he dismisses her with a wave of his hand. He comes to a stop in front of me. One of his followers, a woman with shoulder-length blonde hair and piercing green eyes, winks at me. He holds out his hand, a smile curving his handsome mouth. No bowing. No deference. I have no idea what to do, so I take it.

'Emelia Raven.' His voice is deep and softly accented. 'Allow me to introduce myself.' He inclines his head, light catching a single jade earring hanging from one earlobe. 'I am Joaquin, prince of Jaguar. I come to offer you congratulations on your upcoming reign.' He glances around the room. 'And support.'

Holy shit.

Aside from the political implications, Joaquin is breathtaking. My lips part. Music plays, somewhere in the background, but all I see is him. Power meeting power. The Raven and the Jaguar.

He smiles, revealing fangs that are slightly dropped. 'Shall we dance? They're waiting for us.'

The crowd draws back, leaving an empty space. He pulls me close, his scent, violet mixed with sweet musk, curling around me, his hand coming to my waist. My breath catches. He swings me into the centre of the room, so my skirt flies out like gossamer clouds, light catching the sequins. I tilt my head, one arm held long and free, the other around his neck. I catch a glimpse of our reflection, like twirling figures in a music box, him tall and strong in his black suit, me languid and graceful in cloud-grey, the room glittering as though filled with fireflies.

He glides his fingers along my arm, clasping my hand. The movement is sensuous, his touch awakening fire as he fits me even closer against him. I look up, and the heat in his dark gaze is almost scorching. God and darkness.

We twirl in front of the clapping crowd, the music changing as more couples join us. There's a flash of red as my parents glide past, my mother reaching out to pat my arm. Joaquin brings my free arm around his neck, then both his hands are at my waist as he lifts me, turning so that I laugh out loud. The crowd whoops their encouragement as he does it again and again, until I feel as though I'm at the centre of a jewelled kaleidoscope. I give myself up to it, to the pure joy of the moment.

Eventually, we slow, Joaquin taking me to the edge of the dancefloor, close to the long glass doors open to the gardens.

'Why'd you stop?' I pout at him.

'I thought perhaps you might like a drink? Or to dance with someone else? We've been dancing for a while.' He smiles, the corners of his eyes crinkling attractively.

'We have?' I glance outside, surprised to see how low the moon is. I'm out of breath and, now that we've stopped moving, my feet ache.

I blink, my hand coming to my brow. 'Maybe I *should* have a drink. Or some fresh air.'

'Your choice.' Joaquin gestures and a blood dancer, clad in a few wisps of black satin, glitter sparkling on his muscular body, brings over a tray with several drinks.

'Thank you.' I take a glass filled with sparkling water, draining almost half of it.

'And now, fresh air.' Joaquin plucks the glass from my hand, putting it back on the tray while shepherding me towards the long windows, his hand at my waist. The cool night air feels like heaven on my heated skin, the darkness and relative stillness a relief after the crowded ballroom. But I don't get the chance to enjoy it before I'm snatched up in a powerful grip, held tight against a muscular chest. Air rushes past me and I hastily cling to Joaquin's neck.

'What the hell?'

'I'm sorry. Is this not okay?'

He skids to a stop on the gravel path, next to a long

reflecting pool surrounded by topiary trees, shimmering like a silver mirror. The palace is a distant, gilded wedding cake, music drifting faintly across the gardens.

'I would have appreciated a warning!'

Joaquin puts me down, slowly, so I have to slide against his hard body. I don't mind that. But I'm trying to figure out my next steps. It feels as though the evening has taken a sharp turn, and now I'm somewhere I never expected to be. Jaguar's presence at Versailles is unexpected, but it's very fucking positive. I don't want to screw things up.

'Shall we walk instead, then?' He holds out his arm, like a lord in an old tale of romance. I slip my hand into the crook of his elbow, and we stroll along the gravel path. It's beautiful, the moon a semi-circle of light among feathery dark clouds, stars sparkling like flecks of frost.

I consider what to say next, how to make the most of this. Yet, wandering through darkened palace gardens with a handsome prince, part of me just wants to enjoy myself. Forget about politics, and the Challenge. I can see how seductive, how easy it might be to just go along with things. To take power and enjoy all the privilege and luxury it will bring for my comparatively short life. Why bother to try and change things? It's not going to be easy. The Channel Islands project is proof of that. Laurel's death is proof of that. Humans are food. They always will be. So why am I fighting so hard for them?

Because I'm human.

But also because I'm not. I hate that it goes back to Kyle again, to all that he showed me. He might have betrayed me, but it's clear he also wanted me to see the world as it was. The question is, why?

You have no idea what a difference you could make.

I still remember how it felt, when he said those words. A first glimmer of the idea that I was actually worth something. That I could actually *be* something. He took me to the Safe Zone because I asked him to, but also because it played into his plans to get me off the estate. However, I wonder whether he hoped I might escape Mistral, somehow. He gave me a night; wanted me to experience human existence. There has to be a reason for that.

I've only seen a fraction of the world as it is for humans, yet it's enough for me to want to change everything. Yes, it won't be easy, and I'll most likely have to do it alone.

But nothing worthwhile ever is.

I need to always, *always,* remember who I am. *What* I am. What I saw in the Safe Zones and at the Moon Harvest. Why I want to change things.

'What is it that makes you look so fierce?'

I start. Joaquin is watching me, his face shadowed, his eyes a dark gleam.

'Oh, nothing.' I don't even know where to begin.

'I'm sure it's something,' Joaquin says. 'You are fascinating.'

'You don't know me.'

'Not yet. But I know that you're a human among vampires, yet one who has everything. Who cannot be eaten.' His voice slides along the last word, and I blush, glad of the darkness. I feel like he's not talking about my blood. 'We're more similar than you know.'

'We are?'

'Yes.' The word is a sensual hiss. 'Both of us … heirs. It's a lonely place to be, at times.'

It is. And I'm tired of feeling lonely.

He turns me to face him, then traces a long finger down my cheek, a slow caress. 'I had a sister like you, you know.'

'Like me?' It's hard to breathe.

'Human.' His finger circles my ear, and I shiver. 'You do not want to know what my people do to children like her.'

'My father wanted to kill me, when I was born. He's glad now that he didn't.'

'As am I,' Joaquin murmurs. His finger slides under my chin, lifting my face to his.

Then he kisses me.

Chapter Twenty-One

JUST A KISS

The kiss is gentle, at first. Then it deepens, our tongues tangling as he pulls me closer, his mouth slanting across mine. I tilt my head as his lips trace my jaw, kiss along my collarbone.

It's pretty fucking nice.

But it's not warm. Joaquin is as cool as the stone statues nearby and, even though his touch awakens fire in me, it lacks the heat, the rasp of callus I had with Michael.

This is not the moment to think of Michael.

Joaquin's hands trace my corseted sides, then one slides inside my dress, his thumb rubbing across my nipple as he deepens the kiss further. I gasp, arching into his touch. My tongue slides across his teeth, then catches on one of his fangs, which are fully dropped. I taste blood. It's like a cold shock.

'I'm sorry.' Joaquin pulls back, his hand coming out of my top. 'I can stop, if you like.' He licks his lips, his tongue flicking across his fangs. Tasting my blood.

I blush, hotter than flames. Bloodplay during sex is part of things for vampires, and I can't deny that I'm turned on. But this is madness. I literally just met him, and now I'm alone in a garden, kissing him? I shouldn't be doing this. I turn away, adjusting my dress, not wanting to tempt him any further.

Yet there's a part of me that's tired of doing what I should. The part that led me to run away with Kyle, to witness the Moon Harvest, to find the strength to kill him. Varin told me to listen to the song I carry, the intention in my heart. And I can't deny I'm attracted to Joaquin; I'd have to be blind not to see how sexy he is.

'Is there something wrong?' Joaquin waits, panther-still in the dark.

'No. Nothing's wrong. I just … there's a lot on my mind.'

'Like what?' His lips graze my cheekbone, cold fire.

Like why you're all over me, when we've just met. I take a step back.

'Why are you here?'

'In these gardens, with you?' He smiles. 'Or here, at your ball?'

'Both.'

'I'm in these gardens with you because I want to be. I'm at the ball because you invited me, remember?'

All of this sounds perfectly reasonable. He takes my arm again, steering me along another path, all coiled strength, his presence protection enough for anything that might be out here. Yet something in me is still wary. I've trusted too quickly before, and it led to betrayal.

'What I'm interested in, though,' he continues, 'is why you invited me.'

I pause. 'I invited you because I wanted you to come.'

He huffs out a breath of laughter. 'Is that so?'

I blush as I realise the double entendre. 'I mean, I—'

'The four great families have a tangled past,' he says. 'Yes, we worked together to control humans, when they became out of control. But otherwise … we tend to keep to our own realms. So, it was a surprise, to receive your summons.'

'We're friendly with Lion.'

'Friendly? Even after their prince was killed at your family home?' He raises an eyebrow. 'What is it you really want, Emelia?'

I swallow. Daniel's death was a terrible accident, a casualty of the North Wind bombing aimed at my father. News travels, I suppose, when it's of that magnitude. 'I'm to be crowned soon,' I say, 'and it seemed important to include the other families.'

'Because you want our support?'

'I wanted to know you. And for you to know me. Who I am, and what I stand for.'

'And what is that?' He sounds intrigued, his voice a deep purr.

'I want to change the world for humans, to give them a better life.'

'Is this so?'

I swallow, gazing up at him. A breeze feathers across my bare shoulders, like a kiss. 'It is. I'm starting small. The Channel Islands. A truly free place for humans to live as they wish, to bring up their children without fear.'

'Free humans? Well, that is a marvel,' he says. 'How is it going?'

'It's fine.' I don't trust him enough yet to tell him the truth. I shiver, suddenly aware we're a long way from the palace. The trees rustle as though full of ghosts, ladies with powdered hair and wide silk skirts, a reminder that this has been a place of pleasure for many centuries. 'Perhaps we should head back,' I say. 'There are other people I would like to spend time with tonight.'

Joaquin slides his fingers down my arm, his touch raising goosebumps. He brings my hand to his lips, his dark gaze liquid. 'Are you sure?' His voice hums with sensual promise. And there's a moment where I want it, want him to lay me down on the nearby bench and have his way with me, want to peel off that dark jacket and get my hands on the muscular chest beneath it. That dark well of power in me seems to surge and flex, responding to him.

'I am,' I say, before I can change my mind and do something I'm fairly certain I'll regret.

His dark brows draw together, a subtle movement. 'Of course.' He scoops me into his arms, his hand resting at the side of my breast, as though at any moment those long fingers could slide back into my corset. I cling to him as he speeds me towards the glittering palace. He deposits me outside the long glass doors a few moments later, sneaking another kiss as I slide down his body. Hmmm. I could do far worse than this handsome prince.

So, I kiss him back, then smooth my hands down my dress. 'Am I tidy?'

He grins, tucking a stray strand of hair behind my ear, adjusting the diamond flower. 'You are perfect. Come, let's go inside. I would dance with you again.'

But when we enter the ballroom, Jennie is waiting with a handsome blond vampire. I recognise him as the one who was in my bedroom earlier. His expression, as it lights upon Joaquin's hand at my waist, is tight.

'Dearest Emelia,' Jennie cries. 'Come, meet Deryck Vindhof. He's been waiting half the night to dance with you.' There's a faint reprimand in the words and I raise an eyebrow. I can dance with whomever I choose. But I also know that Deryck, as a Vindhof, is standing with Mistral against us. I turn to Joaquin.

'Thank you for the walk,' I say. 'And our conversation. I'd like to talk again, later.'

Joaquin's dark gaze moves from me to Deryck. 'Of course, dear one. I'll wait for you.' He kisses my hand, lingering slightly too long, staking his claim. Deryck's frown deepens.

I go to him, my arms out, my skirts whispering around my legs. 'It's a pleasure to meet you, Deryck.' I give him my best smile, trying to channel my mother's gracious beauty.

He bows, spreading one arm wide. 'The pleasure is mine, my lady.' He straightens up, offering his hand. 'It's worth the wait, to dance with you.'

'I'm looking forward to dancing with you, too,' I say as I take his hand, wanting to be polite.

'Is that so?' He smiles down at me, seeming mollified.

Not really. Fatigue rolls over me. If I'm honest, I want to go to bed. Alone. Playing politics and kissing princes in gardens and keeping up with tireless vampires is fucking exhausting. But if I'm to meet the Challenge, I need to show no weakness. The show must go on.

So, I dig deep, finding that silver and ebony core once more as Deryck swings me into the dance. 'Of course,' I say.

'What did you think of the gardens? I'd wager you were more lovely than any flower in them.'

I try not to laugh. 'They were very nice. Are you staying long in France?'

'I'm here for a few more nights.' He pulls me closer as we twirl around the room, his fingers splayed across my back. 'Staying in the palace, just as you are. A few rooms down from yours. I hope we can see more of each other.'

I giggle, unable to help it, at his complete lack of subtlety. There's no way in darkness I'll be going anywhere near his room. He swings me around again, pressing me so close my breasts threaten to spill from my corset. Perhaps this dress wasn't the best choice for tonight. Or perhaps it was perfect. I decide to counter his innuendo with a jab of my own.

'Surely your family wouldn't want you anywhere near me. After all, they're challenging my right to rule.' I smile, sweetly.

Deryck's eyes widen, and he momentarily falters in the dance. Then he laughs. 'I'm dancing with you, aren't I?'

'I'm surprised we haven't been dragged from the dancefloor. So, tell me,' I ask, as he twirls me once more. 'What would it take to change your mind?' I know I'm being direct, but something about Deryck, despite his posturing and flowery language, makes me think he'll appreciate it.

He grins. 'Actually, this dance is going some way towards doing so.'

'Oh, really? And how about my voice? Is it really as beautiful as the rest of me?' I can't hide my amusement at this point.

He laughs again, and this time, when he speaks, he doesn't sound as though he's trying to recite sonnets. 'You're smarter than that, surely.'

'I am. So are you. Which is why the over-the-top flirting doesn't make sense.'

'Don't think you're special. I flirt with everyone.'

'You do? Why?' I'm genuinely intrigued.

'Well, it softens people up. But it also means they don't take me as seriously. They think I just spout flowery phrases, that I'm harmless. Which gets me into rooms I might not otherwise be able to enter.'

'You're the scion of Vindhof. I doubt there would be many doors closed to you.'

'Oh, you'd be surprised. I imagine every door is open to you, though.'

I laugh. 'I suppose. Though I have the opposite problem to you. Hardly anyone takes me seriously.'

'I take you seriously.'

'Why? Because of my last name?'

'Because you're pretty.'

'Stop it.'

'All right. Because you're here. You showed up, a human in a room full of vampires – quite a few of whom think you're not fit to rule – and waited until we bowed to you. I think that takes guts.'

Heat rises in my cheeks as we twirl.

'Do I make you blush?' He dips his head close to mine, his blond hair brushing my cheek.

'I told you to stop flirting.' I catch a glimpse of Joaquin standing at the edge of the dancefloor with his arms folded. He's watching me, his dark gaze piercing.

'But I enjoy it so. Especially when it makes pretty girls go pink.'

'So, will you do it?'

'Do what? Stop flirting? Never.'

'Repledge to me. And my crown.'

'After one dance? You've got a pretty high opinion of your skills. It'll take more than that.'

'You've watched me sleep, as well.' I'm enjoying this, I realise. It reminds me of how things were with Michael, how easy it was between us. 'Surely that counts for something.'

Deryck looks up, his lips pursed as though he's thinking. Then he grins. 'Please. A few hours watching you snore isn't going to change my mind.'

'What will, then? And do not say kissing.'

'It's not going to change my mind because I was never against you. My parents went along with Ilias Ravenko and Artos Ravenna because they convinced them to do so. But your mother has already been in my mother's ear about it. You don't need to worry about Vindhof. But if you did want to throw in a few kisses, just to make it look good, I wouldn't say no.'

'Oh! You are outrageous.' I laugh, my head going back as he sweeps me around the room.

'I am. And that Jaguar of yours looks like he wants to tear my head off. Want to make him even more jealous?'

'He's not my Jaguar. And no, I do not.'

Luckily, the music ends before Deryck can do anything else. We slow to a stop and he releases me, stepping back to bow. 'Just one dance, my lady? Perhaps we could wander the gardens, as well.' He winks as he straightens up.

I narrow my eyes at him. 'We can dance again in a minute,' I say. 'And I've no desire to see any more of the gardens.'

'Not even with me?' He flashes a shit-eating grin. I laugh out loud.

'Even with you.'

'Until our next dance.' Deryck bows again.

I do like him. Perhaps he could be a good lieutenant, though I'll need to know more about him, and whether or not his family are definitely out of the Challenge. I spot my mother beckoning to me, my father bringing Joaquin into his conversation with Artos Ravenna. Good. The blood dancer with the tray of drinks is nearby, and I grab one before heading over to my mother.

'Are you having fun, my darling?' She pulls me close. 'Good work with Jaguar,' she breathes, touching the diamond flower in my hair in a pretence of adjusting it. 'Seeing you together has made Vindhof repledge to Raven. They'll no longer support Mistral in that ridiculous challenge.'

'I am having fun,' I say, conscious of watching eyes, preternatural hearing. 'And that's good,' I add under my breath.

'I think your dance partner is waiting.' My mother winks at me, actually winks. It's such a human gesture I stare at her for a moment. She takes the glass from my hand and gives me a gentle push. I turn to see Deryck waiting, one arm outstretched.

I take his hand, and step into the dance once more.

Chapter Twenty-Two

WHY CHOOSE?

We've been at Versailles for three days and, despite my initial qualms, our plan seems to be working. Vindhof are back onside, and my parents are working on Artos Ravenna. Maybe I should have been kinder about Stella, but there's nothing I can do about that now. Stella could have been kinder about me, too. I've seen Ilias Ravenko a few times, and he's always been polite; apparently, he and Father used to fight together, so Father is leaning on that relationship in the hopes of changing his mind.

I miss Sophie, though. She's staying on the coach – it felt safer than bringing her into a palace filled with vampires. We've been messaging and calling whenever we can; she screamed with delight when I told her about Joaquin. I can't wait to be back on board, travelling with her, laughing in the cockpit. But there's still work to do, so I'm making sure I'm seen, every moment I can be.

I woke the day after the ball to a still shuttered room. No crowds of gawking vampires at the foot of my bed this time, though. Instead, just my mother, sitting on her gilt chair, a curious expression on her face. And Joaquin, lounging in long-limbed splendour on a silk-covered divan, watching me. I blushed, clutching my covers, feeling stripped bare.

'He sent them all away,' my mother whispered later, as she brushed my hair to smoothness. 'Told them they'd seen enough, that you needed to be left in peace.' She smiled at me in the mirror. 'I think he may like you.'

I think I might like him, as well.

However, more importantly, I can see how useful he would be. It sounds cold-blooded, but I've been burned twice, first by Kyle, then Michael. Both of them choosing someone else over me. I remember standing in the Costume room, next to my mother's wedding gown, thinking about love, and whether or not Michael was right for me. And how alone I've felt, since he left. I don't want to be at the mercy of love again. It's time for me to choose. And I mean to do so for power, this time.

I'm also conscious of time passing. The next Gathering, where I'll be declared the official heir, is in a couple of weeks. I'll be anointed on the first night; the second night, fealty, when all the families pledge their allegiance to Raven. On the third night, I choose a lieutenant from those assembled. Deryck is a possibility, but he reminds me so much of Michael I'm not sure it's a wise choice. But I don't really know anyone else, despite making the effort to talk to people these past few days.

I wonder whether Mistral will show up at the Gathering, especially as support for their Challenge seems to be collapsing. Not coming to the heir's anointing is tantamount almost to a declaration of war, so it would be a bold move. But showing up to a Raven event, when you've made a big public challenge like that, is also a bold move. I try not to think of Michael, of what he might be enduring with his brothers.

I'm trying not to think of Michael at all, especially when Joaquin's around. It's not difficult to return his obvious affection; his beauty and the magnetic power of his personality are alluring, but I'm still cautious. I don't want to be hurt again.

Yet, as he and I and Deryck lie on more of the ubiquitous silk cushions in yet another glittering salon, both of them feeding me food from silver dishes, I wonder what it would be like. I've been with a vampire before, of course. And I remember how it was when things were good between Kyle and me. How he used to touch me.

'A penny for your thoughts, my lovely.' Joaquin leans forward, a grape held between his long fingers. He pops it into my mouth, his touch lingering on my lips. I chew and swallow, wishing my heart wasn't beating so wildly.

'Oh, they're not worth even that,' I say, heat in my cheeks.

'I would wager they're worth more than rubies.' Deryck hands me a cracker, soft cheese piled on top.

I take it from him. 'Really, they're not. And thank you.'

'I enjoy watching you feed.' He licks his lips, amusement flickering in his darkening gaze.

Oh God. Now I'm totally self-conscious. I glare at him and put the cracker down, reaching for my drink instead.

'Tell me, Deryck,' Joaquin says, 'is your family home near here? You have, what, a little castle, right?'

'It's actually quite a large castle. One of the largest in Europe.'

I get the feeling they're not actually talking about castles.

'Is that so?' Joaquin grins. 'Do you hear that, Emelia? One

of the largest in Europe. Of course, where I come from, our palaces are as large as cities. This place—' he waves his hand '—would just be one small part of it.'

'Tell me, when will you be returning to them?' Deryck's brows lower. 'I hope it's soon.'

'I'll go back when I'm ready.' Joaquin trails his fingers along my shoulder. The blonde vampire reclining opposite us winks at me. It's the same one who winked at me the night of the ball. Joaquin introduced her as Selene, his cousin and one of his closest friends. Her gaze rakes lazily across me, the jade crescent moon hanging from one of her ears catching the faint lamplight. Each member of Joaquin's entourage wears a different earring. Joaquin's is a jaguar, of course.

Selene reaches for the wrist of a blood dancer, his muscled half-naked form reclining with us. I smiled at him as we sat down, but he just bowed his head then looked away. She bites down, suckling his flesh, turning to him like a lover. The movement causes her jacket to gape, revealing one pale breast. I look away.

'Are you shy, lovely one?' Joaquin strokes my cheek with the back of his hand, one corner of his mouth curving. 'Selene does not mind if you watch.'

I turn my head … to see Selene, still sucking on the dancer's wrist, her other hand down the front of his trousers, pumping him. Oh darkness. I can't control my reaction, my lip curling, my brows drawing together.

'What is it?' Joaquin's voice is close to my ear, as he plays with a lock of my hair. 'Do you not like this?'

'No. It's a violation.'

'I agree.' Deryck's lip is curled. 'This is not how we treat our dancers.'

'You don't have sex with them?' Joaquin's voice trails along the word, but I can't take my eyes from Selene's hand moving, grotesque. The young man jerks and shudders, moaning, a darker patch appearing on his trousers.

I get to my feet. This is not my scene at all. Joaquin's hand circles my ankle. 'Selene.' His voice is sharp. 'Take it elsewhere.'

'Or stop,' I say.

Selene releases the young man's wrist, licking blood from her perfect lips. 'But he's so pretty. I've only just started to play,' she pouts. Her gaze moves to me. 'I didn't take you for a prude, Raven, not with how you were kissing Joaquin in the gardens the other night.'

My cheeks flame. 'That's none of your business.'

She shrugs, the crescent moon at her ear dancing. 'Whatever. I know what I saw. Come on.' She pulls the young man to his feet. He looks dazed, staggering slightly.

Joaquin's hand is still around my ankle. I consider stamping my foot. Deryck looks more annoyed than ever. *Thanks a lot*, I think, glaring at Selene's departing form. I just want to go somewhere and be alone for a while.

But Joaquin's fingers glide up my calf, then he takes my hand, pulling me down to the cushions once more. He reaches across me, his body against mine, and retrieves another grape from the crystal bowl. Deryck is pretty much snarling at this point. Gods. I need to defuse this, despite how I'm responding to Joaquin. I scramble back on the cushions, sitting up.

Joaquin turns my head, gentle, as he pops the grape in my mouth. 'Deryck.' His voice is a caress, his hand lingering on my face. 'I'm sorry if I've already trespassed where you wanted to go. She is irresistible, you see. I just had to make her mine.' His gaze sharpens, pure predator, his hand coming to rest at my waist.

Rebellion sparks. I'm not his yet. And I like Deryck. If I want to kiss him, I will. I wrench my gaze from Joaquin's with what feels like an effort.

'Thank you for speaking up,' I say to Deryck. 'I didn't like that.'

Deryck nods, his frown clearing. 'I didn't like it either.'

'I'm sorry,' Joaquin says. 'Where I come from, sex is natural. Nobody minds where you do it, or with whom.' His hand tightens on my waist. I fight the urge to flinch.

'Really? You just … do it, wherever?'

He shrugs one muscled shoulder. 'Sure.' He smiles. 'Like, right now, if I was to kiss you, and young Deryck here wanted to join in, it would be fine.'

'What about what I want?' My mouth is dry. I resist the urge to lick my lips. My God.

'And what is that, Emelia?' His finger is under my jaw, tilting my head. 'Tell me.'

A scream shatters the moment. We all turn. There's a rustle of fabric, the light pad of several sets of feet as a small group of vampires enters the room, all young, a mix of males and females. Some of them are laughing. But there's blood on one of the girls' gowns, droplets on the pale satin skirt.

Joaquin puts his arm across me, the muscles tense. I don't know how to handle this. Bertrand is nearby, though not in the room. However, the second I call his name I know he'll be here.

'Deryck! There you are. We were looking for you.' A young woman sits down, her peach silk dress slipping from one freckled pale shoulder. She giggles. 'Stefan is teaching us to hunt.'

'To hunt?' Deryck glances at me. I keep my face expressionless.

'My father was complaining the other day, about how we're losing our skills.' The young woman in bloodstained satin flops down next to her friend, rolling her eyes. 'I guess he told Stefan's father, who told Stefan, because now he's dragging us through the palace, looking for prey.' She rubs at one of the droplets on her full skirts.

'Prey?' Joaquin's voice is almost a growl. 'Are you hunting blood dancers, then? This does not seem like sport.'

'Stefan says it's important to know how to hunt,' Peach Silk says. 'To remember who we are.'

Stefan. The name rings a bell. Then I remember his father, bending to kiss my ring. Ravenko. My only surprise is that it's not Ravenna.

'Why? It's not like we need to do it anymore.' Satin girl shrugs. 'Our parents are worried about nothing.'

'Please, no!' The cry, anguished, comes from beyond the open doors. A strapping young vampire appears, his fangs dropped, dressed in a velvet suit the colour of chocolate. He's dragging a struggling human behind him, a young woman in dark trousers and a white tank top, scratches on her pale skin, her red hair breaking free of the long braid.

I jump to my feet, Joaquin's restraining hand the only thing stopping me from running forward.

It's Sophie.

Chapter Twenty-Three

AS YOU WISH

'Look what I found, wandering around the grounds. It's like she was asking for it.' Stefan grins, pulling Sophie around in front of him. 'I think it's hot when humans want to be hunted.'

'Let her go!' I put the might of Raven into it, every shred of my borrowed power. How the fuck is this happening?

Everyone turns to look at me. Peach Silk's mouth is a perfect 'o', her blue eyes wide.

Stefan huffs out a laugh. 'The Raven heir. I should have known. Is this one of yours?'

'Let. Her. Go. *Now*.' Rage rises. Bertrand is a moment away. But this is a test. What kind of ruler will I be? One who calls on her guards every time there's a problem, who has to rely on others for protection? But I have no idea what the norm is in this situation. My only interactions with vampires my age have been carefully managed, or born from my own misadventure. None of them have been good.

'Or what?' Stefan sneers, his hand twisting in Sophie's hair. She cries out, tears running down her face.

My rage becomes cold fury. The only thing I can do is what feels right to me. I have nothing else to go on. I have to save Sophie. One wrong move, and she's dead.

'She is one of mine. Which is why I'm asking you to release her.' I make my way between the cushions, sending a silent apology to Sophie, whose gaze is fixed on me. I tamp down my feelings, the way I spent years doing before Kyle helped me change my world. It's one thing I can do well. No one needs to know how scared I am.

I smile at Stefan, as though he doesn't have my friend by the hair. As though I don't want to tear his head from his shoulders. 'And I am indeed the heir to Raven. Your father kissed my ring. I doubt he'd be happy to hear of this.'

'You're a human.'

'Am I? Gosh, thanks so much for pointing that out. I'd never have known, otherwise.' There's a giggle from Peach Silk. 'I am human. So fucking what?' I throw the question down, like a challenge.

'Humans are prey.'

'If that's all you think humans are, ask yourself who it was that built this palace.' I wave my hand. 'Who painted all this gorgeous artwork, designed all these glorious rooms. Because it sure as fuck wasn't vampires.' I smile, sweetly, but there's ice in my tone. 'You couldn't survive without humans. Yet I think humans would survive quite well without you.'

I feel those shadow wings again, as though I'm truly the Raven, a creature of blood and darkness. The room is silent. Stefan drops Sophie, advancing on me. In a flash Deryck is there, helping her out of the room. Thank darkness. I cannot let my relief show, though. This game isn't over. I can almost feel it in my hand, like a puzzle with different pieces. Whichever one I pick next will change how this goes, so I need to choose wisely. I cannot call for Bertrand, even though Stefan looms over me, too close for comfort. Joaquin is a dark presence at my side. The room crackles with power, everyone watching wide-eyed. I refuse to back down.

'Is there a problem?'

Stefan sniffs, deliberately. 'Just the stench of all that anti-feed you're wearing. In the old days, you wouldn't be permitted to exist.'

'Stefan!' Satin Skirt rises, grabbing his arm and trying to tug him away. 'I'm so sorry,' she says, glancing at me wide-eyed. 'I think one of the dancers earlier had something extra added. He's not himself.'

'In the old days, I'd have had your throat ripped out for talking to me like that,' I drawl. Joaquin's hand comes to the small of my back, as though he knows my legs are shaking.

'It could still be arranged,' he murmurs, his dark gaze sharp on Stefan.

Stefan snarls, lunging at me. Joaquin moves quickly; before I know where I am, I'm behind him. And he has Stefan by the throat.

Everyone else is frozen. Stefan pushes against Joaquin's grip, clawing at his fingers. Joaquin squeezes. Stefan chokes, his legs buckling. Holy shit. I place my hand on Joaquin's arm.

'Let him go. Jennie will never forgive us if we ruin her cushions.' I keep my tone light, but I'm freaking out.

Joaquin snorts. 'As you wish. We're in Raven territory, after all. Something he would do well to remember.' He shoots Stefan a fierce glare as he releases him with a shove, leaving all of us in no doubt how things would be if we were in Jaguar territory. Stefan staggers back, his hand to his throat. Black bruises bloom there, already healing.

'I'll tell my father!' he shouts, his voice raw.

'Oh, do,' I say, not hiding my scorn. 'And then I'll let him know how you brutalised one of my friends and disrespected me. This palace is not a hunting ground; I'm sure Jennie won't be happy to hear what you've been up to, either.'

'You wouldn't.'

'I'm not the one who needs to run to Daddy.'

There's another giggle, hastily muffled, from the girl in bloodstained satin. Stefan goes to lunge at me again, but Joaquin stops him, holding up his hand. He shakes his head, tutting.

'You do not touch her. She is your heir and should be respected as such.' There's a growl in his voice and something dark in me responds.

Oh, he could be just what I need.

Chapter Twenty-Four

HOMEWARD BOUND

Less than a night later we're on our way home.

Sophie is resting in my bed, one of the Raven guards driving. I leave her and head downstairs, the coach swaying as we turn out of the huge palace gates. My parents are on the sofa while Varin reclines on a chaise, reading, a faint candle lamp the only light.

'How is she?' My mother reaches out to me. I go and sit next to her.

'She's okay. Deryck healed her wounds, when he took her out of the room. Mentally, though…'

I'm still furious about the incident with Stefan. He finally left the room, perhaps encouraged by Selene returning with several more of Joaquin's people, none of whom seemed particularly impressed by what he'd done. None of his friends left with him.

I went straight to Sophie as soon as he was gone, Joaquin at my side. 'I'm so sorry,' I sobbed, over and over, finally giving into the emotion I'd been holding back.

Bertrand, meanwhile, went to find my parents. They returned a few minutes later in a flash of colour and cool air, Varin and Jennie close behind. Stefan's father, a tall vampire with the same dark hair and sneering expression as his son, arrived not long after.

'Why was she outside, Emelia?' My mother touches my hand. 'Has she told you any more of what she was doing?'

This is the part I don't quite understand. Versailles is bound by deep forest, only the roads leading to the palace cleared. Yet Stefan, when interrogated by his furious and embarrassed father, insisted he'd found her near the front gates.

'I just wanted to see, Emelia,' she sobbed, as we clung together in the aftermath. 'It was my fault.'

'It wasn't your fault! Nothing about this is your fault. You should be able to go where you want without being attacked!'

It was my decision to go home. I'd had enough. We could have stayed longer, but it seemed better to me that we leave. *Prolonging a battle is never necessary.* Another of my father's lessons. As far as I could see, we achieved almost everything we wanted.

Vindhof repledged to us, after the ball. And, following Stefan's actions, his father also vowed Ravenko's support, kissing my ring again. He also surprised me as we were leaving, bowing deeply before grabbing my shoulders and kissing me on both cheeks, in front of the hastily assembled crowd of nobles. 'Ravenko honour Raven, as it has always been,' he'd said, his voice loud enough to carry.

Joaquin also kissed me in front of everyone. On the hand, thank darkness. 'Until we meet again,' he said, all dark promise. 'Which will be soon.' I invited him, and his entourage, to the Gathering. Yes, as a power move, but also because I want to see him again. It doesn't feel like love; we barely know each other, after all. But it feels like … something.

I also spoke privately with both Deryck and Joaquin before we left, thanking them for their support. Joaquin and I may have done more than just talk, if I'm honest. Heat curls in the base of my stomach at the memory of his mouth, his hands on me. I might be choosing with my head, but it seems my body has something to say about it as well.

'She hasn't said much,' I reply. 'And I don't want to push her. I'm just glad Joaquin was there.'

'Yes.' My father looks thoughtful. 'The Jaguar prince seems taken with you. A good thing, I think, though we know so little about them. Him being here, and so obviously allied with you, has strengthened your position immensely.'

'I like him,' I say. 'I hope he comes to the Gathering.' I curl up on the sofa, yawning.

'Go and rest. You can use our bed.' My mother leans in, kissing my brow.

Rest sounds good, actually. I get up, heading into the other ground floor room. My parents' bedroom is draped in red velvet, the bed piled high with soft pillows, the huge ebony headboard inlaid with gleaming mother of pearl feathers. It smells of violets, but also of them: comforting. I flop down on the bed, pulling the blanket around me. Despite the success of our visit, I'm still shaken by what happened to Sophie. If Joaquin and I hadn't been in the room, she most likely would have been killed.

There's a knock at the door. 'Emelia?' My mother comes in and perches on the bed, her skirts settling around her.

'What is it? I thought you wanted me to rest.' I sit up against the pillows.

'I do.' She looks down, sighing. 'But … I need to talk to you about Joaquin, and Jaguar.' She seems serious.

'What about him?' I hug my knees, frowning.

'I think it important you know our history. *All* of it.'

'All of it?' I'd learned plenty during my lessons, or so I thought.

'You know Raven took North America from Jaguar.'

I nod, wondering where she's going with this.

'It wasn't that long ago, in the aftermath of the Red Rising. We were all grappling to secure our territories, and Jaguar … well, let's just say that Joaquin's father was trying to reinstate the old ways.'

'The old ways?'

'His blood temples. Bastardisation of human religion, and utterly, utterly cruel. Children, the elderly. No one was safe.'

'I thought the Red Rising was a bloodbath everywhere.' I feel a bit sick.

'Only because people fought back.'

'What the hell did you expect them to do? Lie down and take it?'

My mother's brow creases. 'I know that Varin spoke to you of the reasons for the Rising. We wanted balance, for the night to belong to us once more. But it became … more complicated, and so the current system was instated. Things settled down. Humans began breeding once more, their numbers rising. And it felt as though balance was returning.'

The Famine and the Blood Agreement. I knew about those. Humans refused to cede control to vampires and were therefore hunted almost to extinction, until vampires realised that they needed to protect their food. The Blood Agreement was brought into place, Safe Zones set up and, at least as I've been taught, human numbers began to rebound once they were able to live safe, settled lives. Of course, the reality of that idyllic vision became abundantly clear when I visited an actual Safe Zone and saw the harvesting plant, the hopelessness of human lives.

'Really?' I don't bother to hide my scorn. There was nothing balanced about it.

'I know it wasn't perfect. But it was peaceful, at least. Then humans began disappearing. Entire Safe Zones cleared out in a single night.'

'Entire Safe Zones?' I never learned about this in my lessons.

My mother nods. 'It became clear quite quickly who was responsible. The one person who refused to set up proper Safe Zones. Whose human population continued to decline.'

'Jaguar.'

'Jaguar. Sending his ships, landing at sunset, overwhelming any guards and simply stealing the humans away.'

'Overwhelming the guards?'

'Jaguar are fierce warriors. But we weren't going to take it lying down and wanted to protect our humans. So, Raven went to war.'

God. This is awful. Those poor people. 'Why just Raven? Why not Lion or Scorpion?'

'Scorpion was dealing with a rebellion already – oh, yes, the North Wind is not the only time humans have tried to take things back – while Lion were happy to stay where they were. So, it was up to us. We drove Jaguar south, to central America, where we had our final standoff. We had the numbers, his forces decimated due to a lack of blood, thanks to the very thing we were fighting for. His poor policies were what undermined him in the end. But we also had no more stomach for fighting. We wanted to return home to our families, to our lives. So, we struck an agreement.'

'You let him keep South America.'

'We did. Out of respect for the family line. A line was drawn at the Panama Canal, with Raven holding everything north of it. Jaguar got to keep everything south. He wasn't happy about it; Prince Joaquin's father is a … complicated man, at best. But he knew he had no choice. He set up Safe Zones, not long after, though I hear they're not as well-regulated as they should be.'

'You hear?'

'You have to understand, the great families… We're close with Lion, but Scorpion and Jaguar went their own way, millennia ago. We know little about their courts or their customs. That's why it was a surprise to see Joaquin at Versailles. Especially when he offered you his support.'

'He told me he had a sister like me. Perhaps that's why he's open to change.'

My mother's brows draw together. 'I see,' she says. 'That might explain things.'

'He said I didn't want to know what his people did to children like me.'

My mother blinks. 'I was *there,* Emelia. I saw the temples, the blood running down the steps, the broken bodies. No humans were safe, no matter their age. It was all so wasteful.'

'*Wasteful*? They were people, not sandwiches!'

My mother's eyes widen. 'Emelia, I didn't mean—'

'Don't you see that humans had no choice but to sign the Blood Agreement? They wanted their children to be safe, the same way you want me to be safe. But did you ever wonder, when you fought for my life, about the world I'd be ruling? If I can't even make small changes, like moving the guards from live food to blood pouches, then how am I ever supposed to achieve anything bigger? You tell me that things take time for vampires, but I don't have time!'

My mother is silent, red lining her eyes.

'Maybe I should have stayed in the Safe Zone, pretending I was living a lovely human life, even though I didn't have to bleed into a bag once a month. My reign will be a novelty, because humans, like me, are seen as food and nothing more.'

'They are food!' My mother's voice is sharp.

I recoil, cold shock running through me.

'But they are so much more,' my mother continues. A red tear slides down the porcelain curve of her cheek. 'You are so much more. We ignore what humans are because it's easier that way, not to face the reality of what we've done.'

'Then help me change it. Help me make it so that humans like Sophie can go for a walk and not be food for idiots like Stefan. You all lived together in harmony, once. I know we can't go back to how it was before the Rising. But surely there's a way for us to make it safer for humans, too.'

My mother is silent, her dark gaze turned down.

'You're right,' she says. 'Of course you are.' Echoes of words spoken in a jewelled chamber. But this time, I think she means it.

'I did what I needed to do here,' I say. 'I showed them all who I was, and we managed to get two families back on our side. I also realise I couldn't have done it alone. That without you, and father, and Joaquin, things might have been different. But that's the whole point. I *can't* do this alone. You and Father say you support me; now we need to show the world that it's not just me wanting to change things.'

My mother nods. 'I did wonder,' she says. 'When you were born. You were so small, so fragile. So inexpressibly beautiful. I knew the path wouldn't be easy, but even then … I felt it could be something wonderful. The biggest mistake your father and I made was bringing you up as one of us, in the darkness. And not realising that things needed to change.'

'You didn't know any different. And I like the darkness.' It's like our roles are reversed: she is the child, and I am the mother, reassuring her. 'I needed to have that experience, so I could appreciate the light.'

My mother comes to sit next to me, pulling me into her arms. I relax against her as she strokes my hair. 'So, what now?' she says.

'I don't know. I can't replicate the Channel Islands, so I need to think of something else. I can't stop blood donations, but I don't want humans to be trapped anymore.'

'We can keep working on it. Look at what you've achieved in just a few months.'

'Do you think Joaquin is a bad choice for me? Because of what happened with his father?'

'What? As a consort?' She pauses. 'I don't think it's a bad thing, necessarily. Though you're young to be thinking of this.'

'It's symbolic of what I want to achieve. A human and a vampire, living together.'

'Yes. But do not sacrifice your own heart for what you think others want to see. It's one of the few choices you, as a ruler, can make selfishly. Don't give it up if you don't have to.'

'He likes what I want to do. I think, even if we don't … I think he could be a friend, if nothing else.'

My mother nods. 'Of course. He wasn't the only one interested in you, though.'

I don't say anything.

'The Vindhof boy.' My mother smiles. 'And Corinna Eligor, if that's your preference. Both would also be very capable lieutenants.'

'Oh.' It's no surprise that Deryck was interested in me. And Corinna, I later discovered, was the girl holding Stefan back when he tried to attack me. 'They both seemed … nice.'

'Yes, they did. You certainly have options, if you want them. I just wanted you to know a little more about what you might be choosing.'

'What about the rest of it?'

Her expression becomes serious once more. 'It is time for change. Let's get you crowned, and we can work out what happens next.' She kisses me on the forehead then leaves the room, a gliding, silken glimmer. I sit there, thinking.

I will do what it takes, to hold the realm. Mistral's Challenge might have collapsed, but it won't be the last I'll face in my reign. As I said to my mother, I can't do this alone. I need someone strong at my side. Combining our territories, our strengths, is a smart way to do that. There's also a kind of poetry to it, a healing of old wounds. I know I'm young, but I don't have forever. I ignore the small tendril of doubt in my stomach. Kyle is gone. Michael is gone.

Joaquin is just what I need.

Chapter Twenty-Five

FIRST NIGHT

The Darkmeadow is as I remember. A wide expanse of grass high in the hills, tumbled boulders all around. But there are no screaming humans here tonight, no blood spattered across stone. Instead, there are crowds and music, billowing silk tents, and a canopy over a raised dais, three thrones set in a row and a semi-circle of Raven guards in front of it. It's hard to believe it's only a few months since I was here, in Kyle's arms, watching death unfold. That I almost died, too, betrayed and alone. I've done a lot, come a long way since then, even though I know I have farther to go. I can be proud of myself for that, at least.

The crowd parts like a wave, two Raven guards holding our standard ahead of me, moonlight catching the flecks of red in their livery. I hold my head high against the unfamiliar weight of a coronet, my trailing cape brushing the grass, my parents with a hand on each of my shoulders. Silence ripples out from us, people bowing as we pass. It's the most surreal experience, a fantasy in silver-grey and black.

The Gathering is held over three nights under the full moon. It's when representatives of all the Raven family branches meet to form alliances, arrange marriages, catch up on news and family gossip. Not just the twelve main families, but all the subsets and minor nobility, too; it's a big crowd. Coaches began arriving last night, sitting shuttered against the daylight. Sophie isn't here; there are no human drivers, because it's too dangerous. Even blood dancers stay on the coaches, under guard. I'm the only human on the field tonight.

Besides, there's no way I want Sophie anywhere near something like this, not after what happened at Versailles. She was quiet on our way back home, though we did return to our usual easy conversation. I gave her a week off when we got back, making sure her small apartment in the Safe Zone was fully stocked with food and fresh bedding, so she could rest. We parted with a hug, and a promise I'd keep her up to date with what happened at the Gathering. Not that I'm expecting much out of the ordinary.

The guards split as we approach the dais, peeling away to the sides and bowing in unison, everything perfectly timed. It's spectacle, imagery, ritual. Just as the Moon Harvest was.

Part of me still wants to rebel, even though I've chosen this path. I remember the market Kyle took me to, the night before it all fell apart. Dancing through the crowd, passed from partner to partner like a bead threaded on a string. How free I'd felt, as though my feet had wings.

And where I'd danced with Michael.

My heart still aches at the thought of him. I suppose it's unfinished business. I don't even know if he's alive. I wonder whether Mistral will show up tonight. I wonder what we'll do if they don't.

Their Challenge has collapsed, of course. My tour, and the time spent at Jennie's, worked well. I'm aware it's a precarious victory, and that things can and most likely will change if I make a mistake. It's why Joaquin's support is so important. He's coming tonight; his messages, full of endearments and sensual promise, have been blowing up my phone since we parted.

My parents ascend the dais first, each standing in front of a throne, leaving the central one free. For me. This is it. This is where the power shifts.

I turn to face the crowd. I've been through the steps, know what I'm supposed to be doing. But being here, feeling the weight of all the vampire families looking at me, is very different from talking about it in the embrace of family.

Stay standing. Wait as my parents both extend an arm to me, then bow. The rustle as the crowd follows suit. It's like watching wind ripple across a field of wheat, bending the stems. Even the guards are kneeling. A moment of power, pure and simple. The power of my family name, of millennia of rule. It's also the power that will allow me to make change. To bring the balance back so there's enough for everyone.

I stand tall, claiming it.

Let the crowd see that I'm a force to be reckoned with. That being human is far more than they could ever imagine. My life may be shorter than theirs, my body weaker, but it's no less full of potential.

'The heir has been chosen.' Varin's voice rings across the field. The crowd parts as he approaches the dais, clad in his smoke-dark chain mail with the Raven crest, holding his unsheathed sword. He places it, point down, on the first step. 'Who brings her to be presented here?'

The words of ritual. A warrior with a sword, should my claim not be accepted by the crowd. Vampires are tough to kill, but it's not impossible. With light, of course. But also metal, razor sharp, wielded quickly enough to sever head and limbs, to create wounds from which there's no healing. My hands are shaking.

'I bring her.' My mother's voice, clear and pure as a bell. 'Blood of my blood, my child, born of my body. Emelia Isadora Raven. Last of our ancient line.'

'Are there any who would challenge this claim?' Varin, hands still on the hilt of his sword, turns to the crowd.

I hold my breath. I don't think Mistral are here. Any objection, and Varin has a choice. He can defend me. Or he can side with the challenger, and kill me.

I don't believe he'd do the latter, not if he wanted to live long himself. My father would destroy him before anyone else could. But tension ripples across the dais as we wait the allotted three beats. The crowd rustles again but, thank darkness, no one says a word.

'And so it is.' Varin picks up his sword, flipping it so it lies flat across both open palms. He kneels before me, offering the weapon.

I take it from him.

Again, there's precedent here. If I suspected Varin of being anything less than loyal, if this first act of fealty was tarnished in any way, I could kill him with his own weapon. I wouldn't dream of it. The arms master has become a friend over these past weeks. I smile and wait for Varin to meet my gaze. His hazel eyes twinkle.

'I accept your fealty, Varin Darksolder.' My voice doesn't shake, and I'm thankful for that. 'Arise, as my champion.'

Varin rises, smooth and lethal in his chain mail, taking his sword back. If he were to strike me down now it would be considered the deepest treason, his name and family hunted down and eradicated. He turns to the crowd, taking a wide-legged stance a step below me, his unsheathed sword held point-down. The message is clear. My mother steps forwards.

'I, Penelope Raven, do officially hand my crown to my daughter, Emelia Raven, on the occasion of her eighteenth birthday. As is tradition for all Ravens, across the centuries.' She smiles, gleaming and triumphant. It is a triumph for her, I realise. Over adversity, over the years spent fearing losing me, of me dying or being rejected as ruler, simply because of my humanity. Vindication of the decision she made to fight for me from the moment of my birth. My heart swells with love, for all that she's done to bring me to this moment. I glance at her, my eyes full of tears. Not part of the ritual, but I don't care. This is about family.

She returns my smile, a faint tinge of red in her onyx gaze. The crowd cheers, howling their support to the stars and bright moon, clapping and stamping. Music starts, a wild beat, as the festivities begin. As I take the next step towards my crown.

Chapter Twenty-Six

MY MOTHER'S DAUGHTER

I'm more relaxed on the second night of the Gathering. The tough part, where someone could have challenged us, is over. Joaquin is supposed to arrive tonight, and I want to see where it can go between us. I sit on my throne, sipping a drink, the Raven ring heavy on my finger, the ruby catching the faint light, like old blood. It's strange to sit here, holding power in my hand; I can see how easily it could overwhelm me. The crowd below dance and mill about, a sea of silver, grey and black, flashes of jewels and beautiful faces. I should join them.

It's not like there aren't people I know here: Corinna Eligor, and a few others I recognise from Versailles. Representatives from Darkwing and Karanlik have arrived, too, their ships spotted offshore a couple of days ago, their coaches joining the others this evening. They've greeted me, unofficially, Darkwing's manner friendly yet distant, Karanlik more effusive. It's progress, I suppose. I spot Deryck Vindhof in the crowd. He winks at me, outrageous as usual. He danced with me last night, dipping me and twirling me, making me laugh.

Perhaps he wouldn't be a bad choice for lieutenant. I have to choose someone tomorrow night, and I've been mulling over the very short list of options. Whoever I pick needs to be aligned with my views, and willing to work with me to change things for humans. But they also need to be noble, and strategically connected. Mistral have held the role several times, most recently for my mother, but they're not an option. Ravenko have also done so, in the past, but Stefan is unsuitable for obvious reasons. I like Deryck, he seems to like me, and I think there could be real friendship there. I just wish I knew more about his politics. And that he didn't remind me so much of Michael.

I'm about to stand when there's a rustle of anticipation, spreading through the dancing crowd like a wave. I sit up, craning my head.

Joaquin. He heads towards me, his entourage following, all rippling power. My parents are also on their way but he arrives before they do, waiting at the base of the stairs, his dark gaze on me. I stand, but otherwise don't move. I don't know the steps of this dance, and don't want to get it wrong.

'Emelia Raven.' Joaquin's voice rings out. The rustling crowd becomes quieter. 'I come to offer you Jaguar's support. But also, on a more personal level, I wish to tell you this.' He puts one foot on the first step. I stare at the curving strength of his thigh, his broad shoulders.

'I come to pay court to you, lovely Raven. To repair what once was broken. What do you say?' His mouth curves at one corner. I remember how it felt to kiss him there.

Oh, he is absolutely what I need.

He holds out his hand. I descend the stairs to take it. And we enter the dance.

Dancing with Joaquin is as it was at Versailles, his strength overwhelming. I don't mind, really. Not when I'm pressed against his muscular chest, his violet and musk scent curling around me, that sensual mouth so close to mine. After a few songs someone taps my shoulder. Joaquin pauses, raising an eyebrow.

'May I cut in?' The cool voice awakens memories, of a dark nightclub and a bone-crushing embrace. And Kyle, protecting me.

I glance at Joaquin. He shrugs. 'If you're all right with it, then I am.'

I turn. Stella Ravenna, my cousin, is standing there. 'Stella. How nice to see you again.'

'And you.' She smiles, and I can see her trying to make it sincere. I wait. 'My father said he saw you at Versailles.'

'That's right. He told me you missed me. And I thought that was weird, because we never hang out.'

Joaquin chuckles, a dark rich sound. 'If you want to dance, let's go. So I can return to Emelia afterwards.'

Stella's brows come together. 'Fine. Fuck … I just… Forget the act, Emelia. I know you're putting your court together, darkness knows why, but here we are. And I want a place in it.'

'Darkness knows why?' I keep my tone cool. 'Not sure what you mean by that.'

'What I mean is, hardly anyone thought you'd survive to be the heir. That's why no one hangs out with you.'

I snort. 'Oh, really? It wasn't because you all tried to eat me at my sixth birthday party?'

Joaquin clicks his tongue. 'Cruel children,' he murmurs, his hand on my waist, his thumb stroking my ribs. 'Although I'm sure you are delicious.' He kisses my cheek. Stella's green gaze widens.

'Look,' she says. 'I want to be part of the court. If you'll have me. We're family, after all.'

'We are. So maybe you need to tell your father that challenging us isn't a very family-oriented thing to do,' I hiss. 'Then, perhaps, I'll see which positions are available.'

Stella rears back. 'What? I don't know anything about that.'

'I find that hard to believe.'

'Would you still like to dance, little cat?' Joaquin moves closer to Stella, his hand leaving my waist.

Her eyes widen as she meets his gaze, and she stumbles. 'Um, yes. Sure.'

Ugh. Whatever. I need a drink, anyway. Joaquin swings Stella into the dance, and I head back to the dais. When I get there my parents are waiting.

'We need to talk.' My father's expression is stern.

'Not here.' My mother's dark brows draw together. 'On the coach.'

The silk at the rear of the dais opens, Bertrand holding it back. My father ushers my mother and me through, a hand at both our waists. My stomach drops. What in darkness is happening?

Varin is already on the coach when we climb aboard, a faint candle lamp illuminating the strong lines of his face. He looks like a knight of legend, Sir Lancelot in gilded black. He's holding a sheet of paper, frowning.

'What's going on?' I can't bear the oppressive silence.

'We've received a message. From Mistral. A letter, in the old way, sealed and stamped. They've also put it online.' My father paces, running a hand through his hair.

'Mistral?' My stomach sinks. Oh no, if they've hurt Michael, I'll—

'They wish to withdraw their Challenge.'

Relief washes over me. 'They do?' I snort. 'Not that they have much choice.'

'They've certainly tried to make it look that way.' Scorn colours my mother's tone. 'Their public message talks a lot about how they want to support you, how they've seen the error of their ways.'

'And the private message?' I glance at Varin, whose jaw is tight.

'It says much the same, though there's a condition attached,' he says.

'A condition?' I will not marry either of them, I don't care if we have to go to war.

'You have to choose one of them as your lieutenant.'

The words slam into me like an arrow. 'Sorry … did you just say I have to choose one of those assholes as my lieutenant? Why in darkness would they think I'd do that? Their Challenge isn't going ahead because they can't get the support!'

'Because if you don't, they'll reveal the true nature of their father's death, and expose his role as Head of the North Wind.'

'So? Let them.'

'It's not that simple, unfortunately.' My mother looks pained. 'Mistral was my lieutenant, and he betrayed us. Many lives were lost, and property destroyed, in that rebellion. If it comes out that Mistral was behind it, it could weaken our position.'

'Why?' I'm furious. 'Why does our choosing to punish a traitor mean we're weak?'

'Because we didn't know about it. He was plotting against me, against you, against the realm of Raven itself, right under our noses,' my father says. 'If they expose this now and spin it so it looks like they've been pressured into accepting you, it could negate any of the gains you've made with the tour and Versailles.'

'Is this about me being human again?' I shake my head. 'No. I did not go through … what I went through, for these two idiots to try and take my realm. Because that's what they want, isn't it? I doubt I'd survive long with either of them as my lieutenant.'

'No one would let anything happen to you!' My mother sounds shocked. I'm surprised at her naïveté.

'So, I'm to keep living my life constantly under guard? I don't want that, either! And I doubt either of them will be interested in what I want to do for humans. Anyone I choose needs to be aligned with my agenda.'

'Who were you thinking of choosing?'

'I'm still not sure. Corinna Eligor, possibly. Or Deryck Vindhof.' Even though he reminds me of Michael. I pause. 'What did it say in the letter? The exact wording? About who they want me to choose?'

'It requests that you choose "a son of Mistral" as your lieutenant,' Varin says, his lip curling. 'In honour of their late father.'

Hmm. 'Not that their father should be honoured in any way, but are there any positives to choosing Mistral?'

'Why do you ask?' My father stops pacing, folding his arms.

'Well, you've always taught me to consider all sides.' An idea is forming. Another gamble.

'Mistral was a good lieutenant to me, until he wasn't,' my mother says, looking thoughtful. 'He stepped aside when your father came into my life—'

'Though it wasn't without tension, my love,' my father interjects. My mother glares at him.

'As I was saying, he served me well. The Mistral line have held the position before. And, of course, it will alleviate any dissent.' Her onyx gaze narrows, briefly. 'The twelve families know the truth of how and why Mistral died, and four of them chose to side with his sons against you anyway.'

'So, if I choose one of them, it will effectively nip that in the bud. Make us out to be the bigger person in all this.'

'Yes. Binding one of Mistral's sons to us also means there will be far higher consequences for their treachery. Loyalty is valued highly among our people, and taking the post of lieutenant sends a message. For one of Mistral's sons to hold the post, then turn on us, would likely be the end of their family line.'

'Just so I'm clear, then, if I don't choose a "son of Mistral", Oliver and Jacques will spend the rest of my reign trying to destabilise me. And if I focus on improving conditions for humans, like I want to, then it will make it even easier for them to turn vampire opinion against me. These are my options.' Such a neat little trick. Darkness flickers within me, something feral rising to meet their challenge. They think they have me. But they don't.

My father nods. 'Unfortunately, yes.'

'What if there was a third option? One that met their conditions, but meant I got what I wanted, too.'

My mother raises one eyebrow.

'Mistral had another son, didn't he? A human son.'

My father looks thunderstruck. My mother's eyes widen.

'Yes, he did. But how—'

'—do I know him? He was my … my friend, in the Safe Zone.' I pause, letting the words settle. I can't give my feelings away.

'If he shows up,' my father says, still looking shocked, 'then yes, I suppose it does adhere to their terms.' He glances at my mother. 'There are no guarantees he's still alive, though. Mistral never cared for human children, as you know. Oliver and Jacques are probably the same.'

I feel sick. He cannot be dead. Why was I so quick to block him?

Because you were hurt, grieving.

'If I choose him, they'll get what they say they want. But I'll also get what I want.'

'Are you sure about this?'

'Yes. This is the kind of court I want to build. A court where humans and vampires hold equal status. Making Michael my lieutenant is a message.' I'm not lying. Aside from however I might feel about Michael, it does make sense. Varin as my vampire champion. Michael as my human lieutenant. Both sides working together, a symbol for how I'd like things to be.

'Choosing Michael…' My father sighs, concern gleaming in his hawk's gaze. 'I understand why you're considering it. It's risky, and bold, and definitely a message to all of our kind. It's the kind of move you need to make as a ruler. But it also puts you in a dangerous position.'

I get it. For the ruler of Raven to be human is precarious enough. For her second-in-command to be, too, is dangerous.

'I cannot choose Oliver or Jacques. I won't. If Michael isn't here, I'll choose Deryck Vindhof. And we'll deal with whatever Mistral brings as a result of that.'

My father glances at my mother, who is biting her lip. She nods.

'The choice is yours,' he says. 'And we'll all support you. Whatever it may lead to.'

There's so much love in his voice it almost breaks me. I know what I'm doing is risky. But it also feels right, for so many reasons.

'Thank you,' I say.

'It's almost time.' My father glances out the window at the moon. 'Are you ready?'

'Oh, I'm ready.' Ready to unleash hell on those assholes. But, as we leave the coach, my mother grabs my arm.

'A moment,' she says, her voice low and urgent.

I wait, wondering what the hell is going on. Father and Varin continue to the dais, taking their places by the thrones.

'Are you sure about this?'

'About what? Choosing Michael? Or not choosing Oliver or Jacques? Because the answer to both is yes. Why?'

'Mistral did what he did out of love for me.'

I'm shocked. It's the first time she's said it aloud, though I know she blames herself.

'Do not repeat the same mistake with his son. You had feelings for him, didn't you; I could see it in your face. And Joaquin is not someone to be strung along. If you choose Michael, you need to be clear what his place is with you, from the start.'

'I'm with Joaquin.'

'Again, are you sure?'

'I don't have a lifetime to wait for love, like you did,' I snap. 'And I have to choose for power, not love.'

My mother's brows draw together. 'We've talked about this. You are Raven, Emelia. You can choose for yourself.'

'No, I can't. And we have to go.' Families are already lining up at the dais. If she doesn't understand this, I don't have time to explain.

My mother sighs, worry still darkening her gaze. 'Just be careful. We're more alike than you think.'

I'm still fuming as we ascend the dais. As if we're alike. Sure, everyone says how similar we look, but we're worlds apart. She is vampire, and I am human. And there lies the main problem with her handing me the crown.

But the wheels are in motion. I have a job to do, the crowd getting restless. Joaquin joins us, standing next to Varin, and the ceremony begins. The families, one by one, approach the throne. Each one announced, their ancient names ringing across the meadow. Each one kneeling, taking my hand and kissing the ring.

There's no sign of Mistral.

As the line grows shorter, the night moving towards dawn, worry sits deep in my stomach. If they want to stand against me, then so be it. I'd love to put the boot into them. I just wish I knew whether or not Michael was alive.

Then I see them. Oliver and Jacques. Tall and blond, looking so much like their father. I plaster a smile on my face as they approach, even though my heart sinks. Keeping up appearances, pretending as though they aren't traitorous bastards.

Then, as they get closer, I realise who's walking behind them. My heart starts pounding.

Eyes like a summer storm meet mine.

Michael.

He's *here*. Oh, thank darkness. Even if it is torture to see him again. Joaquin glances at me, as though he can sense my emotional turmoil. I can barely breathe as first Oliver, then Jacques, kneel before me, kissing my ring. The crowd is silent, as though they know what this means. As though they can see this is so much more than just fealty.

Finally, it's Michael's turn. He kneels, looking up at me.

And there is a world in his eyes.

He takes my hand, his thumb rubbing lightly over the inside of my wrist. A small gesture, hopefully nothing that anyone would notice. But I know what it means. I have to fight to stay cool and calm, to not betray my human emotions, even though my traitorous heart is reaching out to his.

I think of my mother meeting my father, of how in that single moment of him kneeling before her, everything changed.

It seems I am truly her daughter, after all.

Chapter Twenty-Seven

SNOWFALL

We return to the coach just before sunrise. I go straight to my room, close the door and sit on my bed with my knees hugged to my chest.

Michael is here.

It shouldn't mean anything. He walked away. He didn't trust me. He chose his brothers over me. I'm with Joaquin now.

So, what in darkness happened when he knelt before me?

I flop back on the bed, covering my face with my hands. Oh God. How can I possibly have him as my lieutenant? My mother's warning rolls through my mind. *We're more alike than you think.* Maybe I should just choose Deryck and deal with the fallout afterwards.

My phone buzzes. I grab it, hoping it's Sophie. Perhaps she'll have some advice on how to handle this. But it's a message from an unknown number.

Meet me outside. Near the rocks.

My first reaction is to tell him where to shove it. Because of course it's Michael. It's light outside and everyone else here is a vampire, unless some random blood dancer has managed to get my number. But something in my chest seems to tug at me, telling me I need to do this. Maybe it's a good opportunity to talk, with no one else around. Darkness knows I'd like the chance to scream at him. Sighing, I reply.

Fine.

I shrug on my jacket, shove my feet into boots, then head downstairs. My reaction meant nothing. It was the shock of seeing him, that's all. I've shut down the Challenge, I'm two nights into my Anointing, I have a hot new vampire boyfriend, and I'm going to sort this out too. *Emelia Raven, getting shit done*. I should get it on a sweatshirt.

'I'm going outside.' My parents, playing cards with Varin, look up, my mother's mouth an 'o' of surprise. 'Need some air.' I wait until they're at a safe distance to open the door, stepping out quickly, gasping as I'm hit by a blast of cold air.

It's snowing. Fat feathery flakes of white, twirling and dancing in the dawn light, the strange yellow-grey of a snow-filled sky. It's starting to settle, lining the rocks with silver, the dark mass of forest below crowned with white like a wave breaking against the hillside.

It's beautiful, the way snow blankets the world. Making it quieter, smoothing out the rough edges, hiding the flaws. I perch on a rock, staring out across the trees. It's as though the snow is soothing me, too, like ice-cream for my soul. I catch a few flakes, watching them melt against the warmth of my skin, their tiny, intricate designs lost for ever.

'Hey.'

I jump, my head whipping around. Michael stands a few feet away, hands in pockets, wearing jeans and one of his frayed jumpers that I know are so soft to touch, his broad shoulders even more so under a leather jacket.

My resolve melts like the snowflakes on my hand. It's hard to breathe.

I wait, though. Let him speak first, then I can decide where to take this. I keep my expression neutral, but my heart beats wildly, traitor that it is.

He sits next to me, bracing his hands against the rock. And it's heaven and hell combined to be so close to him again, to smell his familiar scent, see those beautiful eyes turned on me. I have to clench my fist to stop myself reaching for him.

'I'm sorry,' he says. 'I should never have treated you the way I did.'

'No, you shouldn't.' Keeping cool, like the snow. Trying to hide my breaking parts, my angry flaws. I watch the rapidly whitening landscape, my every sense on high alert. The cold grit of stone beneath my clenched fists, the endless dark mass of trees disappearing beneath a veil of white, the twisting dance of the snowflakes. The warmth of the man next to me. And the fact I can't touch him.

'You should have told me about my father.' The pain in his voice cuts me.

'I know.' I can't change that now. I can admit where I went wrong, though. 'I'm sorry I didn't. I just … couldn't find the words.'

'I understand.'

'You do?' I look at him, then.

Gods. It takes my breath away. One corner of his mouth is quirked up, his blue-grey eyes warm. There's snow in his hair, a flake caught on his long eyelashes. I remind myself of him snarling at me in a tiny bathroom. Of how hurt I was when he walked away.

'Your trust had been broken, and badly,' he says. 'We hadn't known each other long. But Emelia, I meant what I said to you, that morning on the beach. I am with you. You can trust me. And I'm more sorry than you know that I ever let you go.'

He takes my hand, twining his fingers through mine. I pull it back. Hurt flashes in his gaze.

But he's right. I have had my trust broken. By Kyle. But also by him. And there are other people I need to consider.

'What about the Challenge?' My voice is shaky. 'You must know about that.'

'I didn't find out until I went back to my brothers. I tried to call you and couldn't get through. Went back to the house, hoping to find you, but you were already gone. Damn, you are ruthless.' He grins. Fuck. My heart opens in response.

'I was hurt. And didn't want to prolong it. The Challenge is over, anyway.'

'I know. Well done, by the way.'

'Well done? I did what I had to do. Though your brothers are still trying it on.'

He snorts. 'Why didn't you remind me what utter, complete arseholes they are?'

I laugh, unable to help it. 'What?'

'They're idiots. I hate them. They used to torment me incessantly when I lived at home. Why on earth I thought they might have changed I don't know.'

'I can understand why. They're charming when they want something. Until they get it.'

'Is that what you think of me, as well?'

'No.'

Silence falls between us. My throat feels thick with unspoken words, about all the ways he's not like his brothers, about what seeing him is doing to me.

'What do you think?' There's a thread of vulnerability, of yearning in his voice.

'Of you?' I swallow. 'I … I don't know.'

'Really? Because I think of you a lot, E. I miss you.'

'Why are you here?' I conveniently ignore the way my core heated at his words. *'I think of you a lot.'* I need to remember my mother's warning. My lieutenant is all he can be.

'In this field? Or at the Gathering?'

I'm reminded of Joaquin, in a darkened garden. The same question, and a similar response. But my heart didn't ache in anticipation of his answer, like it does for Michael's.

'Both. You said you didn't want to be part of my world. Yet here you are, standing with your brothers as though they didn't just try to take my throne.'

'I'm here *because* they tried to take your throne,' he says, his gaze intent on me. 'Because of that letter they sent. Do you truly think I would have let either of them near you? Do you not know that I would do anything to keep you safe?'

Oh. Oh darkness. Realisation crashes over me. He knew I had to choose a 'son of Mistral'. And he showed up because he knew, out of the three of them, he was the only one who wouldn't try and murder me at the earliest opportunity. My mouth opens and closes.

'And you're okay with that? Being my lieutenant?'

He nods, one corner of his mouth curving. 'What choice do I have?'

'You didn't have to get involved.' I don't know why I feel

so annoyed. 'I'm the one with no choice, if I want to avoid civil war.'

'Oh, you think I'd just step aside? Leave you to my brothers' tender mercies? You might hate me, Emelia, but I would never do that to you.'

'I don't hate you.'

'No?' His stormy gaze holds me. 'Because it doesn't feel as though you like me much.'

Oh, that is *it*. 'What the hell am I supposed to do, Michael? You walked out of my life, then suddenly you reappear, full of apologies, and say you shouldn't have done it! Maybe I've moved on!'

'With who?' His lip curls. 'That big vampire on the dais last night, acting as though he owned you?'

Guilt stabs at me. ''What the hell is your problem?'

His brow lowers. 'My problem is that I fucked up! I let you go, and I want you back!' He takes my hands again. I pull them back. 'I know you feel what's between us. I saw it in your face last night. We're meant to be together!'

'As my lieutenant. That's it!' We're almost nose to nose and, despite how I want to rip his face off, there's a treacherous part of me that wants to sink into him. To kiss him, wild, rolling in the snow, not caring who sees us.

'That's it? Tell me that's all you want from me. I want to hear you say it.'

We stare at each other, breathing hard. Then I spot something, over his shoulder, moving among the trees below us. It looks like a person, clad in black from head to toe. They're oddly bulky, yet light on their feet. 'Who the hell is that?' I point.

Michael tenses. 'Fuck. Put your arm down. Slowly. And try

not to move.' His voice is close to my ear.

'But why would humans be—'

'Not humans.'

Chapter Twenty-Eight

LOOK AT ME

I stay as still as possible. 'Not humans?' I murmur. 'What the … are you saying these are *vampires*? But it's daytime.' I spot another blur of black, closer to us, moving from rock to rock. Michael is tense as iron.

'Reapers.'

'*What?*'

'Shh. Tell you after.' Michael breathes the words. Light catches the silver blade now in his other hand. My stomach lurches, terror sinking vicious claws into me. We're almost defenceless, out here alone. No one could help us, even if they wanted to.

Another blur of motion, even closer. A figure wearing black fatigues, their head completely covered by a dark helmet and goggles, crouches nearby.

'Don't look at them. Look at me.'

I turn my head. Oh God. He's so close. His warm breath on my face, his eyes darkening as he stares into mine. I almost kiss him, then. Because if I'm about to die a horrible death, it seems like the right thing to do. I close my eyes instead, a single tear rolling down my cheek. Cold air rushes past us both, a faint crackle of snow. I keep my eyes closed, even though the urge to look is killing me. Looking will definitely kill me.

After what feels like an eternity but is probably just minutes, I feel Michael's gentle touch on my cheek. 'They're gone.'

I open my eyes. My heart pounds, my limbs trembling. It's fear, pure and simple. Nothing to do with how close he is to me. I move away. 'Please tell me what the hell just happened.'

He laughs, the sound soft. 'You haven't changed, have you?'

'*Michael!* How are vampires out during the day? And *Reapers?*' I keep my voice low, aware of the nearby coaches. They may be shuttered, but they're not soundproof.

'Fuck.' He pulls back, running his hand through his hair. 'Where to begin?'

'Um, at the beginning?'

'Right. So, after my father threw me out, several years ago, I had to make my own way to the Safe Zone where we met.'

I nod, frowning. That can't have been easy. Mistral's estates are in France. I know he tried to change Michael to vampire, several times, and when it didn't take, he kicked him out. Once again, I wonder what my mother ever saw in Mistral.

'But why come here? Why not go to one of the Safe Zones in France? How did you get across the Channel?'

'I wanted to get away from him. Managed to stow away on a vamp ship, cross the Channel, and made my way east. I don't know what I was looking for. Maybe it was you.'

'Stop being an idiot,' I breathe. 'Tell me what this has to do with Reapers.'

'I … it was tough. I kept moving during the day, because I thought it would be safer. I had my blade, and my father taught me to defend myself, even if his methods were … harsh.' Pain ripples across his expression. 'I was low on food when I ran into what I thought was a group of humans, near the Safe Zone closest to your estate.'

'They weren't humans.'

'No.' He shakes his head, looking down. 'I found out pretty quickly that they were vampires, shielded against the daylight by protective clothing and goggles. I managed to escape them and make it into the Safe Zone. And that's where I found out they were Reapers.'

My mouth drops open. 'But … what the hell? Why would they come out in daylight? It's against every vampire instinct to do so! Shit.' I stare across the snowy landscape, as though it might give away their secrets. 'Is this how they're attacking Safe Zones? Coming in during the day?' I stand up. 'I need to let my father know. If they're planning an attack here, then—'

'They're not planning an attack.'

'How do you know?'

He gestures to the coaches, to the now deserted Gathering field. 'There are hundreds of vampires here, Raven nobility, entire battalions of guards. There's only a handful of them. They'd be wiped out in moments or sent to the Pits. There's no way they'd attack, not with those odds.'

'But we can't just let them go! They must have gone somewhere. These … *monsters* are literally tearing my people apart, and you're just sitting there looking smug.'

'I am not smug!'

'You are so smug!'

'E, it's daylight. Who are you going to get to follow them? They'll be long gone now, probably miles away.'

'But—' My phone buzzes in my pocket. I ignore it.

'You going to answer that?'

'Michael!'

'I bet it's your mother.'

I stick my tongue out at him as I answer the phone.

'Have you frozen to death out there or do I need to send a blood dancer to get you?' My mother's voice is laced with humour but there's an undertone of worry.

'I'm coming back now.' Because if I don't, I'm going to kill Michael. I hang up.

'You're not going back now.'

'Why not? I'd rather not still be out here if those Reapers decide to come back.'

'They're not coming back. And, even if they did, I'd keep you safe, E.'

I swallow. He's too damn close to me. 'How? That blade isn't going to be much use.'

'You'd be surprised.'

'What aren't you telling me?' Because I know it's something. I haven't forgotten my desire to seek out a Reaper, to find out if they are connected to Lady Morvenna. If he knows something, I want to know it, too.

'I'm telling you all I can.'

'Which means you're keeping something from me.'

'Not necessarily. It means I don't have anything else to tell you.'

'Oh!' My fists clench. 'Do you really think I want a lieutenant who keeps secrets from me?'

'No, I don't.' He moves even closer, his chest almost

touching mine. I can't breathe. 'But I imagine you'd prefer me doing this to either of my brothers.' Before I can move, he steals a kiss, his lips pressing against mine. God and darkness! My whole body responds.

I shove him, hard. 'Do not touch me!' I'm so angry I can hardly see. I turn away before I do something I'll regret.

Michael grabs my arm. 'What, that's it? You're just going to walk away?'

'That's what you did,' I snap, pulling my arm free.

This time, when I head for the coach, he doesn't stop me.

I go straight to my room, grabbing a pillow from the bed and punching it before hugging it to me, silently screaming into velvet and feathers. Mistral, *again*. I swear to darkness the entire family was put on the planet just to annoy me. Michael's kiss still burns on my lips, as though my whole body is calling out for him. And then there's the insane fact of Reapers in the *daylight*.

My father taught me that it's better to engage with an enemy you know.

I only hope I survive it.

Chapter Twenty-Nine

BETTER THE DEVIL

Tonight, the dais holds only a single throne. Mine.

I ascend the stairs, holding my heavy velvet skirts so I don't trip. I take my seat, Raven guards in front of me, Varin to one side of the throne, Bertrand on the other. My parents and Joaquin will join us in a moment.

When I returned to the coach after seeing Michael, I'd been too flustered to explain anything about what I'd seen. Reapers, during the daylight? I know I need to talk to my father about it, that it needs to be investigated further. And it will be.

But I need to get through tonight, first. Choosing a lieutenant sets the tone for my reign. It's a position of considerable power; my lieutenant acts in my stead when needed, as well as maintaining diplomatic ties with all the families, and being my closest adviser.

I still don't know what to do, though. I remain steadfast in my decision to not choose Oliver or Jacques, no matter what might happen. Deryck is a safe choice, a neutral yet well-connected heir.

And I like him. But Michael, despite how he frustrates me, is symbolic of the kind of court I want to build. He believes in the same things I do, understands what it means to live in both worlds. He'll also be the first human lieutenant; hopefully, he won't be the last. And if it appeases his idiot brothers, then all the better. Even though it's infuriating to give in to Mistral, after all they've done, Michael is the choice that feels *right* to me.

God and darkness, though, it's not easy! None of this is. Lion are allies, but things have been tense since Daniel was killed. Scorpion still haven't replied to any of our invitations. At least I know Jaguar is with me.

I smile as Joaquin approaches, his sultry gaze finding mine. He's all smooth darkness as he ascends the dais, muscles rippling like his family namesake under the black velvet of his suit. He takes my hand and kisses it, a flicker of his tongue against my skin. Bertrand moves aside so he can take his place next to me, as though he's already my consort.

'Your parents approach.' Joaquin brushes his knuckle along my cheek, then goes to join his entourage, who lounge along the edge of the dais like a pack of jungle predators, scanning the crowd for prey. Selene shoots me a lascivious grin, licking her lips. I blush, frowning.

'Emelia.' Varin moves into my line of vision, blocking me from the crowd and Selene's stare. 'Do you need anything, before this begins?'

'No.' I swallow. 'I'm all right.'

He regards me for a moment, his hazel gaze grave. 'I'm here to protect you,' he murmurs. 'Please call on me whenever you need.'

'Thank you. I will.'

At my parents' arrival the mood in the crowd shifts, expectation building. This is it, then.

My mother comes to me, kissing my cheek, then my father does the same. They flank my throne, a reminder of family and all that's important.

I stand. All eyes come to me as I step forward. Oliver and Jacques are close to the dais, because of course they are. But so is Michael, annoyingly beautiful in a dark suit, his blond hair pushed back from his handsome face. He catches my eye. I clear my throat.

'As my reign begins, I must choose a lieutenant. I already have my champion, Varin.' I gesture to him. He nods. 'I've given the matter a lot of thought.' A lie, but I guess I need to make it look good. And with that, my decision becomes clear. 'The role of lieutenant is one of building bridges, between the Raven and the realm. I have decided, in making my choice, to build a bridge of my own. To close a circle once broken.' I pause. 'Which is why, by the gods and darkness, and the bright silver moon, I choose…'

Oliver, that absolute dickhead, has already taken a step forward. Well guess what, Oliver. You're not getting this job. I always swore I wouldn't have Mistral as my lieutenant when I was crowned. He's dead now, but Oliver is just as bad, if not worse than his father. And Jacques, with his cruel predator's gaze? I don't think so.

Which leaves only one son of Mistral to be at my side.

Engage with an enemy you know.

'… Michael, son of Mistral, as my lieutenant. Raven claw, blood and stone. So be it.'

Snarls erupt from Oliver and Jacques. But Varin is already there, escorting Michael onto the dais before his brothers can do any damage. They have no call to complain, though. I've done as they asked. 'A son of Mistral.' It might not be enough. But as the crowd roars, as Michael comes to stand next to me, it feels like the only option.

My heart is beating faster from excitement, that's all. A dark figure rises to his feet at the edge of the platform. Joaquin's gaze pierces me like a hook, pulling me towards him. Oh darkness.

Maybe I've made a mistake.

Chapter Thirty

LIGHT AND DARK

The coach sways as we head towards home. I sit on the sofa, my knees pulled up to my chest. Michael is on the coach following ours, with the Raven guards, blood dancers, Varin and Bertrand. He's coming back with us because he's my lieutenant. And because I'm fairly sure his brothers will rip him apart if he goes back to them. Apparently, it's quite normal for lieutenants to live on the estate, something I never knew before.

'Mistral didn't live at the estate with us. And he was your lieutenant.' Thank darkness he didn't.

'He did, actually,' my mother says. 'Until I met your father. Then he left and set up his own family.' Her gaze dims briefly. 'It's how things are. Your lieutenant stays with you, as does your champion, until you take a consort. Even then, they might still stay, if your consort doesn't take on either role. So, it's appropriate Michael be on the estate. He can live in the gatehouse. It's where his father was, for a while.'

'He was?' I frown.

'When I met your father … it was complicated. Mistral moved in there initially, before leaving. I suppose he hoped…' She shakes her head. 'It doesn't matter what he hoped. Anyway, the place is furnished, and we'll make sure it's all as it should be for Michael.'

'So, he won't be in the main house?' This might not be a bad thing, to be honest.

'Joaquin is staying in the main house.' Along with his entourage. My parents invited him, in the wake of his declaration to court me. 'He won't stay the entire time, though,' my mother continues. 'He has things to do, he told me, before your coronation.'

Good. Hopefully it will give me the space I need to sort my mind out. We haven't spoken since our argument in the snowfield, but I can't escape spending time with Michael, now that he's my lieutenant. I just need to make it clear there can be nothing else between us. That I'm with Joaquin.

I can do that.

I think.

The passage is as I remember. *No cobwebs,* I told Kyle, when he took me down it to what I thought would be freedom. Now I make my way carefully down crumbling stone steps, one hand on the wall for balance, the other holding my phone torch high to light the way.

I open the door at the bottom of the stairs, letting in bright daylight. No need for me to hide; no one can see me from the house, and I told Bertrand I'd be sleeping and not to disturb me.

I carefully tuck a piece of leather between the door and the wall. I should be back before dark anyway, but I'm not taking any chances. I run across the lawns, my breath puffing in the frosty air. It feels good to be outside. The pale golden stone of the gatehouse's little tower stands out against trees showing the first mist of green, light twinkling in the leaded glass windows. I bang the knocker twice, then wait.

The carved wooden door opens. 'I wondered when you'd show up.' The words are tight, Michael's arms folded.

I blink. 'We need to talk.'

He says nothing, moving to the side so I have to brush past him to enter. We go into a living room with a high ceiling decorated with plaster roses. There's a bay window with a wide-cushioned seat, and a comfortable-looking sofa and chairs, all in shades of blue. A fire burns in the huge fireplace, the room smelling of woodsmoke and lavender polish.

'So, talk.' Michael's hands are on his hips. I try not to notice his long legs, the muscles under his long-sleeved top.

'I need to make sure you know where you … where we stand.'

'Oh? And where is that?'

'You know what I mean! You're my lieutenant, so we have to work together. But that's all we can be.' My hands twist together.

'Work colleagues?' He shakes his head, walking over to the window. 'Fine. If that's what you want to tell yourself.'

'I'm with Joaquin now.'

'Yeah. He seems like your type, tall, dark and bloodsucking.'

'You have no idea what my type is!' I snap the words out. How easily he rouses me to anger.

'Funny. Because I thought it was me, for a while.'

'You walked away, not me! I wanted you to come with me when I left.'

'And here I am.' He moves towards me, his arms wide. 'So, is that it? Or do you have anything else you want to share?'

'You're impossible!' I take in a breath and blow it out, because if I don't, I'll scream. 'I'm trying my best to make this work.'

'Make what work? I want you, E, and I'm not giving up so easily.' He comes closer, looming over me.

'You can't. We can't.' My voice is a whisper.

'Why? He's not here, is he? But you are. Alone, during the day, when no one can see you. Interesting choice, that.' He tucks a lock of hair behind my ear. Oh darkness. I'd forgotten the heat of him, up close.

'You're an ass.' But my words lack bite.

'After all I've done for you.' His hand comes to my chin, tipping my face up to his.

'I should go.' A last breath of defiance.

'You know where the door is.'

I start to move. At least, I think that's what I do. Yet somehow, I end up in his arms, his mouth on mine. Oh God. He's so *warm*. Our tongues tangle, things deepening, until it seems the room is full of sparks. His hard length presses into me as his hands explore, my fingers tangled in his hair.

I should not *be doing this.*

I might want Michael, but Joaquin is who I *need,* for the good of my realm. And kissing my lieutenant, though it might run in the family, is not part of my plan. I manage to get my hands between us, pushing until he lets go.

'E, wait—'

I don't look back, wiping away tears as I run from the gatehouse. Cool air blows the heat from my face, the scent of him from my hair, my clothes. What in darkness was I thinking? I race up stone stairs, not caring about cobwebs or anything except getting back to the safety of my room. Once there, I close the panel, leaning against the carved fireplace. A sob bursts out, despite my best efforts, my chest heaving.

I tear off my coat, pull my gown over my head, rough as though to punish myself for how stupid I am. I run the shower hot, scrub my skin until it's pink, wanting every trace of his touch gone from me, no matter how I might crave more.

I need to be so careful. Joaquin has declared for me. It doesn't mean I have to accept, but I'd be a fool not to. With Michael, I feel like an equal. I've always felt safe with him, from the first time we met. Always felt drawn to his warmth, to the feeling that he is home. Joaquin, on the other hand, feels like … possibility. Complicated, yet exciting. And someone who chose me, in front of all the assembled Raven families. The fact that Michael's touch sets me aflame needs to be set aside. Which would be manageable, if I hadn't chosen him as my lieutenant.

I bang my fist against the tiles, my head hanging as water sluices over me. Eventually, I get out and dress, drying my hair and spritzing myself with anti-feed just to be sure. I wish I could go to bed, but it's Joaquin's first night in my home. And I want to spend time with him too.

I grab a portable candle lamp and leave my room, the golden glow lighting the hallways, glimmering from the sweeping gold banister as I descend to the foyer. It's deserted, apart from two guards either side of the main door. I wonder where Joaquin is.

He emerges from behind the golden curve of stairs, almost as though he heard me thinking of him. 'Emelia, my dove. Where have you been?' He prowls towards me, taking the candle lamp and switching it off.

'What—'

'You don't need it,' he purrs, one hand lifting my hair away from my neck. 'Let me be your eyes in the dark.' A graze of teeth against my throat, a flicker of tongue. My body responds, my back arching. Darkness. 'I've been waiting for you.'

'I'm sorry. I slept late.'

He huffs out a laugh, his hand at my waist. 'You are fascinating.' He draws out the last word, like a lingering caress. 'The way you sleep. The delicious way you smell.' He brushes his lips against mine. His other hand tangles in my hair, pulling so my head tilts, as he sniffs along the line of my jaw. Oh God.

'I find that hard to believe.'

'That you're fascinating? Oh, my dearest, you have no idea. I wish to know you, Emelia Raven.' He's all coiled strength, a violet-scented predator, his voice a rumble. 'In every way a person can know another.'

Darkness enfolds us like a cloak. I feel myself responding to it, to him, something awakening in me. I relax in his arms and he growls, a soft purr against my throat. My vision adjusts and I realise I can see more of him, the dangling jade earring, the angle of his jaw as he leans in for a kiss. He presses against me, his hands sliding down the curve of my hips, his mouth on my neck. I gasp, blushing. I might not be able to see much, but there are guards in here who can. 'We should find my parents. And your friends. Where are they?'

'I sent them out to play. Tonight is about me and you.'

He takes my hand, kissing the inside of my wrist. I remember being bitten there, by another vampire, my body heating at the memory of what we were doing.

'Yess,' he murmurs, his mouth descending on mine once more, 'that's it, my Raven. Let me feel you.' He deepens the kiss until I see stars, my heart pounding as he presses against me. I put my hand on his smooth chest.

'Please.' It's a breathed word, but there are footsteps, the guards by the door coming closer. Joaquin steps back, linking his arm with mine.

'Your parents, I believe, are in the main sitting room.' He sighs. 'I will do this, for you. If you promise to let me take you out tomorrow night?'

'All right.' I can do that. I *want* to do that.

And I'll figure out what to do about Michael later.

Chapter Thirty-One

BLOOD MAGIC

'Tell me what you hear. What you see.'

It's just after sunset. I'm near the fence that borders our estate, where it brushes against the edge of the Great Forest. Joaquin is with me, his hand on my waist.

'When you said you were going to take me out tonight, this wasn't what I thought you meant.' My legs are cold, my short dress and boots not really suited for wandering the grounds at night. I don't really care, though.

'Shh.' His grip on my waist tightens. 'Use all your senses.'

I sigh, doing as he asks. I'm not sure what the point is, other than to show him how bad humans are at this. At first, all I'm aware of is my own breath, the pressure of his hand. Then my vision adjusts and I can see further. The forest, at first a dark mass, now becomes shapes in the darkness. Tree trunks and small things that move. The crackle of twigs, the hoot of an owl. The crashing path of a deer through the undergrowth. I hear the faint sound of rushing water, a whispered thread of noise. Darkness, that can't be the waterfall Kyle took me to, can it? My breath catches. Holy shit.

'That's it. Sink into it.'

'This is amazing. I never knew—'

'—that you could do this? You are vampire, Emelia, just as I am, despite your human form. Your very blood sings with our magic. Do not fight who you are.' His lips brush my ear. I tingle all over. 'We are the reason humans seek light in the darkness. I see you wanting to be that light for them. But there's darkness in you, too.'

'I'm not vampire.' But even as I say the words, I wonder. Yes, I have a human body, human frailties, but my blood, as everyone likes to remind me, is vampire blood.

'No?' He turns me to face him. 'Humans cannot see what you just saw. Nor do they taste each other's blood.'

'I don't drink blood.'

'You've never had blood pass your lips?'

'Not human blood.'

'Maybe you should try it sometime.'

In any other circumstance, this would be abhorrent. But something about being in the dark with him, listening to the forest, brings a wildness to the surface. I wonder what it would be like to be truly vampire, to feed on something living.

Darkness surges in me, the part that only he seems to reach. The crackle of power between us, Raven to Jaguar, that I felt when we first met. It's intoxicating. I'll never have to worry about him betraying me for power, because he has his own. I'll be his consort as much as he'll be mine, equals on our thrones.

He smiles, flash of white fangs, then bites his finger and extends it to me. A single drop of blood, dark red, sits on the tip. 'You are vampire beneath your skin. So drink.'

As I gaze at him, wondering, it's as though the rising wildness possesses me and I grab his hand, bringing his finger to my lips, sucking it. He groans, his eyes closing. He tastes like violets, and something more heated. Then I'm in his arms, his mouth on mine, my back against the cold metal railings.

'Oh yes, my darling,' he murmurs against my mouth. His hands roam over me and I arch into him, wanting more. 'Now let me taste you.'

I tense, wondering what he means to do. His hand slips under my skirt, between my legs, pulling my underwear aside. I gasp, my head going back as he explores me, pleasure pounding through my veins.

'Raven one, Raven two.' The call from a nearby patrol, guarding the fence, brings me back to reality.

Shit. I push at Joaquin. 'We can't do this. The guards…'

He stills, his hand between my thighs, his mouth on my throat. I'm panting, trembling with desire. He pulls back, straightening my clothes, smoothing his hair.

'Perhaps we can continue in the house?' Invitation growls in every word.

I hesitate. I don't know why I'm holding back.

'No?' He nods, once. 'I forget, you think differently here about sex. Very well, my Raven. I shall respect your parents' home, and you. I'm sure I can find someone else to help me out for tonight.' He puts his fingers to his lips and licks them, grinning, his fangs dropped. Fingers that, just a moment ago, were on my most intimate flesh. 'Delicious. Just as I thought.'

Then he's gone, a streak of black in the night. I sag against the fence, my hand to my chest. What the hell just happened?

I've managed to regain my composure by the time I get back to the house. Which is good as I enter the foyer to see

Joaquin, Selene and the rest of his entourage. They all turn their heads as I enter. Selene grins, wiping the corners of her mouth. God and darkness.

Joaquin comes to me, taking my hand, kissing each of my knuckles in turn.

'What's there to do for fun around here?'

'For fun?' It's difficult to concentrate when his tongue flickers across my skin, his gaze liquid on mine. 'Um, there are books and games in the library. There's the ballroom. The Costume Room.'

Joaquin raises an eyebrow. 'That's it? Books and clothing? I wish to take you out, my Raven, not play dress-up. Unless you're into that, of course.' A wicked smile, a ripple of laughter from the group.

'There's a nightclub near here,' I say, feeling strangled. 'It's pretty good.'

Joaquin's face lights up, breathtaking beauty. 'Now that, my darling, sounds much more my scene. Can we go there?'

'Y-yes, of course. I just need to arrange it.' I manage to extricate myself, pulling my phone from my pocket. 'I'll call Ira, the owner, and let him know we're coming.'

'VIP, I hope? Does he have good food?'

'He usually has a selection.' I try not to think about the caged humans behind Ira's bar. 'Free range, mostly. Plus, we can take a dancer if you prefer.'

'I think we've drunk our fill of your dancers.' He grins, revealing dropped fangs. 'Besides, I like to try local flavours whenever I'm somewhere new.'

Thank darkness Ira picks up. I turn away from Joaquin. 'Ira, it's Emelia.'

'I know who it is.' There's a smile in Ira's voice. 'What can I do for you?'

'I have … that is, we have guests, and we'd like to come to the club. Tonight.'

'Raven are always welcome. I'll reserve a table for you.'

'Thank you. There will be eight of us, I think.'

A short while later we're in a couple of cars, heading towards Dark Haven. We pull up outside the Dome, our drivers opening the doors. The line of patrons waiting outside whip out their phones, taking photographs, gasping and calling out. I'm sure I'll be all over social media in a matter of minutes. So different from the last time I was here. For a lot of reasons.

I lead Joaquin and his entourage inside. I haven't been here since that night with Kyle, when we danced and drank, and he carried me home through the flickering dark.

'Are you all right?' Joaquin's hand is at the small of my back. I lean into his strength, finding I need it. I also need wine.

'Lady Raven?' A female vampire, clad in skintight leather, her red hair piled high, comes over. 'This way, please. My name is Ilona, and I'll be looking after you this evening. Anything you need, just ask.'

'Ilona,' Joaquin purrs, his dark gaze wandering over her lush curves. Jealousy stabs me. 'I believe we would like to drink. Wine, for my darling, and your best dancers for the rest of us.'

'Of course.' Ilona is all eyelashes and pouty lips as she leads us to a booth on the edge of the circular dance floor, her body an undulating invitation. I clutch Joaquin's arm and try not to glare. He just laughs, running the tip of his tongue up my cheek, following it with a kiss. Gods.

We squeeze into the booth, Joaquin curving his body protectively around mine. I put my legs over his lap, my arm around his neck, our mouths so close together. Oh yes, I can do this. I can take this handsome prince for my own, for my realm. Maybe he's right. Maybe there is more vampire in me than I thought. It's time for me to explore this side of myself, too. And Joaquin is the perfect companion with whom to do so.

And, as I drink wine and laugh, as Joaquin's hands stroke my thighs, play with the edge of my skirt, graze the underside of my breasts, as his followers gyrate on the dance floor, blood on their mouths, I let myself sink into darkness. I put warmth and light out of my mind, turn towards the cool of night. I think of Varin holding his sword, the idea of balance. I've shown the world my human side. I wonder what they'll think of my vampire side, whatever that is.

I tilt my head as Joaquin runs his mouth along my throat, looking up at the reflection in the mirror fragments embedded in the domed ceiling. A circular dancefloor, curving booths in red leather around the edge of it, as though we're in a flower. And me, draped across Joaquin, his hands on me like he owns me.

'Hey.' Joaquin's hand comes to my jaw, his mouth to mine. He tastes like blood and violets, sucking gently on my tongue before releasing me to refill my wine glass. 'You want to dance? Or you want to go somewhere more private?' His fingertips slide beneath the hem of my skirt. Breathless, I grab my wineglass and drain it. 'Dance,' I gasp. I'm still not ready for anything more, darkness knows why.

'If dancing is what you truly want,' Joaquin says, leaning in to lick droplets of wine from my lips, 'then so be it. But I want *you*, Emelia. And I cannot wait much longer.'

He slides from the booth, pulling me with him, holding me tight as we join the swaying crowd. I cling to him, wondering why the hell I'm resisting falling into bed with him. But later, as we head home, the sky paling towards dawn, my head aching from too much wine, I can't hide from the truth. We head inside, Joaquin's arm around me. 'Shall I tuck you into bed?' he murmurs, all innuendo and heat.

'I'm so tired,' I say, conscious of Selene's mocking green gaze. 'Forgive me.'

'There's nothing to forgive,' Joaquin says lightly. 'One more kiss, though, before you go?' His strong arms come around me as he bends me back. When he releases me, I'm unsteady on my feet. I turn towards the stairs, and see Michael standing there, with my mother. She has her eyebrows raised. Michael's expression is completely shuttered.

And that, right there, is the problem. I'm still hung up on Michael.

Chapter Thirty-Two

THE THIRTEENTH MOVE

'These are all the Raven vehicles on the estate?'

'That's right.' I hold my breath as Michael brushes past, his hand feather-light on my waist. He walks around the Mercedes, his fingers trailing along the glossy trim. For probably the tenth time today I curse the circumstances that led to me choosing him as my lieutenant. If he hadn't come back, if his brothers hadn't been such absolute tossers, then I'd be preparing for my coronation and, most likely, announcing my engagement to Joaquin.

Instead, I'm wandering around my home, trying not to scream with frustration. As my lieutenant, Michael has to know all the ins and outs of how the estate works, as well as understand a political structure going back centuries. My parents are helping him with the latter and I, in what now seems a spectacularly ill-conceived moment of weakness, offered to take him around the estate during the day. So now I'm showing him the outbuildings, all the while doing my utmost not to think of his lips on mine, how he felt pressed against me, the absolute obscene heat of him. I'm furious that I cannot seem to get over him.

'These are the staff coaches? There was a similar arrangement on my father's estate.'

'Yep.'

It's becoming more and more clear that whatever was between us in the Safe Zone hasn't gone anywhere. If anything, my longing for him has increased, especially as I can't act on it. Not because he doesn't want me to, because he's made it very clear he does. But because I have to choose what's best for my realm.

I'm about to turn away when I notice something odd. There are only three coaches here.

'What is it?'

'There should be four coaches onsite.'

'Maybe one of them is on a staff run?'

I check my phone. 'Not at this time of day.'

I don't understand. I checked with the guards when we returned from the Gathering, and the numbers of humans leaving and entering the estate seems to mostly match up now, with the majority of discrepancies explained. But there should be four coaches here.

Michael shrugs. 'Maybe it's something to do with the extra guards in the Safe Zones.' Raven have upped their guard presence in response to the attacks, and we've advised the other families to do the same. I also haven't forgotten my revelation about Reapers, and what they might be. But I'm snowed under with everything that needs to be done before my coronation. Plus, if I want to go to the Pits and find a Reaper I'll have to consult with my lieutenant. And I'm trying to do as little of that as possible at the moment.

'Maybe.' I'm still frowning, though, as we leave the garages and head towards the small guardhouse. I've not found any more clothing left there, despite checking several times. 'So, this is where food deliveries come in, and—'

'E, I can figure this stuff out myself. You don't have to show me around. In fact, what I imagine you should be doing is preparing for your birthday ball.'

Damn him. The ball is a week away, guests arriving soon. It's not like I have to do much except show up, though. I offered to help with organising it, but my mother wouldn't hear of it, telling me I wasn't to dream of arranging my own birthday party.

'You don't *have* to do this at all.' He's grinning now, his arms folded. 'So, the only conclusion I can come to is that you want to spend more time with me.'

My mouth drops open. 'You are truly just…' Words fail me.

'*Just*…?' His grin widens, one eyebrow raised. 'I can't wait to hear what you think of me. Because I know you do. Think of me, that is. I think of you, too. In all kinds of ways.'

'Oh!' Fuming, I turn on my heel and march back towards the house, his laughter following me.

I cannot escape him. Over the next few days, despite my best efforts, I see Michael everywhere. Laughing in the library with my mother. Practising drills with Varin (I stood there, mouth agape, before I realised what I was doing and fled, heat in my cheeks). Discussing strategy with my father in the War Room.

He is *infuriating*.

He's also, I realise, absolutely born to this role. What a fool I was in the Safe Zone, thinking I needed to work out how to fit him into my world. He was born into it, just as I was.

Joaquin is also everywhere. Except, possibly, where he'd most like to be. My bed. But it doesn't stop him from grabbing me at every opportunity, pulling me into alcoves for heated kisses, whirling me around the empty ballroom until I'm breathless with laughter. I enjoy his company, truly. And he's definitely hot. But I cannot bring myself to sleep with him, not yet. Something about the way he waits for me in the shadows reminds me of Kyle, of sneaking around. At least, I keep telling myself that's the reason.

It's what I tell Sophie, too, when we catch up for the first time since the Gathering. She's back at work, seemingly recovered from her ordeal at Versailles. We screamed, throwing our arms around each other when we finally met again. And now, of course, she wants to know everything.

'Half your luck, honestly.'

Sophie, leaning back on a pile of sacks, takes a bite of apple. There's oil smudged across one cheek, more smeared across her grey jumpsuit, the Raven crest in black on the pocket. We're in one of the cavernous garages at the edge of the estate, and I'm telling her my woes.

'What?'

'I only wish I had two hot men after me.' She taps on her phone. 'I mean, seriously. Look at them!' She shows me a news article, with a photo of me at the Gathering. Michael stands next to me, broad-shouldered and serious, beautiful in his dark suit. On my other side is Joaquin, all glowering sexiness.

'Ugh.' I flop back, my hand to my head. 'I knowwww.'

Sophie giggles. 'Things could be worse.'

She's right. Things could be a hell of a lot worse. I sit up. 'I'm sorry,' I say. 'I shouldn't be going on like this.'

'You absolutely should! What are friends for, if not to

discuss the merits of which hot person to kiss? I'm assuming you've kissed them both, anyway.'

I grimace, covering my face with my hands. Sophie squeals.

'What do I doooo?' I groan.

'What you do,' Sophie says, 'is enjoy yourself. Your life is going to change so much, you need to have some fun. You've made no promises to anyone, have you? You're the one with the power here.'

'I guess so.' I pause, overcome. It's just so nice to sit with a friend and have no one expecting anything from me.

'I get it.' Sophie's voice softens. 'I know you have all the boys and dresses and power, but I can appreciate how … intense this all must be. You can always come and talk to me, you know.'

'Thanks.'

Sophie smiles, but something glimmers in her blue gaze. 'Just promise me that you won't give up, that you'll keep trying to change things. Don't let all this coronation shit overwhelm you, or these boys distract you. I saw the Channel Islands, remember? You can do this.'

'I won't.' I blink away tears.

'Besides, there's always Varin if this doesn't pan out,' she says with a giggle.

'Break's over. Back to it!' A tall man walks into the garage, clad in Raven camouflage. It's the guard who drove me back to Dark Haven after Kyle's kidnap attempt. I made sure he got a commendation and a bonus, afterwards. He's also the one whose voice I heard in the guardhouse. When he sees me, he stops short, then salutes.

'Lady Raven. Forgive me.'

'It's fine.' I get up, brushing my hands down my skirt. 'It's nice to see you again.'

'And you, my lady.' He glances from me to Sophie.

'I should get back,' Sophie murmurs, touching my hand. She heads over to the workbench, picking up a polishing rag.

'Can I escort you anywhere, my lady?' The guard holds out his arm.

I smile. 'No, thank you. I know my way back this time.'

He returns my smile, inclining his head. 'Of course.'

I leave the garage, but something makes me look back. The guard and Sophie are standing close together, talking. Then she throws her arms around his neck. I look away, wanting to give them privacy. I'm delighted for her – I don't want to be the only one who's been kissing hot guys. She better be ready to give me every detail next time I see her, though.

But when I look back again, they're both gone.

'Dammit!' I drop the wooden practice sword, my arms and shoulders aching. 'I cannot get the thirteenth strike today.'

'Don't be so hard on yourself. You've only been training a short while, so to have already learnt the Morningstar, even at a slow pace, is remarkable.' Varin, shirtless as usual, folds his arms. 'You remind me of your father.'

I pout, still frustrated. By a lot of things, not just the Morningstar. Joaquin is closeted with his entourage, feeding, and I took the opportunity to come downstairs, hoping time in the practice ring might help burn some of my tension away. But it's just making things worse. 'I just… The angle, when you do it. Could you show me again, but more slowly?'

'Maybe I can help?' Michael's voice is quiet.

I start, then blush all over. I had no idea he was watching.

'Of course. If you don't mind, please remove your shirt, so Emelia can better see the pattern of breath.' Varin nods appraisingly as Michael enters the ring. 'Are you all right with that, Emelia? Michael has been training with me, as you know, and is proficient in these movements.'

'It's fine.' I'm very conscious of being sweaty and dirty, especially when Michael removes his shirt, hanging it over the barrier at the edge of the ring.

God and darkness, he's beautiful. Yet there are scars on his golden skin, biting across his ribcage, along one smooth pec, silvery white marks of trauma. I want to touch them all, smooth the hurt from him.

He takes a practice sword from the rack, and steps into the first position. Then, graceful as water flowing, he moves through the Morningstar. Slow enough that I can see what he's doing, yet with such control and precision I know he can do it far more quickly should he wish. I try not to stare at his bunching abs, the muscles in his arms, his beautiful strong back, as he pivots and strikes.

When he gets to the thirteenth move, I watch carefully, but can't see where I'm going wrong. It looks like what I think I'm doing, yet somehow I'm not.

'Very nice,' Varin nods his head approvingly as Michael finishes. 'Emelia, try it again.'

Feeling as though my entire body is blushing, I start the routine once more. When I get to number thirteen, Michael stops me.

Then, oh darkness, he comes up behind me, fitting his broad chest to my back, his arms coming around mine to clasp my wrists. 'It's the angle, here,' he says. 'Your wrists are slightly out of alignment.' He moves my hand, then takes me through the strike again.

It flows, perfectly.

'Yes!' Varin claps his hands. 'Again!'

We repeat the strike, over and over, Varin clapping the beat for us. And, under cover of one of the claps, Michael's mouth comes to my ear.

'Will you come and see me?'

'I can't. You know why,' I whisper, barely moving my mouth, as Varin claps again.

'How do you know this isn't a work request?'

'Because you would have asked me like a normal person.' I snap, slightly.

He releases me, stepping back. He's breathing harder, perhaps, than he needs to, considering how slowly we were moving. 'I hope that helped.' He is all politeness. But heat lies in his gaze. I feel its answer in my own.

'It really did. Thank you.' I hope Varin puts my flushed face down to all the work I've been doing.

'How's your shoulder, Michael?' Varin asks. 'Did you get it looked at?'

'What happened to your shoulder?'

Michael's stormy gaze slants my way, a grin tugging the curve of his mouth. I glare at him.

'A statue fell as I was passing. In the gallery.'

I grab a glass of water and drink it down. 'Is that where that bruise is from?' I'd noticed it, a smudge of purple across one smooth shoulder, but thought it was from training.

'Hmm.' He gulps down his own water. 'Luckily I spotted it moving and got out the way before it landed on my head.'

He shrugs his shirt back on, and I try not to stare as he does up the buttons.

'Prince Joaquin and his entourage have played several pranks since staying here.' Varin's voice is tight. 'Things that, perhaps, would not trouble vampires overmuch. But they might need reminding that both you and your lieutenant are human, my lady.'

'I'll speak to them,' I say, shaken. What in darkness? I grow cold at the thought of what could have happened, if the statue landed true.

I cannot bear to lose him. But I also cannot have him.

I suppose all I can do is protect him.

Chapter Thirty-Three

BLOOD AND DARKNESS

I stretch up on tiptoes, my hand scrabbling across the high shelf, raising a cloud of dust that makes me sneeze.

'Bless you.'

I whirl, waving my hand in front of my face. Michael stands in the doorway of the War Room, looking infuriatingly handsome in a loose white shirt tucked into dark trousers, his blond hair damp and pushed back.

'Do you need a hand?' He saunters over to me, and I try not to remember how he looked earlier, shirtless with sword in hand, moving through the Morningstar.

'I'm fine.'

'Are you?' He smiles, his stormy gaze darkening, then stretches up, his scent and heat so tantalisingly close, and grabs the book I was trying to reach. It must be how annoying he is that makes my breath come faster, makes me feel as though I might explode.

'Yes,' I mutter. If I keep lying to myself, maybe eventually I'll believe it.

'I'm not.'

'What?' I look up.

'I want you, E. I miss you.' He takes my hand, his fingers twining with mine as he lifts it to his lips.

'We can't.' A breath of resistance.

'Why? Because of your prince?' He drops my hand, his brows drawing together. 'I don't care how many times he kisses you, or how he makes you feel. Didn't I make it clear how I feel, when I came back for you?'

'You didn't come back just for me.' So hard to talk when he's so close to me.

'Oh, I did. But if you don't believe me, perhaps you'll believe this.' He leans in, his heat and scent surrounding me. 'I've wanted you since the first time I saw you, leaning against the wall in the café. I worried for you, every moment, after I lost you at the market that night. And when I found you again, it felt like a piece of me had been restored. When I kiss you, I want to keep doing it for ever. And when you're in danger, even for a moment, I want to tear the world apart to make you safe again. You are everything to me, Emelia.'

I'm going to die, right here. I lean on the shelf, because if I don't, I'll fall.

'We—'

'—can't be together? I can't think of a single damn reason why not.'

'Emelia, Michael. You are needed.'

I gasp. Michael steps back from me, and it's as though warmth leaves my world. My father stands in the doorway, his arms folded, brows drawn together.

'Varin is on his way,' he says. 'There's something you need to see.' He comes into the room, pulling down a screen on one wall. Varin arrives a moment later, all cool elegance in black silks, his long hair tied back.

I'm still reeling from Michael's declaration.

I've wanted you since the first time I saw you.

Our meeting at the café, when I was in the Safe Zone with Kyle and Ruth took me out for the day. How little I knew of anything, back then. But I knew there was something special about him.

My father presses a button, and a video starts playing. All thoughts of Michael leave me. It's the Channel Islands project. I recognise the ferry port, the town centre. And there's a glimpse of me, riding in the open-sided vehicle with Sophie and Jane, Andrew at the wheel.

'The Channel Islands project, seen as controversial in some vampire circles, was nonetheless a valiant effort by the soon-to-be-crowned Raven to promote her human-centred agenda ahead of her coronation.' The voice of the vampire newsreader, visible at the bottom left of the screen, is smooth and polished. 'However, reports are coming in of illegal activity in and around the islands.' Another video, this one jerky, as though the person taking it was running. A moonlit cove and a small boat pulled up on the shore. Climbing out of it, vampires, masked and dressed in dark clothing. 'They're here,' a male voice gasps, excited. 'Let the games begin.'

The camera pans briefly, and I catch a glimpse of a face I recognise. Also dressed in dark clothing, a blade clasped in one scarred hand. It's Andrew.

'What the hell is this?' Michael's voice is raw.

'It's an illegal hunt. On the Channel Islands. Humans letting vampires ashore, unleashing them on the population.' Varin's voice is tense.

'It's Andrew.' I cannot believe the betrayal.

'Yes.' My father is terse, his arms still folded. 'I thought you'd recognise him.'

'Who's Andrew?' Michael directs the question to my father, but I answer.

'One of the leaders of the North Wind. The one who sat in this very room, and told a sob story so I would give him my island project!' Anger bites into me like acid. 'We should shut the whole fucking thing down.'

'I understand you're angry.' My father's voice is quiet. 'As am I. However, there are other things to consider. Take a moment.'

The way he says it, I know he's reminding me of our lessons. My mother isn't here at the moment – she's gone for a dress fitting – which puts me, as the anointed heir, in charge. It's a heady feeling. But it's also one of great weight. Whatever I say next will happen.

In battle, do not act in haste. Take a moment to consider your next moves. Then choose.

I could shut the whole thing down now. Funnel all the humans into Safe Zones, punish Andrew and whoever else is involved in a variety of gruesome ways. And then I'd be back where I started, with rebels in the Safe Zones who have a whole bunch of new reasons to be angry with the House of Raven. I'm still working on ideas for different community models, but don't have anything concrete.

'He'll know that the video is public, if it's on the news. So, they'll be waiting to see what happens next. As will everyone else. Damn! Can they not see that this kind of thing is just going to make it harder for me to change things?'

'There's another possible angle to this.'

I glance at the carnage onscreen again. The boat, and the black-clad vampires. Shit. Of course.

'You think this is who has been attacking the Safe Zones and the nomad communities. They've been capturing humans to hunt. So not Reapers, then.' The attacks on Safe Zones are still happening, though not as often, thanks to our increased guard presence. They've been relegated to an occasional mention in the news cycle. I guess a bunch of humans disappearing or being murdered doesn't mean much to vampires.

'It's a possibility,' Varin says, frowning. 'Though we cannot rule out the Reaper threat.'

'There is no Reaper threat,' Michael says, his jaw tight.

'No? Even though they can move in daylight?' I've been meaning to tell my father about this. Now seems an appropriate time, gauging by the astonished exclamations from both him and Varin. Michael glares at me.

'At the Gathering, when I went outside during the day, I saw them. We saw them.' Oops. I hadn't exactly mentioned that I'd seen Michael that day in the snow. I tell the rest of the story.

'Darkness, Emelia!' My father bangs his hand on the table. 'You were unguarded!'

'She had me, sir.' Michael folds his arms, his grey eyes dark. 'And, as I say, Reapers are not the threat you think them to be. I think it more likely to have been illegal hunters attacking Safe Zones. The attacks were all near the water, correct?'

'Yes,' I say. 'That bothered me, too. Why would they attack the shorelines, rather than the edge of the forest, if they were Reapers?'

'It makes more sense that it was humans and vampires

travelling from the islands, rather than coming from inland,' Michael says.

I shake my head. 'Except the North Wind weren't on the Channel Islands when the first attacks happened. I agree, though, it could still be linked to the hunts.' There's something else, though. A clue that's eluding me.

'So, what do we do?' My father directs the question to me. Everyone else is silent. Again, the weight of power descends, like a heavy cloak. I chew my lip, considering.

'We pull Andrew off the island, and anyone else we can identify in the video. Make sure they're punished appropriately. We also run regular patrols, checking for any illegal activity, as well as figure out where the loading point is on the mainland. We make all this public, put out a statement. Privately, we trace the pathway back further, see if we can get to the heart of who's organising this. We've already got extra guards in the Safe Zones, so hopefully that will deter further raids.'

My father nods, his granite expression softening. 'Good. Why do you want to keep the investigation private, though?'

He knows why. He just wants to make sure I do, as well. 'There are enough people in this realm, including in the twelve families, who think hunting is natural. There are also humans, and vampires, who make a lot of money from participating. Andrew might have got involved as a source of funding for the North Wind, especially once Mistral was killed. I can say I don't allow hunts in Safe Zones or vampire-free zones, but that's as far as I can go, especially with how unstable things are until I take the crown. That's the focus. Then, once I'm officially the Raven, I can make more decisive moves.'

'Good.' My father is still serious, but there's warmth, now, in his golden gaze. 'Let's make it so.'

'Varin.' My champion nods. 'Will you coordinate the removal of the hunters from the islands? Michael, we'll need to talk about punishment, and what form it might take.' The word catches in my throat, remembering his father kneeling in front of my mother, like an avenging angel. But there will be no Moon Harvest this time, no blood and darkness.

'I can help with that, too,' my father says. 'And your mother will need to be informed when she returns.'

A short while later I leave the War Room, feeling wrung out. Punishment has been agreed, Raven guards dispatched to break apart the hunts. A statement is being prepared for the press. All I can do, really. Now I need to feed, and perhaps go for a walk to clear my head. But, as I head down the hallway, a hand catches my elbow. I turn, expecting to see Joaquin. But it's Michael.

'What do you want?' The words snap out more fiercely than I mean.

His brow lowers. 'We have a conversation to finish.'

'We do not.' I keep my voice low, aware of nearby guards, of other ears that could be listening. 'At least, not here.'

'Then when? Where?' His hand is warm on my arm.

'I don't know.' My voice gets louder on the last word.

He leans in closer, almost as though he's going to kiss me. My heart skips a beat. But all he does is murmur the words 'I'll be waiting, then,' before releasing me and walking away.

I watch him go, my breath catching in my throat. Then I realise Bertrand is waiting, and turn on my heel, walking in the other direction. After about ten minutes of pacing the long hallways, I realise I left the book I wanted in the War Room. With a sigh, I head back there, Bertrand still in tow.

When I open the door, the room is dark. That's odd. I'm sure we left a candle lamp on. There's enough light from the hallway to gild the relief map on the table, the faint glitter of blades on the wall.

'I won't be a moment,' I say to Bertrand, taking a step into the room. I touch the switch but nothing happens. Something moves in the shadows. I turn, but the door is pulled shut behind me, separating me from Bertrand. I hear him cry out. And I'm in darkness.

I'm also dead.

Chapter Thirty-Four

JUST A GAME

But as I think this, I'm already moving. I fling myself towards the wall, reaching out, tapping into that extra sense of seeing in the dark that Joaquin helped me unleash. My hand closes over the hilt of a sword and I pull it free, swinging it in front of me. It's so much lighter than the practice blade that it feels almost effortless, the steel part of me.

There's a curse. A hand closes around my throat, pinning me to the wall. My heart pounds, adrenalin coursing through me like lightning. There are thuds outside the room, more shouting. The hand around my throat tightens, lifting me so my feet leave the floor. Fetid breath fans across my face, the scent of violets. Gasping, I change my grasp on the sword hilt. I think of Michael, his hands gentle on mine, taking me through the motion of the strike. And I bring the blade up, hard.

There's a scream. Liquid spatters my feet, and I slide down the wall as my attacker releases me.

The door flies open with a crash. 'Emelia!' Joaquin's voice is a howl of rage. Faint golden light from the hallway illuminates a scene of devastation.

I'm sprawled, panting, in a pool of rapidly spreading blood. A black-clad vampire is curled next to me, groaning, bleeding heavily from a deep wound to his stomach. I can't seem to move, or breathe, gripping my sword so tightly the hilt cuts into my fingers.

Joaquin glances from me to the other vampire, surprise flashing in his dark gaze. I realise, with a start, that it's one of Joaquin's entourage, faint light catching his jade earring. With a growl Joaquin picks him up, tearing him limb from limb in an absolute frenzy. Blood sprays, and I flinch from it, sobbing. There are a lot of guards around us now. One tries to take my sword, but I don't want to let go. Then I hear my father's voice.

'Where is she?'

He enters the room, eyes widening as he takes in the gore spattered up the walls. He crouches next to me, cupping my chin. I flinch, despite his gentle touch.

'Emelia.' His voice is so soft. 'Look at me.'

I wrench my gaze from the horrors around me. I'm shaking so much my teeth chatter, but I don't know if that's because I'm sitting in a pool of blood. I focus on my father, on his lean features, his eyes filled with love, the small crease between his eyebrows that I know means he's worried about me. My breath starts to slow.

Guards mill around us, removing the body, bringing in cloths to soak up the blood. Joaquin squats nearby, his hands dangling between his legs, his expression distant. I suppose he's just lost a friend. I still don't really understand what happened.

My father gently uncurls my stiff fingers from the sword.

He lays it to one side, his eyes never leaving mine. 'You're safe now. Will you let me help you stand?'

I nod. He takes my hands in his and rises, bringing me with him. I shudder as my skirt touches my legs, the damp folds sticky. I retch suddenly, reminded of Jessie, the scent of violets sickening. My father holds me up, rubbing my back.

'Can you walk?'

Another nod. I will not be carried. Not here.

'What in darkness is this!' Varin's voice. 'Prince Joaquin, what has happened here?'

Yes, Joaquin. Why did one of your entourage attack me?

'It was a prank, gone horribly wrong.' Joaquin's voice is strained. 'As soon as I heard about it, I came here. But not quickly enough for my darling.'

A prank? His voice fades as my father takes me into the hallway. What's left of another of Joaquin's minions is there, a broken twisted thing, more blood soaking into the deep carpets. Bertrand sits on the floor, his back to the wall, two guards helping him. There's a cut on his head, his nose a purple bruise. When he sees me his whole expression crumples.

'I'm all right,' I say, my voice a whistle of breath. My neck hurts where I was grabbed, my shoulders aching from being slammed into the wall. But I need to let him know it wasn't his fault. It was no prank, either. If I hadn't been able to defend myself, I'd be dead.

'I did it,' I say to my father, my voice still a wheeze.

'What did you do?' His arm is strong around me, holding me up.

'The M-Morningstar. Moves eight and thirteen.' I think of Michael, his hands covering mine, his chest against my back, his heat and scent all around me. I'm suddenly desperate to see him. It must be the shock.

'Varin has taught you well.' My father's voice catches, and I feel his kiss on my hair. 'But now we must get you cleaned up, before your mother returns and sees you like this.'

Oh God. My mother. I'm not sure what she would have done if she'd been here. I shudder, and my father quickens his pace, lifting me. My skirt is unpleasantly heavy against my legs, and all I can smell is violets. Darkness, is my room truly this far away?

'Will Bertrand be all right?'

'He will. His pride bruised, perhaps, more than anything.'

'Guards on me doubled, I guess. Or tripled. Maybe he'll just wrap me in cotton wool or make me move into the fortified rooms.' It helps to joke about things. But I'm shaking like a leaf, and know that when I close my eyes, I'll see blood and darkness.

My father comes into my room with me, taking a seat on the long chaise. 'I'll wait while you clean yourself up.'

I nod, heading into my bathroom, my hands trembling so much I can barely undo my dress. I step into the shower still clothed, not wanting to get any more blood on the grey tiles. I step out of my dress, stripping off my underwear as I gradually warm up. I remember another bathroom, another moment of violence, rusty stains disappearing in a swirl down the drain.

Blood. It shapes my entire existence. Who has it, what type they have, whether or not it holds magic. It decides whether we're food or nobility. Whether we're strong, or weak. Yet it's something we all have in common.

I lean against the wall, once again feeling as though

something is eluding me, some key that will help me make this work, help me create a world where vampires and humans can live side by side, safely.

I soap my skin, let heat take the ache from my shoulders, calm the tremors in my limbs. But it can't touch the sorrow in my heart. Running separate courts, day and night, won't return things to how they used to be. We cannot go back. We need to go forward. If only I can figure out how.

Chapter Thirty-Five

HEARTS ON FIRE

Tonight is the ball to mark my eighteenth birthday. Another step on my journey towards the Raven throne. I try not to think about the last ball here. My father, broken and burnt. Kyle and I in my room. Death and destruction and lust, all tangled into one terrible evening.

Tonight will be different. Instead of hiding away, I'll be the focus. The hunter, instead of the hunted.

Michael, as my lieutenant, escorts me to the ballroom. There are also several guards following us, on Bertrand's orders. He's recovered from his injuries, as have I, the faint bruises remaining on my throat covered by my Raven choker.

Michael's arm brushes mine as we walk down the long hallway. My bare skin tingles at the contact. He glances over, like he knows the effect he's having on me. I try to ignore how good he looks in the tailored navy suit, so dark it's almost black, his pushed-back golden hair brushing the high collar, his shoulders broad beneath the fine fabric.

I've wanted you since the first time I saw you.

I can no longer deny I feel the same way. I'm stuck between two impossible choices. A fierce vampire mate, uniting two realms, making Raven strong. Or the choice of my heart. I know what I need to do. I just wish it wasn't so difficult.

We haven't had the chance to talk since the events in the War Room. At least, not in the way he wants. He was furious, of course, when he heard about the attack on me. We've also had to manage the situation with the Channel Islands, as well as prepare for the ball. But I've been careful not to be alone with him, even though every part of me wants to fall into his arms.

'You look nice,' he says. A faint smirk, but there's a gleam of appreciation in his eyes. 'Apart from that necklace.'

Joaquin wanted to escort me to the ball, of course. If it were any other party, I probably would have let him. But this one signifies my imminent ascent to the Raven throne. Lion are here, as well as Jaguar. And Scorpion's ships were spotted last night, just outside our waters. I want to show up as a ruler, not someone's date.

Still, it hasn't stopped him from staking his claim. I found a jade pendant on my pillow when I emerged from my shower, with a note.

Wear this for me, lovely one.

Part of me bristled at his presumption. The fact that the pendant perfectly matches the blue-green silk of my dress is beside the point.

'What's wrong with my necklace?' We come to a stop before the double doors. The guards either side go to open them, but I gesture for them to wait.

'Nothing.' Michael's smirk deepens, his gaze travelling down the plunging neckline of my gown.

'Oh! You are infuriating! I should—'

'We should go in. They're expecting us.' He's still smirking. I don't know whether to smack him or kiss him. But the double doors are opening, guards at attention. I smooth my hands down my dress. My mother, already in the room, clad in her customary red, claps her hands once, twice.

Everything stills. The vampires stop moving so perfectly it's like a film being paused. Then, as one, they bow and curtsey as Michael enters the room, followed by me.

I keep my head high, my expression neutral, nodding to the occasional person as we cross the room. I pause at a couple, the man dressed in dark robes. He's tall and lean, his head shaven, his dark-skinned face seemingly sculpted from bone, deep lines at either side of his mouth. Anbesa, head of Lion. I incline my head, while Michael bows. Darkness, I'm relieved to see Anbesa here, though I wonder how it feels for him to be in the room where his son died. I wish I knew what to say. The woman at his side is voluptuous, her figure encased in layers of bright fabric, counterpoint to Anbesa's darkness. Her skin is the smooth brown of a chestnut, her face beautifully angular.

'Greetings, Emelia,' Anbesa says, his deep voice musical. Sadness lurks in his dark eyes. 'May I present Tau, my lieutenant.'

The woman with him smiles, coming to take my hands. 'Birthday blessings,' she says. 'And thank you for inviting us.'

'It's a pleasure to see you both. This is my lieutenant, Michael.' He comes forward, bowing again. Unease ripples across Anbesa's previously impassive countenance. Shit. Michael, of course, is Mistral's son. And Anbesa's son, Daniel, is dead because of Mistral.

The music starts again, vampires whirling in perfect

unison. My mother comes to join us. When she heard about what happened in the War Room, she was so angry she wanted to throw Joaquin and his entourage out of the house. A compromise was reached; Joaquin's people are gone, staying at another Raven property. Only Joaquin remains here.

My mother takes Anbesa's hand, graceful as a willow. 'Will you dance, my lord?'

He smiles, inclining his head. 'It would be an honour, my lady.'

Michael steps forward, holding his hand out to Tau, who takes it. I try not to feel disappointed.

'You wore it.' Joaquin, resplendent in black silk, open to the smooth V of his chest, steps into my path. His tailored trousers highlight his long muscular legs. I swallow.

'I did. Thank you.' I dip my chin. 'It matches my gown perfectly.'

'I know.' Joaquin smiles, his dark gaze liquid with desire. His hand comes to my waist, his violet and musk scent tantalising. 'Shall we dance, beautiful one?'

I nod, letting him pull me close.

'Perhaps,' Joaquin murmurs, as he brings me into the twirling throng, 'we could venture into the gardens again. I would like to take you there. You remember Versailles, don't you?'

I blush, unable to help it, at the innuendo in his words. 'I remember,' I whisper.

'I know. That dress of yours hides nothing.' He grins. My blush deepens. My nipples are hard beneath the silk, pressing into him, my heart beating wildly.

'Shall we?' He dances me towards the long windows at the edge of the ballroom. I remember pulling the old wooden shutters across, my feet and dress sticky with blood. I place my hand between us, on his cool hard chest.

'I can't. Not tonight. This ball is for me, and to leave after one dance would be rude.'

He frowns, covering my hand with his as we sway. 'Of course. I'm honoured, though, that you chose to have your first dance with me.'

I didn't choose that at all. The music comes to an end, the dancers pausing.

'If I may, Prince Joaquin.' Michael stands there, tall and stern.

Joaquin can't refuse, not without making a scene. He releases me, his smile tight. 'Please, enjoy.' As though he owns me and is lending me out.

But then I'm in Michael's arms, the music starting once more. Darkness, this is torture. I can't look at him as we move around the dance floor, weaving in and out of the dance.

On the pretext of twirling me, he pulls me close. 'I want to talk to you. Alone,' he murmurs in my ear, before spinning me away, our fingers the only point of contact. The layers of my silk skirt billow out, twining around my legs as I come back to him, my body full against his for a moment.

'I can't leave.' I keep my voice a breath, conscious of being in a room full of people with preternatural hearing.

'You can. Make an excuse.'

I sigh. He's right. We need to talk. I have to put a stop to this, whatever it is.

'Fine. When I get wine, go to the library. I'll meet you there.' Butterflies dance in my stomach.

He smiles, his hand coming to my waist once more as we move through the motions of the dance. We balance so perfectly, moving at the same pace, on the same beat, as though we're two halves of the same whole. It's different than the abandon of dancing with Joaquin, where I just have to let go while he takes over. We turn and turn again, coming together and apart like clockwork. Michael's grey gaze darkens, his chest rising and falling more than it should, despite our exertion. He looks slightly dazed as the dance ends, kissing my hand before relinquishing me to my next partner, a minor member of Raven nobility from the North, a young woman clad in misty-blue chiffon.

She's pleasant enough, and we talk of this and that as we clap our hands and twirl, threading in and out of the dance. She could be a friend, even if I can't offer more. We part with mutual smiles, and a promise for me to visit. And all the while my mind is whirring, anticipation rising like sap inside me.

I cycle through the dances, counting them down in my head. Six, or seven at most, and then I can plead thirst. Blood dancers enter the room on the fifth dance, some vampires already starting to feed, even though the night is young.

At the end of my sixth dance, I nod to my partner and make my way off the dancefloor. A dark figure steps into my path. 'Hello, my lovely,' Joaquin purrs. 'Shall we dance again?' He stalks around me, his head tilted as he sniffs, breathing me in. It's an utter predator's movement, a claiming.

'No,' I say. 'I need a moment. If you'll excuse me…' The words are polite, but I let him see the annoyance in my eyes. I'm the heir to Raven, his equal in every way, and this is my home. I'm not some prey to be marked and dominated.

His full mouth curves and he steps back, bowing. 'Of course, dear one. Shall I escort you?'

'No, thank you. There are plenty of guards. I'm sure there are many here who'll dance with you while I'm gone.'

'Such a shame, though, that I don't wish to dance with any of them. Only you.'

'Only me?' I pick up a glass of wine from the drinks table, taking a sip, pretending to watch the dancers as they twirl. Out of the corner of my eye I glimpse Michael, heading towards the double doors. Good. I need to nip this in the bud. I remind myself it's the only reason I've agreed to meet him, despite the treacherous butterflies still dancing in my stomach. I return my attention to Joaquin. 'You're such a good dancer. Why you'd wish to hold yourself back with a human like me is a mystery.'

'Hmm.' The sound is a low growl. His hand circles my wrist, lightly. 'But that's the thrill, you see. Your human fragility, the way I can support you, protect you, while letting you express yourself. It's a metaphor for how I see things between us, if you'll have me.'

I swallow. 'If I'll have you? What are you offering, exactly?'

'My support. For now. And you know what else I desire.' He trails the last word, heat flaring in his dark gaze.

I take another sip of wine, my mouth dry. He's the perfect consort for me. Heir to a royal house. Strong. Vampire. Fun to be with. And a damn good kisser. I remind myself that it makes a beautiful kind of sense to unite our houses, especially given our troubled history. So why am I finding him so annoying this evening? I drink more wine, trying to find the words I need. 'You know I like you. You also know I'm about to be crowned. So, my desires, whatever they are, need to be set to the side for now.'

He sighs, taking my free hand, his tongue caressing the knuckles, tasting me. I feel it down to my toes. 'I'll wait. But not for much longer, lovely Raven. So go, and come back soon. I'll be here.'

I drain the last of my wine and retrieve my hand, annoyed and aroused at the same time. I don't need to be told what to do or where to go. I briefly consider telling him to fuck off, that I don't need his support. That we took North America from him, and we could take the rest if we wanted.

Then I feel mean. Joaquin has been nothing but kind to me, making me laugh, awakening a dark side I didn't know I had. He's a wise choice, for a lot of reasons. The fact he's also hot is a bonus. I need to shut down whatever's going on with Michael and focus on Joaquin, for the sake of my realm. So what if Scorpion hasn't shown up. There are three royal houses here, the house fairly humming with power.

I leave the room, taking the most direct path through the glittering crowd. They all part for me as though they're water and I'm a ship, cleaving through. But ships can sink, can be overcome by waves. It hits me again how precarious my position is, how being human makes me more vulnerable than ever. A strong vampire mate is definitely what I need. I hold onto the thought as I hurry down the long hallway, telling the guards I have a human need to attend to.

When I open the library doors Michael is already there, standing at the long windows, his hands clasped behind him. He turns.

'I didn't think you were coming.'

'You said we needed to talk.' My breath is coming fast because I ran here, that's all.

'Just talk?' He comes closer.

'We need to stop whatever this is between us.'

His head tilts, one corner of his mouth curving. 'So you admit there's something between us?'

'No. That's the point. There can't be.' I say this as though my legs aren't shaking.

He frowns. 'No? How do you explain this?'

Before I can move, I'm in his arms, his lips on mine. I melt into him, into his smoky scent, his warmth. Just for a moment. Then I shove him, hard. 'Stop!'

'Stop?' He takes a step back, running his fingers across his lips, his gaze never leaving mine. 'Are you sure that's what you want? Because if it is, truly, then so be it.' He lifts both hands, taking another step back. 'Leave here, now, and go back to him. I'll be just your lieutenant from this day forward until he has me killed, or whatever he has planned for me. And live with the torture of watching him touch you, when I cannot.'

I can't speak.

'I mean it, E. If you want to end this, end it now. You leave the room, and I'll know it's over.' He turns away from me, facing out the window once more. His shoulders move up and down with his breath, the only sign of his agitation.

He's given me the perfect out. Leave the room, and it's done. So why won't my feet move? Why does my heart feel like it's breaking in my chest? I stand there as though trapped in amber, as though I'll be in this room, this moment, for ever.

Michael looks over his shoulder. He makes a sound, a cross between a groan and a growl, and surges towards me. Our bodies collide. He takes my face in his hands, then his mouth slants across mine, possessive and hungry. I'm all heat and embers, blazing in his arms. He lifts my skirt, his touch sliding on my thigh. I'm lost in him, already pulling his shirt free, greedy hands seeking the warm skin beneath. His mouth goes to my throat, and I tense. But he kisses me, soothing me, as though he knows my fears.

'I want you,' he groans. 'So much.' His fingers slide between my legs, and my core becomes liquid, molten to the heat of his touch. He backs me up towards the sofa, both of us still kissing, exploring each other.

'Emelia! Michael! What in darkness do you think you're doing?'

Shit. Michael and I spring apart, breathing hard. I run my hand through my hair, trying to calm myself.

My mother, flanked by two of her personal guards, is standing in the open doorway. But she doesn't look angry.

She looks worried.

Fuck.

Chapter Thirty-Six

WANT AND NEED

'Leave us.' My mother waves her hand.

The guards retreat from the room, closing the doors. I'm mortified, my cheeks aflame. I don't dare glance at Michael, but I'm aware of him, like a fire at the edge of my being.

My mother perches on the sofa. She chews her lip for a moment, her dark brows coming together. Finally, she speaks. 'You cannot be together.'

'My lady, I—'

'Oh, you know it's Penelope.' She waves one slender pale hand. 'Honestly, Michael, I think you'd be a fine consort for my daughter. But she has made promises elsewhere.'

'I'm right here,' I say, stung into speaking. 'And I haven't promised anything to anyone.'

'No, you haven't.' My mother sounds thoughtful. 'Nothing official, anyway. But you're wearing his jewel, at a ball held in your honour. Danced your first dance with him. Did you not think anyone would notice the two of you missing?'

My heart sinks. 'Did Joaquin—'

'Joaquin is with your father, no doubt being shown a series of paintings of illustrious Raven ancestors.' Amusement gleams in her eyes. 'I made sure he was occupied, when I saw that you'd gone.'

'I realise how this looks, Penelope, but I have true feelings for Emelia,' Michael says. 'And I would like to declare my suit, if I may.'

My mouth drops open. 'What?'

He shrugs. 'I'm just asking for what I want.'

'What *you* want?' I feel as though everyone around me has gone insane. 'What about what *I* want?'

'And what is that, Emelia?' My mother's voice is serious.

I look at Michael. He meets my gaze, his handsome face giving nothing away, as though we weren't just clinging to each other moments ago, as though I don't burn at his very touch. I think of Joaquin, how it feels to dance with him, what he can offer me and my realm. Both safe harbours, but for different reasons. It's outrageous that I have to choose.

'I don't know.'

A muscle ticks in Michael's jaw. My mother looks from me to him.

'Michael,' she says, her voice gentle. 'Perhaps you'd like to head back to the ballroom? We can talk about this later. I know the ambassador from Ravenko is keen to speak with you. I'll bring Emelia back with me.'

'Of course.' He glances at me, storm dark, then leaves the room. I didn't imagine the flash of hurt in his eyes. I feel like shit. I'm such a coward.

'Do you really not know who you want?' My mother rises, a shimmer of red silk, and comes over to me. I wish I could fall into her arms and weep. Instead, I shrug, looking away.

'Emelia.' My mother takes my hands in her cool grasp. 'Talk to me. What are you so worried about?'

'I don't want war.' The words spill out, her kindness unleashing my fear.

'What?' She pulls me, gently, to sit with her on the sofa. 'The Challenge has been averted. You don't need to worry about that.'

'It's just a matter of time before the next thing. I'm human and, no matter what I do, I'll never be good enough for some people. I just think Joaquin is a good choice for me. He's strong. He's an heir, like me. And he's vampire.'

A line appears between my mother's brows. 'But—'

'Yes, Lion are here tonight, but you know Anbesa won't agree with what I want to do. Thanks to Mistral and the stupid North Wind, killing his son. Scorpion haven't bothered to show up. Having Jaguar on our side means things will be balanced. If I'm going to choose anyone as a consort, it will probably be him. He makes the most sense.'

'Choosing a consort does not have to be about sense.'

'Oh my God.' I drop my head back, groaning. 'Is this about how when you met Father you knew he was the one, and how romantic it all was?'

'Yes, and no. I understand you wanting a strong mate, but Raven *are* powerful, Emelia. We took North America from Jaguar. We also have substantial holdings, the fealty of the families, and garrisons filled with loyal guards across the realm keeping our borders secure. We're more than strong enough to hold our own, should we need to. You *know* this already. Don't let fear guide your choices.'

'But we'd be stronger with him.'

My mother lifts one shoulder. 'Would we? You don't have to marry someone to create an alliance. There are other pathways to diplomacy. But what you cannot do is string him along.'

'I don't want to do that.'

'Michael has declared himself, and I'd be happy to entertain his suit, if that's what you want. But you're still so young. There's plenty of time for you to find the one you love.'

'I'm also human. I'm not going to live for ever.'

'Neither am I.' Her hand smooths my hair, sorrow in her dark gaze. 'Vampires die, eventually. Or go into the darkness.'

'Into the darkness?'

'Retreat from the world, entomb ourselves. Only the very old ones do this, as they can survive not feeding for so long.' She pauses. 'I don't want to go into the dark. I want to live, with you and Aleks. I want to watch you thrive. See you happy in your life, and your love. I'm the Raven by birth, just as you are. A role thrust upon me, without choice. But you, and your father, are both things I've chosen for myself. And you are both, by far, my greatest joy. I want nothing more than for you to know that happiness, too. So don't give your choices away, not when you don't have to.'

She kisses me, her hands gentle on my shoulders. A tear rolls down my cheek. Of course I want what she and my father have, the kind of love where you can't bear to be apart, where you support and complement each other. She's right. There's time for me to find that.

'You will be the Raven,' my mother continues. 'And that is enough. *You* are enough, by yourself.'

'He came back for me, you know.'

'What?'

'Michael. He knew what his brothers were trying to do and that putting himself forward as an option for lieutenant was the only way to keep me safe.'

My mother says nothing for a moment. 'It's clear he cares for you. And you care for him, too.'

I nod. It's not like she hasn't just seen the evidence with her own eyes, anyway.

'Are you drinking the tea?'

'Mother! I haven't … we're not…' My mother recently switched my regular tea from peppermint to ginger and rue. When I asked her why, I nearly died when she told me it was birth control, one used by humans for a long time, to varying results. Apparently, it's very effective for vampires and, as I have vampire blood, it should be the same for me.

'You don't have to choose anyone yet,' she says. 'But it's good to be prepared. Come on. Let's go back.' She stands, pulling me with her, linking our arms.

'Wait.'

She pauses, beautiful as a rose in her red gown.

'Will you tell Father?'

'Yes. He and I have no secrets. But he'll keep it to himself.'

A few minutes later we're back in the ballroom. Michael is dancing with the ambassador from Ravenko, a tall woman with icy blue eyes and a long sleek ponytail. Blood dancers work the crowd, flecks of glitter floating in the perfumed air, golden light from candle lamps catching silver and gold, jewels and satin. It's like a violet-scented dream.

'I'll go and find your father and Joaquin.' My mother presses my hand, then leaves the ballroom in a whisper of red silk. I head for the drinks table, wanting to ease the ache in my throat. I wish I knew how to choose. Wish it didn't hurt so much to do so.

Then commotion ripples through the crowd. I tense, remembering the aftermath of a bomb blast, my gravely injured father shielded from the light by a group of blood dancers. I spot Varin in the crowd and head towards him, but a guard steps into my path.

'My lady, forgive me.' He bows, deeply, his brow furrowed. 'It is just that Scorpion have arrived.'

Oh God. I know I can do this myself, but this is one moment where I would love my mother's support. Still, it's literally just welcoming someone to my home. The fact they haven't set foot in Raven territory since her coronation shouldn't be a problem. I turn, smiling.

Holy shit. Only the long years of practice holding in my emotions, keeps the smile on my face.

Because it seems to be a problem, after all.

Chapter Thirty-Seven

AN UNWANTED GIFT

A vampire enters the ballroom. She's beautiful, her pale skin so perfect it seems like some other material, flawless alabaster or marble. She's also armoured, overlapping scales of polished steel and gold covering her slender body, the sleeves anchored by metal loops over delicate fingers ending in spiked nails. She has a dagger at her hip and holds a length of chain in her hand. Which is attached to a collar around the neck of a human male.

He's wearing only loose dark trousers, his bare feet black with dirt. His dark eyes widen as he follows her into the room. I say follow, but he's more dragged in, the vampire yanking his chain so he stumbles.

Varin, his face like thunder, stands nearby. Close enough that I know he's there, but not so close it seems like I need protection from my guest. For that's what this woman is, and I need to remember my manners. Despite the fact she seems to have forgotten hers.

'Greetings,' I say, glad my voice doesn't shake. 'Welcome to

Raven. I am Emelia Raven. You must be Jang-mi.' Jang-mi is the ruler of Scorpion. Otherwise, whoever this is should have bowed to me, as a matter of respect.

The woman laughs, revealing teeth like pearl, her fangs dropped. 'The human heir. We'd heard tell but weren't sure whether or not people were making it up.'

The room stills; even the musicians stop playing. My cheeks heat up, but I hold my ground. 'I am the heir, yes.'

'And I am Nari. General and lieutenant to the most glorious Jang-mi, who sends you this gift.' She yanks on the chain and the young man staggers forward, dropping to his knees. Oh God.

'A gift?' I try to keep my voice calm, think of ice-cream and snow and hail, of merciless night and icy stars. But this is an insult. The royal houses were all invited. The heir to Jaguar is here. Lion, in the form of Anbesa and Tau, is here. Scorpion sending a general instead of someone from their family line is … an interesting choice.

'For your birthday, little Raven.' Nari runs one spiked fingernail around the ear of the young man at my feet. 'Although I suppose a dirt-eater like you will have no use for him.'

A hiss ripples around the room. It strengthens me. I bend slightly, placing my hand under the young man's chin, lifting his face. 'Please, stand,' I say. 'What's your name?'

Nari laughs, a tinkling peal of bells. 'Oh, don't bother talking to him. I had his tongue removed, sick of him trying to ask me for things.'

I swallow. Oh darkness. 'He shall be treated with kindness here, as is his right.'

'Oh, yes. We heard about that, too. All your *plans,* to help humans.' She laughs again, then her smile slides away so that she is pure predator, savagery peering out from her beautiful face. 'Here's another gift, from me. Raven lands border our own. If you must free your humans, a spectacularly stupid idea, if I may say so, then don't do it anywhere near to where our stock might get ideas. Because that could become … dangerous.'

Absolute fucking bitch. I wish I was vampire, so I could challenge her to a swordfight, then Morningstar her out of existence.

'What I choose to do in Raven lands is up to me, and me alone,' I reply. 'Right up to our borders.' I smile, not showing my teeth. 'However, surely you've not come all this way to try and tell me how to rule.'

'It seems someone needs to.' She bares her fangs at me.

I raise one eyebrow, hoping she can't tell how much my legs are shaking under my gown. Varin comes closer, the movement subtle.

'Humans deserve to live their lives, just as vampires do.'

'So, it is true. You would give up all that your parents fought to achieve. I was *there,* child, at the Rising. I fought with my queen until our swords were red with blood, and we gloried in it.' She leans forwards, hissing the last few words.

'That was a long time ago. Things change. And I cannot see how what I do in my own realm affects you.'

'Why would you?' Nari snarls. 'You're a child. A child who, in my realm, would not be suffered to live.' Suddenly Nari is pressed against me, one hand around the back of my head, pulling it to one side. Exposing my neck.

There are gasps, then silence, like a breath held. Raven guards surround us immediately.

But I already have a dagger to her throat. *Her* dagger. *Thanks, Varin,* I think as I hold it there, pressing the tip into her flesh.

'Don't carry a weapon unless you want it to be used against you,' I hiss. 'Though I'm not sure why you felt you needed to carry one here. After all, I'm just a human.'

Nari laughs, throwing her head back so the dagger scores her skin, blood running down her neck. 'So, this Raven has claws, after all. You know you cannot kill me with that.'

'I know,' I say. 'But I can slow you down long enough that they can.' I nod at the guards, swords drawn, and Varin, poised to strike.

She releases me as suddenly as she took me, snatching the dagger from my grasp. Before anyone can stop her, she throws it.

There's another gasp. The young man on the chain slumps to the ground, the hilt protruding from his chest. Nari jerks the chain, dragging him to her, biting into his throat. He trembles in her iron grip, blood dripping where her nails pierce his skin.

'What the fuck?' I can no longer hold back. 'Help him, somebody.'

But it's too late. With a swift twist, Nari snaps the youth's neck, letting his body slide to the ground. 'Hmm. Tasty. And so very easy.'

Air displaces, darkness at my side. Joaquin. His fangs dropped, lips drawn back, eyes blazing. And on my other side, heat. Michael, his expression just as ferocious.

Nari just laughs, wiping blood from the corner of her mouth, the movement delicate. 'It seems I've outstayed my welcome, such that it was.' She nods to Joaquin. 'Interesting.

We heard tell of this, too. Is it true, then? Does the Jaguar stand with the Raven?'

Joaquin's answer is a snarl.

'The Lion also stands with Raven.' Anbesa, his robes swirling like smoke, comes to me. 'And we do not tolerate such displays, Nari.'

'I think it best you leave.' The words cut through the tense atmosphere, brittle as ice cracking. My mother stands nearby. My father is behind her, all ash and granite, a sword in his hand.

'Lady Raven.' Nari bows her head a fraction. Darkness, she has nerve! 'Thank you for such a lovely evening.' Her lip curls as she takes in the ballroom full of shocked guests. 'I'll be sure to tell Jang-mi the depths to which Raven have fallen. I'm sure she'll be *very* interested.'

Then she's gone in a whoosh of air, a stunned silence settling in her wake. My mother claps her hands, and the music starts once more. Then she comes to me. My father and Varin are also gone, I suppose to make sure Nari leaves the estate.

'Are you all right?' Her voice is low, rage glittering in her onyx gaze.

'I'm unharmed.' Shaken, but that seems to be the way of things at the moment. I take in a breath and blow it out. Joaquin waits nearby, as does Michael. Darkness, what a mess this night has been. I try not to look at the dirty bare feet of the dead youth, curled on the floor. Guards are already around him, lifting him.

'Penelope, we must take our leave.' Anbesa's mouth is pursed with disapproval as he takes in the scene. I'm embarrassed, and furious. If I were vampire, none of this shit would be happening. Scorpion wouldn't dare to show such disrespect to a vampire heir. And with that thought comes the knowledge of who I have to choose.

'Will you not stay longer?' My mother sounds surprised. 'We have rooms prepared for you.'

'I'm truly sorry, Penelope, but after what happened to Daniel, and now this … I hope you understand.' He pauses, turning to me. 'I told the truth when I said Lion stand with Raven,' he says. 'And we will not be involved in any … unpleasantness. However, I bid you be careful. Yours will be a reign unlike any other. I cannot say I wouldn't do the same, if I had a child like you. But it is not an easy path you wish to tread.'

My mother purses her lips, blinking. 'We want to change the world, Anbesa. Can you not see that? The old ways no longer work for us.'

'All I see is that you have a human child, and it's changed how you view things. I have a dead child. Can you not see how that would change things for me, as well?'

He takes Tau's hand. She inclines her head to me, her dark eyes soft with sympathy. Then, with a whisper of silk, they're gone from the ballroom.

The body is gone, too. People dancing, as though someone's life hasn't just ended. Poor young man, buried so far from home, another casualty of all the twisted shit vampires have done to humans. That's why things need to change. That's why, despite how I feel about Michael, I need to stay with Joaquin.

I sit down, heavily, on a nearby chair. I'm exhausted. And this night has been a disaster.

Chapter Thirty-Eight

WHERE YOU GO, I GO

I don't know where Sophie is.

I went to find her after the ball, wanting to talk over everything with her. There hasn't been much on the news, thank darkness, apart from official photos, though a few images made it online. I'm still embarrassed, though. About being caught with Michael, and how close I came to screwing everything up, then the Scorpion debacle.

At least Joaquin is gone for a few days, taking his entourage to 'see the sights', as he put it. He made a big show of kissing me passionately before he left, despite the audience of Michael, Varin, my parents and a host of guards. Or perhaps because of it. I'm glad he's gone, to be honest.

But Sophie, when I look for her, isn't in the garage or anywhere else on the estate, even though she's supposed to be back on shift. Nor is she answering my messages. What if she's ill? I haven't had a lot of time to spend with her, but I'm doing the best I can at the moment, with everything else going on.

Worry curling in my stomach, I head down to the basement office, Bertrand in tow.

'Is there any mention of her on the lists?'

A different guard is at the computer today, looking just as nervous as the previous one. I suppose when Bertrand is towering over you, dressed in the red-flecked livery of my personal guard, it's enough to shake anyone's confidence.

'I'm sorry.' She clicks her mouse. The printer in the corner whirs, spitting out several sheets of paper. Bertrand catches them, running his finger down the list of names.

'It says she last left the estate three days ago,' he rumbles. 'Why has no one followed up on her not returning for her shift?'

'That's the thing.' The young woman looks even more worried. 'We don't usually do that, because sometimes humans … well…' She glances at me, apologetic.

'Humans what?' My stomach drops. 'They *die?* They're still people, though, each with their purpose!' I snarl the last few words. The guard flinches. Bertrand glances at me, his eyebrows raised. I pull my anger back with an effort. 'If people don't show up for work, they need to be checked on. Please make sure this happens, going forward.'

'Of course, my lady.'

God and darkness, this infuriates me! This division between vampire and human, neither one knowing what the other is truly doing.

'Raven don't share their concerns with us.'

Words spoken by the human guard commander, the one who helped me get home after Kyle's death. Oh *shit*. Realisation hits me like a hammer blow. I can't speak for a moment. Bertrand's head snaps up, his blue gaze on me.

'My lady?'

'It's fine,' I manage to say. 'Um, keep looking, please? I, er, I just remembered I'm supposed to be doing something.'

I leave the room. Bertrand follows me upstairs. He doesn't say anything, but I can feel him glancing at me.

'I need to rest,' I say, when we get to my room. My mind is whirring.

'My lady?'

I pause, my hand on the door handle.

'Wasn't there something you needed to do?' He's frowning. I know he knows I'm up to something.

'Um, yes, but I realised on the way up I had the time wrong. So, I'm going to rest first.'

His mouth twitches. 'Of course. Let me know if there's anything I can do.'

I nod, closing the door. I sit on my bed, needing a minute to sort through everything in my head. But, oh darkness, it feels as though pieces of a puzzle are clicking together, faster than I can make sense of them.

The human commander who saved me wore a red flower in his lapel. As did the driver I saw that day at the guardhouse, when it was clear humans had been taken from the estate. I saw the same human commander hugging Sophie, that day in the garage. And I overheard his voice when I was hiding, when he cleared away the clothes left behind in the guardhouse. The same guardhouse where Kyle swapped a secret for a pass off the estate. It all seems connected to the mysterious red-flower symbol.

Which is also tattooed on Ira's wrist. Oh God. I lie back on my bed, my hand on my mouth, tears starting as I realise where else I saw it. Sitting in a booth, gazing up at a domed ceiling studding with mirrored fragments, a cracked funhouse reflection of what was below.

Six curving red booths around a circular dancefloor. A red fucking flower.

More puzzle pieces, flickering through my mind. *Ira* was the one who brought Andrew and Jane to us. The same Andrew who let vampires on my islands to hunt. What if the North Wind didn't surrender? What if it was some sort of plot, with Ira, to get what they wanted? Freedom. And I just fucking gave it to them, like an idiot, instead of punishing them for their crimes. The human commander knew Ira, too; knew he was sympathetic to humans, or so he told me. Yet he keeps them caged in his bar, their blood on offer to customers. Doesn't seem very sympathetic to me. Ira was also at the Moon Harvest, where vampires hunted humans as punishment for the North Wind's crimes. And, perhaps most damningly, he knew Kyle from before he was in the pits, before he came to work for us and betrayed me. And I know Kyle was a Reaper, because he told me. Just before I killed him.

What if Reapers and hunters are working together, capturing humans? It would tie in with the timing of the attacks on the Safe Zones, which my father said showed clear signs of vampire involvement and which, despite our increased guard presence, are still happening. Oh *God*. What if Sophie's been taken, tricked somehow into going with them? My stomach lurches and I sit up, a violent wave of nausea hitting me at the thought of her being savaged, running in darkness, unable to escape. I run into my bathroom and vomit, then curl up next to the toilet, tears running down my face.

My head feels as though it's splitting, too much to keep inside. I can't tell my parents, or Varin, or Bertrand, not without concrete evidence. There is someone I can confide in, though. Someone whose job it literally is to support me.

I wipe my face and brush my teeth, then head back into my room. I dig around in the bottom of my cupboard, pulling out my old Raven sweats and putting them on. Then I press the carved leaf on my fireplace and head down the dark stairs and out of the hidden door at the base of the tower, blinking against the afternoon sunshine. Crocuses nestle beneath the trees, daffodils nodding their golden heads, the first breaths of Spring in the air as I race across the lawns.

Michael, dressed in jeans and a T-shirt, opens the door as soon as I knock.

'E? I wasn't expecting you—What's wrong?' He pulls me inside, steering me into the living room. 'Tell me.'

'It's Sophie.' I tell him all I've realised, stumbling on the words in my haste to get them out. 'She's disappeared. I can't lose her, not like this. If it's a hunt, I need to stop it.'

'You absolutely do not.'

'What?'

'You're *the Raven*, Emelia. Or you will be, in a week or so. You cannot go running off whenever you feel like it. Oh, don't look at me like that. You made this choice, remember? And I'm your lieutenant. I'm supposed to talk you out of shit like this.'

'I thought you were supposed to support me,' I snap, stung.

'This is me supporting you! You can't do stuff like this anymore!'

'Why not? If I'm the Raven, why can't I do whatever the hell I want? My friend is missing, and I need to find her!' My voice catches. 'So excuse me for wanting to do something right.' I get up, heading for the door, but he grabs my arm. 'What are you doing?'

'Stopping you.'

'From going back to the house?'

'From doing whatever hare-brained scheme you've come up with.'

We glare at each other, heat simmering between us. Then he sighs. 'Tell me what this is about.'

'I have to do something, Michael! I'm going to be the Raven in a week! And then my life will be … fuck. I'll be as trapped as I was before. I'll have to marry Joaquin and rule the realm and I just … I want my friend back. I want one final adventure. Yes, I chose to be the Raven. But it doesn't mean it's easy.' The words tumble out of me like release, sorrow I hadn't realised I was carrying.

Michael's throat moves, his stormy gaze on mine. 'Why do you have to marry Joaquin?'

'I don't know. I don't know anything! I thought … you know when we saw those Reapers, in the daytime? I wanted to go and find one, in the Pits, and ask them for help. That's how desperate I am. I want to change things, but I can't figure it out. I can't figure anything out.' The last part is a wail. 'And maybe if I marry him, people might take me seriously.' Tears come to my eyes.

'First of all, plenty of people take you seriously. You pulled a dagger on a vampire general!'

'So? She still insulted me to my face.'

'And second of all, what in darkness do you mean, you wanted to find a Reaper?'

And I break. I tell him all of it, about Lady Morvenna and the red flowers and why the Channel Islands won't work, why I'm struggling so much. At some point he takes my hands, his fingers gently rubbing mine. When I finally finish, the love in his eyes almost breaks me.

'What,' I mutter.

'You don't have to do this alone. I'm here, E. I'm with you.'

Oh God. I want him so much. But it's much more than just lust. He *sees* me, in a way no one else does. He feels like home, like safety, like the warmth of a fire on a dark night. And I cannot have him.

'Michael, I—'

'You don't need to marry him, or anyone. Not if you don't want to. You are more than strong and capable enough to rule by yourself.'

I stare at him, my lips parting.

'Your heart matters, too. What happened between us, at the ball… I know you feel as I do. You would have left the room, if he was what you truly wanted.' He moves closer, his hand coming to my chin. My eyes close, every nerve ending on my body alight, responding to the heat of him, the pull between us igniting once more. His lips brush mine, then he pulls back. I open my eyes.

'If I start kissing you now,' he says, his voice a low growl, 'I'm not going to be able to stop. And I want you to have choice. Even if everyone and everything else takes it away from you, I will always fight for your right to choose.'

It's as though my heart breaks, over and over, each time he retreats from me. I could reach out, now, and he'd be mine. The thought of doing so feels like wings, lifting me. But the weight of responsibility drags me down again. I know that ruling demands sacrifice. I thought I was willing to pay that price. But now I'm wondering, as he pulls back from me once more, whether the price is too high.

He sighs. 'Go on, tell me your plan.'

His hands are still at my waist. I'm finding it tough to concentrate. If I really could choose, it would be to leave here with him, find Sophie, and somehow figure out a life together. I can only do one of those things.

'I'm going to get on the next shift bus, and head to the Safe Zone to see if I can find Sophie. And if I can't find her, I'm going to go to Ira and ask him what he knows. Because I *know* he's connected to this, somehow.'

Michael frowns. 'Ira? Why not go as the Raven?'

'What, after dark, with a bunch of guards? You know why.'

'Speaking of guards, where do they think you are at the moment?'

'In my room, resting. One advantage of them not really understanding how much humans need to sleep.' I grin. 'So I'm going to catch that bus. And I'm telling you because, if I don't come back, you'll know where I am.'

Michael gets up and opens a drawer, pulling out a knife in a leather sheaf, which he checks before tucking it into the back of his waistband. Then he shrugs on a hoody and holds out his hand. 'If you think I'm letting you do this alone, E, you are sorely mistaken. Where you go, I go.'

Oh.

Chapter Thirty-Nine

RED FLOWER RISING

We make it to the shift bus just in time, joining the queue of humans climbing on board. I keep my head down; even dressed in Raven sweats with my hair tied up, there's a chance I could be recognised. Michael stays close, his hand in mine, his warmth steadying me. We sit at the back, then file off with everyone once we reach Dark Haven. I smile to myself, despite everything. If I'd figured this out earlier, I could have saved myself a lot of heartache. Simply got on a shift bus and disappeared into the Safe Zone, rather than going through all that I did with Kyle. But then I wouldn't be who I am now, I suppose. I wouldn't have chosen to be the Raven or feel strong enough to do it. And I would miss my parents, desperately.

I know what I'm doing is risky, and stupid. But I meant what I said to Michael. The weight of responsibility, of doing the right thing, is getting to me. I need some space away from it. A few minutes later the second bus arrives, taking the familiar route along the curving road leading to the coast.

We get off at the Safe Zone, heading down the hill past the harvesting plant, the usual line of people waiting outside. I breathe the fresh sea air, dreaming of a day when humans won't have to donate blood anymore. Vampires survived before the Rising without harvesting plants; they can damn well do it again. I just need to figure out how.

'It's this way, isn't it?' Michael tugs on my hand. We're in the town centre, crossing the square where he and I first danced, where rebels and guards once clashed, fire exploding into the night. Being here with him again is bittersweet. It feels natural, as though I'm still living in my small white house, waking to the sunrise in his arms. It's so tempting to go back to that life, dancing at the night markets, walking on the beach, kissing on the sofa.

Sophie's small apartment is down a side street – I checked the staff records before leaving the house – and seems the best place to start looking.

But when we press the buzzer set into the side of the door, a male voice answers. 'Yeah?'

'Hi, I'm looking for Sophie.'

'Sophie doesn't live here anymore.'

'Anymore?' The only response is a click. 'What the hell?' I press the buzzer again, but there's no answer. Michael, finally, pulls my hand away.

'Let's go,' he says, gentle. 'Are you sure this is the right address?'

'Yes!' I show him the scrap of paper.

He studies it. 'Yeah. It's correct.'

'So, where the hell is she? What if he's holding her prisoner up there or something! We need to help!'

He shakes his head. 'You can't. No, listen,' he takes both my hands. 'You cannot do anything. You need to come back as the Raven. That's the only way you're going to get in there. Even then, I doubt you'll find anything.'

'Why?' I frown at him. There's something in his voice, something he isn't telling me. 'Why wouldn't I find anything?'

'Because people disappear! There are ways in and out of Safe Zones, if you know where to look.'

'She wouldn't do that! Not without telling me! God!' I think for a moment. 'Has she gone to one of those nomad settlements, near the Great Forest? Maybe we can send guards to search them all and—'

'Do you think that's a good use of Raven resources?'

I don't say anything.

'If she's gone, she would have had good reason to do so. And she would also have had her reasons for not telling you.' He wraps his arms around me, his warmth comforting. 'I'm sorry,' he continues. 'But wherever she went, she probably won't want Raven guards following her, either.' Still so gentle. I know he's right. And I hate that.

'She's my *friend*.' My throat aches with unshed tears. I glance back at the apartment door, up at the shuttered windows.

'She's also human, in a world that isn't kind. Come on.' He keeps his arm around me as we walk back through the town square. I lean on him, loss stinging my chest. How stupid I was, to think we were friends. What other option did she have, when the heir approached her? She probably felt she couldn't turn me down. But I swear there was true joy between us, laughing among the stones at Stonehenge, watching the road unfurl as we talked, sharing our hopes and dreams.

We turn down a side street, taking a shortcut through an

alleyway that will bring us to the main road, where we can catch the bus to Dark Haven.

'Shit.' Michael tenses, his arm tightening around me as we run into a small crowd of people, all in the process of getting into the back of a battered-looking van. Before we can retreat a guard dressed in Raven camouflage prods me in the back.

'Get in, now,' he hisses. 'Raven have already made it hard enough for us. We don't have time for stragglers.'

'But—'

'Keep your head down,' Michael mutters. 'I'll get us out of this.'

I obey, tucking my face into the curve where his neck meets his shoulder, breathing in his smoky butterscotch scent. The last thing we need is for me to be recognised.

'We're not with this group,' I hear Michael say.

'Stop fucking around.' A rough hand grabs my arm, pulling me from Michael and shoving me into the back of the van. 'Get in, or I'll shoot.'

I stumble, sitting heavily on a seat. I hear Michael shouting, then the door opens again and he's pushed in, sprawling on the floor. I glimpse a gun in the guard's hand before the door clangs shut. I also spot something painted on the alley wall, like a sign. A red flower.

There's a rumble, the van swaying as it starts to move. I help Michael to one of the rough benches running either side of the interior, panic curling in my stomach. There are half a dozen humans in here, and every one of them is staring at us. I go to knock on the driver's partition, but Michael pulls me back.

'Sit, girl,' a woman says, her tone admonishing. 'You know

better than to disturb the driver. We'll none of us get out of here if you do that.'

I swallow, then sit down. Michael puts his arm around me. I lean my head on his shoulder, trying to quell my rising fear.

'Nervous, is she?' A man opposite nods at Michael. 'Ah well. It's not an easy choice, is it? But it'll be worth it when we get there.'

'When we get where?' I whisper. 'What the hell is happening?' Everyone in the van is dressed in outdoor clothing, fleeces and cargo trousers and padded jackets, as though we're going for a hike. Oh God. My breath comes faster and faster. I try to relax, but I can't.

I think we're about to be hunted.

I know there are humans who enjoy the challenge, and the money they earn for their families. They feel as though it lets them choose their death, and if they can take down a few vampires in the process, even better. God and darkness. Michael kisses my brow, but I can feel he's as tense as I am. I dig in my pocket for my phone, and realise to my horror it's on my dresser at home. Wherever we're going, we're trapped. I huddle against Michael, going through every move I've ever learned from Varin in my mind. It helps, a little.

'We've stopped,' Michael murmurs, a while later.

Adrenalin spikes and I'm instantly alert, my heart pounding.

The doors open with a clang, revealing the guard who shoved me into the van. 'Everyone out.'

I hang onto Michael as we climb out, everyone staying close together. The guard closes the door and jumps in the passenger side, then the van leaves, so quickly it sends up a spray of dirt.

I look around. Our surroundings don't fill me with confidence. We're in a forest clearing, the surrounding trees dark and impenetrable. The sky is purple, a few faint flickers of golden sunset remaining. Floodlights spill bright white light across the clearing, as though we're on a stage. It makes it even harder to see beneath the gathered trees. To see what, or who, might be there.

The other humans are wide-eyed, but I can't tell whether they're afraid or excited. It's possibly the first time they've been anywhere outside the Safe Zone. Pain flickers in my chest. I suppose if we're all going to die here, at least they have this brief moment of freedom. It seems a pretty poor return for their lives, though.

'Do you still have the knife?' I whisper.

Michael nods.

'Do you have any other weapons?'

He glances down at me, one corner of his mouth lifting. 'Another knife, tucked into my boot.'

'Can I have it?' Screw this. If this is a hunt, I'm not going down without a fight.

Michael bends down, then hands me a small, sheathed blade. It's warm and makes me feel a little less vulnerable.

Then the lights go out, plunging the clearing into darkness. Someone screams. As my vision adjusts, I see the woman who told me off in the van running, blindly, her hands out. I can see, but realise she, and the other humans, can't see much at all. I remember standing at a fence, Joaquin's hands on me as I stared into the depths of the forest. And then what we did after. Oh, darkness. We cannot be here. *I* cannot be here.

'We have to get out of here,' I say.

'Agreed.' The tension in Michael's voice matches my own.

'What's our best option? Fighting back-to-back? Damn. I wish I had a larger blade.'

Michael laughs.

'What?'

'You're amazing, you know that?'

'Just don't want to die today. And I'd be pretty happy if you could avoid doing the same.'

'No one is going to die today.' The voice is cool, and female. 'Not even you, Michael, though darkness knows you deserve it.'

I realise, with a start, that the clearing is full of figures dressed in black.

Vampires.

Chapter Forty

SECRETS AND LIES

A figure comes forward, moonlight faint on her face. She's tall and curvy, with long blonde hair. Her face is pretty, almost doll-like, with her cupid's-bow mouth, pointed nose and wide blue eyes, a sprinkle of freckles across her pale skin.

'How does she know your name?' I take a step away from Michael, the knife clutched in my hand.

'Yes, tell her, Michael. How do we know each other?'

'Cut the bullshit, Cass.' Michael's voice is low and fierce.

Cass? The female comes so close that her black leathers brush against me as she kisses Michael on the cheek. Then her attention turns to me.

'Who the fuck is this?' She bends her head, sniffing.

I stiffen, lifting my chin. I don't care who she is, or who she thinks Michael is to her, but I'm not prey to be scented. 'Stop sniffing me.'

'She smells like you.' Cass lifts her head, her eyes wide. 'Is she another blood-borne human? I thought they were all murdered.'

'Her name is Emelia.' Michael grits out the words.

I've had enough. 'Who the fuck are you?' I hiss. 'If you're going to hunt us, just get on with it. Or let us go.'

'Hunt you?' Cass bursts out laughing. There's more laughter, from the other vampires in the clearing. 'Have you told her nothing, Michael?'

'Just get on with it.' Michael's voice is hard, his arms folded. Then, to me, 'They won't let us go.'

'He's right, I'm afraid.' Cass grins, her dropped fangs delicate points. 'Come on. It's time to show you your new home.'

Our new home? I'm so furious I barely notice as the vampires close in on us, herding us towards a path through the trees. Michael reaches for my hand. I pull away. Hurt lances, deep in my chest. I storm ahead of him, but he catches my arm.

'Let go of me!'

'You need to stay close.'

'Why? What's going to happen if I don't?' I pull my arm free. Michael grabs it again.

'What the hell is your problem?'

'God and darkness, Michael, if you don't tell me what's going on I'll hunt you myself,' I hiss. I swear the vampire nearest to me snorts with laughter.

'This isn't a hunt!'

Oh, that's it. I'm going to burst into flames. 'Then what—'

'Save your lovers' quarrel until you're settled in, chickens.' Cass folds her arms. 'We're here.'

Michael's arm slides around my waist as we come to a stop. I'm about to pull away when I take in our surroundings. My jaw drops.

We're in the middle of a huge square clearing, deep in the

woods. Trees rise, tall around us. And, bordering the clearing, are houses. Smoke comes from the chimneys, faint lights twinkling in the windows. Ivy shrouds most of them, green curtains softening their shapes, offering only the occasional glimpse of brick and timber. Lights shimmer, deeper in the trees. More houses, I realise, dark shapes among the soaring trunks.

There are whole villages in there.

It's like being in a fairy tale, glimmering candles and ivy-strewn dwellings deep in the forest. But the vampires surrounding me, clad in black, tell a different story.

'Welcome to the Greenwood. I am Cassandra, captain of this cell.' Cass turns, taking in the group of wide-eyed humans. One of them, the woman who spoke to me, is sobbing, relief in every gasping breath. 'This is your home, now,' Cass continues. 'You have passed through, leaving all sorrow, all fear behind. In the name of Lady Morvenna, I welcome you.'

I stiffen. Lady Morvenna? What the fuck? But if this is one of the settlements, does that mean… 'You're Reapers,' I breathe.

'We are.' Cass smiles as she turns to me, her fangs dropped. 'And so is Michael.'

'You need to tell me *everything*. Now.'

Michael and I are in a small bedroom on the top floor of a house, with its own adjoining bathroom. A dormer window in the sloping ceiling frames a square of dark purple sky and black branches, a few stars visible. Rose-patterned paper covers the walls, more roses on the soft bedspread, the huge iron-framed bed the only piece of furniture in the room apart from a chest of drawers. A smell of cooking drifts up from below, indicating we're not alone.

I fold my arms, leaning against the wall. I need answers. I'm also aware that we're both missing, and that's going to be a huge fucking problem. Answers, and then a way to get out of here.

Michael paces back and forth, dragging his hand through his hair. 'What do you want to know first?' His voice is strained.

'How about we start with who Cass is? Your secret girlfriend?'

'No.' He laughs. I want to smack him. Or kiss him. 'Gods, no. She would laugh her head off if she heard you say that. She's my sister. Half-sister, to be exact. Not that anyone knows. My father liked to fuck around, which is probably no surprise.'

'Your half-sister?' This is the absolute last thing I expected. I gape at him. 'She's Mistral's daughter?'

'Don't ever call her that. Not if you want your throat to remain intact.'

'Okay.' I blink, shaking my head. 'Tell me the rest.'

'The rest?'

'All of it. How are you a Reaper? That story you told me about escaping from a Reaper patrol was bullshit, wasn't it?'

'Not all of it. I did escape,' he says. 'Just not quite as I told you. Cass helped me come here after my father threw me out.' He pauses. 'You've seen my scars, right?'

I nod, remembering what I saw in the practice ring. Realisation dawns. 'Your *father* did that to you?'

'Yeah. Him and my brothers, after he tried to change me to

vampire and it didn't work. I ran away but they caught me, savaged me, then left me for dead. Cass had heard, somehow, and she was there, waiting in the darkness. I wouldn't have made it, otherwise. She brought me here and they healed me. I was a good fighter, so they trained me as a Reaper. But then Cass and I argued and I asked to leave. She refused. I was so pissed off that I ducked out on my next day patrol. I was lucky to get away.'

'What do you mean, get away? Couldn't you just have caught the bus out of here?'

'When you come here, you leave your life behind. There's a place here, I'll show you tomorrow, where you can get your Raven mark removed.'

'Is this where Sophie is?'

'I don't know. It's pretty likely, though. She was trying to get out of the gates at Versailles, wasn't she? There's a connection point very close to there.'

Shit. Realisation rolls over me, accompanied by sorrow. 'Why wouldn't she tell me?'

'The opening might have come up at short notice. Or … E, I'm sorry, but you are the Raven. She might have felt she couldn't say anything.'

I'm silent, fighting back tears. I understand. 'Can we look for her?'

'We can. But she most likely won't be in this cell. There are other cells.'

Other cells? God and darkness. Then something else Michael said hits me. 'What do you mean by "when you come here you leave your life behind"?'

'Once you're in the network, that's it. Reapers hold their borders incredibly tightly. There is no leaving. No chance that the Reapers' secret will be told. This is a one-way ticket, Emelia.'

I stare at him, horror cold inside me. 'We can't leave?'

He shakes his head. 'It was bad luck we turned down that alley when we did. Once I realised it was a Reaper transport, my plan was to get us out the same way I left. But Cass will be onto me.'

'I'm going to be crowned in less than a *week*,' I hiss. 'If we disappear, Raven will unleash darkness knows what to find me. We can't let that happen!'

'I know. If worst comes to worst, we might have to come clean to Cass about who you are.'

'Who I am? She'll kill me.'

'I won't let her do that. You know I won't. Gods, Emelia. I'd let her kill me before that happened.' His gaze softens.

I hold on tight to my anger, not yet willing to yield. 'This is bullshit.'

'What, me giving my life for yours? No, it isn't.'

'Oh, that definitely is. There is *no* way I would let you—'

'E.' He comes closer, close enough I can feel the heat of him. He caresses my cheek. 'We're alone. In a room. Together. Do you really want to spend the time arguing?'

'Yes,' I say, even as I close my eyes, pushing into his hand like a cat.

'Yes?' He chuckles. 'Because I can think of far better things to do.' His other hand comes to my waist, pulling me hard against him. Oh, darkness.

'We shouldn't do this.' My arms twine around his neck, giving the lie to my words.

'No?' His lips brush mine, feather light. More kisses,

butterfly gentle, but I can feel the restraint behind them. 'Are you sure about that?'

'We really shouldn't … I'm with…' I don't even know what I'm saying anymore. But his hands tighten on me.

'You are *mine,* Emelia. Not his. And you know it. Just as you know I'm yours.'

My lips part, my whole body screaming for him. *You are mine*. Those words, growled, do something to me. I'm just getting it out of my system, I tell myself, as his kisses become more heated, as he moves me towards the huge bed. Just this once, and I can move on. He lays me down gently, still kissing me as his hands go to my waistband. He pauses, as though to give me a moment.

I don't need a moment. I need him. I lift my hips so he can slide my sweats from me.

'Hmmm.' His voice is a rumble against my throat. 'While I like how you look in these, those gowns of yours make for much easier access.'

'Pig.' I smack his shoulder, moaning as he grinds against me, his hardness teasing me.

'You know I'm right,' he murmurs, smiling against my mouth as he kisses me, long and slow. He pulls back, bracing himself with one arm either side of me. His eyes are dark, his lips swollen from my kisses. Light caresses the strong planes of his face, the gold of his hair.

'Michael, I—'

He shakes his head, leaning in to kiss me again. 'No more talking,' he murmurs. 'Just kissing.'

His lips trail lower, down my neck and over my collarbone. Then his weight leaves me, and I feel warm hands sliding up my calves. I open my eyes to see him kneeling before me.

My heart pounds, my breath coming in short gasps as his hands move higher, tracing fiery circles on my skin. Then he brushes a soft kiss on the inside of my knee. He looks up at me.

'Don't stop,' I gasp.

His hands curve around the back of my hips and he pulls me towards him so I'm at the edge of the bed. He kisses my inner thigh, his tongue sliding across my skin like a touch of flame. I collapse back as his hands trace across my underwear, his mouth teasing me. Then he pulls my underwear aside and kisses me, right at my sensitive core. My hands clench on the quilt, my head going back. Pleasure bursts through me like a firework as his tongue flickers against me, like nothing I've ever experienced before. My body arches into his mouth, into the fire of his touch, wanting more.

My pleasure crests, sweetness rolling through me like a wave, and I cry out as his fingers slide inside me, as friction builds like embers catching, as his tongue swirls around the delicate bundle of nerves. I'm crying his name, wanting more as I shudder against him.

I finally come down, blushing as I realise how loud I've been. Yet at the same time I feel wonderful. Michael lowers himself onto me and kisses me, my hands in his hair, our tongues tangling. I can taste myself, a faint musk, and wonder how he would taste on my tongue. I reach between us, to the hard length straining against the front of his trousers. He groans as I free him, guiding him to where he needs to be. I moan as he rolls his hips, sliding into me, filling me.

He swears, his mouth against my neck, his hands gripping me tight. Then he withdraws, pulling back. He's so beautiful, his blue eyes darkening, the hard length of him.

'Why'd you stop?'

'We do this, we do it properly,' he growls. With one smooth movement he pulls his hoody over his head, dropping it on the floor. He takes off his trousers, everything, until he's naked. Holding my gaze the entire time.

I bite my lip. He's all muscled hardness, rippling abs. I want to explore every inch of him with my mouth, my hands. I pull my top over my head, then go to undo my bra, but he stops me.

'Let me.' His hands are so beautifully warm, and I can barely breathe as he leans over, unhooking the clasp then pulling it gently from my shoulders, dropping kisses as he goes. His mouth closes over one peak, and I arch against him, crying out. I've never felt this trembling need for someone. Even Kyle, when I thought I loved him, never made me feel this way.

Michael kisses me, pulling my underwear away. And then his weight is on me, all heat and hard muscle. His gaze is ocean-deep, so tender. I could stare at him for ever, do this with him for ever.

'I need to tell you one more thing before we do this,' he says, his hand moving between my thighs.

'You do?' I don't care what other secrets he has. I just want him to not stop what he's doing.

'I love you, Emelia Raven. And I'm with you, to the end.'

His finger trails down my core, and I gasp as it slides inside me. He gasps as well, a slight groan, when he feels how ready I am.

'Please,' I whisper.

He shifts his weight, nudging at me. I reach down and guide him home.

Oh God. Oh *God*. Words leave me as he starts to move,

thrusting in and out. He takes it slow at first, filling me to the hilt, all heat and hardness. I lift my hips to meet his, grabbing at his shoulders, wanting the heat and friction. He speeds up, each thrust teasing my sensitive core, pleasure coiling deep inside me. I wrap my arms around his neck as it builds, and we kiss and kiss and kiss some more, as though neither of us can get enough of each other. He pulls back, kneeling, and hauls me up against him. I straddle him as his hands find my hips, as he thrusts upwards, filling me again, moving harder, deeper, as I ride him. Oh G*ods*. I moan his name, my head going back as the pleasure intensifies. He groans, his pace quickening to match mine and we find our release together, circling through universes, stars bursting around and through me.

I sag against his chest, his arms around me. I run my hands down his back, along the ridged muscles, the trailing scars. He kisses me, long and deep, our bodies still joined. I don't want to move, don't ever want to be apart from him.

'Are you okay?'

I almost laugh. I'm so far beyond okay I can't find the words. I'm blissful, joy radiating through me. I run the back of my hand along his cheekbone, wanting to imprint the memory in my mind. The beauty of his face, the softness of his expression, this moment of our first joining. He kisses my fingers, his eyes never leaving mine.

This is not getting it out of my system. This is a realisation. Of who I truly want. Who I've wanted, all along.

He risked everything to come with me, to make sure I was safe. To make sure I wasn't alone. I've spent my entire life feeling alone. But as we cling to each other, all warmth and joy, I know that, whatever happens, we'll be all right as long as we're together.

Because I love him, too. I can't hold it in any longer. 'I love you so much,' I say.

His lips part, and there's such joy in his gaze. He cradles me, leaning me back until we're lying down again, skin to skin. He strokes my hair, soft kisses like butterflies.

'There's no one else for me, ever.'

I can't offer him the same promise. Not with Joaquin still hanging around.

Chapter Forty-One

WONDERLAND IN GREEN

'We should go downstairs, see if there's any of whatever they're cooking left.'

I grimace. 'Maybe you could go, and bring me something back?'

Michael and I are tangled together on the bed. His hand moves lazily along my spine, warm tendrils of pleasure radiating through me. I'm also conscious of how loud I was.

'No one will mind. That's if they even heard us. We're the only room up here, apart from the bathroom. So you can moan my name as loudly as you like.' He winks at me.

'Oh God.' I bury my face in his shoulder. He shakes against me, laughter a rumble in his chest.

'No one is even going to care. Come on.' He peels himself off me and starts getting dressed.

'I might have a shower,' I say, sitting up. 'Before we go downstairs.'

He pauses, then lets his trousers drop to the ground, his gaze darkening.

'Good idea. I'll have one with you.'

Later, we head down to the kitchen together, hand in hand. The shower … let's just say it took longer than usual, and there wasn't a lot of showering going on. I glance at Michael as he glances at me. He grins, and I blush.

Despite our situation, I like this.

Like being here with him, just us, together. It's how it should be. The Raven house, with its towers and shadows, seems a million miles from the warm kitchen with its green tiles and scrubbed wooden table, hanging lanterns casting pools of golden light. A pot of something bubbles on the stove, and a man sits at the table, a bowl in front of him.

'Hey,' he says, as we come into the room. 'You both new here?'

'Just arrived.' Michael holds out his hand. 'I'm Michael, and this is Emelia.'

The man gets to his feet, shaking Michael's hand. 'Welcome, welcome to you both. I'm Paul. Have you eaten? There's stew on the stove, or fresh fruit in the fridge. Plus, I think there's some of Sarah's fresh-baked bread left.'

Stew and bread sounds pretty amazing. I can't remember the last time I fed. Paul opens a cupboard, handing us a couple of bowls, then gets spoons from a drawer.

'Help yourselves. You'll soon learn where everything is. We all muck in here, there's a job schedule on the fridge so you can put your names down in any empty spaces. You planning on staying at Greenwood, or moving on?'

'Moving on?'

'Sure. The network has plenty of openings, depending on what you want to do. The universities are in mid-terms now, but they take applications right up to the end of the school year.'

Universities? I must look stunned, because Michael grabs my hand, pulling me over to the stove. 'Here.' He takes the bowl from my slack fingers, ladling stew into it and handing it back to me.

'Come and sit, Emelia.' Paul pats the bench.

I sit down, putting my bowl on the table. 'Universities?'

'There's only two in this country, though I think they'd like to open a third at some point. But if you want to go elsewhere, you'll have to wait for a spot to open up on the ocean transports.' His brow creases. Maybe because my mouth is hanging open. 'You can get all the info at the community hub.'

'Eat up before it gets cold.' Michael sits opposite me, nodding towards my bowl as he plonks a plate of buttered bread between us.

'I know it's a lot to get used to at first,' Paul says, taking a mouthful of his own meal. 'But this is the best possible way,' he continues, once he can speak. 'It's worth everything to be able to live like this again.'

He finishes, getting up to wash his bowl at the sink, drying it and putting it in the cupboard. I eat my stew, my mind racing. What in darkness is this place?

Paul leaves the room, and it's just me and Michael and the scrape of spoons on our bowls. After a moment he puts his down. 'What?'

'There are universities here?'

He smiles, his entire expression softening. 'Yep. It's … this is a pretty wonderful place, Emelia. You'll see, tomorrow.'

'Why in darkness wouldn't you have told me about it?'

'If I'd revealed the secrets here to Raven of all people, they would have hunted me down and killed me.' He takes my hand, playing with my fingers. 'It was bad enough I left like I did. I'm glad I did, though. Because I wouldn't have met you.'

'Stop distracting me,' I breathe. 'I need you to show me everything.'

'Now?'

'I don't know. Is it open at night?'

'It is, but more for vampires. Do you want more stew?'

'No. I want answers.'

'We can go out now. Or we can go back to bed and try to sleep. I'll show you around tomorrow.'

I raise my eyebrows. '*Try* to sleep?'

He shrugs. 'I can't guarantee I'll be sleeping much. Not if I'm in bed with you, with nowhere to go and no one to interrupt us. Especially with how loud you are.'

My breath catches. 'I can be quiet.'

'I hope not. I like how you sound when you're unleashed.'

I blush, heat curling at my core. 'Well, then.' I stand up and take our dishes to the sink. I run the water, filling the bowl, squirting soap. Michael comes up behind me and kisses my neck, his hands sliding down the curve of my hips.

'I need to do this first,' I gasp, as his touch becomes more intimate. 'What if someone comes in here?'

'Then hurry up.'

'If you help it'll be faster.'

He groans, grabbing a tea towel to dry the dishes as I wash them. My entire body is tingling with anticipation, evidence of his arousal apparent.

'Enough,' he says, grabbing my hand when I go to put the dishes in the cupboard. 'Leave them. We can apologise tomorrow.'

'For leaving the dishes out?' I say, as he pulls me towards the stairs.

He glances back at me, a wicked grin on his face. 'For how loudly I'm going to make you say my name.'

Oh, darkness.

Chapter Forty-Two

THE HEART OF THE FOREST

I wake in Michael's arms. His face is relaxed in sleep, light soft on his full mouth, catching the gold in his hair. I drop a kiss on his shoulder.

'Hey.' His eyes open, and he smiles. And it's just this perfect moment as we gaze at each other. For a moment I let myself imagine how it could be if there was no crown, no world to change. No Joaquin. If we could stay here together and live our lives, among green leaves and the scent of fresh-baked bread.

He sits up, throwing back the covers. I clutch the quilt, enjoying the view as he rummages in his trouser pockets. He returns to bed a moment later.

'I have something for you. I meant to give it to you on your birthday, at the ball. But you know how that turned out. I've been carrying it with me ever since, waiting for the right moment. And, well, this feels like it.' He holds out his hand. A small velvet pouch sits on the palm. I take it, opening it to reveal a delicate silver ring.

His stormy gaze softens, the way it only does for me. 'It was my mother's.'

I tip it into my palm. Tiny silver flowers studded with diamonds twine around an opal, which glimmers with green and pink fire. 'Are you sure … I mean, I can't take this.'

Michael takes my hand in both of his. 'There's no one else I want to give it to,' he says, his voice soft, his eyes iridescent in the gold light of morning. 'Consider it a promise. That I'll always be there for you. Wear it on whichever finger feels right.'

There's a lump in my throat as I slide the ring onto my ring finger, on my right hand. It fits perfectly. I look at it, then at Michael.

'I love it,' I say. 'So much.'

'I love you,' he says, gathering me to him, taking my hand with the ring and kissing it, then kissing me as we slide down among the feather pillows, the soft sheets, tangling together once more.

A while later, freshly showered, we venture outside. Morning light slants between branches misted with spring leaves, huge trees like guardians around the edge of the clearing, shading the rows of ivy-shrouded houses. Children play on green grass, laughing as they kick a ball around. It's so beautiful, so carefree, it brings tears to my eyes.

Michael slings his arm around my shoulders as we walk across the clearing, towards a gap in the houses. When I see what lies beyond them, I gasp.

'They built a town?'

'The town was already here. Abandoned, the forest growing up around it after the Rising. There are thousands like this, across the globe. It's how the cells were able to expand.'

We're at the beginning of a street, more houses visible down side streets leading into the deep woods. Humans stroll past shops filled with goods, a greengrocer with gleaming displays of fruit and vegetables, a bakery with shelves of pastries and golden loaves. I pause at one window filled with jewellery and tiny enamelled boxes, just like ones I saw in Old London. Another shop sells perfume in gilded glass bottles, while another has clothing and shoes. It's a world away from the Safe Zone, from the market with its worn and patched stalls, shops filled with second-hand goods. These are like vampire shops but staffed by humans. The scent of freshly brewed coffee drifts from a bustling café, tables and chairs filled by people talking and eating. There's no illusion here, I realise, as we head further down the street. It's what I thought the Safe Zone would be like. But this is the reality I was seeking.

Except…

'What about the blood?' I keep my voice low. 'Surely humans have to give blood, for the Reapers. Or, darkness forbid, they're not *hunting*, are they?'

Michael points to a low brick building, a sign with a red flower on it next to the door. 'There's a bleeding house in every cell. But it's voluntary. Most people are happy to donate blood regularly, seeing it as the price to pay to live like this.'

'A bleeding house? But … if they can't leave, and they still have to bleed, how is it different from a Safe Zone? Apart from everything being a bit nicer. Aren't people just as trapped here?'

'No. Not at all. You can't leave the network, but it doesn't mean you're tied to one place. You can go anywhere in the world, as long as it's within a Reaper network. Everything is digitally connected, plus there are trade networks bringing in goods, which is why everything is so nice.'

'This is *global*? What the hell, Michael? Why couldn't you tell me?'

'Look around,' he says, his voice soft. 'And think about why.'

I look around. At the children playing, the happy people in the café. The gleaming shops and comfortable homes. I think about the small ships I saw, crossing the Channel. And I understand, even though it stings, why he might not have felt he could tell me. We barely knew each other in the Safe Zone, and we'd both been betrayed. I kept my secrets from him, he kept his secrets from me.

'How do people get here?'

'You saw the van, in the Safe Zone. The numbers are tightly controlled. Though the network is still expanding, it's limited by the expanse of forest. Wherever a red flower appears, there's a connection point. And when spaces open up, people are brought in. They call it "passing through".'

'*That's* what the red flowers mean?' I laugh, shaking my head. This is beyond anything I could have ever imagined. It explains so much. The humans going missing from the estate. The woman on the bus, crying about someone she knew passing through. And Ira… Oh my God. The Dome must be a connection point.

A couple of young women come out of the bleeding house, arm in arm, both laughing. One has a sugary cake in her hand, while the other carries a small paper bag.

'Did they just…?'

'Yes.'

It's so different from the industrialised misery of the

harvesting plants in the Safe Zone. No shuffling line of people. No blood ports. And I doubt anyone was offered cakes.

'I understand,' I say. 'I'm still pissed, but I get why it's so important to keep this a secret. What I don't understand, though, is how no one has ever found this place, or any of the others.'

'We're deep in the woods. Like, miles deep. Vampires don't fly, so they'd have no way of seeing this place. Even if a cell was discovered, there's a protocol in place to shut things down immediately and disconnect them from the network, keeping it safe.'

'There is?'

'And there's a reason Reapers have such a fearsome reputation.'

Of course. It makes sense. Vampires stay out of the Great Forest, not wishing to tangle with Reapers. But… 'I thought all Reapers were vampires. How were you one?'

'Humans can be Reapers as well. It's not easy for vampires to go out during the day, even with protection against the light. So they train humans as well.'

'That's how you know the Morningstar.' And how he knew to disable Jessie, when she attacked me.

He says nothing, just kisses my hair, his arm tightening around me as we continue on.

'So, Reapers lay down their lives to protect the network, and in return humans just have to donate blood?'

'That's pretty much it. No boundaries on human/vampire relationships. Just coexistence. Balance.'

'And that's how we like to keep it.' A black clad figure bumps Michael with her shoulder. I can't see her face, but her voice is instantly recognisable. Cass.

I tense. There's something off-putting about the Reaper. The mask and goggles don't help, especially when she turns to me.

'He showing you around?'

I nod.

'Good.' Cass turns her attention to Michael. 'I missed you, dickhead.' She punches his shoulder. 'So, you better not pull another fucking stunt like that again, or I'll kill you myself.'

Shit. This doesn't bode well for us getting out of here.

'Hey, I'm just messing with him.' The goggled head swings my way once more. 'I do that to all my lovers.'

'Ew.' Michael shoves at her. 'Stop it, Cass. She already knows we're related.'

She laughs, her head going back. 'Fine. Sorry. And I'm sorry about being a dick when you got here, too.' Genuine affection laces her tone. 'So, is this your girlfriend?'

'No,' Michael says. 'She's much more than that.' He smiles, hugging me closer.

Despite the goggles, I get the feeling Cass has just rolled her eyes. 'All right, get a room. Have you told her much about the place?'

'A little,' I say. 'It's … amazing. How things should be.'

'Yeah. It is.' Cass pauses. 'You seen the lady's shrine yet?' Her voice softens.

'The shrine?'

'Right. Come on.' She pulls Michael by the arm, dragging us down a narrow pathway, branches either side arching over us so we're enclosed in green.

The path leads to another small clearing, but there are no buildings here. Just the green woods, echoing with the sounds of spring.

'This place is sacred to Lady Morvenna, our founder. And

the flower that symbolises everything we stand for.' Cass bows her head.

I shake my head, unbelieving. It was right under my nose, the entire time.

A small statue stands at the centre of the clearing, which is almost perfectly circular and carpeted with flowering plants. Small red flowers.

Chapter Forty-Three

THE SHRINE

Four pathways made of pale grey pebbles bisect the circular clearing like a cross. The weathered shrine at the centre is shaped like a roosting bird, wings curved around its body, a pool of water on its back reflecting the trees and sky. It's a silent, beautiful place.

'Is Lady Morvenna real, then?' I whisper.

'Real? I suppose she was, once. No one really knows. There are stories of her returning to help at times of need, a bit like the human legend of King Arthur, I suppose.' There's a smile in Cass's voice.

'And the red flowers?'

'The scarlet pimpernel. That's a fairly recent symbol. A counter to the red moons of the Rising.' Scorn now colours her words. 'It's based on a story, a human book.'

'Oh!' A memory comes back to me. 'I think I read it once. About a man in, er, France. During the Revolution. He smuggled aristocrats to safety, didn't he?'

'That's right. It felt appropriate for us, apart from the

aristocrats. We have no time for any of them. Reapers hold fealty to no one except the Lady.'

Oh, so that's good, then. I glance at Michael.

'We're all sworn to her, sworn to protect the humans who nourish us, to share the world with them as equals. Wherever you see the red flower, you can find a pathway here. But I suppose you'd know that already.'

I know now. But, like everything else in this place, it just brings up more questions. If Kyle was working for Ira, helping smuggle people into the Reaper network, because he was a damn Reaper, after all, then why the hell was he also working for Mistral? Even if he did love Jessie, how could he betray his principles like that?

Because he was good at betrayal.

The words whisper through my mind. I clutch Michael's hand, as though he can chase the shadows away.

'How do you know when she's going to return?'

'You don't, really. She chooses her time. There's a legend that when the pimpernel flowers turn blue, she'll walk among us once more. But I've never seen a blue flower here.'

'She didn't show up during the Rising?'

'Reapers had no part in the Rising, because we saw no point to it. More violence never breeds peace. The world was overrun, by both humans and vampires; it was time for it to be rebalanced. But when the last few remnants of the human armies retreated into the woods, Reapers intercepted them.'

'What happened?'

'They were offered a choice. Join our cells and give up their old world or die. Most chose the former. And, with their help, we grew to the global network we are now. A world of day and night, humans and vampires living together, still following the original blueprint of the first settlement.'

'This is why Reapers have such a fierce reputation.'

Cass nods. 'We let the legend grow, a shield to keep us all safe. It's why we do what we do.' She glances at the watch on her wrist, then claps Michael on the shoulder. 'I have to go. But I'm glad you're back, brother.' She flashes from the clearing, leaving us alone.

I'm amazed. But I'm also aware of time passing. My parents will be frantic with worry, Raven forces no doubt being mobilised across the realm, looking for me.

'We need to get out of here,' I murmur.

'I know.' The same worry is evident in Michael's voice. I get it. There's so much at stake here. I cannot be found. 'And we will. I have a friend I can ask for help. We'll catch up with him later.'

'What will we do until then?'

'Come on.' Michael's thumb rubs my shoulder as he tucks me into his side. 'Let me show you around.'

A short while later we stroll along the main street. Despite my concerns, I still can't get over how perfect it is. Or the fact that it's hidden away, and it's global, the legend of the dark knights keeping vampires out of the Great Forests. Why would they come in here, after all, and risk the Reapers' wrath? They have everything they need, in their cities built by human hands, their art and porcelain and blood all provided whenever and however they desire. I understand why vampires felt they had to act, to take back the night. But I cannot understand why that meant the wholesale destruction of an entire way of life. If I could, I'd stay here for ever, not return to that world of blood and shadows beyond the trees. It sickens me to think of it now, my paltry efforts to change things almost embarrassing, yet still more than anyone else has ever tried to do.

This is what I want, I realise, as we cross the bustling main street, taking a side street lined with houses. I glimpse comfortable furniture, soft curtains, a child's play set in a back garden as we go past. *This* is what will work. Not vampire-free zones or hunting grounds or some fucked up amalgamation of everything else. *This* is how we can coexist, vampires and humans.

However, I need to tread carefully. Reapers won't want their secrets exposed, especially to Raven. The network is closed, the entry numbers controlled, so me asking to open it to everyone isn't going to work. What I need to do is learn all that I can about it then replicate it, beyond the trees. *This* is the future.

We continue wandering past shop windows, kissing in arched doorways. We pass a statue of a weeping angel on a huge plinth, photographs set into the base, vampires and humans. A legend is engraved into the stone. *In memory of the fallen.*

I pause. 'What's this?'

'It's a memorial,' Michael says, his voice soft. 'To fallen Reapers from the Southern Network.'

'Oh.' I scan the photographs, the men and women, human and vampire, all of them dedicated to the marvel of this place, to the point of sacrificing their lives to keep it safe. Then my breath catches. I'm glad Michael's arm is around me. I might fall, otherwise. In the bottom row is a picture of a dark-haired vampire, his handsome face split in a familiar grin. It's Kyle. Seeing his face again … my chest feels as though it's caving in.

'Is that…?' Michael's voice is low. His other arm comes around me and he holds me while I break against him. Even though I thought my love for Kyle died when he betrayed me, it seems there are still little tendrils left, barbed things lurking in the depth of my soul, ready to tear into me at any moment.

'Come on.' Michael tows me gently away. I get a vague sense of green leaves and dappled sunlight. 'Just breathe, E. Keep breathing.'

But how can I, when all the oxygen seems to be gone? I curl into him, burying my face in the curve of his neck, gasping against his warmth.

'Come on, let's sit.'

I open my eyes. We're at the edge of a rocky outcrop, the forest falling away beneath us, rising to the hills behind. Dark figures move among the trees, one of them raising their hand to wave.

I collapse onto a nearby rock. Michael sits, too, his arm around me. I lean on him, breathing in his quiet strength, until I feel a bit calmer.

'I want to let him go.' The words surprise me.

'Kyle?'

I nod. 'I don't love him anymore. But there are still questions.'

'I know what it's like.' He takes my hand, twining his fingers with mine. 'Loving a vampire … it's an intense experience.'

I glance at him. He drops a kiss on my temple.

'The first girl I ever loved was a vampire.'

Chapter Forty-Four

LOVE STORY

'Really?'

'Yep. I was sixteen, still living with my father. And she was ... on the estate.' He frowns. 'We were friendly, I guess. But after my father tried to change me, he left me pretty torn up, and she ... er, she looked after me, while I was recovering. No one else even cared. My mother was already dead, and my father washed his hands of me when it became apparent I couldn't be made vampire.'

I swallow against sickness, hugging him closer. Blood-borne humans can't be changed. I know that all too well. 'Why did he let you live in the first place? I've always wondered that.'

'My mother ran away from him after I was born. She was a Vindhof, as you know, and they took her in, sheltered us. I don't remember much about it.'

'Really?'

Michael nods, his blond hair falling forward. 'When she ... after she died, he came to find me. I suppose I was happy to see him. I was young, though. Too young, really.' Pain flashes across his face. 'Anyway. I met Bonnie, and she was like a ray of light.'

'Oh.' I hate Bonnie already.

He grins. 'Jealous?'

'Keep telling me your love story, sunshine.' I bump him with my shoulder.

'Not much more to tell. She looked after me until I healed, then … continued looking after me. I thought she loved me.'

'Why wouldn't she? You're very lovable.'

'You're just biased.' Another kiss on my temple. 'Anyway. I thought she loved me and, once I was well enough to leave, I asked her to come with me.'

'And did she?' This is so like Kyle and me, leaving the Raven estate together.

'Yeah.' Michael's gaze darkens. 'Right up until the moment she betrayed me to my father and brothers. Turned out she was fucking all of them, too, often at the same time. I was nothing but a joke to her. That hurt almost more than the beating they gave me, to be honest.'

'Oh, darkness.' I turn his face to mine, kissing him. 'I'm so sorry,' I murmur against his mouth. 'I want to kill all of them for you.'

'Fierce girl.' I feel him smile. 'I don't know what happened to Bonnie. Nor do I care. And my father … you know about him. I don't mind if you want to flex some of that Raven power on my brothers, though.'

'Consider it done. There are perks to sleeping with the heir, you know.'

'Hmm, yes there are.' He gently tugs my hair, angling my

head as the kiss deepens. 'You flexing your power isn't the first one I think of, though.'

God. I want him so much. I don't know how we can make this work, once we get out of here.

'What is it?'

'What's going to happen when we get out of here? With…'

His expression darkens. 'Joaquin? You love me, not him.'

'I do love you. But—'

'There are no buts. You love me, end of. If you think for one moment I'm going to give you up and let you go back to him, you must be fucking kidding yourself.'

He's right, of course. If our situations were reversed, I would fight for him until my last breath. How can I expect him to feel any differently? I don't say anything as he pulls me to my feet, as he leads me through the woods past more shops, more houses, a primary school with a climbing frame in the playground, fashioned from cut timber. All of it sheltered by soaring trees. I become aware of noise up ahead, cheering and clapping, the occasional roar of frustration.

'Where are we going?'

'You'll see.' We pass under an archway constructed of logs lashed together. A carved wooden sign hangs from it, shaped like a sword and shield, the shield bearing a familiar red-flower emblem. We follow the path to a clearing, where a circular arena has been carved into the forest floor. Tiers of wooden seating rise around it, the ground inside trodden hard. There are humans in the seats, as well as vampires, clad from head to toe in black, wearing goggles like the others I've seen.

Two more vampires are in the ring, wielding swords. Fighting. Their swords have timber blades, I realise, as we get closer. Michael leads us down between the seats to a spot in the front row.

The fighters circle each other, then one darts in, arrow-swift, swinging their sword. The other fighter blocks, pushing their opponent upwards so quickly it forces them into a backflip. I gasp, my hand to my mouth. The crowd cheers, the crack of blades echoing through the clearing.

'They're so fast!'

'Yes, but watch. You'll notice when they're about to strike, how their muscles bunch up. It's a subtle tell. Most humans can't see it. Unless they're like us.'

'What?'

'Just watch. See if you can spot it.'

I focus on the ring. At first, it's a blur, the two fighters moving so quickly I can barely make out what they're doing. Then I see it. A tiny movement, like the smallest of breaths taken before each strike, each darting slash.

Now that I know what I'm looking for it's easy to see, even when the fight becomes more intense. I wince at one particularly brutal strike, slicing under the arm to the ribs, the crunch of bone audible. The crowd groans.

'Shit.'

'Don't worry. This is just a friendly competition. People lay a few bets but it's all in fun.'

'Doesn't look very friendly.' The struck vampire has fallen to their knees, one hand to their side.

'It's part of training. A real enemy wouldn't hold back, so we don't, either.'

'We?' My stomach lurches. 'Are you telling me you've fought in this arena?'

'How do you think I learned the Morningstar?'

'Are you fucking kidding me? You trained to fight with vampires?'

'Isn't that what you're doing with Varin?' Michael keeps his voice low. He's grinning, though. 'This is how Reapers keep their skills sharp. Human and vampire.'

The crowd roars. The downed vampire sweeps their sword, knocking the other fighter to the ground. Swift as a flash they're on them, a blade to their throat.

'Fight's over. A blade to the throat is the end goal. A vampire can heal from a lot of things, but not from having their head removed.'

'Holy shit.' I clutch his arm. People around us are clapping and groaning, money changing hands.

'Michael?' One of the fighters comes over to us. 'Is that you?'

He gets up, shaking the vampire's hand. 'Good to see you again, Eddard.'

'Is it? Last I remember I put your arse in the dust in here. I thought that might have been why you left.'

'You put my arse in the dust? Was that before or after I almost took your head off?'

I close my mouth, which is hanging open. This place is one revelation after another. I remember my first time in the Safe Zone, how the sky looked, how it felt to see things in the human world. This is ten times as intense.

I realise the black-clad vampire is looking at me, head tilted.

'Sorry. I was miles away.'

'I was just asking your boyfriend if he cared for a rematch. And he's making excuses.' Laughter threads the smooth tones coming from under the mask. 'Says he needs to stay with you or some bullshit.'

I blink. 'Er, well, I guess he does and—'

'Bollocks. You're perfectly safe here. Flynn will sit with you.'

Flynn is the other fighter. He lopes over to us, vaulting the barrier and sitting next to me, slinging an arm around my shoulders. Up close, the masked face and goggles are disconcerting, but there's a sly smile in his voice. 'Yeah. I promise I won't hit on you too much.'

'You guys are both dickheads, you know that?' Michael, grinning, bends down and kisses me thoroughly. My breath is unsteady when he lifts his head. 'You going to be okay?'

'Go on.' I give him a little push. 'I know you're dying to.'

Eddard hands Michael a moulded leather chest guard, forearm and shin guards, which he straps on, plus a helmet with a metal faceguard. It doesn't seem like enough, not for facing a vampire. I push down my worry as they head to the rack of practice blades. People clap, calling out as Eddard moves to the centre of the ring. Michael, twirling his sword nonchalantly, comes to face him.

Eddard drops into a crouch. Michael's sword comes up, instantly. And it's on.

My nails dig into my hands and I try not to cry out as Eddard strikes, arrow-swift. But Michael, somehow, blocks him, countering with one of his own. Move number 13 from the Morningstar, I realise, remembering his body against mine.

'Don't worry.' Flynn leans closer to me. 'He'll be fine out there. Even if he is a bit rusty.'

'A bit rusty?' Michael is trading blows with Eddard, moving so quickly I can hardly make out what he's doing. If that's rusty, I wonder what he'd be like at full power.

'Is it harder … I mean, wearing the goggles, does it make it more difficult to…'

'Eddard is fighting at full capacity,' Flynn says. 'But yeah, it's weird. Takes a lot of time and training to get used to it, especially when you're blood-borne. Goes against all our instincts to be out here in the light.' The goggles swing my way. 'Plus, of course, you can't see how pretty I am.'

I grin.

'You and Michael known each other long?'

'Long enough.'

'Hey, just asking.' Flynn raises both hands, sitting back. I feel bad.

'Sorry. I mean, he and—Michael!' He's gone down, groaning, holding his left arm. I half-stand, but Flynn pulls me back, gently.

'Don't worry. He's tough. Eddard has hit him harder than that before.'

'That seems hard enough!' But Michael is already back on his feet, his blade spinning as he unleashes a flurry of strikes. Eddard parries, laughing. As I watch, a pattern emerges. For every two of Eddard's moves, Michael does one. It's as though he can anticipate what comes next.

Then all of a sudden, they come together, a blade at each other's throat.

'Ha, nice one!' Flynn gets to his feet, clapping.

The other spectators clap, too. Eddard and Michael shake hands. Michael is limping but, as he takes off the helmet, he's grinning, his entire face alight. His shirt, damp with sweat, clings to his muscles. Oh darkness. He racks all the equipment then comes over, still breathing hard, a wild light of joy in his eyes. Before I can speak his lips are on mine, his arms around me. Then he picks me up, slinging me over one shoulder.

'Hey!' I smack him as he carries me away from the ring, Flynn and Eddard's laughter ringing behind us. 'What do you think you're doing?'

'Taking my woman back to our place.' His hand slides across my backside, squeezing.

'You cannot carry me all the way back to the house!'

'I'm pretty sure I can.'

'Put me down!' I pinch him, hard.

'Ow!' He stops, releasing me so I slide against him, kissing me. I taste sweat and a faint tang of blood, his smoke and incense scent curling around me.

'What's got into you?' I say, once I can talk. 'Not that I'm complaining.'

'I want you, E. Now.' His voice is a growl. 'In that nice bed of ours. Or the shower. Actually, both.'

My knees go weak. 'I want you, too. But you don't need to carry me around like a sack of potatoes!'

He grins. 'Then walk faster.'

'Oh, just watch me.' I stride ahead of him, as fast as I can. After a minute or so I realise he hasn't caught up. I turn. He's walking a few metres back, his stormy gaze intent on me.

'What the hell are you doing?'

'Watching that nice arse of yours and imagining what I'm going to do to it.'

'Oh my God.' I maybe let my hips swing a little as I start walking again. Then I'm scooped up, flinging my arms around Michael's neck and laughing as he carries me the last few steps to the house, taking me over the threshold then setting me down. My body tingles with anticipation, need curling in my stomach. Michael's shirt is already off by the time we reach the top floor and head into the bathroom together, locking the door.

When I see his arm, I gasp. 'Michael!' There's a huge red welt, already turning purple, across one bicep.

'What?' He's already out of his trousers, sliding down his underwear.

'You're hurt.'

'You can kiss it better. I'm injured in a few other places, as well.' He winks, then steps into the walk-in shower, turning it on.

A few moments later I join him, pressing my lips to the bruise on his arm, my hands already exploring his body. 'Does that feel better?' At his growled assent, I grin. 'Just tell me where it hurts.'

Chapter Forty-Five

CHOICE AND CONSEQUENCE

I'm curled up against Michael, my whole body sated. I never imagined it could be like this, with anyone. I don't ever want to leave. I definitely cannot go back to Joaquin. But my coronation is only days away.

As though he knows what I'm thinking, Michael pulls me closer, all muscle and heat. 'I spoke to Eddard, while we were fighting. About the transports.'

'And?'

'He can help.' Michael's hands stroke lazily up and down my spine, his lips tracing fire down my throat.

'Michael.' I manage to get my hands between us, braced against his muscular chest.

'Hmm?' His mouth trails lower as he rolls me onto my back.

'Unfair,' I gasp, as he reaches a sensitive spot. 'Stop distracting me. You need to tell me the plan.'

'Do I?' He lifts his head, humour in his stormy gaze. 'Because I can't quite remember it at the moment.'

'We can't stay in bed for ever!'

'Again, not sure why.' His teeth graze my nipple.

'Gods!' This man will be my undoing, I swear. I tried to muffle myself with the pillow, earlier, but he just laughed, taking it from me and tossing it across the room.

'Do you want me to stop?'

My head goes back, and I almost give in. 'Stop,' I pant.

He stops, though his breath is coming as hard as my own. 'Fine. There's another transport coming in, tonight. We need to wait until the humans are cleared, then get on it.'

'That's the plan? Get in a van and go back?'

He grins. 'Yes. But listen,' he says, as I start to protest. 'It's not as easy as it sounds. Cass leads the clearings, so she'll be there. We'll have to time it to the second.'

'You really think she wouldn't let us go? What if I tell her who I am?'

'She won't care. She guards these borders too tightly to let anyone through, even the heir to Raven. Especially the heir to Raven.' He's not smiling any more. 'Eddard will signal when things are cleared, then we go.'

It sounds so simple. 'What about the driver?'

'We'll have to bribe him. Or you could pull rank. But there's no guarantee that won't freak him out. So that's a last resort.'

'Okay.' I turn the ring on my finger, thinking.

'What is it?'

'Nothing.' It's not nothing. I feel as I did when I travelled around my realm, when I laughed in Stonehenge, walked through ancient palaces, danced under painted ceilings at Versailles. All the while with an ache in my chest. I feel the same ache now. 'Do we have to go tonight?' It's a whisper.

'We've already stayed too long. Your parents will be frantic,

Raven searching for us. All it takes is for one person to have seen us in that alleyway and they could already be on their way here.'

'I know.' I do know. It's been an almost constant thread of worry since we got here. 'I know we *have* to go. But I don't want to.' I sit up, running my hands through my hair. 'We're going to have to come up with a story as to where we've been.'

'Maybe we should tell the truth.' He takes my hand, playing with my fingers. 'That we wanted to spend time together. Alone.' His blue gaze is unwavering, fixed on me. I know what he's saying.

'You want me to tell Joaquin it's over.' I shake my head. 'I don't know if I can, yet.'

'Darkness, Emelia! You love me, not him!'

I don't say anything.

'I watch you, day after day, dealing with shit you don't want to deal with, putting everyone else first, making decisions based upon what's best for humans, or for the realm, or to protect your family. I see you with him,' his lip curls, 'the way he puts his hands on you, moves you around like a doll, never asking you. Where's *your* choice in this? What do *you* want? Forget Raven, forget the crown, forget all of it! If you could have anything in the world, what would it be?'

My breath hitches in my chest. 'You,' I say. 'I want you. And to stay here, in this beautiful place.' The ache in my chest worsens, like a heavy stone pressing on me. 'I've fucked everything up!' I groan, rolling onto my side away from him. 'My mother told me not to string him along. She told me to choose for myself who I wanted to love.'

Michael fits himself against me, heat all down my back, his

arm around me. 'So why can't you?' His breath is warm on my skin.

'Because I'm scared.'

'Someone very wise once told me that courage isn't the absence of fear; rather, it's how you overcome fear.'

I laugh, despite my torment. 'That sounds like my father.'

'It was. Though he told me the words came from someone else. A human.' He kisses my shoulder. 'And you, my darling Emelia, have overcome your fear time and time again. When you left your home, not knowing what would happen, but knowing it would be worse to stay. When you witnessed the Moon Harvest. When you had to kill Kyle. When Jessie attacked you. When my brothers challenged your crown. When Joaquin's follower attacked you. When Nari tried to humiliate you at your own birthday ball. Each time, you faced up to things. You didn't shrink away. So why are you so scared of doing this?'

I don't say anything.

'Is it because you have feelings for him?' Tension threads his voice.

I turn to face him. 'I'd be lying if I said I didn't like him. Didn't find him attractive. I don't want to hurt him. There was a time, after you left, when I thought he could be right for me. But…'

'But?'

'I don't love him. I love you.' The ache in my chest eases. I don't want to leave because I don't want to return to what's waiting for me. I'm going to hurt Joaquin, which I never wanted to do. But this is my mistake and I need to face up to it. Perhaps there's a way for us to remain friends, for our realms to stay aligned. As my mother said, there are other paths to diplomacy. I have her, and my father, and the entire might of Raven behind me. Michael is who I want at my side. A choice I'm making for me. 'I'll end it. But without mentioning your name. We need to keep this under wraps until after I'm crowned.'

'You don't have to protect me.'

I silence him with a kiss. 'I absolutely do. We don't know what Jaguar are capable of.'

He pulls me closer, nuzzling my neck. 'So secret meetings, is it? I'm up for that.' He's also up in other ways, I can feel, pressing against me. But there's one more thing I need to say.

'I want to come back here, once I'm crowned, and speak to Cass. Tell her who I am.'

His kisses pause. 'What? Why the fuck would you want to do that?'

'Because I think this place could be the answer to changing everything.'

He tenses. 'What do you mean?'

'Before I went to the Safe Zone, I thought it was somewhere humans could live their lives the way they used to. But it became clear very quickly that wasn't the case. The Channel Islands … you know why it won't work. But this way of living is perfect. And it's global. Everyone gets what they want.'

'No way. No fucking way.' He rolls onto his back. 'Fuck, Emelia. Reapers *kill* to protect the cells. They've been doing so for centuries. If you expose this, you risk bringing the whole lot of them down on Raven.'

'I don't want to expose them! I want to learn from them.'

'What do you mean?'

'There are more abandoned towns and cities; darkness knows I saw plenty when we were travelling. I want to set up my own cells, using the same model, for whoever wants to go there, vampire or human. I can link them to the Safe Zones and set up a network for humans to move through, just like the Reapers have done. Raven guards can protect them, just as the Reapers do. And I'll make sure they're run the same way.'

'It's not going to be that easy.'

'Oh, I know that! Everyone tells me things aren't going to be easy. Nothing is fucking easy. Nothing worthwhile, anyway. No one thought I'd survive to adulthood, but I did. No one thought I could be crowned Raven, but I'm going to be. And no one thinks I can change the world. But I'm going to. This is what I'm here for.'

Michael still looks doubtful. 'Reapers won't let you blow their secret open.'

'I don't want to do that! I just want to use this model. Nobody needs to know.'

'You know it won't work like that.'

'What else can I do? What other option do I have?'

He doesn't seem to have an answer.

I know I have to leave this place, plunge back into the swirling politics and darkness of my regular life. Just as I know I need to end things with Joaquin, whatever the fallout may be. But I dare to dream of a life like this. A court of light and darkness, of daylight and dreams.

A few hours later we crouch in bushes at the edge of the clearing where we first arrived. It's dark, the forest rustling softly. We both reek of anti-feed, courtesy of a bottle Michael found in the bathroom.

'What in darkness?' I exclaimed when he opened the cupboard and grabbed it.

'Every house has some.'

'But it's…'

'Expensive? Yeah, I guess. But it's made from distilled vampire blood. It's not just humans who donate blood here. Maybe it's only expensive in our world because we've made it that way. Every household here has some, so humans can travel safely between cells.'

Another piece of information to tuck away, to rage against. Another difficulty we've imposed on humans. Yes, of course, make the one thing that keeps humans safe expensive. It's a good way to keep them down.

'Not long now.' Michael breathes the words, his breath warm on my cheek.

Darkness, I hope this works. But there's no alternative. We have to leave. Still … I turn and kiss Michael, putting my whole heart into it, the love and joy and warmth he gives me.

'Wow,' he breathes, when I pull back. 'What was that for?'

'Because I love you. And if we don't make it out of here, I want—'

'We'll make it out of here,' he growls. 'Even if I have to kill them all myself.'

I believe him. I love him so much. 'You won't have to do that. We can do this.'

'We can.' He presses another kiss to my lips. 'But if things do get rough, follow my lead.'

I nod.

Headlight beams slant across the clearing. A van appears, black against the shadowy trees, stones crunching beneath the tyres as it comes to a stop. A few moments later several figures stagger from the back.

'Be ready.' Light catches the blade in Michael's hand.

The van stutters into darkness. Someone cries out, like a bird. Dark shapes appear in the clearing. Moonlight silvers the golden fall of Cass's hair as she approaches the stumbling humans. Michael cups his hand around his mouth and makes several soft hooting noises, like an owl. One of the vampires moves closer to us, holding his clenched fist behind his back, three fingers raised.

Three minutes.

At least, I'm guessing so.

The vampires round up the humans, escorting them from the clearing. Eddard is last, closing his fist but not looking in our direction.

'Now!'

Michael and I burst from the bushes, running towards the van. The door is still open, the driver climbing back into the cab.

We almost make it. Almost.

'What the fuck is this?'

It's Cass.

Chapter Forty-Six

IF ONLY

The Greenwood at night is like fairyland, or at least how I imagine it. Despite our situation, I can't help but feel yearning for the life I see.

Faint golden lights decorate the buildings, more glimmering deep in the woods, like fireflies in the dark. During the day, the street hummed with human activity, people shopping, dining in cafés, socialising. It still hums, but this time with vampires. Shops are still open, cafes filled with elegant lounging figures sipping from blood pouches. It's a parallel world, a world of night. There are humans here, too; a young man working in a café, a woman sitting with a group of vampires while one of them drinks from her wrist, the gesture gentle and affectionate, all of them talking and laughing. An older woman with a small crate of blood pouches, nodding to the shopkeeper before heading down the street. It's fascinating.

And it makes so much sense.

Desire burns in me, brighter than ever, to implement the

same system across my realm. But I need to tread carefully. Especially now Cass, who is escorting us along the street, has caught us trying to leave. Our only option now is to tell her who I am and use it as leverage in the hopes I might be allowed to leave, instead of having my throat ripped out. My hand comes to my neck as Cass bangs on the front door of a large red-brick building, long windows with leaded glass lining both storeys.

The door opens.

A tall handsome vampire, broad-shouldered, clad in grey sweatpants and a tattered T-shirt that does nothing to hide his muscles, is standing there. He runs a hand through his tousled brown hair, then breaks into a crooked grin. 'Captain. And Michael, with the lovely Emelia. Come on in.'

How in darkness does he know who I am? But his voice is familiar and, after a moment, I place him. Flynn, who'd sat with me at the fighting ring. He leads us down a long corridor towards the back of the building, pausing to turn on a candle-lamp set into the wall.

'Nice of you to bring Emelia to see me without my mask, Michael.' His tone is teasing as his gaze moves to me. 'I told you I was pretty.'

I snort, despite our circumstances. Michael shoots me a fierce look. 'You're prettier,' I whisper.

'You just haven't got to know me yet,' Flynn drawls, winking at me. Damn vampire hearing! Cass brings us through to a large room running along the back of the house. Couches sit on soft rugs, bookcases lining the walls. There are several vampires in the room, relaxing on the couches.

'Look who came to call.' Flynn flops down on one of the

sofas, folding his arms. 'I'm just trying to convince Emelia that I'm the better option.'

'Stop fucking around, Flynn.' Cass's voice is sharp. 'I just caught these two trying to make a run for it.'

'Can we talk about this?' Michael's tone is casual, but his arm is tense against mine.

'Talk about what?' Cass tilts her head. 'About why you were trying to escape again, or why you've brought the heir to Raven into our cell? Because I'd really, really like to know, *lieutenant*.' She snarls the last word.

God and darkness.

Michael and I both freeze. Every vampire in the room sits up, their eyes on me. I guess they didn't know, at least.

But how the hell does Cass know?

She clicks a remote control, and a TV on the wall above the fireplace comes on.

'… teams are still searching for the missing heir to Raven, who appears to have run off with her lieutenant.' Footage shows a photo of Michael and me, then battalions of Raven guards searching the Safe Zones, busloads of them heading to different destinations. 'It's a shock move by an heir some already see as controversial, and could not come at a worse time, with her coronation only days away and the situation on our borders with Scorpion. Raven need a strong leader, not one who leaves at the first sign of danger.' More footage, this time showing vampires running through precise battle drills, their layered armour bearing the Scorpion crest. My stomach sinks.

'What have Scorpion done?'

'Keep watching.'

The footage changes to a city on the water, a domed cathedral with green-topped towers now with a hole in the roof, one of the towers toppled. 'The incursion happened without warning, a battalion crossing the border and using light flares to temporarily overwhelm the Raven garrison. There are reports of several casualties, as well as damage to the city itself, though the Scorpion forces were eventually overpowered and retreated. Jang-mi has issued a statement, that it was a rebel group of guards and offering her sincere apologies to the House of Raven. However, increased Scorpion activity along our borders does hint at something larger brewing. Is this just sabre-rattling or something more ominous?'

'Fuck them.' I cannot believe it.

'Oh, but there's more. Your boyfriend seems to have something to say.' Cass's voice drips with scorn.

'Prince Joaquin has made a statement to the press,' the newsreader continues. The footage now shows Joaquin, clad in black, standing on the steps outside my home. Michael squeezes my hand. I feel sick.

'I don't believe Emelia would leave me of her own accord,' he says, sorrow lacing every word. 'Not so close to sharing our news with the world. I had my doubts about her choice of lieutenant, and they have now been proven correct.'

'Fuck.' Michael swears, hard.

'We will find you, either way.' Joaquin looks into the camera, ferocious, fangs dropped. 'And it will not go well for you. The house of Jaguar will not be insulted—'

'Turn it off.' I put ice in my tone, the command of Raven.

'I don't obey your orders.' Nonetheless, Cass turns it off. 'Now. Tell me what the fuck you're doing in my cell.'

'We came here by accident.'

Cass snorts.

'She's telling the truth.' Michael's voice is a low growl. 'You've seen the footage. Let us go.'

'No fucking way.' She sounds so much like Michael. 'You know how it works. Just because you got out before doesn't mean I'll let you go again. And especially not with her.'

My lip curls. 'I'm right fucking here, for starters. And second of all, do you really think your Reapers could withstand the entire might of Raven?' Fuck this. Everything is on the table now. I bare my teeth, advancing on Cass. All the other vampires in the room are still. Flynn is watching me, eyes wide. 'Do you think I fucking *like* seeing my realm threatened? My people killed? I want to change the world, not see it torn apart! But if I don't get out of here, things will be destabilised. We risk war, globally. And that will affect you. I'm here because I had no choice. Yet what I've discovered … your world…' I pause. 'It's *beautiful.* It's how things *should* be. The last thing I want is Raven coming here and breaking it apart. I can keep your secrets. The only thing I ask is that you work with me, not against me. Together we could change everything. But if you aren't willing to let me go, you can kill me right now.'

'Emelia!' Michael sounds frantic.

Cass stares at me. I think I glimpse something like respect in her blue gaze. Then she claps, slowly. 'Nice speech, little Raven. Some lovely promises in there. But no way of knowing whether you'll keep them. Tell you what. We'll let you go. But he stays.' She points to Michael.

'No!' We both say it at the same time.

Cass shrugs. 'It's the best deal I can offer. I need something, after all, to ensure your silence.'

'Is my word not enough? I am Raven.' Panic makes my voice shake, but I don't care. I cannot lose him.

'We hold no fealty to you.'

'Emelia, you need to go. You're the one who can change things.' Michael's arms come around me.

'Say your farewells, and I'll escort you to the border just before dawn. A transport will arrive early, to take you back to your estate.'

Tears spill down my cheeks, my hand on Michael's face. He kisses my palm, damp on his lashes as they brush my skin. 'I'll find my way back to you,' he murmurs. 'No matter what. We're meant to be together, E.'

'I can't leave you,' I whisper. 'Please. I can't do this without you.'

'You can.' He kisses me, a sweet press of his lips. 'You can.'

I shake my head, tears flying. It's as though a hand is crushing my chest, as though all the air and warmth is being squeezed from me. 'I can't lose you again.'

'You won't. I'll never stop loving you.'

'I'll never stop loving you, either. No matter what.' I sob. I can't leave him. I think it will break me, if I do.

'Cass, have a heart.' Flynn's voice is faint in the background. 'Can't you see that—'

'What's going on here?'

There's a shocked weight to the silence that falls, my sniffling the only sound.

'General.' Cass sounds stressed. 'To what do we owe the pleasure?'

General?

I lift my head, wiping my eyes. A huge figure stands in the doorway, dressed in black. He winks at me, then lowers his brows over his icy gaze as he surveys the room. Every vampire snaps to attention, including Cass.

Ira stalks into the room, pulling the cuffs of his jacket as he inspects every vampire in turn. I cling to Michael.

'Ira is a general?' I whisper.

'Commander, actually,' Ira says. 'Of the Southern Reaper Cells.'

Chapter Forty-Seven

BACK TO REALITY

What in darkness?

Ira raises a scarred eyebrow as he continues to inspect the vampires. 'A little casual for being on call, don't you think?' He pauses in front of Flynn, looking him up and down.

'Uh, I'm off-duty tonight, sir. Just visiting.'

'Hmm.' Ira nods. He continues to Cass. 'Report, Captain.'

'Sir?'

'Your report. I would very much like to know why the heir to Raven is in tears in your living room.'

'Sir! She came here under false pretences—'

'I did not!'

Ira holds up his hand. I stop talking.

'She says they came here by accident, even though she's with Michael. And now they want to leave. I agreed to let her go. But Michael stays.'

Ira turns his attention to me. 'Is this true, Emelia?'

'Yes. I was looking for a friend in the Safe Zone when I …

we got pushed into a van. We were in the wrong place at the wrong time,' I say. 'I'll keep your secrets; I just want to work with you! I've tried explaining this, but Cass wants to keep Michael as collateral. I can't leave him here, though.'

'Why?'

'Because he's my lieutenant. He has a role to play in my coronation. And beyond that, for all the changes I want to make.'

'When you say you want to work with us, what do you mean?'

I take a moment, wanting to get it right. 'Everything I've seen here, the way vampires and humans coexist, it's exactly what I'm trying to do. I'm dedicating my reign to making a better world for humans and vampires. And I believe the Reaper model is the perfect solution. I don't want to expose your network. I just want to use the same model.'

'And if we won't work with you?'

'Then I'll keep your secret.'

'You've seen the news footage?'

I nod. 'Cass just showed me. Another reason I want to get back. I need to fix this, not hide in the woods.'

Ira's eyes narrow briefly. 'All right. Let them both go.'

'But General—'

'That's an order, Captain.'

Cass's mouth tightens, then she nods. 'Sir.'

'You both leave on the next transport,' Ira says. 'I'll escort you personally.'

'Thank you.' Relief overwhelms me, my knees wobbling. 'Thank you so much.'

We reach the clearing as the sky pales, the first fingers of sunrise reaching through the dappled leaf cover. A van pulls up, nondescript, the paint a faded blue. Ira, masked against the light, opens the back door. Inside are seats, set against the walls. 'Get in.'

Michael and I climb in, and Ira pulls the door closed behind him as the van starts to move. There's a click, and a portable candle lamp blooms in the darkness, the glow faint but enough to see by as Ira pulls off the mask and goggles.

'Do my parents know?'

'That I'm a Reaper? No. And I'd prefer it remained that way.' His voice is a rumble. The van sways.

'And the club?'

'Is a front. A transport point, for humans passing through. Sometimes they work in the bar while they wait for a space to open up.'

'Like Toby?' The young man I saw in a cage, the first time I went to the Dome. And who died in a dark meadow, torn apart by Mistral.

'Yeah.'

'How did he end up at the Moon Harvest? I know he wasn't a rebel.'

'How do you think?'

Sickness rolls over me. 'Kyle.'

'He fucked me over. He was a Reaper, as you know, but then got caught and sent to the pits. When I saw him with you at the Dome, I couldn't believe it. He started working for me again, helping humans onto the network. But he was also working for Mistral. And sometimes, people didn't end up where they were supposed to be. Toby, poor kid, was in the wrong place at the wrong time.'

'Is that how you knew to check on me?' Ira sent wine, after seeing Kyle and me at the Moon Harvest. A ruse to check I made it home safe.

'I had my suspicions, but no proof. But I knew there was a leak somewhere in the network. It wasn't until Kyle died that I figured it out.'

'What about the North Wind? Did Jane and Andrew really knock on your door, like you said?'

'No. They got picked up by a Reaper patrol after an illegal hunt, then brought to me. We thought they were prey, not the organisers.' His tone darkens. 'They asked for the meeting with your parents; told me they wanted to surrender. I think their funding was running low, once Mistral was killed. Perhaps they thought it was a way in.'

'And I gave them a whole new community.' I shake my head. 'I'm an idiot.'

'You were trying to make a difference. Never feel bad about that. You weren't to know they were hunters.'

'Did you see the footage of Andrew?'

'Yeah.' His voice becomes a growl. 'I'm glad you shut that down. Otherwise let's just say the next boatload of vampires he let onto the islands would not be there to hunt.'

'Thank you,' I say. 'For everything. For getting us out today. For listening to me.'

'I believe in you, Emelia Raven. I believe you'll make the changes you want to make.'

'Does that mean you'll work with me?'

He shakes his head. 'Not up to me. Reaper cells work as a collective. There's a hierarchy of command and they'll all need to be in agreement. I'll do what I can, of course.'

'I appreciate that.'

Ira smiles. 'Did you like it there?'

'I loved it,' I say, my mind going back to dappled green woods, to firefly lights and the feeling of sun on my skin. 'Every moment.'

Weary, I lean against Michael, the van swaying as we head towards the real world once more.

Chapter Forty-Eight

AFTERMATH

'I hope you understand.'

I knew it would be difficult when I got back home. I came up with a cover story, even though Michael told me it was ridiculous. I don't care. I won't expose him to Joaquin's vengeance.

Ira's van dropped us at the gatehouse. It was still daylight, so there was time for us to go inside and make sure our stories were aligned. We also may have aligned in other ways, and I made sure to shower thoroughly before trekking across the lawns to the main house. I let myself in through the dancers' quarters, wanting a moment before facing whatever lay before me. But the chorus of gasps when I appeared, dancers rushing over to hug me, put paid to any hope of respite before the storm hit.

My mother was the first to greet me, flashing down the hallway in a blur of red silk, alerted by the guards who spotted me the moment I stepped out of the dancers' quarters. 'Emelia!' She alternated between shaking me and hugging me, red smearing her cheeks to match her gown. My father arrived a moment later, his expression grave, sorrow in his golden gaze that cut me to the quick.

I apologised, profusely, saying I didn't mean to be gone so long. That I decided to take a trip to the Safe Zone, then on impulse continued to Stonehenge. I spun a tale of Sophie going missing, weaving truth with lies, and the pressures of my coronation, and needing space. Of how Stonehenge made me feel as though anything was possible, and I wanted to have that feeling again. Michael followed me, I told them, to talk me into coming back. But I always planned to return, to take my crown. I said that several times, with more apologies, eventually breaking down in tears.

I know I hurt them by disappearing again. My mother didn't feed the entire time I was gone, triggered by memories of my kidnapping. How stupid I've been! I only meant to find Sophie, to do something for myself before the yoke of power was placed around my neck. I never meant to be gone for so long, despite how it changed my world.

I hold onto that seed of hope now as I meet with Joaquin in the ballroom. Hope is the one thing that makes how horrible this is worthwhile.

I ask Bertrand to wait outside. He'll come in, if I need him. I hope I don't.

'I don't understand any of this!' Joaquin paces up and down, his dark hair rumpled. 'Why the hell would you take off to what, see some tumbledown stones? How could you leave me like that? *Nobody* knew where you were!'

'I know. It was stupid of me, and irresponsible. Surely you understand, though, the pressures of being the heir? I just needed to get away.'

'You could have talked to me.' Joaquin's voice is raw. 'Gods, Emelia, we are almost engaged!'

Are we? I try not to frown, wiping my hands down my velvet skirt.

'I cannot have you thinking you can run off like this, once we're together!'

Okay, now my eyebrows are raised. 'I have no plans to run off anywhere. But I want to take my crown as I am and work out for myself what it means to rule. I'm too young to tie myself to anyone yet.' A lie. My heart is already taken.

Joaquin drops to his knees, taking my hands, resting his face on them as he groans. 'You were supposed to be my redemption!' His voice cracks and, when he looks up, there's blood on my fingers.

Oh God. I kneel as well, my heart aching. 'I don't want to hurt you.' I smooth the blood tears from his cheeks, run my hand through his dark hair. 'I'm so—'

Before I can finish, he captures my mouth with his, his arms coming around me, bending me back. I respond, despite myself, to his violet and musk scent, the coiled power in his touch. There's a falling sensation, then I hear Bertrand's voice.

'Please put my lady down.'

I realise we're at the door to the ballroom, Joaquin carrying me. Darkness, what is he thinking? I untangle myself, sliding down his body as he releases me. His hand comes to my cheek.

'I'll stay until your coronation.' His expression is dark, shuttered. 'Then we can talk.'

Chapter Forty-Nine

IT BEGINS

My robes are stiff, heavy with beading.

I used to dread them, when they were on their mannequin in the Costume Room. Run my hands over the white satin, the Raven insignia beaded in silver and black on the high-collared cloak, the corseted waist and full skirt. Wonder how I could ever wear them. Vow that I never would.

Yet here I am.

I chose this, I remind myself, as I put on my Raven necklace, the long silver chain unspooling down my front. The Raven emblem, a black enamel bird with wings outstretched, surrounded by a circle of diamonds, glitters in the half-light. My hair is braided, coiled low against the nape of my neck. My head bare, ready for the crown.

There's a knock at the door. 'Emelia? It's almost time.'

My parents and I are staying in a palace not far from here, an ornate wedding-cake of a building with high railings out front, once home to human royalty. But now I'm sitting in fortified rooms deep below Old London. Waiting to meet my destiny.

I take a deep breath, smoothing the front of my skirt, Michael's ring on my right hand catching the light as I open the door.

My mother is also in white, silk draped around her slender curves, her long dark hair loose. She looks like a nymph from a painting, all onyx eyes and red lips, her perfect face shimmering in the faint light. Her smile dims slightly when she sees me.

'What?' I touch my hair, wondering if I've somehow messed it up.

'Nothing.' She puts her hands on my arms, pressing a kiss to my brow. 'It's just … I've dreamed of this day, Emelia, since you were born. And feared it, as well. Wondered if it would even happen.' She pulls back, a red tinge to her gaze. 'Pssh.' She blinks, flapping one slender hand. 'I cannot cry. The dressmaker would never forgive me if I got blood on my dress.'

I throw my arms around her, emotion welling in my chest. 'I love you so much,' I whisper, kissing her smooth cheek. 'Thank you. For everything. For being my mother. For fighting for me.'

She hugs me close. 'Now, come,' she says after a moment, her voice rough. 'We must go.' She rubs her thumb across my cheek, catching a stray tear. Then, hand in hand, we leave the room. With every step it's as though power settles around me. Bells toll, marking my steps as I approach the crypt.

The scandal of my 'disappearance' seems to have died down, and all of Old London is festooned with Raven banners, black and silver in the moonlight. My parents and I put out a statement, saying my leaving was a misunderstanding now resolved, then praising Jaguar for their support, talking of old family ties and long histories. And mentioning that, while we're enjoying Joaquin's company, I'm far too young to tie myself to anyone at this point. I haven't seen him since our conversation in the ballroom, but he'll be at the coronation tonight.

'You were supposed to be my redemption.' I'm still trying to figure out what he meant, and his tears. Another thing to address once this is over. Apart from not wanting to lose a powerful ally, I'd like to stay friends if nothing else. I definitely don't want to hurt him anymore. So Michael and I will keep our love under wraps for a while longer. I wish Sophie was here, so I could talk to her about him, but after seeing the Greenwood I can't be anything but happy for her that she's found a new life. I miss her, though.

I stop walking. My mother turns, her eyes wide.

'They're waiting for you.'

'Let them wait. I need to tell you something.'

My mother frowns, then nods to the guards escorting us. They keep moving, leaving us in the hallway alone.

'When Michael and I were away … well. We're in love. I think he's the one.'

My mother's face lights up. 'Truly?' She hugs me, squeezing me. 'Oh! I'm happy for you.'

'You're okay with it? We won't say anything, not until everything is resolved with Joaquin.'

She cups my face in her hands. 'All your father and I want,' she says, 'is for you to be happy. It's all any parent could want for their child. Your life is your own, Emelia. And it's time for you to live it.' She smiles, her eyes lined with red.

'Come, my gorgeous girl. Let's claim your crown. The world awaits.'

A short while later I wait behind a set of double doors. They're ancient, the timber so dark it's almost black. Ravens are carved into the wood, their wings spread.

My parents flank me, my father's white silk shirt glowing in the gloom, his jewelled sword-belt slung low, catching faint flickers of light.

'You know what to do?' This is my father.

'I'm ready.' I grab both their hands, looking first at my father, then my mother. 'Thanks to you both, I'm ready. And I love you so much.'

Varin, in front of me, resplendent in chain mail, turns his head, a faint smile on his lips. 'It begins.'

Music starts playing beyond the wooden doors. Soft at first, the faint strains of violins. The sound swells, the melody twining around us. This is it. This is where everything changes.

Varin draws his sword, a whisper of sound, holding the shimmering blade upright in front of him. As my champion he goes first, clearing the way.

Michael is next, shoulders broad under white and silver livery, holding the Raven sceptre. As my lieutenant, it's his job to hand it to me once I'm crowned. I wish it could be more, wish I could declare my feelings to the world. But Joaquin is in the crowd waiting beyond the doors, a place of honour as befits his status.

A guard approaches, holding a crown on a white satin pillow. It's simple, a delicate circlet of diamonds, the Raven emblem on the front in black enamel, a huge diamond on the raven's breast winking like a star. My mother takes it, putting it on for what I realise is the last time. Then she smiles at me.

As Raven, she'll crown me herself. She's the only one qualified to do so, and it signifies her power passing to me. I get a sense of the crushing number of centuries, the weight of history on my back. The feeling that I'm another bead on a chain, being moved along to the next position. The music swells to a crescendo, and the double doors open.

It's time.

Chapter Fifty

FIRST, LAST, EVERYTHING

I've watched old ceremonies of human kings and queens, flickering images of gold and jewels, of crowns and long processions.

This is similar, yet altogether different.

We're underground, in a vaulted catacomb lit by candle lamps. These are for mine and Michael's benefit only. No humans are usually at Raven coronations. I wonder what it would be like to be in the airy confines of a great abbey, light streaming through multi-coloured windows, instead of this gold-tinted darkness.

We weave our way through the jewelled throng, a carpet the colour of blood leading to a dais with a single throne. Guards in the liveries of all the different houses stand to attention on either side of the carpet, a wall of protection between me and the crowd. It's like the Gathering again, times about ten thousand in terms of intensity.

What my parents are doing is unprecedented.

If there was ever another human child born to the house of

Raven, those records have been lost. They were no doubt killed at birth, just as I was supposed to be. Even if they did survive, I cannot imagine a world where they would be elevated above all vampires in the realm. No one would have dreamed of such a thing. But my parents, my mother, dreamed differently.

And a human is about to take the silver and black crown for the very first time.

It's surreal to be here, for it to be actually happening, after all the years spent dreading this moment. I wish I could hold Michael's hand, his warmth an anchor in the chill darkness.

This ceremony, with its jewels and darkness and old traditions, is the price I'm willing to pay, so that humans everywhere can be free. I remember the artwork I saw, the beauty of ancient palaces and stone circles sheltered by wild mountain peaks. A network of cities, hidden by forest, protected by darkness. A place where the human spirit, in all its beauty, can flourish once more. I think of a young man, his bare feet dark with dirt. Another, dying in a blood-soaked meadow. A small girl who just wanted a book. I'm doing this for all of them. Taking this step so the cycle of death ends here. If it takes my entire life, I'll change things, restoring the balance once more.

I am the last Raven. Last of the old regime. And I'm also the first Raven. The first to straddle both worlds, to truly understand what it means. And the one who'll bring them together.

I make my slow way through the jewelled crowd, heads bowing as I pass. It could be a thousand years in the past. Yet, as I approach the throne, all I see is the future, and hope for what it might bring.

When Varin reaches the dais he turns, standing one step

down and slightly to the left of my throne. His dark eyes scan the crowd, his sword still unsheathed. A show of power, and a threat.

Michael takes his place to the right, muscular arms holding my sceptre steady. It's carved and gilded, the top a single huge diamond topped with a tiny ebony raven, wings spread and beak open, screaming to the world.

Then it's my turn.

I ascend the dais, facing the huge silver throne etched with patterns of curving feathers, inlaid with ebony enamel. The high back is shaped like wings, curving down towards the arms, topped with a raven's head, rubies gleaming in its enamelled eye sockets. My parents, standing to the left of the throne, both look as though they're holding back strong emotion. I get it, totally. I glance at Michael. His gaze shifts to mine, just for a moment. But long enough so I know what he's thinking.

I'm with you.

He is with me, thank darkness. As long as we're together, everything will be all right.

I turn to the assembled throng.

Everyone is here, which is as it should be. I spot Stella and Artos Ravenna, Deryck Vindhof and a few other faces I remember from Versailles. Jennie De Corbeau is smiling, arm-in-arm with her handsome husband, their family around them.

Oliver and Jacques are also here. I didn't want to invite them, but it's all part of the show, even though it infuriates me to pander to them this way. Once I'm crowned, I'll shut them down. I've no doubt Michael will stand with me in doing so.

My gaze flicks to Joaquin. He's close to the dais, dressed in his usual black, his handsome face impassive. Strange.

His entourage are with him, also dressed in black, but Selene is nowhere to be seen. She doesn't have to be here, but it's odd that she isn't.

'Assembled Ravens.' My mother's voice rings through the vaulted space, echoing from ancient stones. The crowd becomes still, preternaturally so, as though collectively holding their breath. Perhaps because none of them, apart from Michael and me, actually need to breathe.

I can do this. He's with me.

'Just over two centuries ago, I stood before many of you assembled here tonight, and took my own vows to Raven,' my mother continues. 'To uphold the throne, to govern our vast realm, and fulfil my duty of providing an heir.' She gives me a fond glance. 'And so it has come to pass. Emelia, child of my blood, do you take this vow? Do you take this throne? Do you pledge your very life to our name?'

'I do.'

Yes, I fucking take it. I fought for this, just as my mother did. Fought against it, too. I think of the costume room, the shadows of my ancestors, the power I sometimes feel, burning inside me. I draw on the shadows, just as I do the light. Stand tall as my mother comes to me, lifting the crown from her shimmering dark hair, holding it high above my head.

'And so, in view of all gathered here, I pass on my crown. To my blood-borne child, heart of my heart, bone of my bone.' Her eyes are lined with red and she blinks, the world in her onyx gaze. I'll remember this for ever. This moment when she hands me her power, when she lets me know how much I'm loved. I wouldn't be here if it wasn't for her. I smile at her, my heart full.

She lowers the crown onto my head. It's surprisingly heavy for such a delicate piece, like a band of ice around my head.

My mother drops into a low curtsey, her skirts crumpling like petals. She rises, taking my hand and leading me to the throne. I sit. Michael comes to me and, on one knee, presents the sceptre with both hands. His fingers brush mine, a brief touch, as he bows his head. A reminder of what I'm here for. Of what we're going to try and do. Together.

'All hail the Raven,' Varin shouts, raising his sword.

'All hail the Raven!' The crowd, as one, drops to one knee, heads bowed. As do Varin and Michael. And my parents.

I remember my mother telling me, in a jewelled room, that power lies in performance, as much as anything. And I'm the star of this show.

It's time for me to shine.

Chapter Fifty-One

DARK WINGS

I am Raven.

A year ago, hell, even six months ago, I would have raged at anyone who thought this would actually happen. Would have cried and gone to hide in my room, all the while plotting my escape. But that was before Kyle changed everything. If it wasn't for him, I would never have known what I could become.

Never have met Michael.

I know I had a lot to do with it as well, through the choices I made. But Kyle helped me realise what was possible. And with that thought, something dark and hard inside me finally dissolves, as though I still held a little piece of him. I let it float away, sending a silent thank you, just in case he might be somewhere, listening.

The crowd is a swirling mass of brocade and silk, almost as though they're dancing, as the families line up to swear fealty. I stand near the edge of the steps, Michael just behind me, my mother to one side. And, one by one, the Raven families come to offer me their swords.

It's a blur of gleaming steel, of bows and curtseys and murmured congratulations, as each representative kneels before me with their blades. I take them, just as I did at the Gathering, accepting their loyalty to the throne. To me.

Then it's Mistral's turn. Oliver comes forward, sword in hand, candle-lamp light gleaming on his golden hair, so like that of his father and brothers.

I accept his fealty. And give him back his sword.

As I do I see it.

The tell. The small bunching of his muscles, like a breath drawn in.

The room explodes into a blur of movement.

Michael pulls me back, violently. At the same time there's a ripping noise like silk tearing. A thin line of red droplets sinks into the white satin of my skirt. I stare at it, unable to comprehend what's happening. Michael drags me away, blood on his hands smudging across my dress.

'Get her out of here.'

My father's voice sounds ancient, inhuman, like the creak of a glacier, the scream of an eagle. His sword is drawn, his face a mask of fury. More blood sprays.

But my mother…

Michael pulls me from the dais, through a doorway where I'm lifted into Bertrand's strong arms and run at speed towards the fortified rooms. The screaming from the throne room gets quieter, yet doesn't lessen in my mind.

I'm pushed into a soft chair. Someone is breathing hard, the sobbing sounds loud in the small room. They should stop doing that, really. There are so many vampires in here.

I'm vaguely aware of someone kneeling in front of me, taking my hands. I'm cold, the room withdrawing slowly so everything seems far away.

'She's going into shock. We need to get her lying down, elevate her feet.' I'm lifted, moved from the chair and laid down on something else soft. Someone places a cushion under my feet, I don't know why. The sobbing noises continue. I wish they would stop, because something just happened, something just…

'Emelia.' A voice I know, and love. Someone lies down next to me, their entire body against mine. Warmth seeps into my icy bones. A gentle hand strokes my cheek. I start to come back to myself.

And I realise I'm the one who's sobbing.

Michael lies next to me, his body half covering mine as though to protect me. Blood is smeared across his face, his eyes dark with sorrow. I try to speak but I can't. Something's choking me, and I know when it comes out I'll break again. Because something just happened and I can't, I cannot, I…

'Is she safe?' A door closes with a clang. My body trembles so much I can't control it.

'Uninjured. But she's in shock.'

'We all are.'

All these voices around me. Michael keeps stroking my cheek, holding me as though I might break into pieces if he lets go.

'Where's her father?'

'He's still out there. He won't come in here until it's finished.'

I flinch, whimpering.

'Shh, Emelia. I have you. I'm with you.' Michael kisses my

temple, and I can feel wetness on his face, his voice choked. 'You're safe in here.'

'You need to move away from her. Mistral are finished now.' The voice is stern, and Michael is gone, suddenly.

I scream, reaching for him.

'Let him go.' The other voice sounds like Bertrand, but the iciest, angriest version of him I've ever heard. 'He is not part of this. She'll have need of him in the times to come.'

Arms come around me again, wrapping me in warmth. Tears trickle down the sides of my face, catching in my ears. It's as though the scream has cracked whatever's choking me, and it's starting to spill out. But I can't go back, don't make me go back to what just happened, I cannot, I…

Chapter Fifty-Two

BLACK HOLE

'We leave. Now.' I flinch at the ice and darkness in the voice, the crash of the door opening.

'My lord, you are—'

'I want my daughter out of here. Now.' A rasp of death. I've never heard him speak like that. I remember being near a bomb blast in the Safe Zone with Kyle, and feeling as though I was underwater, time stretching around us like some strange bubble. It's the same now. As though a bomb has gone off and I'm lost, scattered, waiting for my pieces to come back together.

'I'll bring her.' Michael's arm comes around my shoulders, sitting me up.

My father stands in front of us, almost entirely covered in blood. Sword in hand, gore still sliding from the long, curved blade. Splashed in great gouts across the white silk shirt, the finely cut dark trousers. Smeared across his lean face, in his dark hair. I only know it's him by the hard golden glitter of his eyes.

Joaquin is next to him. Also covered in blood, his sword raised, his face a snarling mask of rage. For a moment all is still, just the dripping of blood onto stone. Then his sword drops.

My father meets it, mid-air, with his own blade. 'The kill is mine, if needed,' he growls.

The kill? Nothing makes sense, nothing… I don't, I cannot. Please don't make me….

As though in a dream I watch my father lift his blade again, pointing it at me. No, it's pointed at Michael, who still has his arm around me. 'Did you know?' The words are a howl of pain. '*Did you fucking know?*' I don't think I've ever heard my father swear.

'I swear I did not. I swear it on my life. I would never—' Michael's voice breaks.

The blade hangs there, blood stippling tiny spots on the floor. So much blood. It's all over me. My gaze goes again to my skirt, to that straight line of droplets cutting across the white satin. I draw in a shuddering breath.

'The dressmaker would never forgive me if I got blood on my dress.'

'He is brother to those traitors! He should die, like they did.' Joaquin snarls at Michael.

I put my arm across him, as though I can protect him. Even though I couldn't protect … I couldn't…

Joaquin tries to pull Michael away from me. I hang onto him, baring my teeth, snarling. 'He stays with me.' It's all I can say. Each word feels like lifting a slab of rock. 'He … he stays…'

Joaquin snorts, releasing Michael. He drops his sword with

a muffled clang. 'Fuck this.' He turns away, heading for the door.

'Bertrand, get them back to the palace. Take as many guards as you need. I will…' Agony ripples across my father's face. 'I will bring her.' He turns, leaving the room.

Michael and Bertrand try and help me stand, but I can't see, can't breathe, my legs unable to bear my weight. Bertrand swings me into his arms, Michael next to me as we speed through the underground corridors, a phalanx of guards around us.

All I see is blood.

I can't stop the replay in my head, can't hold it back any longer. Oliver swearing fealty then taking his sword back, his smile turning to a snarl. The slight bunching of his muscles. Michael grabbing me, pulling me back as Oliver swings his sword, as he breaks the most sacred vow a vampire can make. My father and Varin starting forwards.

My mother. Throwing herself in front of me. Fighting to protect me, as she has done all my life.

And Oliver's sword slicing through her neck, separating her head from her body. The two distinct thuds as they both hit the floor. I don't know if I'll ever stop hearing that. There's no vampire healing to save her, no blood to be drawn to put her back together again.

My mother. My world.

Is dead.

I'm screaming again, but all that come out are husks of sound, whispering shrieks, my throat raw. There's a hole inside me, where a connection bound me to her from the moment I was conceived. Now broken, now gone.

More memories. My mother's head, rolling, her mouth a perfect 'o' of surprise. A line of blood, *her* blood, sprayed across my skirt. Michael pulling me away as my father, his blade moving so quickly it's like a lattice of steel around him, slices Oliver in half. Taking out Jacques, coming to his brother's defence, with another shattering strike. Varin and Joaquin going for the Ravenna guards who stepped forward in Mistral's defence. The crowd screaming, more guards coming to Varin's aid, the Ravenna contingent swiftly overpowered. And Joaquin, moving through the crowd like a wild animal, he and his followers cutting down anyone who resisted. More violence. More pain. More death.

'Change is coming, but this time it cannot come with blood.' I said those words, so long ago, to the North Wind. Thought I was doing the right thing. That I was going to change the world.

But now everything is broken. So much change. So much blood. And I don't know if I'll ever be whole again.

Chapter Fifty-Three

FIRE AND FURY

The building is old and crumbling, smelling of damp and the nearby river. The clocktower soaring above it is dark, the clock face tarnished and broken, its bell silent.

I don't care.

I don't care about much of anything, really. Apart from Michael.

I refused to go back to that underground room where my mother's blood still stains the stones. I don't care that it's tradition, the place where Raven holds court in Old London. As far as I'm concerned, they can fill the whole place in like the grave it is.

My mother isn't there, of course. Her body waits, shrouded in muslin, to be returned to the family estate for burial. My father hasn't left her side. It would break my heart, if it wasn't already shattered.

I asked if someone else could do this but apparently, as the crowned Raven, it's up to me. I refused the sceptre when offered it, remembering it splashed with red, bright as the rubies adorning the Raven throne, brought here for today's events.

I stand on a hastily assembled dais, the Raven crown heavy on my brow, Varin to my left, Bertrand behind me. And in front a row of Raven guards, swords out, separating me from the assembled crowd. Michael is to my right. If it wasn't for him, I think I'd go down there and beg for someone to end this pain, to send me to join my mother.

A horrible way of thinking. I know it's wrong, but I'm shattered and shredded, unable to pull myself back together. Michael's arms hold the broken bits into a semblance of Emelia, but the old me is gone, taken for ever in the sweep of a blade. Tears threaten, and I shove them back. This Raven will not cry. Not here, anyway.

Bertrand's hand comes to the small of my back, steadying me as I sway. There's so little air in here. Michael glances over, his expression stern. I have to do this. For him, as much as anyone else.

I take a breath and blow it out. My fists clench. Then I step forward. The crowd, almost all of them dressed in black, sink to their knees in a rustle of fabric.

I resist the urge to smooth my palms down the front of my skirt. The black velvet feels heavy, almost stifling. It wasn't supposed to be like this. My mother was supposed to be with me. It's like a wail in my mind, tears threatening again. I push them back.

'We're assembled here tonight to bear witness.' My voice is clear and doesn't tremble. 'And judgement. Rise.'

The crowd obeys. I observe them as though from a

distance, as though I've found a small safe space in which to hide while someone else does this for me.

'All who are here witnessed the events of my coronation.' A slight tremor. Michael, Varin and Bertrand all move closer. 'Raven is a family. One with close ties across the realm. There are names here tonight whose history goes back for more than a millennium. And others whose names, once spoken tonight, will never be heard again.'

Somebody sobs. I'm pretty sure I know who.

'Ravenna.' The sobs grow louder. I'll ask Stella to leave if she doesn't stop. 'You stood with Mistral and, therefore, against your royal house of Raven. You are to be stripped of your name, confined to your estates in darkness, and—'

'No!' A roar of protest. Stella has a younger brother. Tough shit. I had a mother.

'Be grateful you're losing nothing more than that,' I snap. 'You'll find no friends here to defend you, should I change my mind.'

The room is silent. Waiting.

'Mistral.' The word echoes through the space. I try not to snarl, though several in the crowd respond that way. 'Your line stands broken. No more will your name be held as part of Raven, no more will it be spoken. Your estates have been confiscated. And all who hold the name have been ended. Except one.' Michael knows I'm doing this. We spoke about it as he held me on the bed in the gatehouse, sunlight gilding his hair.

'My lieutenant is the son of Mistral. Yet he holds no affiliation to that house, nor has he for many years. Silence!' The word is a whip-crack, cutting through the murmuring in the room.

I turn my head. 'Michael, approach.'

He comes to kneel before me. Varin moves, smooth and lethal, his blade hovering above Michael's bowed head. The crowd's silence changes, becoming heavy, like a held breath. I hate that I have to do this, so much. But it's the only way I can keep him alive.

'Do you disavow any association with the house of Mistral, darkened be their name?' Gods, I just want to be done with all this. Just want to kiss him and tell him it's all right.

'I do.' His voice is deep, strong. 'I revoke their name, and everything to do with it.'

'And do you give up your role as my lieutenant, and any future claim to it? Knowing that you stay alive only at my pleasure?'

'I do.'

'Then I give you one gift, Michael, in recognition of your flawless service. And in memory of my mother, who loved you like a son.'

His head comes up slightly. Varin's stance remains rock solid, but his dark eyes are on me. Neither of them knew I was going to do this. I wasn't even sure I was. But it feels so horrible, stripping everything from him in front of a crowd. I want him to have something back. He saved me, after all.

'Henceforth, you'll be known as Michael Raven. Do you accept?'

He lifts his head, and there's so much love in his stormy eyes that I almost gasp. 'I accept, your Grace. It's an honour to bear your name.' He smiles, and my heart clenches in response. He's my light in the darkness, the one who risked it all for me, over and over. The one who'll help me change the world. I don't need him as my lieutenant to make that happen. I just need him.

I nod to Varin. He steps back, sheathing his sword. 'Then let it be so.'

Michael gets to his feet, then bows, deeply. He takes a position to my right once more. I lift my chin, glaring at the gathered crowd.

'I did not wish to start my reign with blood and darkness. But I will do what needs to be done, for the sake of this realm. Like it or not, I am now Raven.' I let my lip curl. 'If—'

The doors to the chamber fly open, crashing so hard against the walls that plaster rains down. Two figures stand in the doorway, holding a large chest between them. Both male, both armoured, both vampires. And both with the Scorpion crest on their layered breastplates.

Varin is already in front of me, sword out. Raven guards flash through the crowd, surrounding the two figures with a ring of silver and black. Everyone draws back, but no one leaves. I suppose they want to see whatever spectacle happens next, another disaster to gossip about. Fuck them all.

'We wish to approach the throne.'

The entire room waits on my command. Do I kill them now, or wait to hear what they have to say? What kind of ruler do I want to be?

'Let them come closer.'

The guards part to allow them passage, but stay close as the two warriors approach the throne with their bulky chest.

'Stop,' I say, when they reach halfway. I don't really care what happens to me, but Michael is here, as well as Bertrand and Varin. 'Check the chest.'

But before the guards can do so the two warriors tip it forward so that the hinged lid opens. A slurry of dark liquid pours out, along with a jumble of objects, hitting the ground with a wet splat.

'Get out.' Varin, his voice like death, starts forward, quick as a flash.

'Varin, wait.' He pauses, sword raised, at my command. I am so, so angry, dark rage rising as I walk down the steps, through the silent wondering crowd. 'What the fuck is this?' There's a murmur at my expletive. I don't care.

'We bring a message,' the warrior closest to me intones. 'From the most high and brilliant Jang-mi. From the Scorpion to the Raven. She does not send greetings, nor does she offer wishes for a long and healthy reign. Instead, she wishes to remind you how easy it is.'

My skirts almost touch the spreading slurry of liquid and, now that I'm close, I can smell it. The smell of the charnel house. Of death. 'Tell Jang-mi I do not accept her message,' I say. 'I've had enough of blood.'

I want to scream to the heavens at the insult. I want to burn the whole fucking thing down and start again. A small hand, severed at the wrist, lies in the pool of blood at my feet. Along with a whole jumble of body parts. Human. The message couldn't be clearer. *She wishes to remind you how easy it is.*

'Execute them,' I say, turning away. 'And send their heads back to Jang-mi.' I don't care what it means. I have to do something. To be humiliated like this, during my coronation week. It's already a declaration of war.

There are screams, and light flares in the chamber. I turn.

The two Scorpion warriors are wearing bulky helmets, made of layered metal like their armour. Light, brilliant as sunshine, now leaks between the layers, smoke starting to rise. Every vampire in here is flattened against the walls, trying to avoid the dazzling streams of light. God and darkness.

The Scorpion warriors are burning themselves alive.

I stand there, ice in my heart, and watch them burn.

Chapter Fifty-Four

DARK QUEEN

Michael is gone.

Another piece of me, lost. I can't believe this is happening.

He had no choice, though. I gave him my name, but it wasn't enough to keep him safe. The first attempt on his life came before we left Old London. An arrow, poison-tipped, shot between the guards as we left the building following the judgement. Luckily Bertrand managed to deflect it, so it clattered harmlessly to the ground.

The second was more serious. A bomb, placed under our car. Only found because Bertrand insisted on upping my security to ridiculous levels, inspecting every inch of my rooms, cars and belongings, each time I made a move. I understood, though. The fact I didn't want Michael to leave my side meant I was in danger, too. I couldn't guarantee he'd be safe on the estate, either, though I tried my best. He would have been a prisoner, and he is not someone to be caged.

He sent me the message, early.

Come to the Gatehouse.

I knew what it meant, was already sobbing as I crossed the dew-spangled lawns, tendrils of mist curling among the trees. But I had to do it. I had to let him go.

He, too, was crying as he opened the door, folding me in his arms. I clung to him, breathing in his heat, his smoky incense scent. He didn't say a word, simply drew me into his bedroom and undressed me, tenderly, kissing me as he went, then removed his own clothes before making love to me with a wild desperation.

Afterwards, he cradled me in his arms. 'Come with me,' he murmured, dropping soft kisses on my brow, my cheeks, the brush of his lashes on my skin.

'You know I can't.' Each word a knife, cutting me deeper. I knew where he was going, of course. The one place he could disappear to, but where he knew I could find him.

Back to the Greenwood. A one-way ticket; Cass won't let him go a third time. Ira will keep an eye on things and let me know how he's doing. If I need him to, he'll take me there. A small thread of hope, in a howling darkness.,

So I tried to be brave, even as I stroked every part of him I could reach, breathed him in, memorising each line and contour of his skin, the warmth of his touch, telling myself that I could do this, that I could let him go. But when I heard the rumble of the van pulling up outside, I broke. 'I can't do this alone,' I sobbed.

He took my hands, kissing the ring on my finger.

'You can, my love,' he said. 'You have it in you to make all the changes you want to make. You are strong, and fierce, and the bravest person I know.' He was crying, his tears mingling with mine. 'I'll always believe in you, not just because I love you. I believe you can make a better world. And that we'll be able to share it, one day.' He kissed me, salt on our lips. 'What happened to your mother … fuck.' He wiped his eyes. 'I would give my own life to change that. To bring her back.'

'No!' I wrapped my arms around him. 'You do not give your life for me. Ever.'

He stroked my face. A single tear, crystal-bright, rolled down his cheek. 'I would, though. If it meant keeping you safe, I would give everything.'

'I love you,' I said through my own tears. 'So much.'

I watched him get dressed, kissed the tears from his eyes, ran my hands through his golden hair as I kissed him one last time. Then, when the door closed behind him, I screamed into pillows that still smelled of our love, shredded the sheets, howled my rage and sorrow to the uncaring skies. Then I dressed and crossed the lawns, a queen of snow and shadows.

Now I'm lying on my bed in my room, alone. The curtains are open, the shutters disengaged on my order, sunlight sparking off the mirror, the velvet and carved wood. I don't want anyone else coming in here.

Tears slide into my ears as I huff and arch my back. I don't know if I'll ever stop crying. I know I have things to do. A whole realm to rule. But God and darkness, can I not have time to grieve my mother? My broken heart?

There's a sharp knock on my bedroom door. 'Emelia?'

The voice is raw, broken, as though whoever is speaking has been screaming for a long time. Perhaps they have. I wipe my face, taking a moment to pull myself together. I go to the door, but don't open it.

'Father?' I haven't seen him much since my coronation, both of us too bound in our own grief. The court is in mourning, which means no events. No parties, no meetings. Nothing but the most essential of work.

Joaquin is still here. I've only seen him a handful of times, always with Varin. He seems genuinely shaken by my mother's death, expressing his sorrow, his dark eyes liquid with pain. I can't find it in myself to ask him to go.

My mother is due to be buried shortly. I suppose Father has come to talk to me about that, though arrangements have already been made. A private funeral. Neither of us can deal with anything more. Or maybe he wants to update me about the Scorpion situation, whatever that is.

'You need to come out here, now.' Pain cracks in his voice.

'Stand back.' I wait a moment then open the door, squeezing out through the smallest possible space. My father is a few feet away, a tall shape in the darkness. No candle lamps, now. We all prefer it that way.

'What is it?'

He turns and walks away, beckoning me to follow. It's torture to be in the house, my mother's presence permeating the very walls. Apparently, my father tried to destroy her clothing in the Costume Room. Varin managed to stop him before he did too much damage, or so Bertrand told me, though apparently her wedding dress is shredded beyond repair.

Father leads me to the War Room, ushering me inside. It's dark, apart from flickering images on the screen pulled down against one wall. I try not to gasp at his ravaged face, his golden eyes dulled, dust in his dark hair as though he's been sleeping in a crypt. Varin and Joaquin are already here, both watching the screen with their arms folded. Cameras pan past destroyed buildings, bloodstained streets, then rise higher, showing a town that looks as though a bomb hit it. I frown, unsure what I'm seeing.

Then I spot a familiar ferry terminal. Or rather, what's left of it.

I choke down sickness. The camera drops down, revealing a pile of human remains on the edge of the dock, next to scattered luggage. As though they were waiting to escape when whatever hit the island did this. As the scene zooms in on a bloodstained teddy bear, I look away.

'Scorpion?'

I've heard nothing more from them since the events of the judgement. Our borders remain quiet. The incinerated guards left nothing behind but melted plates of armour, no hint of whatever technology had been fitted into their helmets. If it was a declaration of war, I'm still waiting for the other boot to drop. And trying to decide whether or not to drop it myself.

'No.' My father turns his head, his expression dark. 'Reapers.'

I keep watching. The report is worse than I could have imagined. The majority of the remaining population, including children, were slaughtered. Those few who did manage to get away spoke of dark figures in the night, arriving out of nowhere. It happened a couple of days before my coronation, but it took the survivors that long to be picked up, floating in their small boats.

'We finish this, now,' my father growls. 'It's time for the woods to be cleared, the scourge of Reapers to be gone. It's time, Emelia, for Raven to deal with this.' He gestures to the screen. 'It cannot go unanswered!'

The news report is damning. Public sentiment seems pretty clear. Everyone, not just my father, wants me to blow the Reapers apart. The Channel Islands project was my big gesture, and they destroyed it. In any other circumstance it would be the normal thing to do. Except I know it wasn't Reapers. I cannot risk their secrets being exposed. Sophie and Michael are both in the network. I can't jeopardise their, or anyone else's safety.

'How will the new Raven respond?' the newsreader says, black ribbon garlanding her desk. 'Sequestered still in mourning, the realm waits to see what her response to the Reapers will be,' she continues, as the camera pans past the wreckage. 'Despite the ill-advised nature of this settlement, we can't escape the fact that Reapers have been the scourge of the Great Forest for too long. Perhaps it's time to put an end to this lawless menace, once and for all, as Scorpion are trying to do in their own realm.'

Everyone in the room is looking at me. Even though I'm not wearing my crown I can feel it. Like a band of ice around my head, around my heart. Anger rises, darkness and flame.

'Clear the islands. Move the human survivors to the mainland and kill any vampires you find there. We'll discuss Reapers after my mother is laid to rest.' So easy, if I don't feel anything, to make these choices.

My father nods. 'All right.' His voice is monotone. I want to scream, to shake him.

'How do we know this isn't Scorpion, anyway? That … *gift* of theirs had to have come from somewhere.' My voice is cold, hard, as though when Michael left, he took all that was soft and warm about me. I cannot share my sorrow at his loss; I have to keep it locked inside. They'll find out he's gone, soon enough, and I'll act as surprised as anyone else. 'Increase the guard presence on all our borders. Let them see that it's not going to be easy, after all. Let them see this Raven has teeth.'

I feel my power flex, the wildness in my blood. I am the Raven, both human and vampire. And I am ready to unleash darkness.

Chapter Fifty-Five

IN THE GREENWOOD

Michael

The clearing is empty when I arrive. I make the long whooping call, cupping my hands around my mouth, putting my whole breath behind it.

A moment later I'm surrounded by dark shapes, stark against the bright green forest.

'Michael?' Flynn's voice, recognisable through the mask.

'Is Cass here?'

'I'm here.' My sister grabs the back of my neck, squeezing perhaps a little tighter than she needs to. 'But why the fuck are you?'

I twist out of her grasp. 'It's a long story.'

'It's good to see you, man.' Flynn slings an arm around my shoulders, bringing me along the familiar pathway towards the settlement. 'How's Emelia?' His voice changes, darkening. 'We saw … I mean, fucking God and darkness. What a shitshow. Is she all right?'

'She's broken.' An ache in my chest, echo of her pain. 'About as well as you could expect.' I hate that I had to leave her; would never have done it, if there was any other option. But I need to stay alive, for her. For us. She knew it, too, that she couldn't keep me safe for ever, not without caging me. I was a marked man from the moment my brother swung his sword, one last terrible twisted gift from my family. I have to lock away my pain, my sorrow, and thank my lucky stars I have somewhere safe to go. Ira, at least, will keep us connected. We'll be together again one day, I know it.

'Give her my love,' Flynn says. 'And I don't mean that like a dick.'

'No can do.' I bite the words out.

'Are you out, brother?' Cass falls into step with us. There's an uncharacteristic gentleness to her tone. 'I thought she gave you her name.'

'She did. It wasn't enough to protect me, though.' The forest rises around me, a glimpse of cloud-flecked skies above the treetops. Last time I was here, Emelia was in my arms, her soft skin, her scent all around me. It's hell to be apart from her.

I took the long way here, Ira getting me on several different transports, moving me around so with each stop I shed a part of who I was, until I was just Michael, another orphan looking for a new life. Except for her. She's given me her name; I wanted to give her mine, but this is better. A piece of her I can hold onto until we see each other again.

I saw the news report, about the Channel Islands, and how they think it's Reapers. My heart aches for her, knowing she'll do what it takes to keep our secrets. But whoever is attacking Raven lands risks bringing the wrath of Raven onto us, destroying what we protect with our lives. If someone is trying to implicate Reapers in massacres, I'm going to stop them. They want blood, I'll give it to them.

'Is that why you're here? You've come back to hide out? Or are you just the first wave of whatever attack she's going to unleash on us, now that she knows where we are?' The usual sting is absent from Cass's voice, though. I know she liked Emelia and is probably shaken by what happened.

'You know she won't say a word.'

'Even with the entire pressure of Raven on her?'

'She's stronger than you know. I'm here because I have to be. She'll keep us informed of any developments, via Ira. There's no threat.'

'Come on, Cass, give him a break.'

Flynn. My brother in every way except blood. We've fought together, many times, and I know he has my back. They all do. My sister stares at me for a moment, then bumps my shoulder with hers. It's the closest thing to a hug we'll ever do, I guess.

'Okay. You're back in. But I cannot let you leave again. You're our insurance, now.'

Fine. If that's how it's to be. I'll stay here under dark trees, with my memories of her. Stay true until we're together again, and safeguard this way of life until she can make it happen on the outside.

'I know. But I'm in, Cass. I want to wear the black.'

My sister nods. Flynn whoops as we head into the heart of the woods, shadows closing around us.

And I am a Reaper once more.

Chapter Fifty-Six

DARKNESS RISES

It took all I had to hold it together long enough to make those orders. But it's done, now. I watched the newsreel as long as I could, then left the room. No one followed, apart from Bertrand. I went to the library, waiting while he flashed around the room, not caring if there was any threat there. Let them come.

Now I'm sitting on the sofa, my knees pulled up to my chest, staring into space.

'Are you all right, little bird? I'm so very sorry about your project.'

The cushions move as someone sits next to me. It's Joaquin. There's a moment of panic, but his dark gaze is so kind, his hands so gentle as he pulls me into his violet-scented embrace. I put my hand on his chest, trying to make myself feel something, anything apart from the deep well of despair. But there's nothing. No warm heartbeat beneath my hand, no heat of breath, no softness. I can't stop my tears.

'Ah, my sweet.' Joaquin sits me up, gently. He tucks a lock

of my hair behind my ear, his hand lingering, cupping my chin.

'Thank you,' I say. 'Thank you for being here.' The words are broken, but I mean them. Despite the fact I don't love him, he's been a friend.

He tilts his head. 'Do you cry for your mother?' His dark gaze narrows. 'Or is it for your lover?'

Shock ripples through me, a lightning bolt fissure in the darkness. 'What?'

'Do you think I didn't know?' Pure predator, now. His hand tightens around my jaw, holding me in place. 'Do you think I didn't smell him on you? You will be *my* wife, not his. And you will not dishonour me any further.'

'I don't remember agreeing to be your wife.'

'Who said anything about agreeing?' He smiles, slow and poisonous. 'I said you were meant to be my redemption, and that is still the case. With you at my side, my child in your womb, my father can no longer refuse to crown me.'

Horror sluices through me. I push back against his hand, baring my teeth. 'You can't do this!'

'Oh, but I can.' He leans in, brushing my lips with his. I open my mouth, about to scream for Bertrand. But Joaquin catches me in his dark gaze, and it's as though I'm snared in a glittering web of silk and gold, criss-crossing my entire mind.

'That's it,' he murmurs, kissing me again. He takes my left hand, slipping an emerald ring on my finger. 'Not as romantic a proposal as I'd hoped, but this should do.'

I try to speak, but it's as though the web is choking me.

'There, there, my pretty raven.' Joaquin gently smoothes the tears from my cheeks. 'It's not such a hardship, is it? I will be good to you, while you live. And when you're gone, I'll rule our realms as they are meant to be.'

I push against him, but it's no use, my screams trapped inside me. I remember Mistral trying to pull me into a similar trap, my mother shocking me out of it. But she isn't here, and she never will be. There's no one to save me.

I am alone.

Acknowledgments

It's been such a joy to step back into the violet-scented realm of Raven and continue Emelia's story. I've been amazed and overjoyed by the reader response to the first book, and hope you've all enjoyed this instalment (despite how it ended) and how Emelia's world has expanded.

Once again, I must thank the brilliant team at One More Chapter, including my lovely publisher Charlotte Ledger, my fabulous editor Ajebowale Roberts, and everyone who worked to make my book the very best it can be, from the beautiful cover design to the promotion and support. I truly couldn't do this without you all!

To my agent, Laura Bennett, thank you for continuing to believe in this vampire world, and for helping me navigate the publishing side of things.

To my lovely beta readers Kat and Michelle. Both of you were such amazing support through what was a very rushed first draft, and I truly appreciate you both. Michelle, you are and continue to be a valiant WhatsApp partner, an appreciator of haunted dolls, and an all-around brilliant writer friend. You are the best, and I could not get through this insanity without you.

And to all the readers who messaged me and commented to let me know how much you enjoyed *The Last Raven*, thank you all so much. Putting a book into the world is a leap of faith, and to know that the story connected with so many of you has meant so much.

To my beloved husband, thank you for continuing to believe in me and the stories I want to tell. And to my sweet daughter, thank you for continuing to inspire me. May your star always shine brightly.

The author and One More Chapter would like to thank everyone who contributed to the publication of this story...

Analytics
Imogen Wolstencroft

Audio
Fionnuala Barrett
Ciara Briggs

Contracts
Laura Amos
Inigo Vyvyan

Design
Lucy Bennett
Fiona Greenway
Liane Payne
Dean Russell

Digital Sales
Laura Daley
Lydia Grainge
Hannah Lismore

eCommerce
Laura Carpenter
Madeline ODonovan
Charlotte Stevens
Christina Storey
Jo Surman
Rachel Ward

Editorial
Rosie Best
Kara Daniel
Charlotte Ledger
Lydia Mason
Jennie Rothwell
Tony Russell
Sofia Salazar Studer
Emily Thomas
Helen Williams

Harper360
Emily Gerbner
Ariana Juarez
Jean Marie Kelly
emma sullivan
Sophia Wilhelm

International Sales
Peter Borcsok
Ruth Burrow
Bethan Moore
Colleen Simpson

Inventory
Sarah Callaghan
Kirsty Norman

Marketing & Publicity
Chloe Cummings
Grace Edwards
Katie Sadler

Operations
Melissa Okusanya
Hannah Stamp

Production
Denis Manson
Simon Moore
Francesca Tuzzeo

Rights
Ashton Mucha
Alisah Saghir
Zoe Shine
Aisling Smyth
Lucy Vanderbilt

Trade Marketing
Ben Hurd
Eleanor Slater

The HarperCollins Distribution Team

The HarperCollins Finance & Royalties Team

The HarperCollins Legal Team

The HarperCollins Technology Team

UK Sales
Isabel Coburn
Jay Cochrane
Sabina Lewis
Holly Martin
Harriet Williams
Leah Woods

And every other essential link in the chain from delivery drivers to booksellers to librarians and beyond!